Other titles by this author
Bequia Mystery Series
Dead Reckoning
Deadeye
Deadlight

Science Fiction
Geborah's Seed

Map of the Eastern Caribbean and The Grenadines

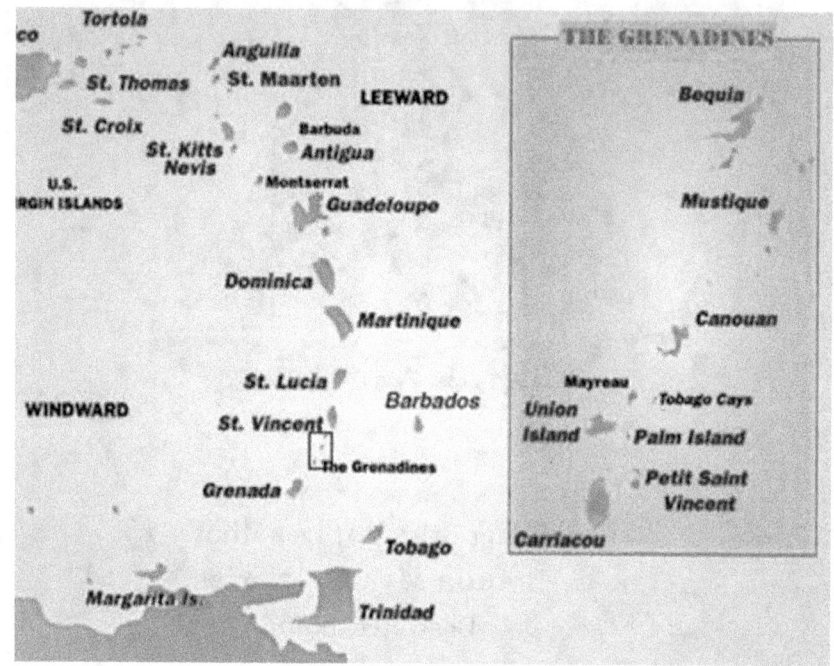

Bequia Map

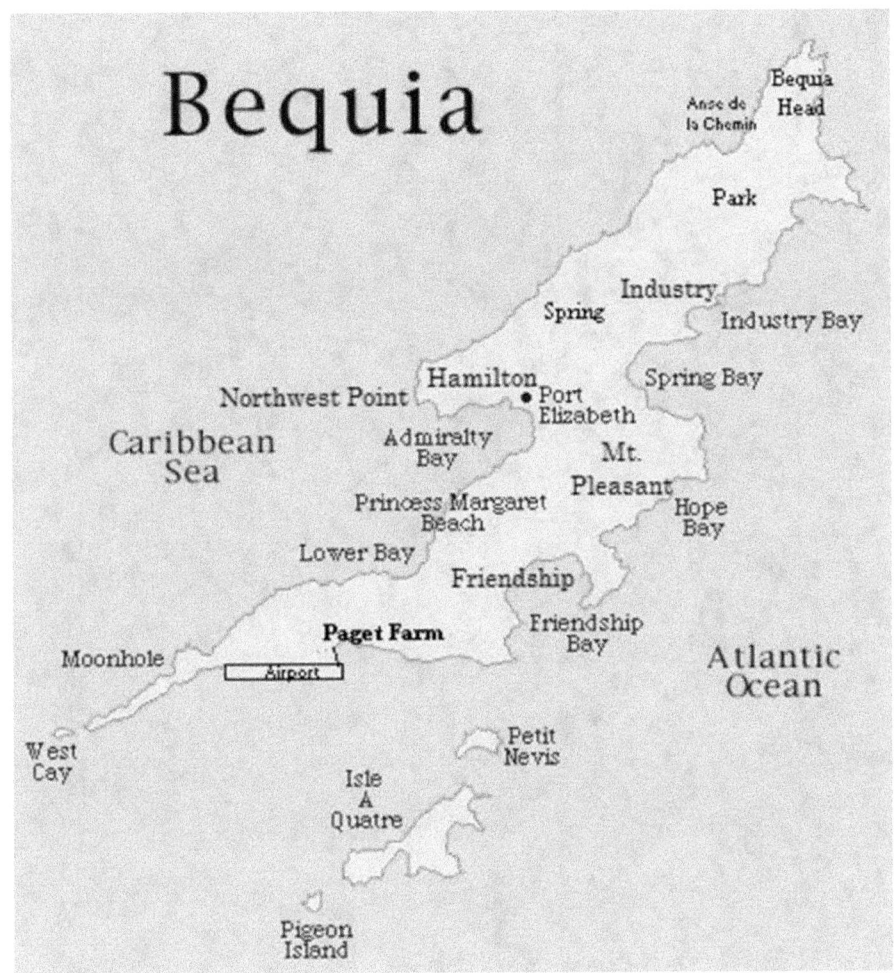

Union Island Map

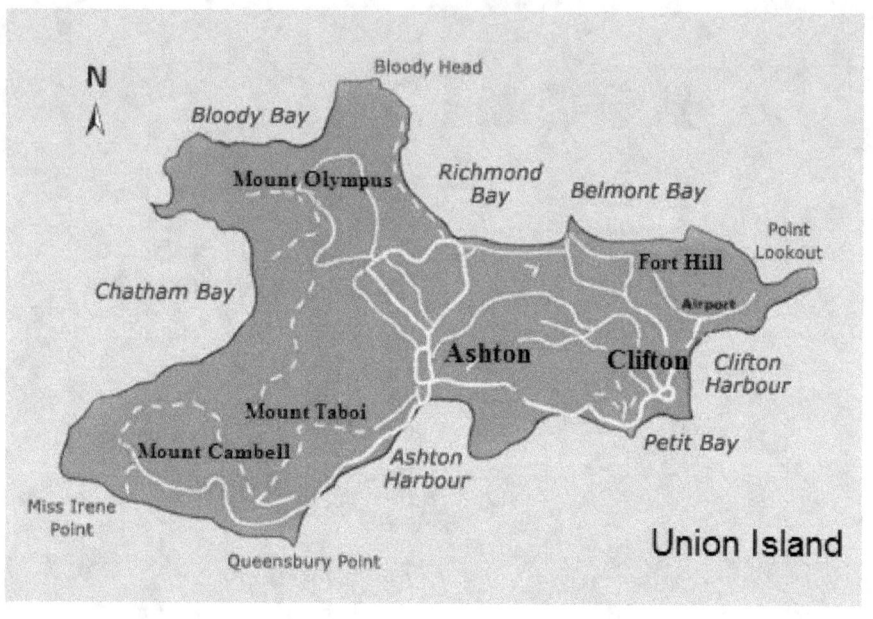

Deadeye

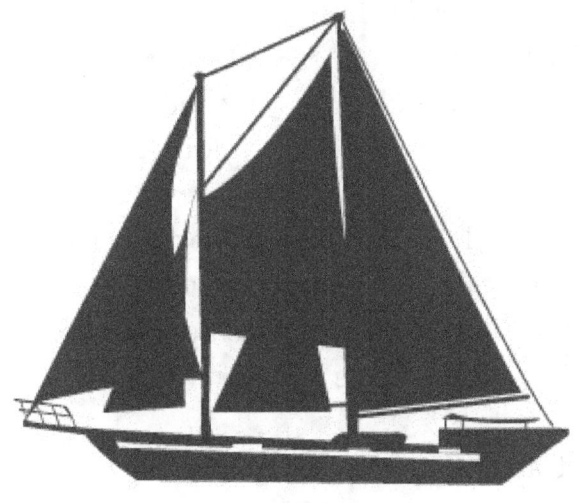

A Bequia Mystery

Michael W Smart

Copyright © 2012 by Michael W. Smart
First published 2014
Available in print ISBN: 978-0-9914008-3-6
Availabe in ebook ISBN: 978-0-9914008-4-3

Cover Illustration Copyright © 2013 by Michael Smart
Cover design by: Denise Kim Wy
http://www.coveratelier.com)
Editing by: Amanda Hough, Progressivedits
http://www.progressivedits.com
Author photograph by: Camilla Sjodin
(www.sjodinphotography.com)

Published by Michael W Smart at CreateSpace

to Judy, Audrey and Rachel;
who provided the place and space to write.

Deadeye:
A flat hardwood disk with a grooved perimeter around which a shroud line is rove, and pierced by three holes through which lanyards are passed to draw and tension the shrouds.

CHAPTER 1

Confusion and chaos greeted me at the scene. Horns blared in the midmorning heat. Vans piled up one behind the other, their drivers lending voice to the loud animated shouting already present at the roadside. The disordered dissonance smothered the pleasant afterglow of my flight down from Bequia, the first time I'd flown Mike's Seneca on my own.

Pedestrians milled about, lining both sides of the narrow mountain road; women carrying laden baskets on their heads; children in school uniform who should've already been in their classrooms; goats grazing at the roadside; men apparently having no place they needed to be. A chorus of voices raised in excitable animation.

A uniformed constable stood amidst the chaos. Unable or unwilling to control the mess, contributing yet another loud voice to the cacophonous chorus.

Alighting from the battered police Toyota 4runner I noticed yellow police tape stretched across a section of the road. Each end of the tape tied to stakes made from cut tree branches and driven into the ground. Off to the side, away from the crowd, a full-figured, buxom woman in a simple pink batik sundress, and sensible grey flats, silver buckles across the toes, stood before a distraught older man. She said something to the man before heading in my direction.

Zelina McIntosh, late twenties, one of the few female CID detectives on the Royal St. Vincent and the Grenadines Police Force. And among the handful who investigated criminal complaints beyond the limited purview of sexual and family offenses; the reason she'd accepted the Union Island station assignment. As the only CID detective on the island, Zelina investigated all criminal complaints. While she didn't have as many cases as she might on St. Vincent, she'd make her bones quicker on Union Island than on the mainland. I considered myself fortunate to have her in my Division.

Reaching me, she stood at attention and saluted. I returned the salute, before flashing a welcoming smile and shaking her hand.

"Suprintendent," she greeted in a lilting Vincentian contraction of Superintendent, releasing my hand.

"Cut the formality Zelina. Jus we gurls heah."

She smiled in turn, a pleasant, broad separation of full lips revealing straight, pearl white teeth. The smile lifted the chubby flesh covering her cheekbones. A thin patina of perspiration glistened on her ochre toned face.

"Before I forget, terrific job on the Delves case," I said, referring to a fatal stabbing on the island she'd successfully closed.

"So what we have heah?" I asked her.

She flipped pages on a spiral stenographer's notebook in her left hand.

"Passahsby discovahed de vehicle approximately seven o'clock dis mahnin," she began, consulting her notes. "Dey made a repoht at Clifton Police Station. Names are in de repoht at de station. Sargent Baptiste and Constable Quashie responded to de scene."

"Where is Baptiste by the way?" I asked, interrupting her.

"Said he had business back at de station since dis a CID case."

"I see," I said.

Her exasperated expression informed me she did too. Baptiste deliberately avoiding me. Fine by me.

"Anyway," she continued, "De registration plate is listed in de ownership of...." she flipped more pages, "Samuel Gooding. Dats im ova dey," she pointed, indicating the man she'd been speaking to when I'd arrived.

"Accordin to Mr. Gooding he loaned de vehicle to an American frend."

"When? When de las time he see de vehicle?" I asked.

She flipped more pages. "Accordin to Gooding, last evening jus befoh dahk."

"And de name of dis friend?"

"John Smith," she said reading from her notes.

"John Smith?" I repeated.

Zelina noted the skeptical inflection in my voice. "Yuh noh dis man?"

"I noh it's probably a false name," I said.

"How come?"

"Is an American ting. Smith and Jones are common aliases. Any description of dis friend?"

"White, American, late fifties about. Big. Dress in dahk pants, and a light blue polo shirt wid dat horse ting on it."

"And he's supposedly staying on PSV?"

"Dat accordin to Mr. Gooding."

"What yuh think of im?" I asked.

"I tink he hire out de vehicle fe money. Is a criminal offense, but no way to prove it widout de American or de money."

"And what being done to locate dis American?"

"Nuttin yet. Sergeant Baptiste stop doin anyting aftah yuh call me. And I didn't have a chance to staht inquirin into dat yet. Anyhow, if he been drivin he might be down in de wreck."

"Dats de reason de Commissioner give CID de case and why I'm here," I said, recalling the astonishing phone call earlier that morning from Commissioner of Police Mike Daniels. He'd ordered me to Union Island to personally take charge of the investigation. A vehicular accident was not usually assigned to the CID, unless it involved a fatality. And usually handled by an investigator well below my rank. An American staying on the resort island Petit St. Vincent might be involved he'd explained, a situation requiring delicate handling. He'd also suggested, practically commanded, I save time by flying down in his personal Piper Seneca.

His call had set my heart racing. He'd dispatched me into a lion's den. First, the situation had the potential to blow up in our faces given the combination of a wealthy American tourist, and a foreign owned island resort where the management vigorously protected their guests' privacy.

Secondly, I'd have to contend with Union Island's Station Sergeant, Garrett Baptiste, a misogynistic, incompetent bully who used his position to conceal his own insecurity and ineptitude.

Primarily my heart had raced at the prospect of flying the Seneca, and also the chance to see Gage. He'd sailed down island from Bequia two days before.

I'd missed him even after just two days apart. Missed waking up beside him; watching him get dressed; smelling his scent; reaching for him at night and feeling his arms close around me.

But the scene before me dominated my attention and monopolized my thoughts.

"Corporal Radcliff," I shouted, turning to the constable who'd driven me out from the airport.

"Ma'am," he said, stiffening to attention.

"Move dis police vehicle off de road and you and de odder constable start moving dose people and vans. I want dis road clear in five minutes."

"Yes ma'am," he acknowledged.

"Constable Johns," I called next, searching for the gangly nineteen-year-old rookie who'd accompanied me from Bequia. I'd shanghaied him for this assignment. He wasn't complaining. It meant an exciting change from his usual boring routine. And the flight down had transformed him into a wide-eyed kid on a fantasy adventure; when he wasn't clutching his seat in white knuckled apprehension.

"Ma'am," he said, materializing like magic at my side.

"Mek sure dat man don't go anywhey," I instructed, pointing to Samuel Gooding.

"Yes ma'am," he acknowledged, running off.

Loud voices rose from the roadside. Corporal Radcliff's above everyone else. He and his partner gesticulated in wild abandon, shooing, prodding, cajoling at the top of his voice; moving the knot of people and vehicles along the roadside.

The road clear, I called out to Corporal Radcliff again. When he arrived I gave him further instructions.

"Okay. One of you at dat end of de road," I said, pointing in one direction, "the odder ovah dat end," pointing in the opposite direction. "Keep any traffic moving and dis road clear." I shouldn't have had to direct them, but neither had taken the initiative to control the scene.

I walked to the opposite side of the road, to the yellow tape. Far down in a steep ravine, maybe a hundred meters, the tail end of a yellow Volkswagen 181 'Thing' stuck out of the treetops. The dense packed trees had arrested the compact jeep's fall. It had left a trail of smashed rocks, torn foliage, and vehicle debris in its tumble down the ravine. The soft, convertible canvas top had been shredded. A small portion of the front end visible from the road appeared crushed.

A sudden thought occurred. I turned to Zelina surveying the scene alongside me.

"Why didn't Gooding drive de jeep himself? Why give it to de American?"

"I was jus gwoin ask im dat when yuh ahrived."

"What about photos of de scene?" I asked.

"I tek some wen we was putting up de tape," she said, fishing in the cloth handbag under her left armpit. She extracted a small Nikon digital camera, powered it up, selected playback mode and handed it to me. The jeep had plunged off a narrow winding road halfway up Mount Olympus, northwest of Ashton Township. It had tumbled over a cliff of rock and dry forest. Zelina had photographed the jeep's destructive path, including mangled bits of yellow and red debris. Her activities at the scene since receiving my call earlier in the morning to take charge of the investigation, those of a professional investigator.

Still an hour before high noon. The sun a blinding silver orb high in a pale azurine, almost cloudless sky. Scattered cumulus hovered over Union island. The remainder of the sky clear and bright. Frequent rainy season showers had nourished the verdant landscape and brightened the vibrant reds, oranges, purples, yellows and blues of fruit trees and wildflowers.

From our vantage point on the mountain, Union's entire three square miles spread out before us. The green sloping landscape gave way to white sand and turquoise bays surrounded by a sapphire sea. Mayreau, Canuoan, Bequia and St. Vincent all visible to the east and north. Palm Island and Petit St. Vincent to the southeast. The Grenadian islands Petit Martinique and Carriacou lay to the south. And in the distant haze, the volcanic peak of Grenada itself.

I rummaged in my handbag, retrieved my cell phone, and dialed the Coast Guard dispatch desk in Calliaqua Bay on St. Vincent. I requested an ETA on the cutter Commissioner Daniels had dispatched. I'd flown over it on the trip down, a forty-foot aluminum cutter throwing a white bow wave as it plowed south for Union. I waited while the dispatcher radioed the vessel. The background noise of multiple active radio frequencies heard through the phone. Twelve minutes the dispatcher informed me. I hung up and turned to Zelina.

"Let's go see Mr. Gooding."

"If I may suggest Suprintendent."

"What?"

"Follow my lead."

She stood directly in front of Samuel Gooding. Zelina shorter by a head, but her authoritative presence clearly intimidated him. He bowed his head, eyes focused on the ground while she addressed him.

"Mister Gooding, yuh know we can bring a chahge gainst yuh fe unlawful hire of a vehicle. Dis is Suprintendent Johanssen of de CID." She emphasized my rank, as if by itself it increased the seriousness of the trouble he faced. In fact, absent evidence demonstrating he'd hired out the vehicle, we couldn't charge him.

"Why yuh no drive de jeep yuhself?" She continued in the same aggressive tone.

"I tell yuh me nevah hire out de jeep. Me loan it to a fren," he insisted, his gaze still downcast.

"Okay. So yuh loan it," she said, going along. "Yuh see him drivah license? Him have permit to drive on St. Vincent and the Grenadines? Why yuh no drive him yuhself?" She repeated more forcefully?

"He say he meeting sombady in private."

"Who?" She pressed him.

"How me fe noh? Him no tell me an me no ask."

"Whey dis meetin supposed to be?"

"Me no noh."

"Yuh no noh? Yuh len him yuh jeep and yuh no noh whey he gwoin wid it? Yuh edah stupid or lyin. So now we goin ahress and chahge yuh."

Zelina's threat produced muted muttering from the intimidated man before us. He hadn't done anything wrong, he insisted. Just being neighborly and helpful to a visitor. Didn't know nuttin bout nuttin. Repeated 'Lord have mercies' liberally interspersed in his mutterings.

Zelina turned to me, a knowing expression on her face. I nodded. We wouldn't get much more from him. She informed him he was under arrest and we left him guarded by Constable Johns.

We returned to the spot where the vehicle had left the road. A typical rural Vincentian road. Narrow, winding, poorly maintained and potholed, having dangerous drop-offs sometimes marked only by a low stone wall. Local drivers knew the dangerous stretches and deadly curves. A stranger had no chance, especially at night.

Evidently he'd been headed down toward Ashton. He'd misjudged the sharp curve, and half mounted, half plowed through the stone wall. It meant the jeep had been moving fast. But if the driver had been aware of impending disaster, the scene showed no evidence of it. No skid marks; no other indication the driver had tried to avoid hitting the wall. The jeep didn't appear to have hit side-on and rolled. Rather the destructive path indicated it had travelled straight over the low wall before tumbling end over end.

If one could believe anything Gooding said, I wondered who the driver planned to meet. Why it had to be kept private. It might mean a woman. I wondered if he'd been on the way to or from the rendezvous.

I walked over to Gooding again who remained under the watchful eyes of Constable Johns.

"Mister Gooding," I said approaching him, his gaze still firmly fixed on the ground.

"Look at me when I speak to you," I commanded.

His gaze slowly left the pavement and rose to meet mine. He had deep-set eyes in a heavily lined coal black face.

Dark irises, surrounded by dull chalky sclera; red streaks in the corners.

"Where yuh len dis man de jeep?" His gaze moved back and forth across my face, not focusing, avoiding my eyes.

"In Clifton, ma'am," he eventually answered, making momentary eye contact before quickly averting his gaze. His entire manner meek and submissive.

"What time?"

"Time? Time? I dohn noh time. Was jus gettin dahk."

"And how much he give yuh?"

"Him give me...." he began before catching himself and shutting his mouth. I glanced over at Zelina. She stifled a laugh.

"He nevah ge me nuttin, inspector... officer... suprintenden...." he continued in a nervous stutter.

"Riiight," I said. And when he supposed to return it?"

"Was fe leave it by Clifton Harbor wen he done wid it."

Satisfied, I returned to the still chuckling Zelina.

"So what now Suprintendent?" she asked.

"I need to get down to that jeep," I said in non-patois English, glancing at my watch. "And whey de hell de Coast Guard be?" I asked, lapsing right back into it as my exasperation grew, again checking my watch. Checking it every few seconds wouldn't get the Coast Guard and SSU officers on site any sooner. On these islands things occurred on Vincy time.

Mon ostie de saint-sacrament de câlice de crisse! My silent frustration switched from patois to French, one of three languages I'd grown up hearing in my household.

"Suprintendent, how we gwoin bring up de jeep from down dey?" Zelina asked, channeling my own thoughts. I'd been contemplating the problem on and off since arriving on the scene. Anywhere else, it'd be a no brainer. Call in a crane, a hoist, whatever. Haul it up. But in the Grenadines it presented a challenge requiring creative thinking. Another reason to get a move on. No telling what this operation might entail and how long it might take.

"Not sure yet," I said to Zelina. Won't know til I get down dey, see wha we have. Yuh have yuh VHF?"

"Yeah Suprintendent."

"Call de Coast Guard. Find out whey de hell dey be," my patience running on empty.

She fished in her handbag, extracted a handheld VHF and tuned in the Coast Guard frequency. The cutter had to be in range of the portable radio by now. Standing next to her, I heard both sides of the exchange.

"We jus leave de harbor, be dey just now," came the answer to her inquiry. 'Just now'. A distinctly Vincentian concept. A subset of Vincy time, indicating an indefinite period which might be soon, maybe later, but in practice meant whenever.

We waited in the tropical heat. The scenery magnificent and unchanging. Distant specs of white sail appeared motionless in the blue expanse. Zelina and I discussed what we knew so far, formulating theories regarding the accident. I told her my idea the driver might've been meeting a woman, wanting to keep the meeting discreet.

He'd picked up the jeep in Clifton, and judging from the angle it went off the road, he might've been on the way back. Did he meet the person and drive up here together? Or did the meeting take place farther up the mountain? Not much up there. No villas or hotels. A few rudimentary island homes sparsely scattered in the dense forest; a few clearings offering spectacular views. Maybe they'd wanted the view and privacy; an impromptu lover's lane.

Who had the driver met? And was that person also in the vehicle when it went off the road and down the cliff? I wondered.

Merde! I needed to get down to the wreck.

CHAPTER 2

'Just now' arrived when a grey Land Rover transporting two Special Service Unit constables and a Coast Guardsman approached the scene. The Special Service officers dressed in green camos. The Coast Guardsman in a navy blue jumpsuit. All three wore U.S. supplied combat boots. The Special Service officers wore holstered side arms.

I recognized all three men disembarking from the jeep. The St. Vincent and the Grenadines Police Force was a small group, in a small environment. Its eight hundred fifty members distributed among the constabulary, various CID units, the Fire Service, Coast Guard, and the small Rapid Response and Special Services Units. Units I'd trained with, both as trainee and instructor.

The ranking constable, Inspector Dillon Lewis, enjoyed a certain celebrity on the Islands. He'd been a gifted cricket player who'd played on the national team for a short time. He also played steel drums in a popular calypso band. He had a reputation as a lady's man, a 'playah', parlaying his minor celebrity, bachelorhood, and disarming charm to 'lime' any female who entered his orbit.

As evidenced when he greeted us. "Ladies, ladies. Good day and ow y'all doin?" a broad smile on his pleasant, if not exactly handsome features. His dark eyes, set in an angular face of smooth dark skin, held a mischievousness gleam. He had a flat nose, and wore a groomed moustache above thick lips.

"Suprintendent," he said more respectfully when he noticed the glare I'd leveled at him. I didn't need him to come to attention or salute, but he needed to be reminded this was work, and I his commanding officer. Early in our association I'd had to forcefully dissuade him of the notion we'd be anything but commander and subordinate. There'd been no problem after that early dressing down. But flirting lived in his DNA. I didn't mind it. Had long ago ceased minding such foolishness from men around me, as long as it wasn't inappropriate and didn't interfere with work. Lewis and the other men on the force knew well enough by now not to play the fool around me.

An effective police officer when not playing Casanova or the class clown, Lewis had made his bones under fire training with the Philadelphia Police Department. I'd lived in Philadelphia attending U Penn for my Master's Degree, and we shared a few places and even a few acquaintances in common.

He turned his charm on Zelina instead. "How yuh doing detective?"

"Dohn play wid me fool," she retorted. I suppressed a smile. Zelina couldn't be less interested. And though he outranked her, she didn't take crap from anyone. One of many things I admired about her.

His usual charm getting him nowhere, Lewis turned to help his colleague unpack the jeep and assemble the climbing gear.

Sergeant Colin Williams, two years younger than Lewis, and two years junior to him on the force, had a more professional air about him. And a promising career on the force. His name on a list of candidates Commissioner Daniels and I'd been keeping a special watch on.

The Coast Guardsman, Able Seaman David Sammy, a youngster close in age to Constable Johns; no more than nineteen or twenty. His round cherubic face and fleshy cheeks appeared to still possess its baby fat.

"Las one down buy de beahs," Inspector Lewis shouted over at me, stepping into his harness and cinching the straps.

"Dis isn't a training exercise or contest Inspector. Dis a crime scene, yuh heah me? Yuh watch yuh footin and step carefully so yuh dohn disturb any evidence."

My admonishment diluted his levity. But he still wore a distressingly familiar condescending smirk. Being male in a patriarchal culture intrinsically ascribed greater capability to him than to women, solely by virtue of his gender. A notion he continually needed to prove; to women, to himself, to his peers.

But despite his outward cavalier attitude, I noticed he paid close attention to his equipment. We both noted Williams anchoring the lines to the jeep. The clap of metal on metal and the whirr of uncoiling ropes filled the surrounding air as our practiced hands passed rope through metal, and snapped carabiners into place on our harnesses. Lewis clipped an ascender to a carabiner snapped to his harness. We'd need the ascenders later for the climb back from the wreckage. He fed his line through an ATC descender which functioned both as a rappel and belay device.

I paid attention to his knots. He fashioned an autoblock knot, a safety precaution in case he lost control on the descent, and also a stopper knot at the bitter end of the line.

I checked his technique and progress while performing the same tasks on my own equipment. Before donning worn and dirty leather gloves, I attached a fanny pack to a carabiner on my harness. I transferred a few items from my handbag to the pack and the cargo pockets of my pants. I handed the handbag to Zelina for safe keeping.

Finally ready, standing side by side, Williams completed a final check of us both.

We dropped the static lines over the side. I watched the fall, ensuring we had sufficient line to reach the wreckage. As we stepped backwards over the remnants of the stone wall, Williams placed a short piece of rubber hose, cut longitudinally, over each rope to prevent chaffing where it rubbed against the stone wall.

Before starting down I cautioned Inspector Lewis again. "Remembah, walk it down slow. Look fo anyting dat might be evidence. Blood, personal items, and pieces from de jeep."

"Yes Suprintendent," he replied, still smirking, though his demeanor a bit more serious after stepping over the edge. Concentration etched his broad black forehead, glistening with the first bands of sweat. His gloved hands competently managed his lines. His left fed the rope through the descender, his right braking hand just below his right buttock.

We continued down, side by side, walking backward at maybe a seventy degree angle to the rock face, our booted feet planted solidly against it. One step at a time. Our eyes searched the slope in front, to the sides, below.

We'd climbed past the rock face into the brushy brambles and trees growing at odd angles from the mountainside. We followed the path of smashed and uprooted foliage plowed by the Volkwagen. Stripped leaves and torn branches, the white flesh exposed beneath ripped bark, formed a thick carpet underfoot. The pungent scent of cottonwood and cedar rose from the mangled foliage.

Something caught my eye. A flash of color against the rusty brown and green. A piece of fabric, light blue. Didn't bode well for what I might find in the wreckage below. A knot formed in my stomach.

"Belay," I called over to Lewis. He halted his descent, directing a questioning gaze at me before wrapping a few turns of the rope around his descender.

Similarly belayed, I pulled Zelina's camera from the fanny pack and snapped a few shots of the broken branch and shard of fabric. I returned the camera and pulled a clear Ziploc bag from the fanny pack. I stuffed the piece of fabric into it. That too went into the pack.

I motioned to Lewis. We continued our descent. The heavy cottonwood branches which had arrested the jeep's plunge, now directly below. The road seemed a long way up. The spectators above observing our progress shrunk to doll size.

We descended into the leafy treetops, almost on top of the wreckage. We'd transitioned from climbing down a cliff to climbing trees, maneuvering through branches as thick as utility poles. A few yards from the Jeep I called to Lewis to belay again.

I didn't know how much more weight, if any, the branches holding the wreckage might bear. Or if the slightest disturbance might send the jeep plunging deeper into the trees, maybe completely off the cliff into the rocky ravine below.

Amid the topmost branches, I belayed myself again. I perched in the fork of two branches, steadied myself, and shot close-up photographs of the wrecked jeep, now scant feet away. Close up I saw more of its front end, pushed in like an accordion. A large flap of the ripped and shredded canvas top hung over the still intact roll bar, obscuring my view of the driver and passenger compartment.

Merde. I needed to get even closer.

I didn't relish this situation at all. Physically I was hot and sweaty. Perspiration trickled down my temples and cheeks, into my eyes, down my neck, under my shirt collar and beneath the snug bra. The tight climbing harness dug into my buttocks and crotch.

Emotionally, I recognized my precarious situation. Any number of little things, or combination of things, might conspire to ruin my day. Not just my day, but my subordinate's too. He was my responsibility.

As the thought occurred, I glanced over to check Lewis's position. I didn't need him upsetting the delicate balance of little things preventing a disaster from occurring. This wasn't the time or place for macho bullshit.

The expression on his sweat glistened face assured me of his own awareness and concern. The smirk no longer present. His eyes intently focused, concentrating on his own precarious perch.

The knot in my stomach grew. My stress level increased, intensified by my physical discomfort, the imminent danger, and an image of what I fully expected to find in the wreckage, or hanging in the trees close to it. Adrenaline rushed into my bloodstream, infusing my tissues, heightening my stress.

I could've delegated this job to Williams. He'd had similar training. At least as competent as Lewis or I. But the responsibility fell to me. I led from the front, facing the same risks as the men and women under my command. In a male dominated culture it had gained me a measure of their respect.

"Inspector," I called over to Lewis. He'd been awaiting instructions and seemed relieved to finally have something to do. I tossed him the extra coil of rope attached to my harness.

"Anchor dat to de tree and toss me de end. Anchor your second line and belay yuhself to it."

I observed him tie off the lines, paying close attention to his knots. I didn't doubt his competence, but my life depended on that anchor.

Now we both had two new rappelling lines extending past the wreckage into the trees. I lowered myself from the tree limb I'd been sitting on, braking when I reached a lower branch wedged behind the Jeep's left front tire. I straddled the thick branch, pulling myself forward to the front end of the jeep.

The odor reached me first. Unmistakable. A nauseating blend of methane and hydrogen sulfide. And a loud buzzing drone assaulted my ears.

Up against the jeep, I belayed my line. I exchanged the worn climbing gloves for purple Nitrile gloves. I grasped the crumpled passenger side door. Cautiously raised myself to a standing position on the thick branch. The slight amount of pressure I exerted against the jeep hadn't budged it. The wreck remained tightly wedged. My confidence grew as I worked my way over it.

The horrendous buzzing emanated from a dark hovering mass of flies covering a body in the front of the jeep. The driver pushed against the back of the front seats. Broken and bloody, blackened and bloated.

Even discolored I discerned a white male, approximately sixty-years old. Dried blood streaked and matted the wisps of white hair. A ripped polo shirt also soaked in blood, now a dark shade of brown, dotted by small patches of light blue. Similar brown stains covered the upholstery and door panel.

The lower half of the body, from the waist down, remained hidden. Buried and pinned beneath the dashboard and engine block jammed against the front seats. The disintegrated detritus of a motor vehicle surrounded and covered the corpse. Beads of shattered glass, ripped pieces of upholstery, dashboard fittings, and bits of molded plastic. Swarms of flies and armies of ants already at work on the remains. I'd expected it. Had fortified myself for it. The gruesome reality still came as a gut wrenching shock.

The knot in my stomach turned to a bubble, threatening to burst and spew its contents. I suppressed the urge. Lifeless bodies weren't uncommon in my line of work. I'd encountered them in many forms. Mangled by steel and carbon fiber in vehicular accidents; punctured by knives and hacked by machetes; shredded by bits of metal propelled from a firearm. Though familiar, I still hadn't grown quite used to it. Hoped I never would.

I retrieved Zelina's camera from the fanny pack and photographed the body and wreckage.

I used my cell phone to call Zelina. I didn't want the report going over the police band or VHF airwaves. It'd make the discovery common knowledge within the hour. The topic of small island gossip and speculation. Inevitable. But at least I'd delay it for a while longer.

"Zelina," I said when she answered. "Keep this just between us for now." For some reason patois had deserted me. "There's a body in the jeep. Fits the description of the American. There's no way to remove the body. We have to bring the whole jeep up and cut it out."

"Understan." Zelina a quick study. She didn't identify the speaker on the other end of the call.

"Any ideas on how we're going to bring it up? I asked.

"I was tinkin de fire tender at de aipoht. It have a winch. But de constable tell me de winch not wokin."

"Can they fix it?"

"No. Is a paht dey waitin on."

Sacrament. Typical, I thought. "Okay. I'll get back to you," I said, disconnecting.

Not surprising. Next I speed dialed Mike's satellite number. Commissioner of Police Mike Daniels answered promptly, like he'd been anxiously awaiting my call.

"What you got JJ?" he asked. No greeting or preamble.

"I'm down at the wreck Chief. There's a body trapped inside. Fits the description of the American."

I heard his sigh through the phone. A sensitive man, the Chief. Hard but compassionate. The political and media complications attending the death of a tourist didn't help.

"Thing is Chief," I continued. "We won't be able to extract the body without bringing the jeep up and cutting it out. The fire tender at the airport has a winch but the winch isn't working."

"Of course it isn't," he responded. No mistaking the exasperation in his voice.

"I don't know what's available locally for cutting, and we'll need to move the wreck once we get it up. I'll also need a bag for transporting the body."

"Okay. I'll make the arrangements on this end. But nothing will probably get to you before nightfall, more likely early in the morning. You'll have to secure the scene for the night."

"I figured," I said.

"Call me when you're able to give me a detailed report. Talk with you soon JJ." He broke the connection. My attention returned to the body.

I mentally constructed a timeline. Rigor had fully set in, and full livor mortis too. His clothing obscured the extent of lividity, but the skin, where it hadn't been ripped open, had stretched and cracked, displaying a greenish black color. And the odor indicated the onset of putrefaction and decomposition.

He'd obtained the vehicle from Gooding between six and seven the previous evening. The wreck had been spotted around seven am and reported to the police. Twelve hours. Two in the afternoon now. Another seven hours. He'd been dead anywhere from twelve to nineteen hours.

He wore a wristwatch, smashed and broken. Reaching across the corpse I noticed the jeep's seatbelt still bucked across his waist, now buried in the folds of bloated flesh. Curious the Volkswagen even had one. The 181 'Thing', or 'Safari' as some called it, was an older vehicle, before seatbelts became standard. And most Vincentians dismantled or cut the seatbelts in their vehicles.

I swatted away flies and ants to reach and unclasp the wristwatch. Stopped at ten o'clock. As good an indication of time of death as any. He'd been dead for sixteen hours.

Inspector Lewis had been uncharacteristically patient and quiet on his perch above. Finally he called down.

"Suprintendent. Wha yuh see?"

"Stan by Inspector," I called back. I called Detective McIntosh on the cell phone again.

"Zelina, we wohn be able to move de jeep til mahnin. I need yuh to send down a tarp or somethin to covah de bahdy." I'd slipped back into patois.

"I figah dat. Getting one ready now."

"Yuh de best gurl. Send it down when yuh ready. Also if yuh have a small fire extinguisher up dey send it down too."

I pocketed the phone and called up to Lewis.

"Inspector, dey sendin something down just now. Wen yuh get it bring it ovah heah fe me."

"Yes ma'am."

Nothing to do for the moment but wait. And contemplate the corpse before me, and not for the first time, the vagaries of life and death. In college and graduate school it'd been an intellectual exercise. In the world of police work it'd turned into reality. Up-close and personal. People were mortal. Myself included, I reminded myself. Death ever present. I didn't dwell on it. Its reality didn't consume me. But it did provide a certain perspective.

Who was this man? I wondered. Had he felt the same way? Contemplated his mortality? Imagined how he'd die? I doubted it. Most people didn't think about their mortality until it stared them in the eye. How had he lived? Had it been constructive and fulfilling, or full of regret? Who'd he leave behind to mourn and miss him? How'd he come to be in this place? I'd have the answers in time. In death he now belonged to me.

"Suprintendent," I heard from above.

I gazed up to see Inspector Lewis securing a bundle to his harness, careful to keep it from entangling his lines. He lowered himself to the tree limb, inching his way up behind me.

"Hole up Inspector," I said when he reached me. "Lemme reposition."

I'm not sure he'd heard me. His eyes were locked in a fixed stare on the corpse. He'd seen his share of dead bodies, as I had, but he'd been raised in a religious and superstitious culture. As much as he might deny it, and as much exposure as he'd had to the world outside these islands, those childhood influences remained lodged in a primal corner of his mind.

"Yes ma'am," he said. A deferential tone in his voice I didn't quite expect.

I'd had time to study the arboreal terrain enclosing the wreckage. I'd determined how and where to move around it. I unfastened the brake on my line, gave myself slack, and carefully repositioned myself on the opposite side of the wreck. I brushed away flies taking a sudden interest in me, threatening to envelope me.

"Inspector," I said. "Dey send down a fire extinguisher?"

He unwrapped and unfolded a bundled green tarp and held out a small red extinguisher.

"Spray it ovah de body," I instructed.

He pulled the pin from the neck and squeezed the metal trigger. A jet of white spray enveloped the corpse, scattering the flies which rose in a black buzzing cloud above the body.

The extinguisher foam covered the corpse in a thin patina of white resembling talcum powder. The spray scattered the ants too, but they'd be able to get at the corpse again. So would other crawling insects. Not so much the flies after we covered him.

We passed the tarp under and around the body as best we could. From my cargo pocket I retrieved a Tanto tactical switchblade, a gift from Gage, who'd declared a girl must never leave home without one.

Funny, I thought, that many of his gifts to me were weapons.

I forced myself to concentrate on the task at hand. I knew all too well how easy it'd be to lose myself thinking of him. Many of the gifts, but not all, I smiled.

Inspector Lewis hadn't noticed the black aluminum handle concealed by my gloved hand. I heard his surprised inhalation when the spring loaded blade snapped loudly into place. The webbed seatbelt material no match for the sharpened, partially serrated stainless steel blade.

The tarp wrapped and secured around the corpse, Inspector Lewis and I prepared to depart the scene. We tied the rope ends to the jeep and climbed back to the branch where he'd anchored them. There we tied off the ends of the rappel lines leading up to the road. Time to climb.

Almost an hour to reach the road. We arrived winded and soaked in sweat. Neither worse off than the other. No bragging rights for Lewis today.

"Well done Inspector," I said as we stripped off our gear. "Good job." The compliment well deserved and acknowledged by an appreciative smile.

Zelina had bottles of water ready for us. We guzzled them like frat boys in a beer chugging contest. When we'd finished the first bottle we each reached for another. Lewis poured the contents over his close-cropped hair, spraying everyone when he shook his head from side to side like a drenched dog.

No hair dousing for me. But I poured most of the bottle around my neck. The cold, soothing liquid flowed down my back and chest.

Zelina and I walked off to the side while the men stowed the gear.

"How bad?" she asked in a sympathetic voice.

"Bad. He be down dey almost sixteen hours."

"Poh man," she said, the sympathy in her voice, extended to both the dead man and to me, also reflected in sad eyes.

"So, everyting on hold til tomahrow?"

"Looks dat way," I said, glancing at my watch, closing on five o'clock, and noticing a distinct change in her demeanor. A mischievous grin spread across her face.

"Good ting fe yuh." She said

Wha yuh mean?"

"De Wherever in Clifton," her grin wider as she delivered the punch line.

"Yuh terrible gurl, yuh know dat?" I smiled.

"Uuh uuh," accompanied by a conspiratorial wink and a lascivious laugh.

"Get away from me," I retorted in the same spirit.

Still enjoying herself Zelina pulled her cell phone from her handbag, opened it, and made a call.

"What yuh doin?" I said.

"Not to worry Suprintendent. Lemme andle dis."

When the other end answered she said, "Connect me wid Sergeant Baptiste."

My ears perked up.

"Sergeant Baptiste?" she said after a pause. "Detective McIntosh. I gwoin need two constables to wohk ovahnight. One till midnight and a releef from midnight till aight am. I might need dem aftah dat too. Right now I need to close off de Mount Olympus road from Ashton."

A pause before she spoke again. "De Suprintendent busy right now. We have fe secure de scene until tomahrow." Another pause. "Yes Sergeant. Dat is correct. I gwoin need some equipment too. I sendin Corporal Radcliff fe bring it."

While Zelina made her arrangements I briefed Lewis on the situation. When Zelina returned the teasing girlfriend had vanished, replaced by the efficient CID detective. Corporal Radcliff departed in one of the police Toyotas, accompanied by the other constable.

My stomach rumbled. I realized I hadn't eaten all day. I needed to wrap things up before I fainted from low blood sugar.

"Inspector Lewis has his instructions," I said to Zelina. "He'll schedule his detail to secure dis location until we can start again tomorrow."

She nodded. "I have a pohtable genaratah and floodlights coming," she told them. "And de road close off from below wid constables on post."

"What about food?" I said as my stomach growled again.

"I'll mek ahrangements. De poliss have accounts wid Tan'N in Ashton and Olivia's in Clifton."

"Okay," I said. Everything seemed to be covered. "You might as well head back now too Zelina. You still need to book Gooding into custody. And Inspector Lewis," I said turning to him, "I'll wait until the equipment gets here and then Constable Johns is yours until tomorrow."

While I waited I called Mike and updated him on the situation, including the arrangements for securing the scene overnight. I told him I'd upload all the photos from the scene to him when I had the chance.

The call to Mike completed, I displayed the number of another encrypted cell phone and sent a text message.

I received a quick reply.

CHAPTER 3

By the time I arrived in Clifton Harbor the accident scene had receded to the hindermost parts of my mind. My subconscious brain still worked the case. Synapses continued to send and receive their chemical messages, categorizing, analyzing, associating, memorizing.

But the primitive parts of my brain dominated my conscious mind. The parts directing emotion and physical sensation; particularly sexual desire and arousal.

He'd texted me where to meet him. My pulse raced in anticipation as I crossed Clifton's main square to Lambi's, a popular bar and restaurant on Clifton's waterfront. The bar and dining room, partially built on stilts over the water, provided a panoramic view of Clifton Harbor, and the low silhouettes of Palm Island and Petit St. Vincent in the distance.

I scanned the open air room as I entered, the way I'd seen him do countless times. I'd acquired the habit, without conscious thought or effort. I knew where I'd find him. A location providing the best view of the entire room and all the entrances and exits.

As expected, he sat at the circular bar in the center of the room, his back to the kitchen. A cocktail glass of his preferred drink, rum and coke, on the bar before him. He'd just turned fifty five, still a solid hunk of manhood in a six foot one inch, one hundred ninety pound frame. His weathered, chocolate colored face topped by close-cropped curly salt and pepper hair, thinning on the top.

He possessed an understated sexuality, even at his age. Maybe because of it. A fully formed, self-assured man. A woman would have to be dead not to notice, or not be affected by its compelling attraction. I assumed he'd seen me enter, but he gave no outward sign. Instead his eyes, sometimes soulful, sometimes cold-blooded, continued their casual scrutiny of the room.

No one around the bar but Gage. A few early diners, itinerant yachtsmen, occupied tables around the room. Still too early for the nightly steel band. And being midweek, Lambi's wouldn't get as packed, as loud, or as crazy as on the weekend. Especially this time of year.

When his gaze finally rested on me it had the same effect as a jolt of electricity. Still had that effect on me. Even after three years together. At odd moments our relationship still confounded me, like something in a dream. It had seemed entirely implausible when we'd first met. A twenty year difference in our ages for one. And neither of us had appeared the least interested in the other.

Not entirely true. He'd piqued my interest, as in a fascinating psychological subject. It being my field after all. I'd been intrigued by an ineffable aura surrounding him. A depth, a hardness; disturbing and perhaps dangerous. Barely perceptible, unshakable, and under tight control. His piercing brown eyes as cold as ice one moment, as tender as a child's the next, with a disconcerting way of looking at me, like looking into me, or through me. When we'd first met I'd sensed a guarded reticence. A cold distance. Until I'd discovered he also possessed a warm, charming, even tender side.

I'd liked him. Not in a romantic way. Rather an instant comfort around him. Nonthreatening. And he hadn't reacted to me as most men did. From our first meeting he'd treated me as a real person, not some Barbie doll type eye candy to be seduced, possessed or showcased. And he'd exuded a refreshing honesty. Not exactly the forthcoming type, even now he seldom spoke about himself, his life, his past. But he'd projected forthrightness. A distinct impression of meaning every word he said.

A startling revelation, unexpected, had crept upon me like a microscopic organism burrowing under my skin, forcing me to acknowledge a different set of emotions the longer I knew him. Strange and confusing. An attraction for a man I hardly knew, but who I could.... maybe.... possibly.... might even be able to......fall in love with.

And a shock, though not altogether surprising, the morning I woke up in bed curled against him, realizing I'd made love to a man I knew little about, but who I'd inexplicably fallen in love with.

I'd given up trying to analyze and rationalize it. In the same way I'd eventually given up trying to suppress my burgeoning feelings for him. It'd been a futile exercise. In the final analysis my feelings for him were visceral and deep. I loved him. No rhyme or reason for it. It simply felt right. Not just some of the time. But all the time. Whoever had said love wasn't something you can account for or predict had sure as hell been referring to me.

While his face remained impassive, his light brown eyes held a sensual welcome, conveying without words everything I needed to know. A warm flush raced through my body.

"Hi sailor," I said, sliding onto the bar stool next to his. "Buy a girl a drink."

"What's your pleasure?" he asked. An amorous twinkle in his eyes.

I returned the look, enveloping him in my gaze; losing myself in his. Another flash of heat surged through me.

"Well, I'm drinking whatever you're drinking. As for my pleasure, that's a whole other matter."

Full lips parted in a characteristically genuine and infectious smile, encompassing his entire face, enlivening the sometimes cold, distant eyes. It smoothed out his rougher edges. I kissed him lightly on his parted lips. The soft hairs of his moustache tickled my nose.

"Salty," he said, running his tongue over his lips.

"I've heard you like a woman who knows how to build up a sweat."

"Depends on the activity," he said, still smiling. "I hear you like to spend your afternoons climbing down cliffs."

That he knew how I'd spent my afternoon didn't surprise me. He had an uncanny awareness of everything occurring in his proximity.

"What else have you heard?" I asked him.

"That you might've found the body of an American tourist in a wrecked jeep."

"News travels fast."

"Just the broad strokes. So far you still have a lid on the details."

He paused when Denise, the bartender, approached. A stout, fulsome woman, she wore her hair close cropped, male style, and dyed bright red. She wore a v-neck tee shirt, 'Bermuda' stenciled across the chest.

"Wha'll yuh have Suprintendent?"

"Same as de gentleman Denise," I said. "And I'm stahvin. Can I get a likkle plate of stew chicken please? De smell from dat kitchen mekin me stomach growl."

"Shoh ting. What a dreadful ting fe appen. Dat poh man."

"Shoh nuff," I said, derailing any further attempt to draw information from me. Denise placed my drink on the bar in front of me before heading to the kitchen.

When she'd gone Gage said, "I guess that was you in the Seneca this morning."

"Oh my God Gage. It was beyond awesome. Like my first solo. I still can't believe Mike let me take his baby up by myself." The words flew from my mouth in an excitable rush.

"You've a terrific pilot. You have enough time in type. Wasn't anything for him to worry about."

Spoken as a statement of fact, conveying unquestioning confidence and trust. Just one of the countless things I found endearing in him. A genuine respect, non-begrudging, freely given as from one peer to another. His quiet, egoless strength and confidence; his self-certainty, made him easy to be with, and allowed me to be completely myself around him.

We ate at the bar. Usually I'm not a big eater, preferring small portions I can pick at and savor. What Gage teasingly described as eating like a bird. But my hunger felt like it'd been building for days. I plowed into the steaming, aromatic plate of boneless chicken, stewed and smothered in a brown curry sauce. Rice and green vegetables on the side.

Gage resumed his silent vigilance through my first heaping forkfuls. Without turning his head his gaze shifted across the room, table to table, out onto the dinghy dock, and the harbor beyond. Around the bar he searched the bottles and glasses arranged on the shelves. For what? I couldn't tell. Then sudden clarity. He'd been scanning their reflective surfaces. Constantly aware of everyone and everything around him. I wondered why he still considered it necessary.

Incorrect premise, I concluded. Not a matter of necessity. Autonomous. As natural to him as breathing.

When I'd convinced my stomach its connection to my mouth still existed, I laid the fork on the plate and inhaled a deep breath. The plate still held a sizable portion. I'd put a dent in it, but not by much. Gage had probably figured as much and hadn't ordered anything for himself. Usually I picked from his plate. I offered him my fork.

"Want to help me finish this?"

After a few forkfuls he asked, "Any anomalies regarding your dead guy."

His question elicited a smile. I'd anticipated it. Figured he'd voice it sooner or later. His mind instinctively going there, in the same way his eyes never ceased scanning and filtering for what he called anomalies.

"Two minor ones," I said. "But it's early days yet. The case is just getting started."

"When it involves someone being dead there's no such thing as a minor anomaly," he proclaimed. "Same goes for coincidences."

"Your paranoia's showing again."

"If it wasn't for what you call my paranoia, I might not be sitting here having this conversation with the most beautiful woman I've ever set eyes on."

I think I blushed. A flush of blood rushed to my face. Accompanied by a tingling along my spine, travelling from my head, spreading out between my legs, and down to the tips of my toes. Spoken by any other man those words might've evoked an entirely opposite reaction. From Gage they meant much more than mere flattery.

"How's Wherever's water tanks?" I asked, my breath coming in short gasps.

"Full," he said.

"And Rodney?"

"Back on Bequia until tomorrow."

"Good. Because I have another hunger I need to satisfy. But first I need a bath."

Gage's fulltime home, and my home away from home, was a fifty eight foot Herreshoff designed staysail schooner named Wherever. She, Gage insisted on the feminine pronoun, possessed spacious and comfortable accommodations below decks, and a personality under sail any sailor worth their salt might term endearing. She and Gage had been together a long time. And not only did he insist on the feminine pronoun, he referred to her as if she were a living, breathing friend. He'd remarked more than once how she'd given him back his life.

The setting sun turned the western sky blood red as Gage navigated Wherever's dinghy through Clifton's crowded harbor. I hardly noticed, anticipating the full length bathtub in the master cabin, and the activity to follow.

I began stripping off clothing the moment I reached the bottom of the companionway steps inside the main hatch. Gage climbed down behind me, pulling me into his arms. His mouth met mine, pressing and opening. His tongue reached in, seeking mine. Strong arms enclosed me, folding me against his firm body.

I practically tore the tee shirt off him, breaking the kiss momentarily as I whipped the shirt over his head and tossed it aside. His fingers worked on my belt, and the buttons and zipper of my slacks.

I gripped his back and sank against him, my flesh melting against his like molten clay. My fingers scraped against his scars. A jagged three inch knife wound on his upper left arm; the gunshot wound by his right ribcage. Others I'd come to know intimately. I'd explored them countless times as he lay in bed beside me; wondering about each one.

He removed my bra, tossing it aside. Cupped my breasts in his hands, caressing them. He kissed one, pulling and suckling on the nipple. Then the other. A moan from deep inside me escaped my lips. I pulled at his jeans, he at my pants, impatiently trying to shed them. Our mouths met again.

We slid to the teak cabin sole amid discarded clothing. My legs responded like automatic doors to his weight pressing down on me. They opened, knees drawn up, cradling him, my hips arching to meet him, inviting him in; surrendering myself completely.

The cabin faded upon his initial thrusts. The thick delicious fullness expected and yet surprising. Unleashing a flood of rippling sensation; my insides coming apart. I lost my mind entirely when the first convulsive spasm hit.

The soak in the tub came after, not before. And we made love again after I emerged from a leisurely soak. A slow, lingering coupling the second time, savored like dessert after the main course. And later, holding each other in the dark aft master cabin, Wherever gently rocked us to sleep.

I awoke suddenly. Still snuggled against him. His arm around my shoulder. Gage in the throes of a dream. Muscles in his arms and legs tensed and flexed in rapid spasms like the quivering flanks of a racehorse after a fast gallop. Spasms strong enough I'd felt them through my skin, pressed against his. Strong enough to wake me. He moved very little while sleeping, or dreaming. He never made a sound, even as the tension grew inside him.

As I'd done many times before I wrapped my arms around him, cradling and rocking him. Whispering in his ear: "It's okay. You're safe. Shhhhh."

He awoke startled, yet silent and unmoving. Only the wide, frantically shifting eyes betrayed his inner agitation. I marveled at the discipline and conditioning it required.

The tension dissipated while I held him, and rocked him. Soon he returned to normal sleep, his head nestled between my breasts.

I felt his pulse against my skin slowing, almost disappearing altogether. The first time I'd experienced the phenomenon it'd scared me half to death. In a panic I'd felt for his pulse, afraid he'd suffered a coronary. But the pulse had been there, so slow and light against my fingertips it'd been barely palpable, but rhythmically steady. I'd since grown accustomed to this thing he did to his heart rate. But just the same I put my hand on his chest, like I always did, just to be sure.

I wondered where his dreams had taken him this time. And whether I'd ever be able to help him quiet the demons haunting him.

CHAPTER 4

I awoke early, to the rising sun. To the sound of water lapping softly against Wherever's hull instead of roosters crowing outside my window. Refreshed and whole again. Bathed in a sexual afterglow. Gage still asleep, or so I thought.

"You're up early," he said as I disentangled myself from his arms.

"Got a full day," I said, stepping toward the head and shower. "I need to make sure we get the wreck up today. Poor man's been down there long enough. And I need to get this investigation going. By the way, I have to send some photographs to Mike. Can you encrypt and send them over the secure server for me?"

"No problem."

When I'd finished in the head, and after a quick shower, I heard him moving around the galley. The aroma of eggs, toast, and mountain roast coffee filled the cabin.

I stepped to the starboard hanging locker and opened it. I didn't keep much in the way of clothes on board. Mostly odds and ends, swimwear, a few sundresses. I hoped to find something suitable for the day ahead.

The top locker drawer held a small assortment of underwear mixed among bikini tops and bottoms. After pulling on panties and a soft cotton sports bra, I searched for pants and found only jeans. A dressy enough pair suitable for the day. A white uniform shirt I didn't remember leaving on board also hung in the locker. I donned the shirt, tucked in the tail, and ran a brush through my damp curls before securing them in a ponytail.

When I passed through the galley Gage had already set up on the opposite side of the bulkhead at the nav station, booting up his laptop. On the dinette he'd set a plate of scrambled eggs, another of toast next to an open jar of homemade orange marmalade, and a steaming mug of coffee flanked by milk and sugar.

I fixed the coffee to my liking, spread marmalade on a slice of toast, and joined him at the nav station.

"You have the photos?" he asked.

"Yeah," I said, glancing around and not remembering where I'd left my handbag or briefcase. The cabin neat and tidy. No discarded clothing on the cabin sole. I had no memory of tidying up.

"Have you seen my bag and briefcase?"

"Over on the settee," he said.

I walked over to the salon on the starboard side, a step down from the main cabin floor. On a plush robin's egg blue settee running the length of the salon sat my handbag and briefcase. On the cabin sole next to a mahogany coffee table I found my boots, and on the varnished coffee table itself, my Kel-Tec, the switchblade, and other items I'd had in the cargo pockets of the pants I'd discarded on the floor.

The compact Kel-tec PF9 millimeter handgun had been a present from Gage. The tan cowboy style ankle boots too. In fact, the entire birthday gift had included the boots, and the

Kel-tec tucked snugly into a soft leather strap sewn into the inside lining.

I gathered my things, put the switchblade in my jeans pocket, pulled the boots on over a pair of borrowed socks, and secured the petite nine millimeter. I found its small size and light weight incongruous with its lethality. As incongruous as the reality a lethal weapon had become part of my everyday attire. Not just one, but two, since the petite Kel-tec served as my backup weapon.

From my handbag I retrieved Zelina's camera, removed the memory card and walked it over to Gage.

"I seem to remember leaving a mess in here last night," I said. "What'd you do with my clothes?"

"Put them in the washer," he said, taking the postage stamp sized card and inserting it into a slot on the side of his laptop. "I'll do a laundry later."

Moments later thumbnail images of the crash scene, the jeep, the body, scrolled onto Gage's laptop. One after the other in rapid succession, filling the screen. Gage continued to browse them even after they'd finished uploading.

"Anything jump out at you?" I asked.

"Nothing. But things are rarely ever as they seem at first glance."

A Gagism. Like anomalies and coincidences. Among many others. He encrypted the images and forwarded them to Mike via a secure server. Only six people in the world, including Mike and me, had access to Gage's server. Eight months before while searching for the person who'd tried to kill Mike, Gage had given us access, and installed the encryption keys on our personal laptops. He'd also provided encrypted cell phones capable of satellite access and uplink.

A man of many parts. And many secrets. A man whose past I knew little about. Over time, he'd shared brief glimpses of that part of himself. Especially after Mike had been shot.

I'd learned of his access to surprising resources, including money. And his extensive network of contacts. His use of private aircraft to travel. Entering and exiting countries in unorthodox fashion. I'd met two people he called friends. No. Brothers. People he trusted. And over time, I'd come to understand the reasoning behind his secrecy, and the stakes involved.

It hadn't always been that way. I'd thought his secrecy, shutting me out of such a large part of himself, doomed any chance of a relationship. And it'd been a struggle for me. He'd waited. Patiently and exasperatingly disengaged. Providing the space I'd needed to resolve my feelings on my own, devoid of pressure or argument or interference.

Except for my mother's voice in my head. 'Fait dahr evryting an luv bahr evryting'. 'Faith dares everything and love bears everything'. One of many sayings my two brothers and I heard repeatedly growing up in her household.

And another, 'Wha is fe yuh cyan be no fe yuh'. 'What is for you will be for you'.

I thought I'd forgotten my mother's many Vincentian folk sayings after leaving home. But they'd spontaneously pop into my head when I needed their wisdom most. They'd helped me sort out the unexpected feelings I'd developed for this man. And as she'd done so often when I still lived under her roof, her quiet wisdom helped me to make a decision, and be at peace after making it.

I sat at the dinette finishing the eggs, a second cup of coffee, and loading the images onto my own laptop when my cell phone rang. Mike.

"Morning JJ, trust you had a restful night." His sarcasm unmistakable.

He'd known Gage had sailed to Union Island. Besides being my boss, mentor and friend, Mike had taken upon himself the role of surrogate father. He'd been as reticent of my increasing closeness to Gage as I'd been. But he too hadn't interfered. He'd offered his advice and unconditional support, leaving me to make my own decision.

"Very," I said, loading the single word with unmistakable ambiguity.

Mike had eventually accepted my relationship with Gage. And even seemed to bless it. Neither had ever mentioned discussing it, but given their close friendship, I'm sure they had.

"We've hired the MV Barracuda to make an unscheduled run to Union," Mike said, switching to business. "It'll be bringing a tow truck, acetylene equipment, a stihl saw, and a body bag. Should be everything you'll need. Should be arriving there between eight thirty and nine. I'm sending you a doctor too. A pathologist I've assigned exclusively to this case. The ferry will wait to bring the wreckage back here to St. Vincent, and the Coast Guard will transport the body."

"Got it Chief. Thanks."

"Anything else you need?"

"That'll do it for now."

"What about ID on the body?"

"It's the American, but I'm pretty sure he gave the vehicle's owner an alias." It caught Gage's attention. Questioning eyes locked on mine.

"Once we have the wreckage up I can search the body for identification."

"Okay JJ," his businesslike tone softening. "Take care," he said, and hung up.

It suddenly occurred to me, in all our conversations since I'd arrived on Union, he hadn't once asked about his Seneca or my flight.

"An alias?" Gage asked.

"One of the anomalies I've yet to explain. The other is his insistence on driving himself. He said he needed to meet someone in private. Who? I have no idea. I'm thinking maybe a woman he didn't want to be seen with. And the final anomaly, what was he doing up on Mount Olympus? There's nothing up there. Is it where he met this unknown person, or had the meeting already taken place somewhere else? According to the timeline I've been able to piece together he died three to four hours after acquiring the vehicle."

Gage listened in silence. Not interrupting my flow of thoughts, absorbing it all. It'd been helpful to verbalize my thoughts out loud. It provided a place to start as I ordered and prioritized my tasks for the day. The questions I needed answered.

I called Zelina. Already headed back to the wreck site to supervise the shift change at the roadblocks. I filled her in on the Chief's arrangements, told her I'd meet her at the site later.

At eight thirty I climbed topside onto Wherever's deck, shaded by a large blue canvas awning. I gazed across at the

Ferry wharf. Empty except for the Coast Guard cutter. But to the northwest, in the brightening morning sky, out past white surf crashing against the reefs sheltering Clifton harbor, a black and white inter-island ferry bore down on Union Island.

"Gage," I called down the hatch. "I need a ride ashore."

I gathered up my bag from the cockpit where I'd dumped it. My briefcase I'd left below. I waited for Gage to pull the hard bottom inflatable dinghy alongside, and climbed down into it.

Dodging between moored and anchored yachts crowding Clifton Harbor Gage leaned toward me, his voice raised above the outboard's steady drone.

"I'd thought of heading farther south for a few days, maybe Carriacou or Petit Martinique. It's getting as crowded as Port Elizabeth around here. But I'll stick around if you're going to be here for awhile."

"I'm not sure where I'll be," I said over the outboard. "I hope to transport the body to St. Vincent today. I'll fly up to meet it, or maybe I'll accompany it on the cutter. I haven't decided yet. In any case I'll have to be back here ASAP. This investigation has to begin here."

"Okay. I won't decide anything till I hear from you."

At the wharf we didn't prolong the goodbye. A quick smooch, exchanged "I love yous" and "see you laters", and we parted. He headed back through the harbor. I headed toward the Coast Guard cutter.

As I stepped off the cutter's boarding ramp the duty officer on deck stamped smartly to attention in that peculiar British manner I considered both hilarious and disconcerting. He raised his right arm in a stiff salute, palm forward, the back of his fingers lightly touching his dark forehead.

"Good morning," Petty Officer, I greeted him, returning the salute.

"Mahnin, ma'am," he said. "Welcome abohd. Can ah get yuh a coffee or sumting?"

"No tank yuh. De Captin aboard?"

"Yes ma'am. In de cabin. Dis way," he said, motioning me to follow him.

The cutter, CGV Hairoun, an aging forty foot patrol boat, had been supplied by the United States, one of the original vessels commissioned into the newly created Vincentian Coast Guard back in the nineteen eighties. Open decked fore and aft, a small superstructure in the center housed the mess and elevated bridge. On the foredeck stood a tripod mount for a heavy caliber machine gun.

Officers' cabins and seamen's berths were forward of the mess, below the waterline. The Captain, a Sub Lieutenant, equivalent to the rank of Police Inspector, sat at the mess table finishing a cup of coffee. He stood to attention and saluted when I stepped through the hatch.

" Mahnin Leftenant Hazell," I said, returning the salute. "Good to see you again. "Ow's Suzette and dose adohrable gurls?"

"Just fine ma'am. Getting biggah evry day," he smiled.

"Say hello to Suzette fah me."

Many of the Coast Guard Officers were married. I'd met the wives over the years at various functions. Suzette Hazell among a handful of wives I called friends. Her open, friendly manner had created an instant rapport between us. Unlike some of the other wives, who'd been standoffish, and radiated an unspoken, disguised, but unmistakable resentment.

Perhaps due to my appearance, my rank, or being in the field alongside their men.

"I will," he said. "And I want to tank yuh again fe de help wid Lisa."

"Glad to do it Leftenant, no need to thank me. Any wohd from Inspector Lewis?" I asked, switching to business.

"Not since las night. He detail sum crew and dey been gone since las night."

"De MV Barracuda docking just now," I said. "Wen dey unload I'll drive ovah wid dem. We'll bring de remains back heah for transpoht to Calliaqua."

"Aye Suprintendent," he acknowledged.

"Dat's dem now," I said, as a loud blast from the ferry's horn shattered the morning calm. I turned and headed for the hatch. He followed me out on deck, where we watched the ferry, its engines surging, its propellers churning the water into white foam, maneuver against the wharf, tie up, and lower its vehicle ramp.

A yellow flatbed tow truck drove down the ramp onto the wharf. The word 'Jammin' emblazoned in large black fire-tailed lettering across the hood.

After checking the equipment I introduced myself to the doctor, a young American woman I estimated to be around twenty six or twenty seven years old. We hadn't met before, and her youth surprised me. By the expression on her face, I appeared to be a surprise to her too.

Doctor Eileen Gash had a petite build, no taller than five-foot-four I estimated, about a hundred and ten pounds. An attractive face, a becoming, somewhat shy smile, and thick silky shoulder length auburn hair tied in a ponytail. She wore a simple blue and white, short sleeved calf length sundress.

Belted at the waist, and buttoned discreetly to conceal her chest and cleavage. Her modest attire didn't completely conceal the hourglass figure beneath, especially when a passing breeze pinned the material against her body.

Being Caucasian, and young, I'd initially assumed her to be a student at the medical school in Kingstown. Surprised again to learn she'd postponed a fellowship in Pathology to join the Peace Corp. She'd been assigned to St. Vincent and the Grenadines which had a desperate need for pathologists. She intrigued me, and I hoped I'd have a chance to spend more time getting to know her.

After introductions we squeezed into the tow truck's cramped, cluttered and garishly decorated cab. The interior reeked of marijuana. Orange felt covered the dash, and large green and black felt dice hung from the rear view mirror. Strings of colored glass beads bordered the headliner, and photographs had been pasted on every conceivable surface.

The driver, missing an upper front tooth, and wearing a red, yellow and green Rastafarian tam covering long strings of matted dreadlocks, barreled through Clifton's narrow streets. Apparently unconcerned by the presence of a police officer in the cab. He seemed equally unconcerned for other traffic and pedestrians in his way. His hand remained pressed on the horn, leaving it only to change gears, which he did frequently and aggressively, each time surreptiously brushing his hand against the doctor's thigh wedged against the gearshift.

"Driver!" I shouted over the incessant horn and screeching reggae music pounding from blown out speakers. "If yuh dohn slow down, an if yuh keep brushin yuh hand pon de doctah, I'll drive de truck meself cause yuh rass be in jail. Airee?"

He turned toward me, his jet black face and bloodshot eyes a mask of innocence. He noticed the expression on my face and immediately returned his attention to driving. Less aggressively, and never once touching the gearshift until the steep climb up to the crash site. I acknowledged Dr. Gash's silent sign of gratitude.

At the crash site the Rastafarian studied the scene. He maneuvered his truck into the best position and set out his equipment. As he worked he danced to imaginary music only he could hear. I'd insisted he keep the truck's music turned off. I didn't want any distractions, and besides, the ailing speakers gave the music a fingernails on chalkboard quality. He pumped his arms, moved his hips, shuffled his feet and twirled to the imaginary beat. But for all his obvious faults, and the likelihood of being as high as the moon, he appeared to know his business. While he did his thing I introduced Dr. Gash to Zelina and the rest of the detail.

"Your turn Sergeant," I said to Williams when the climbing gear had been laid out. Yuh an Lewis tek the cable down and attach it. Den come up wid de jeep. But stay to de side, clear of de cable."

Both acknowledged, smiled at each other, and busied themselves gearing up. The Rasta man meanwhile had inclined and lowered the truck's flatbed. He unspooled all the cable, and attached the cable's stout steel hook through a link in one end of a coiled length of heavy chain. He picked up the other end of the chain and fed it over the side.

"Eh Babylon," he called approaching Lewis. "Yuh have fe wrap de chain, one so an one so round de axel," he indicated using his hands. "Den fassen dem wid de shakles."

"Bwoy shut yuh mout!" Lewis responded, his voice loud and belligerent. "Yuh no have fe tell me wha fe do."

"Airee," the driver said, a gap-toothed grin aimed at Lewis. He danced back to the truck as though Lewis's rude retort had never occurred. Probably accustomed to that sort of treatment from police. I didn't condone it, but let it pass. This being neither the time nor place to address the matter.

The operation proceeded smoothly. Lewis wrapped each length of chain around the Jeep's rear axle and attached shackles, forming a yolk. Williams observed from the side, ready to assist if needed. Everything set, and Lewis and Williams safely out of the way, the Rasta engaged the winch motor, bopping his head to the imaginary beat. The cable wound onto the drum, taking slack out of the chain, until a straight taut line of cable and chain stretched from the truck to the jeep.

The Rasta stopped the winch. Competent, I concluded, high or not. We'd reached the point of greatest danger - the jeep wedged too tight to budge; the chain ripping the axle apart; the cable snapping and whipping through the air with a force and speed capable of ripping flesh and amputating limbs.

The Rasta engaged the winch again. It labored under the strain. The jeep remained fixed in the trees. The strain increased. The sound of the winch motor turned to a high pitched whine, the drum not turning at all.

A loud explosive crack signaled the wreck breaking loose of the treetop's grip. The winch drum groaned. The jeep jerked again. The drum screeched around. A final shudder and the wreckage jerked free of the trees.

The Rastafarian disengaged the winch again. He checked motor, drum, cable, and twirled a pirouette. When he reengaged the winch, the drum turned smoothly, winding in the cable. The wreck moved up the steep sloop accompanied by the shriek of grinding metal, leaving a trail of deep gouges in the hard rocky ground. Lewis and Williams followed its torturous progress, remaining well out of its way and the taut chain hauling it up.

Half way up the winch had wound in all the cable. The Rastafarian disengaged the winch. He grabbed a short length of chain attached to a ring on the truck's rear steel bumper. He slipped the large hook at the end through a link of the chain holding the Jeep. He reversed the winch, letting out slack. The short length of chain attached to the bumper grew taut, holding the wreck in place. He unhooked the slack cable and pulled its full length off the drum.

"Eh Babylon," he called over the side, feeding down the cable. "Yuh have fe hook de cable pon de chane down dey agane."

Williams crabbed sideways on his rappel line and grabbed hold of the cable. Using short, careful steps, keeping clear of the taut chain, he walked the cable down until it had no more slack. He reset the hook through a link, moved out of the way and signaled hoist away.

The Rasta reset and engaged the winch, just enough for the cable to take up the strain and put slack in the short length of chain attached to the bumper. After he detached the short chain, the winch resumed its task of hauling up the wreck. The shriek of metal grew louder and closer. Soon the tail end of the jeep appeared at the road's edge.

The Rastafarian had positioned his tow truck past one end of the damaged stone wall, allowing cable, chain, and eventually the wreck, an unobstructed path. I admit to being impressed. The operation had gone more smoothly than I'd expected. The mangled heap finally sat on the road. No one had been hurt. Time to get to work.

A nauseating odor emanated from the wreck. I checked the time, eleven fifteen am. The sun high and hot in a cloudless sky. I mentally did the math. The body had been trapped in the wreck for close to thirty-four hours. The flies reassembled around the corpse, their loud buzzing as irritating as their physical presence.

"Constable Johns," I called. When he appeared next to me I said: "Tek de driver down de road ovah dey. Keep im dey. And anyone come up de road yuh stop dem and keep dem away."

"Yes ma'am," he acknowledged, attempting to avert his eyes, and at the same time unable to resist glancing at the tarp covered form.

"Seaman Sammy," I called next, and gave him similar instructions for any pedestrians approaching from the other direction. The roadblock in the valley and posts at the scene had effectively kept the road clear. But the possibility still existed of an errant passerby happening upon the scene during extrication and examination of the body.

I pulled Zelina's camera from my bag and handed it to her as Lewis and Williams climbed onto the roadway. They set about retrieving the ropes and other gear. I'd need their expertise shortly. But first I wanted Zelina to photograph everything again, now that we had access to the entire vehicle.

I also wanted Dr. Gash to get started on her preliminary examination.

She'd donned a blue apron, tied at her back, a surgical mask, safety glasses and blue latex gloves. I did the same, minus the apron. We approached the jeep. She unwrapped the tarp gingerly, exposing the corpse, and silently examined it. Pronounced bloating. The stretched skin cracked, blackened and discolored. White blotches of extinguisher foam exaggerated its macabre appearance.

While Doctor Gash examined the body, I examined the wreckage enclosing it. I meticulously studied the debris for anything out of place. I examined the torn and stained clothing. I searched the side and back trouser pockets on the corpse's left side. Empty. The pockets on his other side still inaccessible. I studied the wreckage encasing the body's lower half. Still unsure we'd be able to extricate it in one piece.

"Doctor," I said. "If we can't cut away this wreckage, we may have to dismember the corpse to remove it."

She gazed up at me, the lower half of her face hidden by the surgical mask. Concern apparent in her blue eyes.

"What do you think?" I prompted her.

"Let's cross that bridge when we get to it," she said, a confidence in her voice I hadn't expected. "And please, call me Eileen. Right now I'm puzzled by this white substance covering the remains."

"Oh. That's extinguisher foam. When we realized the body had to remain here overnight we covered it with this tarp. We used a fire extinguisher to disperse the insects and flies before covering it."

"Good idea. Seemed to have inhibited insect activity a bit. Might make it harder to pinpoint a definite time of death though."

"We've a pretty good idea on that. A wristwatch he wore got smashed in the accident." As I voiced the words I had a strange sensation of something odd regarding what I'd said. I pushed the thought aside.

"What can you tell me at this point?" I asked.

"Nothing you can't see for yourself. Male, Caucasian, around sixty; multiple trauma, fractures and lacerations, rigor and the onset of putrefaction. I can't tell anything more, including cause of death, until I perform an autopsy."

My gaze lingered in one long last examination of the wreckage and remains. Nothing more to learn from observation alone. Zelina had finished photographing and stood waiting. I called for her, Lewis, and Williams to join the doctor and me.

As members of the Special Services Unit, Inspector Lewis and Sergeant Williams had more experience in search and rescue, including extrication of trapped victims.

"So what yuh guys tink? Tink we can cut aroun de body?"

"Yeah Suprintendent," Williams said confidently. Lewis focused his attention on Doctor Gash.

"We cut heah and heah," Williams continued. "Rite down to de frame heah. Most is jus liftin all dis heah. Easy wid de winch."

Williams in charge, the operation commenced. Eileen covered the remains and cautioned Williams on how to prevent damaging it while cutting. I pulled her and Zelina aside, out of Lewis's line of sight. And well away from the sparks flung by the stihl saw slicing through metal.

"When we get to the Harbor," I said to Zelina, "I want you and Doctor Gash to accompany the remains to the morgue. An mek sure Lewis dohn play de papyshoh," I finished in patois, using the colloquial slang for fool. She understood my meaning.

So did Doctor Gash, even if she didn't quite understand the words. She turned to me, a shy smile parting her lips. "You don't have to worry about me Superintendent. I've been here long enough to learn how to take care of myself."

I returned the smile. I'd rather put Lewis in the tow truck accompanying the wreck than anywhere near Doctor Gash. But putting him and the Rastafarian together for any length of time seemed equally unpalatable. Either option carried the potential for a mess I'd have to clean up later. I hoped having Zelina close to Doctor Gash would be sufficient deterrent to stifle Lewis's skirt chasing proclivities.

"Whey yuh gwoin be?" Zelina asked.

"It's time I paid a visit to PSV," I said.

"I shud go wid yuh."

"Not dis time," I said. "I tink low key be bettah for now. Yuh stay wid de doc. I want she start de autopsy soon as yuh reach de morgue. I'll fly de plane up an meet up wid yuh latah."

Doctor Gash turned to me, a mixture of surprise and curiosity in her animated eyes and face.

"You fly your own plane?"

"I'm a pilot," I chuckled, infected by her enthusiasm. "But the plane belongs to the Police Commissioner. You fly?"

"I wish."

"Maybe we can go up together sometime," I suggested. "It's a great way to see the Grenadines. A schooner being the other."

Zelina cracked a laugh, grinning from ear to ear.

"I'd love to," Eileen said, a nervous uncertainty in her voice as she eyed Zelina's amused giggling.

The wreckage lay in three sections on the road. The crushed front end had been cut away. The engine, spouting an array of cut hoses leaking fluids, lay between it and the jeep's rear section. The body finally accessible. Its lower half crushed and mangled like the remains of the jeep.

Doctor Gash examined it briefly before Lewis and Williams lifted and placed it in a zippered body bag. I searched the pockets and the rest of the clothing. Nothing. No wallet, no ID, no passport, no money. Not even a scrap of paper.

Along Ashton's and Clifton's narrow streets pedestrians paused in their activity. Shop keepers ran from their shops. Vehicles pulled off to the roadside. All stared at the solemn procession passing by. A police Toyota 4runner carrying me, Zelina, and Doctor Gash led the way. The tow truck in the middle, Constable Johns riding in the cab and the crumpled sections of jeep on the flatbed. The open backed land rover carrying Lewis, Williams, Seaman Sammy and the remains, brought up the rear.

At Clifton's wharf the tow truck drove straight onto the ferry's waiting ramp. The crew of CGV Hairoun unloaded the body bag onto a folding canvas stretcher and carried it aboard like pall bearers.

I watched the ferry and cutter depart the wharf, one behind the other. The vessels crossed the harbor, threaded the entrance, and turned north. Once in open water both vessels throttled up, the cutter spreading a wide wake and racing ahead.

CHAPTER 5

I walked from the wharf, headed along the shoreline toward the 'yacht club', short hand for the Anchorage Yacht Club Hotel and Marina. The complex had recently been rebuilt to include a marina providing dockage for fifteen moderate sized sailboats, and included a restaurant, bar, and a small hotel of six rooms and four beachfront cottages. The best place to find a local water taxi at that time of day.

I needed to carefully consider my approach to Petit St. Vincent, a private, foreign owned island resort. Technically I had jurisdiction. In practice St. Vincent allowed the resort a fair degree of autonomy. Typical PSV guests included celebrities, business titans, and other well-heeled foreigners seeking a private hideaway. They paid exorbitant prices for the privilege, and the resort's management zealously protected that commodity.

A cordial relationship existed between the owners, management, and Vincentian authorities. The Island presented no security, crime, or political problems for us. In exchange we pretty much left them alone. The Chief had assigned me this case to ensure nothing rocked that particular boat. I needed more information before heading over there. If they sensed me just fishing, they'd stonewall.

I sought out Seckie's water taxi. Spotted it at the end of the yacht club dock. A sturdy center console launch, built locally, inboard engine, seating for eight passengers under a full length green canvas bimini on a wood frame. Seckie ceased whatever had been occupying him at the helm when he heard my approach. He turned in enthusiastic anticipation of a fare. His wide sun baked face lost its enthusiasm when he recognized me. But not the ever present smile.

"Suprintendent," he beamed. "Yuh down heah seein bout de dead man in de jeep." A statement, not a question. The news already taking wing.

"Dat's right Seckie. But I need a ride ovah to PSV, an sum infamashun maybe yuh can help wid."

"Shoh Suprintendent. Whatevah yuh need."

A big man in both height and girth, middle age and a lifetime of beer had culminated in a sizable paunch. It hung like a roof over the lower half of Seckie's body. I wondered how long since he'd last seen his feet. He still had some salt and pepper hair on his balding pate. And like most Vincentians of his generation, a number of missing teeth. Pleasant and gregarious, he'd be a bountiful source of information. Especially as he had an arrangement to transport PSV staff to and from Union Island.

"When yuh wahn go PSV?" he asked.

"Now." I said. "On de way yuh can tell me who yuh noh wohkin ovah dey."

"Well, lemme see now," he said, preparing to cast off. "Yuh have..." and commenced rattling off a string of names.

"Hole on! Hole on mahn. I have fe rite it down," digging in my bag for a pen and notepad. "An tell me if yuh noh wha work dem do."

He began again, providing names and occupations of Union Islanders working on PSV, while the fast launch cleaved the stretch of blue water between Union Island and Petit St. Vincent. Wind bellowed beneath the bimini, forcing us to raise our voices to be heard. Frequently he'd lapse into gossip about someone he'd named, which didn't interest me. But his detours gave my hasty scribbling in the bouncing launch time to catch up on the names pouring from his mouth. As good as getting an employee list from PSV's manager. Something I knew wouldn't happen.

When he'd exhausted his memory, I asked him, "Yuh ever tek a white mahn, American, bout six foot, hundred ninety pouns, maybe sixty yeahs old? Las time him was weahin dark pants, an a lite blue shirt wid a horse ting on it so," my hand over my breast indicating the position of the embroidered polo pony trademark.

"But me noh dat mahn," Seckie exclaimed. "Is him dead? Lord have murcy," his face an open expression of shock.

I didn't answer his question. "How yuh noh him?" I asked instead.

"I tek him ovah couple times. An bring him back too. I remembah cause he always tip me. He was weahin dem close like yuh say, las tim I tek him was when.......?"

His face contorted in concentration, conjuring the memory of when he'd last seen the American.

"Toosday. Yeah Toosday. I membah now. Jus befoh dahk."

"Yuh noh dis mahn name Seckie?" I asked, holding my breath, hoping against hope.

"Nevah heah him name. But I noh who yuh fe ask."

Lost in conversation I hadn't noticed our approach to PSV until Seckie throttled back to ease into the lagoon and approach the dock.

Petit St. Vincent lived up to its description as an island paradise. One hundred and fifteen acres of lush, rolling greenery, and a bewildering variety of bright colors bursting from wild flowers, orchids, fruit trees and other vegetation. Surrounded by white sand beaches, clear green water, and spectacular coral formations. At night the sweet subtle fragrances of its flowers perfumed the air.

Seckie tied the launch to the dock. The area pleasantly quiet. Not much activity in the blistering midday heat. A small dock house stood on the beach a short distance from the dock, surrounded by multicolored Hobie Cats, Sunfish, windsurfers, and kayaks lined up on the sand.

A row of rope hammocks were evenly spaced further along the beach. The hammocks slung between wooden posts sunk into the sand, shaded by roofs of dried coconut tree branches. The hammocks empty except for one occupied by a guest swinging lazily while engrossed in a book.

"Roy." Seckie called over to the dock master attending the water toys. When Roy met us on the dock Seckie asked, "Yuh noh de American me tek ovah a Union toosday, a him dead yuh noh."

"Whey yuh say," Roy exclaimed, shock registering on his face. "Fe shoh?"

"I bring de Suprintendent. She say so," Seckie explained. I'd said nothing of the kind.

"Yuh noh him name?" Seckie asked.

"Nah mahn," the dock master said, shaking his head. He turned and pointed to a young man climbing out of a Mini Moke at the beach end of the dock.

"Derrick mus noh. He drive de guess roung de island. And he bring de American to de dock."

Derrick had apparently observed the water taxi's arrival. He'd driven down to the dock expecting a guest. When he joined us on the dock Roy related the latest news.

Yuh noh de guess yuh bring down Toosday go a Union, a him dead in de jeep."

"Wha," Derrick said, expressing his own shock at the news.

"Wha he name?" Roy asked.

"Mistah Mansfield. Charles Mansfield. He ahrive las weeken, stahin in cottage twenty."

I digested this news while they animatedly discussed theirs. The news would soon spread among the resort's staff. It'd make no difference if I denied it, or asked for it to be kept quiet. I needed to get to the manager before he got wind of it. In any case, in my mind the trade off had been worth it. I now had a name to go with the body.

"Derrick," I said, interrupting their discussion. "Mind givin me a ride to de office?"

"No problem Suprintendent," he said, leading the way.

"Seckie," I said before following him. "Wait for me, unless yuh get another fare."

"I be heah suprintendent."

I boarded Derrick's Mini Moke, the only vehicles permitted on the island. Resembling golf carts, the handful of Mokes transported guests and staff around the island's luscious acres. I climbed out at the entrance to the main building housing the resort's main open air dining room, bar, and offices. Empty when I arrived except for staff. I made my way to the offices in the rear.

A petit young Vincentian woman, her straightened black hair framing a pretty, dark cocoa face, sat behind the receptionist desk. She spoke in heavily accented, non-patios English.

"May I help you?"

"I'm Superintendent Johanssen of the CID," I introduced myself, showing her my badge and ID. "I need to speak to your manager regarding one of your guests."

A deer in the headlights expression typical of most Vincentians when dealing with the police replaced the welcoming smile.

"One moment ma'am," she said, picking up the telephone handset on her desk and pressing a button on the console. After a moment she spoke into the handset. "The poliss is here wanting to speak with you concerning a guest." Again she waited. "A Superintendent Johanssen of the CID," she said after the pause. She replaced the handset on its cradle and gazed up at me, evident relief on her smiling face.

"Mistah Forester, the Generahl Managah, will be right out to see you Superintendent."

A door to the right of the reception area opened. James Forester, tall, robust, mid-fifties, strands of unruly white hair receding from his lined sun tanned forehead, approached.

Since my time with Gage I'd gained an appreciation for the physical attractiveness of middle aged men. More attuned to the facial lines and expressions the years had wrought. And how different men wore them. James Forester's tanned, leathery face, and his neatly trimmed salt and pepper moustache and beard, conferred a distinguished sexy appeal. Then again since Gage, no other man, regardless of age, measured up. Forester strode over and offered me his hand, his smile open and welcoming.

"Superintendent," he gushed, "Please come in," he said, his British accent discernable.

We'd met socially on a number of occasions. Originally from the UK, he'd abandoned a career in aeronautical engineering to settle in the Grenadines. His other passion being competitive sailing.

"So good to see you again," he said, indicating a leather armchair facing his desk. His office offered a view of a rolling hillside of landscaped lawns and flower beds awash in color. An admirer, he'd eventually given up hitting on me after numerous rebuffed attempts. Didn't stop him from openly flirting whenever we met.

"I understand you're inquiring about a guest," he said, observing me closely as I settled into the armchair and crossed my legs. "How may I help you?"

I flashed my most ingratiating smile and aimed for the top prize, aware we'd eventually settle for something less.

"I need a list of your guests currently staying on the island," I said.

He returned the smile, and stroked the neatly trimmed hair covering his chin. The game afoot, as his countryman might say.

"I'm afraid I have to disappoint you Superintendent. One of the reasons, the most important reason, our guests come to PSV is privacy. We take that responsibility quite seriously."

"I can appreciate that," I said. "As I'm sure you can appreciate the fallout of one of your guests being involved in a fatal motor vehicle incident."

The smile fell from his face, replaced by concern. The conversation had taken an unexpected turn.

"Are you referring to the tragic accident on Union Island everyone is talking about?"

"I am."

"And you believe a guest on this island is involved."

"Not believe. I know."

"I'm not questioning your information Superintendent, but it's inconceivable one of our guests would be involved in something like that and not report it."

"That's why I need to see your guest list, so I may make the appropriate inquiries," I said.

He shook his head, his mahogany brow furrowed in thought.

"I sincerely wish to assist your inquiries Superintendent," he said. "But what you're asking...." The sentence dangled in the air, unfinished, while he pondered an appropriately helpful alternative. One which wouldn't compromise his primary responsibility to his guests, and Board of Directors.

"Superintendent," he began again. "I sincerely hope there is some other way I may assist you. Maybe if you told me who this guest is I might arrange a private meeting between you. You could then make your inquiries discreetly."

The opening I'd been waiting for. Time to sink the harpoon. "You misunderstand me James," I said, deliberately using his first name and pausing for effect. "Your guest is the victim. He's deceased."

My words had the intended effect. His mouth opened, but no sound issued from it. The implications of what I'd told him very different from what he'd been contemplating.

"Who?" he said finally.

"A Mister Charles Mansfield," I said. "Arrived last weekend, staying in cottage twenty."

"You're sure of this superintendent?" he asked, dark blue eyes staring into mine, imploring me to be mistaken. I almost felt sorry for him.

"We found identification on the body," I lied.

"So what happens next?" he asked, deflated.

He probably had a clear idea of what happened next, but sought confirmation anyway. When he spoke to his board of directors he'd be able to report his information had been provided by the Police.

"The body is being transported to the morgue in Kingstown as we speak," I said. "We will notify the American Embassy in Barbados of course, and they will notify any next of kin in the States. In the meantime we'll conduct our inquiries for the coroner's inquest, including an autopsy."

"Quite," he said. "And how may I assist you?"

"You may allow me to examine Mr. Mansfield's cottage. And I will require it be sealed for the time being."

I saved him worrying about the unsavory implications by quickly adding, "I can take a quick preliminary look right now with your permission. Your guests needn't know this is a police inquiry. Just a prospective guest inspecting the accommodations. And I assure you, the cottage will be released before the weekend, and I'll be out of your hair."

I'd used the entendre deliberately, prompting him to visualize his fantasy - me in his hair. It lightened his mood, as

I'd hoped. I know how to flirt too. But bottom line, he hadn't been forced to give up much, and I'd obtained precisely what I wanted.

Petit St. Vincent, like other resorts in the Grenadines privately owned by foreigners, had its own private security. James Forester called PSV's head of security to his office to brief him, directing him to accompany me to the cottage rented by the late Charles Mansfield. He'd have to break the same news a few more times to the rest of his management staff, his Assistant General Manager, his head of Guest Relations, and the principles on the Board.

I waited in the still empty dining room. I used the time to place a few calls. Zelina and Doctor Gash were minutes out of Calliaqua. The ferry another thirty minutes behind. Gage, in the middle of maintenance chores, said he'd be aboard when I returned from PSV.

PSV's Chief of Security Peter Wellington and I, only slightly acquainted. Another UK transplant, I'd met him briefly on a couple of occasions. He looked about forty. Difficult to tell. A hardness about the face and eyes. Like Gage.

He drove in stoic silence along the twin concrete tracks laid out for the Mini Mokes through the landscaped gardens and evergreen tunnels around PSV. Exotic sights, sounds and scents inundated my senses as we drove across the island. Color everywhere. And occasionally a glimpse of the blue Caribbean peeking through the tropical jungle of rubber, banyan, and palm trees.

The twin tracks we'd been driving on abruptly ended at a heavy wood door built into a stone wall. Overhanging tress and foliage hid the door from view until you came upon it. Wellington held the door open and motioned for me to enter.

Cottage 20 sat nestled into a forested bluff overlooking a cove on the southern part of the island. The door led onto a terraced stone sundeck, providing a panoramic view of the Caribbean on one side, the Atlantic on the other; the Grenadian islands to the south and Tobago Cays to the north. The deck furnishings included a low rectangular table, two cushioned lounges, and a rope hammock slung in one corner.

Large French doors led into the living area. The cottage's open design favored the northeast trade's fresh cooling breezes. Like all the resort's cottages it possessed no air conditioning, no TVs, no telephones, and no locks.

I entered the main living room. Walls constructed of local blue stone divided the interior, the other rooms accessed through arched openings. A lofty peaked ceiling overhead. Mahogany bladed ceiling fans and chandelier lamps hung from its exposed purple-heart beams. Against one wall sat a plush white sofa, a day bed against the other. The other furniture included slate topped coffee and end tables, and cushioned armchairs placed around the room.

I extracted Zelina's camera from my shoulder bag. I methodically photographed the cottage, moving into the bedroom, dressing room, and bathroom. Mansfield's clothes neatly hung in closets and laid out in dresser drawers. Toiletries spread along the bathroom counter. Fluffy bath towels and soft white bath robes hung in place awaiting use. The bed unmade.

No personal items. No books. No papers. No jewelry. No wallet or passport, or airline tickets either. Not in the cottage. Not on his body. A red roller suitcase, its telescoping handle extended, stood in a corner of the bedroom. I opened it. Searched its zippered compartments. Empty.

I sensed a huge anomaly.

"Has anyone, staff, or anyone else, been in the cottage since Mr. Mansfield left?" I asked the security chief.

"Not that I'm aware," he said, speaking for the first time. "A red flag was on the hoist outside."

"Red flag?" I said.

"Each cottage has a message box attached to a small flagpole," he explained. "Place a request for service in the message box, hoist the yellow flag, and a staff person will pick up the request. Hoist a red flag and you won't be disturbed. If he'd used room service the tray is left by the message box and is picked up by the staff. No need to disturb the guest.

"So the red flag you saw outside meant Mister Mansfield hadn't requested any services and didn't want to be disturbed?"

"It appears so Superintendent," Wellington said.

But nothing's ever as it appears at first glance, said Gage's voice in my head. Following a final scrutinizing gaze around the room I departed the cottage.

"Mr. Forester explained the cottage is to be sealed?" I said, noticing a small red flag fluttering in the breeze atop a bamboo pole.

"Yes Superintendent. I'll see to it personally.

"Thank you Mr. Wellington."

"Please, Peter," he said, smiling for the first time.

CHAPTER 6

I'd seen Gage just long enough for our parting to induce a forlorn ache. I planned to return to Union Island the next day. Saturday at the latest, I'd assured him. He'd said he'd already contacted Rodney, his deckhand. Told him not to bother heading down to Union. Gage said he'd remain in Union until I returned. Following a long ardent kiss he ferried me ashore by dinghy and walked me to the airport.

Flying the Piper Seneca to St. Vincent partially assuaged the ache. The aircraft climbed into a clean, clear and calm sky, a pale shade of blue. My heart soared, and the view beyond the cockpit melted my earthbound woes like smoke dissipating in the wind.

From two thousand feet the Grenadine Islands stretched north and south like a string of emeralds in a cobalt setting. The sea flat and motionless. The short flight, fifteen minutes, didn't diminish the exhilarating sense of freedom I experienced each time I took to the sky. The feeling never got old. And the Seneca and I performed a flawless duet from liftoff to touchdown.

The heat of E.T. Joshua's sun baked tarmac hit me like a blast furnace when I stepped from the cockpit. An unmarked police Toyota Tacoma waited to ferry me into Kingstown. Mike wanted me to report directly to his office upon arrival.

After two failed attempts I connected to Zelina's cell.

"I just landed," I informed her. "But the Commissioner wants me to report straight to his office."

"No worries," Zelina replied. "Doctor Gash jus now prepahrin to x-ray de body."

"I'll meet you there as soon as I'm done," I said before disconnecting.

The main road from Arnos Vale twisted and rose as we climbed the heights separating St. Vincent's southeastern coast from the valley in which the Capital, Kingstown, lay. The breeze created by the Toyota's swift passage offered little relief from the hot, stifling air.

Three months before, a hurricane had roared across St. Vincent, destroying twelve hundred private homes, public buildings, roads, infrastructure, and crippling the twin pillars of the island's economy, agriculture and tourism. The devastation still evident along our route. Collapsed homes on the side of the road. Flood borne debris strewn across empty yards and fields. Felled and uprooted trees littered large swaths of torn up ground.

The road also wound through my past. A time of fond childhood memories. Dorchester Hill on my right, where my family had lived until I turned four years old. The area undeveloped back then, providing wide open spaces where my two older brothers and I played, flew kites, and raced home built scooters and go carts. Where I'd eaten my first raw carrot right out of the ground.

"Lemme try" had been a constant refrain in my attempts to keep up with them; to try whatever they did.

"I kan help meshelf," had been another, as I fought to assert my independence even at that early age.

Passing Cane Gardens on our left I recalled afternoons spent in the company of friends, or at the homes of friend of my parents. On the outskirts of Kingstown proper we passed the preparatory school my brothers had attended, across the playing field from my father's office.

Barefoot, carefree times I recalled fondly. As a child, St. Vincent, and the Grenadine Islands, had held an idyllic magical charm. Fun filled days spent at the beach, squeaking ceiling fans, mosquito nets, and the smell of kerosene lamps. My brothers labored twice a day at an old hand pump, providing water for the house. A chore they despised and cursed. As the baby sister I didn't have to pump, but insisted on my short entirely ineffective turn anyway. Whatever they did I wanted to do too.

One day my parents informed us we'd be leaving St. Vincent. Daddy had a new job and we'd be moving to our other home. The first time I'd heard of having another home. My parents packed up the house, and packed up us kids. For some reason which I don't remember, we weren't all able to stay together the night before departing St. Vincent. My mother dropped me at her friend's house. The rest of the family overnighted at a separate location. I'd spend the entire night in panic stricken fear I'd been abandoned and left behind.

The next day we all boarded the 'Goose', a seaplane which flew us to Barbados, where we boarded a bigger airplane. My first time in a jet airliner. The airliner whisked us to a magical land of large shiny cars, tall buildings towering into the sky, and more fair skinned people than I'd ever seen in my life.

In Kingstown the constable negotiated narrow congested streets choked by pedestrian, vehicular, bicycle and hand cart traffic. All jostling for maneuvering room. Horns blared and tempers flared in the shimmering tropical heat. Music screamed from every vehicle, every open store front, every sidewalk stall. The capital a chaotic cacophony of sights, sounds, smells, people, and vehicles.

Yet a logical rhythm existed amidst the madness. An ebb and flow allowing vehicles, carts and pedestrians to move along in bewildering harmony, like the musical chords of a Chinese opera.

Before long we pulled up to an imposing colonial era red brick building dominating Bay Street. A large circular glass structure at the center of its roof, like you'd see at the top of a lighthouse. Large arched openings covered the building's first floor windows and entrances.

The building housed the Kingstown Central Police Station, headquarters of the Royal St. Vincent and the Grenadines Police Force. It contained a jail for short term prisoners, and the main immigration office. We drove through large metal gates into an interior courtyard, where I disembarked and thanked the driver.

I entered the all too familiar colonial building. I'd spent a large part of my police career in it. Especially after Mike's appointment as Commissioner of Police. Its historic office lined halls conjured ghosts of a colonial past. And bittersweet memories of my time inside its walls. Some triumphs. Some failures. Colleagues I respected and cared about. Others I'd rather see dismissed from the force.

I'd been on the verge of resigning the force myself, relegating my decision to join in the first place a huge mistake. A misguided and frustrated urge for justice. Chalk it up as a lesson learned. Time to find another way.

Then Mike Daniels had arrived and everything changed.

I approached his office suite on the top floor, at the end of a long hallway spanning the length of the building. His office overlooked the courtyard on one side, Bay Street's busy thoroughfare on the other, including Kingstown Harbor and the four story Government Administration building on the opposite side of Bay Street. Mike's Secretary Cecilia, who only the Commissioner called Cissy, greeted me as I entered the outer office.

"Superintendent, so nice to see you again," she said in proper but accented English, a welcoming smile on her usually stern, matronly face. She protected the Commissioner with the fierceness of a lioness. The friendly smile transforming into a ferocious, forbidding snarl for anyone attempting to cross her, or get by her.

"They're in the conference room. You can go right in, he's expecting you," she said.

Even so, she ushered me to a door which provided direct access from the outer office to the conference room. No one approached the Commissioner's offices unless Cecilia personally escorted them.

She opened the door and ushered me through. I heard voices through the opened door. Mike speaking. He turned toward me as I entered, a warm smile greeting me.

"Superintendent Johanssen, finally," he said formally, but conveying a warmth in his eyes only he and I were privy to.

"Commissioner," I said, observing the formality and proffering a salute, which he dismissed by a quick "at ease", directing me to a seat at the conference table.

My formality had been directed more to the other officials in the room. Superintendent Nigel Mitchell, Commander of the Criminal Investigative Division, and Deputy Commissioner Reginald Huggins.

Also attending the meeting, Assistant Superintendent Vincent Taylor. Eight months earlier he'd been promoted to the Public Information Office, a new department created in response to Deputy Commissioner Coffe's public information debacle.

Coffe had been a pain in Mike's ass since the day of Mike's appointment. His narcissistic arrogance had eventually been his undoing. Not to mention his incompetence. He'd created a mess of the investigation into the attempt on Mike's life eight months earlier, and the disappearance of a visiting tourist named Sarah Holmes. His handling of both cases had devolved into a national embarrassment. On international TV no less. In the aftermath he'd quietly accepted early retirement.

Taylor possessed a natural talent and aptitude for the new department. Light-complexioned, charismatic, camera friendly, and smart. Next to the Commissioner, the public face of the Royal St. Vincent and the Grenadines Police Force. The office had since been renamed the Public Information and Complaints Department, responsible for also handling citizen complaints against the police.

I chose the chair next to Taylor. Deputy Commissioner Huggins sat at the far end. Superintendent Mitchell on the opposite side facing Taylor and me.

Commissioner of Police Michael Daniels stood at the head. Three years older than Gage, and a fifty-ninth birthday approaching, he didn't possess Gage's rugged handsomeness, or dangerous aura. Shorter than Gage, at five foot eleven, and heavier, around two hundred pounds. His complexion darker than Gage's. Like Gage he wore his hair close cropped to his scalp, grey liberally sprinkled among the tight black curls. Observing him, being back in the building, reminded me of the battles we'd fought together. And how he'd changed the trajectory of my career, and my life.

He'd been given a mandate to transform the ill trained, ill equipped, understaffed, and under resourced Police into a professional force. A tall, arguably impossible order. He'd inherited an unyielding bureaucracy moribund in a patriarchal, often misogynistic male culture. A force possessing no expertise in criminal investigation, forensics, or an understanding of community service. And recalcitrant senior police officials who resented his being parachuted in over them. Who considered him an outsider. Officers like Coffe. And Superintendent Mitchell, sitting across from me.

Mike Daniels had accepted the challenge. He'd retired to Bequia following a long successful law enforcement career as Monroe County Sheriff in Southern Florida. Part of the reason he'd been offered the position. The Florida Keys and St. Vincent and the Grenadines shared a similar geography. And both shared the distinction of being gateways for narcotics entering the United States.

Given the uncertain outcome of elections due next year, Mike's tenure might be drawing to a close. His priority, after surviving the attempt on his life, had been to cement the hard won gains he'd achieved in the police force. We'd both been on the lookout for like-minded professionals to promote into key positions. Like Sergeant Williams, and Detective McIntosh.

The list also included Deputy Commissioner Huggins, waiting expectantly at the foot of the table for Mike to begin. He'd been promoted to replace Coffe, and had proved himself a thorough professional. Not a street wise or intuitive cop. His approach more intellectual. But smart, possessing extraordinary administrative and management skills, and politically astute. A believer in the reforms Mike had instituted. Definitely a contender for the top job following Mike's departure.

Across the table from me Superintendent Mitchell, another contender for the top job, fidgeted. Impatient. A disapproving glare directed at my attire. He'd risen through the ranks, stuck in the old ways as Coffe had been. A walking textbook of psychological disorders. He craved respect but didn't know how to respect others. He affected an officious, overbearing manner to conceal his insecurity and incompetence. He harbored a narrow-minded misogynist attitude and an obsession regarding his own self-importance. He routinely downplayed and excused police misconduct, and encouraged his officers to 'pile on' in his words. His quiet lobbying for the top job and attempts to undermine Mike's reforms hadn't gone unnoticed by Mike and his allies on the force.

"As you're aware by now," Mike said at last, "there's been a fatal vehicular accident on Union Island. The deceased is believed to be an American visiting St. Vincent and the Grenadines, a guest on PSV. I assigned the investigation to Superintendent Johanssen. She's spent the past two days at the scene. I wanted all of you to hear her preliminary report first hand, at the same time, and discuss a coordinated strategy on how to proceed."

"From de repohts I hurd, dis a straight forward vehicular accident. I'm sure de Superintendent can handle dat widout help from us," Mitchell interjected, his manner condescending. The dark centers of his pale reddish eyes dared me to challenge his assessment.

The challenge came from the foot of the table. Deputy Commissioner Huggins sneered at his subordinate from stern eyes behind black framed glasses fixed on the flat bridge of his nose.

"Dere are matters beyond just de investigation dat bear consideration," he upbraided Mitchell. "Matters of a delicate nature. And I foh one want to know what repohts you're referrin to when de primary investigator just now returned from de scene."

"Superintendent," Mike said turning to me.

"The investigation so far," I said, ignoring Mitchell's stare and marshalling my thoughts. "Indicates the deceased, A Mister Charles Mansfield, an American renting a cottage on PSV, obtained the vehicle from a local man on Union Island, name of Samuel Gooding, around six thirty pm Tuesday evening. We believe Gooding illegally hired the vehicle to the American, but there's no evidence to substantiate that," I added parenthetically.

"Evidence at the scene indicates the vehicle went off the mountain road into a steep ravine at ten pm Tuesday night."

"What evidence?" Deputy Commissioner Huggins asked.

"A smashed wristwatch worn by the deceased. I believe the victim died close to that time. We have to wait on the autopsy to confirm it. Evidence at the scene also indicates the vehicle had been travelling at a rate of speed making it impossible to negotiate the turn where it went off the road. Other than the wristwatch no personal effects or identification were found on the body."

"How'd you identify him?" Mike asked.

"By interviewing a water taxi operator, and staff on PSV."

"How'd it go on PSV?" Deputy Commissioner Huggins asked.

"Very well sir. I'd obtained the information on the deceased's identity prior to speaking with the General Manager. He granted me access to the deceased's cottage and has sealed it until I release it."

Thin eyebrows on Deputy Commissioner Huggins's dark forehead rose above his glasses in silent approval.

Superintendent Mitchell sat in stone faced silence, his disapproving stare still leveled at me. Jowls on both cheeks, delineated by deep frown lines running from the bridge of his nose to his square chin, formed a severe parenthesis around his broad nostrils and thick downturned lips.

"One odd anomaly," I said, catching the subtle smile on Mike's face. "There were no personal effects in the cottage either. No wallet, no passport, and no airline tickets."

The statement prompted a rise from everyone in the room, including Superintendent Mitchell. His expression something resembling interest.

"So the only source of identification is the folks you interviewed?" Mike said.

"That's correct sir," I said. "But I believe the ID is solid, based on physical description. All we need is confirmation."

"Immigration records?" Mike asked.

"Haven't had the chance yet. I'll be able to tomorrow. I'll also have another look through Mr. Mansfield's cottage. And I plan to have Detective McIntosh interview as many PSV staff as possible, see if we can reconstruct the victim's movements and activities since his arrival. Our information is he may have been meeting someone on Union Island the night he died."

Superintendent Mitchell appeared ready to comment but Mike interrupted him.

"What about the man who owned the vehicle?" he asked. "What was his name again?"

"Samuel Gooding," I said. "He's still in custody on Union Island. But I don't believe we can charge him. There's no evidence he did hire out, or intended to hire out his vehicle."

"We can get a confession," Mitchell said, the only contribution he'd made to the discussion.

Typical, I thought. His methods tended to be bullying and abusive, unconcerned for the individual's rights.

"Even wid a confession, wid no other corroborating evidence de public prosecutor won't take up de case." Deputy Commissioner Huggins said.

"Release him," Mike decided. "We know where to find him if we need to. We have to get moving on this. I'll contact the Foreign Secretary's office and brief them on what we have so far, and the tentative identification. After they notify the

American Embassy maybe the Americans can help to confirm the ID."

Turning to Assistant Superintendent Taylor Mike said, "I want a lid kept on this. I'm sure the story's already spreading, and we'll probably get inquiries from the news media soon. We're not releasing any information for now. If the press asks, we confirm the broad facts, no details. We can't comment on an ongoing investigation, blah blah blah. You know the drill. Thank you all. Dismissed."

The meeting ended in a general shuffling and scraping of chairs on the wood floor. Deputy Commissioner Huggins turned to me before exiting the room.

"Superintendent, where is de wreck now?"

"At the Calliaqua base sir."

He nodded and exited into the outer office, where Superintendent Mitchell stood waiting for him. They departed down the hall deep in conversation.

What the hell is that about? I wondered. As I headed for the door Mike motioned me through another door leading to his inner office. He asked his aide to get a car ready.

"I'm coming to the morgue with you JJ," he said, dropping the formality once the others had departed. "We can ride over together. Good job," he said, a smile spreading across his brown face.

"Especially how you handled the PSV situation. I know I handed you a can of worms when I asked you to take charge of this case."

"Not like I haven't been there before," I said. Both of us veterans of bureaucratic, personal, and political trench warfare fought in these halls.

The streets quieter by the time we departed the station shortly after five pm. Kingstown's business offices and stores closed for the day. Busses and mini vans dangerously overloaded with passengers raced out of the capital in every direction.

The sun descent in the western sky cast lengthy shadows across Kingstown's deserted streets, reflecting in bright golden splashes from the building's glass surfaces.

"How were the flights down and back?" Mike asked.

I suppressed the urge to gush. To give the memory free rein. Allow it to burst forth with the same soaring thrill as the actual experience. A modicum of formality still needed to be observed. We weren't exactly sitting on Mike's verandah in Friendship Bay enjoying a beer. He was the Commissioner of Police, even in the absence of the drab grey uniform and official braid which he hated wearing. And we were riding in his official police vehicle, driven by a uniformed corporal who periodically cast covert glances at us through the rear view mirror.

He recognized my suppressed excitement, smiled, and instead asked, "What'd you think of Doctor Gash?"

"My first impression. Young and inexperienced. Until I saw her in action. She knows her way around a cadaver. Did you know about her before assigning her to this case, or was she just someone available at the time?"

"I made it a point to get to know her and her resume when she first arrived. I've had a request in to the Peace Corp for a pathologist for a while now."

"I like her actually," I said.

"Good," he said. "You both have a lot in common. She reminds me of another smart, capable, underestimated young woman I met back when I first took this job."

I smiled.

"By the way, I'm gonna need your written preliminary report first thing in the morning. Before I contact the Foreign Secretary's Office. You can stay over tonight and finish it up. You look kinda beat."

Besides the home he owned in Friendship Bay on Bequia, Mike maintained a rented home in Montrose, his official residence on St. Vincent, staffed by civilian and police personnel.

I noticed the driver's quick glance in the rear view mirror. But it wasn't my primary reason for declining Mike's offer. I did feel beat, and reasoned I'd be up late constructing the case file and working on the report. I wanted to be in my own house, in my own bed, using my own shower, and a fresh change of clothes in the morning.

"Thanks Chief," I said. "But I want to get home. And I need to check in at the Port Elizabeth Station in the morning. Then it's back down to Union."

We crossed the Leeward Highway intersection and arrived at the Milton Cato Memorial Hospital complex. A 211 bed facility named for the first Prime Minister of St. Vincent and the Grenadines following independence. It also housed facilities of the recently established Trinity School of Medicine, which attracted students from around the Caribbean. And a few students from Canada and the United States who'd been unable to gain admission to the more competitive institutions in their home countries.

A pungent odor greeted our approach to the morgue. A mixture of formaldehyde, organic decay and scented fragrances. When we entered I noticed why. Spaced around the room, a dozen or more scented candles flickered in the harsh fluorescent light. A shroud-covered figure occupied one of three dissecting tables.

Doctor Eileen Gash and Zelina McIntosh stood in conversation at the far end of the room, studying a series of x-ray images clipped to a viewer mounted on the wall.

"Doctor Gash," Mike called, startling them both.

"Commissioner Daniels. Superintendent." She greeted, regaining her composure. "I'm sorry. I didn't hear you enter."

"No worries Doctor," Mike said, smiling and crossing the room to shake her hand.

Zelina had not moved, standing in a stiff posture, not exactly at attention, but a close approximation. She made an attempt to salute but Mike interrupted her, "At ease, Detective," offering his hand instead, his other hand patting her on the shoulder while they shook.

"Good to see you again Zelina," he said. "Thank you for the good work you did down there." His sincerity apparent in his smile, in his dark brown eyes, and the tone of his voice.

"Just doin de job sah," she said.

"Wish I had more who did the job as well as you," he said.

He turned to Eileen, "What do you have so far Doctor?"

"I've just got the x-rays back." she said. Haven't started on the autopsy yet."

"Do you mind putting in some extra time Doctor? We need to expedite this investigation."

"I'd planned on it," she said.

"Thanks," Mike said. "Anything you need is at your disposal. X-rays tell you anything so far?"

"Nothing I didn't expect. Massive trauma, multiple fractures extending over most of the skeletal system, including his fingers. See, here, and here," she said pointing to areas on the x-rays.

"Unusual," she said, squinting her eyes at the images and scrunching her long, elegant nose in concentration. "But consistent with the rest of his skeletal injuries."

"The most significant finding so far," she continued, Are these areas here, around the heart. See," indicating them on a chest x-ray. "He had advanced atherosclerosis, hardening of the arteries. A heart attack waiting to happen. He may have suffered a massive coronary while driving. If so, it'll show up in the enzyme and toxicology screens."

Mike digested this information. We all did.

He said, "Okay Doctor, we'll leave you to it. When do you think you'll have a report for me?"

"I'll have preliminary findings by morning. The lab results will take longer. Depends on, well you know.... " she said, not finishing the sentence or needing to elaborate on the deficiencies of the local laboratory.

Equally aware Mike said, "This has priority Doctor. Whatever we're not equipped to handle here we'll send out. Barbados. Or Stateside if we have to. What about identification?" he asked.

"Oh," she said, as though suddenly remembering a forgotten detail. She picked up a brown envelope from the table below the x-ray viewer. "Dental x-rays," she said, handing it to him. "They can be used to identify him if you have a set to compare them to. Same for DNA. I've already collected samples, but again, you'll need a comparison sample."

"Thanks Doctor," Mike said. "I'll be in touch."

Outside in the hospital courtyard I said to Zelina, "I'm heading back to Bequia for the night. You're welcome to stay over at my place. We can head down to Union together in the morning."

"Tanks, but I feel like spendin de nite at home."

She meant her family home on St. Vincent. Stationed on Union, she didn't see them much. Even though visiting entailed only a short ferry ride. For Vincentians it seemed more like taking a trip from New York to Florida.

"I'll drop you at the airport," Mike said to me. "Can I give you a lift somewhere Dectective?"

"Anywhere close by Heritage Square sir. I can catch a van from dere."

He nodded. "I'll dispatch CGV Hairoun to return you both to Union in the morning. Zelina, be at the base at oh eight hundred. It'll stop in Bequia on the way and pick you up JJ."

We all climbed into the vehicle, Zelina in front next to the uniformed corporal. Our day done. Almost.

I flew the short hop to Bequia. Secured the Seneca in its usual tie down spot. The house depressingly dark when I arrived home in Lower Bay. It possessed a lonely, unlived in feeling. I'd been away only two days. I thought.

I switched on lights, but the unoccupied feeling persisted. Subsiding only after a long, leisurely shower, a few bites of cold leftovers from two days before, and a Toni Braxton CD on the player.

Even then not entirely. Something still missing. A piece of home. A piece of me.

And something else unsettling my equilibrium. That time of the month.

I poured myself a glass of Pinot Noir, opened my laptop, and lost myself in work. First I categorized the digital images, placing them in appropriately named folders. Crash Scene, Victim, Cottage. I scrutinized each one as I sorted them into the various folders.

I listed the physical evidence on an Excel spreadsheet, surprised at the shortness of the list. I'd been aware of the paucity of physical evidence, aside from the wrecked Volkswagen jeep. But seeing the actual list provided a dismal perspective. When I listed the broken wristwatch, a vague memory tried to assert itself, but failed to take hold.

But it opened a new train of thought. In a document separate from the case file I listed the apparent anomalies. The most glaring being the lack of identification. Not on the body. Not in the cottage he'd been renting. At the very least he'd have had a passport, and a return airline ticket. He couldn't have entered the country without possessing both. What had happened to them? And secondly, the lack of personal items and effects. None on his person or in the cottage. As if he'd been attempting to conceal his identity.

Next I listed unanswered questions. Who had he planned on meeting? And where? But the supposed meeting was based solely on the word of a witness who'd been trying not to incriminate himself. Was his statement credible? And why had Mansfield driven up Mount Olympus? Not the most obvious place for a meeting. Nothing up there. Maybe that'd been the point.

Staring at the typed questions provided no answers. I poured another glass of wine and turned to composing the preliminary report.

CHAPTER 7

I slept the sleep of the exhausted. I hadn't dreamt. At
least I didn't remember any dreams upon waking. I awoke at
my usual time, to the accompaniment of roosters outside my
window. The space next to me in the bed empty. I'd rolled
onto his side of the bed, expecting to feel the warmth of his
naked body against mine. My sleeping mind forgot his
absence. I decided to take a run. First I needed to pee.

Still dark outside as I trotted down to the beach. The
landscape materialized from the darkness as dawn's first faint
light crept across a cloudy eastern sky. The salty morning air
crisp and refreshing, bearing the scent of rain.

Along Lower Bay's shoreline fishermen prepared their
nets and fishing boats. Rolling surf lapped around their ankles
and onto the beach in a rhythmic boom and sigh. The sand,
like fine powder, crunched beneath my running shoes as I
pumped along the beach. Out in the small cove a white
fiberglass mooring buoy bearing red lettering marked the spot
Wherever normally lay. Now empty. Like his side of the bed.

I'd run the length of two football fields when the beach
ended. Ahead a steep promontory separated Lower Bay beach
from Princess Margaret beach. This next part not a run, but a
hike.

I stepped onto the well-trod trail at the edge of the tree line, and climbed through the thick, thorny brush lining the path. Dense woods soon obscured the view of the beach behind, the beach ahead, and the open bay on my left. Sweat ran in rivulets down my sides, back, and stomach. A cotton headband held the salty moisture from my eyes.

At the crest the bay emerged in spectacular view. The rising sun, hidden behind a elevated ridge running like a spine down Bequia's center, colored the eastern sky raspberry.

December, the congested harbor reminded me. Christmas three weeks away. The height of tourist season. Transient sailboats of every type and kind packed Admiralty Bay, their masts rising like a forest stripped bare after a fire. Maybe a hundred, or close to it. More on the way.

The crowded harbor the primary reason Gage had sailed south. He hated this time of year, when charter yachts engorged the harbor, and cruise ships disgorged hordes of tourists upon the island. He claimed it disturbed his quietude, and he'd sail south for quieter shores. But those increasingly difficult to find. The Grenadines continued to grow in popularity as a vacation destination for winter refugees.

The influx of visitors disturbed my quietude too. It multiplied my workload and strained my Division's resources.

I pushed thoughts of work from my mind. Paid closer attention to my footing as I half-jogged-half-climbed down the steep side. Until I had sand beneath my feet again. The white expanse of Princess Margaret Beach curved away ahead of me, bordered by lazy lapping surf on my left, a forest of coconut, breadfruit, and mango trees on my right. I picked up the pace.

Activity in the tree line drew my attention. More fishermen. Some recently returned. Others just starting out, hauling the ubiquitous Bequia double-ender fishing boats from beneath towering coconut trees down to the shoreline. A young boy staked out the family goat for the day. I waved and acknowledged their greetings as I ran past.

I loved to run. Gage hated it. I loved the time alone, enclosed in my solitary cocoon, experiencing the sensations of my body, the invigorating physicality of it. Muscles stretching and contracting, joints flexing and straightening, heart pounding, lungs inflating and deflating; all working in harmonious physiological concert. Running cleared my mind, allowing random thoughts free rein to ricochet around my brain, meeting, colliding, connecting; generating unexpected meanings, insights and clarity.

Gage preferred to swim. As comfortable in the sea as though he'd been born in it. He effortlessly swam five or more miles in a morning. He'd head far out past the points bordering the bay. Out and back. Strong, steady, even strokes propelling him through the water like a creature of the sea.

At the end of Princess Margaret Beach the rock stepping challenge began. Another steep promontory separated this beach from the next. A tunnel eroded through the rock connected the beaches. At low tide the exposed sand between boulders formed a path through the tunnel. At high tide, stepping from boulder to boulder formed the path.

I jogged-stepped through to the other side, where the beach fronted the Plantation House Hotel. I picked up the pace again. Ran along the beach past the hotel's neatly trimmed lawn and landscaped plants. Farther along, a stone footpath and seawall protected the beachfront establishments from the encroaching sea. I ran along the concrete topped path, past the pizzeria, the Green Boley restaurant, the

Gingerbread Hotel, the Whale Boner, and finally the Frangipani Hotel on the edge of Port Elizabeth.

The harbor itself bustling and busy. The first ferries to Kingstown in the process of loading. Under the emerging dawn's pale light pedestrians and minivans jostled for space along the Harbor road and on the wharf.

At the Anglican Church I turned for the run back to Lower Bay, by way of the main road. It'd be a climbing run the entire way, until the Lower Bay turnoff. There the road declined steeply toward Lower Bay.

Bequia morning sounds filled the air. Roosters crowing, goats baaing. The incessant beep-beeping of minivan horns declaring their presence behind hairpin turns in the road. Calypso and Soca music blared from their speakers. Drivers and passengers hailed me: "Mahnin Miss Jolene." Or, "Miss Super", using a friendly contraction of my rank. I waved in response. The muscles in my thighs and calves stretched and tightened as I pushed upward and onward.

At the Lower Bay turnoff I halted, bent at the waist, head lowered, hands on my hips, blowing draughts of air through my mouth. My thighs and calves ached, but not terribly. The circuit I'd run less than four miles. My sweat drenched tee shirt clung to my torso, and a glistening layer of moisture covered my exposed skin. I sucked in a deep breath of fresh salty air, straightened, and commenced walking at a pace to cool myself down. A cooling draft on my skin as the sweat evaporated.

I approached a turn in the road, Gage's favorite spot. It overlooked the panoramic expanse of Admiralty Bay, including the three smaller bays and crescent shaped white sand beaches within it. The breathtaking view emerged in a cinematographic fade in as the sky lightened from the east.

Back at my house I commenced stripping the moment I skipped through the door. First the beach soaked, sand filled running shoes and ankle socks, abandoned by the door. Then the sweat soaked tee shirt as I crossed the sitting room. In the kitchen I set coffee brewing. At the bedroom door I pulled the tight fitted, seamless white cotton sports bra over my head. A silent sigh of relief as breasts fell free of the bra's supportive stricture. The cut-off sweats and underwear removed as one as I hop scotched to the bathroom door. I dropped the bundled clothes into the laundry hamper and stepped over the tiled shower sill.

Hot showers a luxury on Bequia. I'd had a hot water heater installed in the house, but I used it infrequently. I preferred the bracing splash of a cold shower, especially after a run or workout. I lathered using homemade body wash containing natural ingredients, inhaling the fragrant floral scent. My shampoo also homemade, containing natural liquid soap, spring water, coconut oil and crushed lavender flowers.

following a long leisurely rinse I turned off the shower. I reached outside the curtain for a full-length bath towel. Wrapped and twist tied a smaller towel around my hair and stepped to a long stone counter littered with the usual bathroom items. A large clamshell shaped sink occupied the middle of the counter. Above the counter and sink I faced a large wall mounted mirror.

I stared into the mirror while brushing my teeth, wondering what to wear, and about my hair, which on any given day tended to be uncooperative.

As a teenager I'd dreaded my hair. It'd been the instigator of angst driven consternation, frustration, hair product expense, and delays in getting ready to go anywhere. I'd tried to tame the unruly mess of natural curls using hair gel, straightening irons, cutting and tying. All to no avail. At some point I'd come to terms with its natural proclivities.

I brushed it out, still wet. I'd ceased using a hair blower long ago too. My hair would dry by itself soon enough in the tropical heat, and take on its characteristic unruly frizz. I gathered it at the sides, pulled it tight at the back, and secured it with a black velvet scrunchie.

The face staring back at me possessed a combination of features inherited from my Vincentian mother and French-Canadian father. I had his hazel eyes, his straight nose, delineated jaw line and dimpled chin. I had my mother's forehead and delicate brows, her wide mouth, and full lips.

I decided not to apply makeup. I seldom used any.

I hung the damp towels and walked naked to the bedroom closet. I pulled on a pair of black lace panties, and chose dark lightweight slacks and a thin black leather belt. Rummaging through the drawer for a lightweight bra, the ballistic vest Gage had given me caught my eye. It looked, felt, wore, and even washed like a short sleeve tee shirt, long at the waist to cover the pelvic area. The only difference its weight. Not heavy, but the layers of woven anti-ballistic fabric extraordinarily dense, comprised of some super-secret material providing protection against all ballistic projectiles and bladed weapons.

According to Gage the vest and everything about it remained classified. I didn't bother asking how he'd acquired it, especially a female model, its elastic breast cups comfortably accommodating my size and shape. Much of Mr. Nicholas Gage remained off limits and 'classified'. I'd grown used to that too.

I'd marveled at the comfortable fit the first time I'd worn the vest. He'd given it to me during the investigation into Mike's shooting. Concerned for my safety. I'd worn it often since then, more like a garment than a shield, and enjoyed the freedom of not having to wear a bra when I wore it.

Since I planned to spend most of the day in the field, and would be away from home for a while, I pulled it on. I donned a teal short sleeved shirt over it, buttoned the front, tucked the tail into the waistband of my pants and buckled the belt.

Shoes next. Here I had choices capable of creating a time delaying dilemma. But I chose the comfortably broken in pair of tan cowboy style ankle boots I'd worn the day before. The Kel-tec snug in my boot, I walked over to the night stand on my side of the bed. I opened the drawer and retrieved my other weapon, a nine milliliter Glock 19 and its fifteen round magazine. The official sidearm issued to armed response constables of the Royal St. Vincent and the Grenadines Police Force.

I wondered, not for the first time, about the unexpected turn my life had taken. That I'd become a cop, a 'babylon' in the local vernacular. A decision triggered by an event I'd sealed in the back of my memory, and seldom mentioned. My occupation astonishing enough. That armed police had become a necessity in St. Vincent and the Grenadines seemed equally incomprehensible.

Unfortunately violent crime had infiltrated our tranquil existence. Firearm related robberies, assaults, and murders on the rise, fueled by increased trafficking of drugs and guns. Less than a year ago Mike had been callously gunned down by drug traffickers who'd brought their war to Bequia's shores. If not for Gage's involvement we'd probably never had closed the case. And only a handful of people, including me, Gage, Mike, and two friends from Gage's past he'd enlisted to help, knew the full story of those events.

I carefully checked the Glock and inserted the loaded magazine. I partially pulled back the slide to glimpse the gleaming brass cartridge I'd left lying in the chamber. I double checked the engaged safety, and placed the weapon in my shoulder bag which also held my police badge and ID, a belt holster for the Glock, a telescoping metal baton, and other personal items.

I consigned the unmade bed to my housekeeper. She came twice a week regularly. More if I needed her. She handled the housecleaning, cooking, laundry, and other required housework. I packed a weekend bag before exiting the bedroom.

In the kitchen I poured a cup of coffee, added a splash of cream, one level teaspoon of brown sugar, and sipped the hot brew while loading the laptop and notebooks into my briefcase. Running late I skipped breakfast.

Velma stepped through the side door at the back of the kitchen at the same time two loud bleeps of a horn sounded from the front.

"Morning Velma," I greeted her as I slung the shoulder bag strap over my shoulder and gathered the weekend bag and briefcase.

"Mahnin Super," she greeted me in turn. Plump and sturdy, Velma possessed the pleasant easygoing manner characteristic of Bequians. And a bawdy sense of humor, an infectious laugh, and an endless repertoire of hilarious local gossip. Eminently trustworthy, she was as protective of me as if I were one of her own five children.

"I'm going down to Union for de weekend," I told her. "Close up de house fe me when you finish."

"Yuh go cahful yuh heah. Dem bad bwoys out a street gone crazy wid dem gunplay. Lord have mercy."

"Tanks Velma," I said, accepting her warning as sincerely as it'd been given.

The changing nature of crime on the islands had set people to worrying about things they hadn't had to before. Fear of being robbed at gunpoint, or being shot, an unfortunate and increasing reality. Especially among shop owners. Months after the occurrence, people still spoke in hushed, frightened tones about the shooting of Commissioner of Police Mike Daniels. And it seemed not a week went by without a new gun related incident for people to talk about and worry over.

An older model open bed Toyota Tacoma in blue, white, and stripped yellow police livery, blue beacons affixed atop the right and left sides of the windshield, waited on the road at the end of the path from my house.

Constable Chester 'Johnny' Johns, who'd accompanied me to Union Island, stood next to it. His dark honey hued face a mask of invented seriousness, an affect betrayed by the youthful exuberance in his large, dark brown eyes, and a standard sized uniform hanging so loosely on his tall slender frame, one couldn't resist laughing.

I liked Chester Johns, seconding him frequently as my driver and assistant. He possessed a sense of punctuality for one thing, rare among Vincentians. And his cheery enthusiasm for learning police work evoked the mentor in me.

"Mahnin Suprintendent," he greeted as I approached, stamping his feet, straightening to rigid attention. His right arm raised in a stiff salute, the back of his fingers lightly touching the oversized uniform cap obscuring his forehead.

My answering salute a wholly non-regulation sweep of my hand somewhere in the proximity of my brow.

"Good morning Constable Johns. At ease. How you doing today?"

"Fine Suprintendent. All good Ma'am."

"Good. Den le we go."

CHAPTER 8

The first rain shower raced across Bequia during the drive to the station. It poured in intermittent squalls, moving from southeast to northwest, drenching different parts of the island as each squall passed, leaving the landscape fresh and clean.

"Suprintendent," exclaimed Station Sergeant Dennis Lucenti, as usual the first to notice me entering the station. As if he maintained a daily lookout.

"I didn't noh yuh was back Ma'am," he said, stamping to attention and saluting. The uniformed constables preparing for the day shift heard the thudding sound of his boots on the wood floor, noticed my presence, and followed suit.

"As you were," I said loudly enough for everyone to hear. "Came back last night," I said to Lucenti. "But leaving for Union again just now."

Short, stocky, carrying a bit of a beer paunch, Lucenti exuded an infectious ebullience. Friendly, jovial, and loquacious, he enjoyed chatting up people, especially tourists who stopped into the station seeking information, or any other strangers with whom he happened to strike up a conversation. He possessed a penchant for tall tales, often keeping his listeners guessing at the veracity of his stories.

But his most important trait lay in his ability to wrangle the younger, lackadaisical, and inattentive,- some might say scatterbrained - constables. Especially the rookies. While his easygoing soft-spoken manner tended to lull the uninitiated, testing his patience often resulted in a sudden snappishness, akin to a dog guarding a cherished bone from an incautious interloper.

Before I had the chance to ask him the whereabouts of Detective Inspector Desmond Cato, the detective entered through a solid, heavy oak door at the rear of the building. He might've been an older version of Constable Johns. Tall and lean, his face possessed a serious countenance he didn't need to affect. an impression accentuated by a small mouth and lips so thick they appeared to be perpetually pouted.

A uniformed constable stood guard by the door Desmond had exited, which only occurred when the holding cells were occupied.

"Suprintendent," he said, striding over to greet me. "Sorry Ma'am, didn't know you was back. We have a development in de case."

"My office," I said, turning and heading for the stairs.

Before my sudden departure for Union Island I'd dropped two open cases in Cato's lap. I'd meant to handle them personally, until I'd received Mike's call. One involved a complaint by a visiting British couple of valuables stolen from their Bungalow. The other a shooting of a Port Elizabeth man by an assailant who'd we'd located and arrested. The Director of Public Prosecutions needed more background on the relationship between the victim and assailant. And we still needed to know how and where the assailant had obtained the handgun used in the shooting.

Detective Cato launched into his report as a heavy downpour pelted the station's zinc roof, creating a sound overhead like popcorn popping.

"I was talking to people around de wharf yesterday," he said in non-patois, heavily accented English, pushing wire rimmed spectacles higher on the flat bridge of his nose. "I was asking if dey knew anyone trying to sell jewlry and such on de wharf. I was told about dis fella, known as Natty Dred, real name Calvin Smalls, resident of Canuoan. Anyway, I waited to see if he'd show up on de wharf, which he did, and I observed him attempting to sell some watches and jewlry. I questioned him and he can't explain how he came into possession of de jewlry. So I take him up and brought him to de station for questioning. When we searched him we found more jewlry in his pockets. Some of de jewlry matched items stolen from de Cummings. Some matched stolen items from tree odder open cases."

"What'd he say when you questioned him," I asked.

"He claims not to know bout any robberies. Claims some friends gave him de jewlry to sell."

"You buy that?"

Cato's thick lips stretched into a grin, the corners of his eyes crinkled behind his spectacles. "We charged him wid handling stolen goods. Dat's at least six months in prison, so he start talking. He gave us descriptions of dese supposed friends, three fellas from St. Vincent. Claims dey gave him de jewlry. So me and DeSilva from de Paget Farm station been making inquiries and think we have a location where dese fellas staying. We was going to look for dem this morning."

The information constituted the breakthrough we'd needed to close a string of thefts and burglaries against tourists.

"I was about to call you and update you on all dis when I see you come in. I didn't know you was back from Union."

"Dat's some excellent work Inspector." I said, not especially surprised he'd provided the break in the case. A smart, intuitive detective, Cato didn't merely plod through cases like so many of his colleagues. He didn't like unanswered questions and loose ends, and presented solid cases to the Director of Public Prosecutions. Among the best, if not the best in the entire CID, possessing exactly the sort of dedicated professionalism Mike sought to instill in the force.

Cato hailed originally from Lowmans on mainland St. Vincent, and like me, he'd lived and been educated abroad. I'd often though he'd be the ideal CID commander, instead of the idiotic Mitchell. On the other hand I appreciated having him in my Division. I relied on him, both as an investigator and a partner in the field.

"How'd you plan to handle it?" I asked.

"Well I just talked to the prisoner again. He don't know if dese fellas have any firearms. Said he never seen any. But it doesn't mean dey don't have any. I was thinking me and DeSilva approach de house. Have constables covering de road and yard outside."

"Okay. Put your team together. I'll come with you." I thought about waiting for the Coast Guard. Zelina and the crew could provide additional backup. But it'd also mean a larger armed presence in a volatile situation. I nixed the idea. If at all possible I didn't want this arrest to turn into the OK Corral.

The house, in reality a dilapidated shack, sat nestled on a hillside between La Pompe and Paget Farm. Small, wood planked, the ramshackle structure had a rusted corrugated tin roof. The planks old, warped, rotted and loose, leaving large gaps between them. A dense growth of breadfruit, mango and banana trees concealed the shack from the road.

Wearing ballistic vests, 'POLICE' stenciled on the back, we assembled at the foot of a dirt path leading up from the main road. The bulky older generation vest I wore redundant. But I couldn't reveal to the others the classified vest I already wore beneath my shirt.

The only ones armed, Cato, DeSilva and I checked our weapons. Cato directed DeSilva and two constables into the bush and trees on either side of the path, to take up positions at the rear of the house. He directed two other constables to remain at the foot of the path. The two of us cautiously approached the house from the front. The path and yard around the shack muddy and slippery from the early morning rains.

A flimsy, cracked and crooked sheet of plywood constituted the front door. Two outward opening wood shutters hung on either side of the door. The door and shutters were closed. Even so we remained out of the sightlines as we approached. The crooked ill-fitting door and shutters didn't completely cover the openings.

Pulsating soca rhythms poured from the house. And the unmistakable odor of marijuana. So far there'd been no sign of movement, or any indication of occupation. Cato crouched in the muddy ground on one side of the door. I at the other. After a silent count of three I yanked on the plywood door. Cato went through in a crouch shouting "Poliss!" His weapon up and ready. I followed on his heels. We heard a crash from the back and DeSilva bellowing 'Poliss" as he entered from the rear.

The interior dark. Sparsely lit by narrow shafts of sunlight through gaps in the wall planks. The dim light illuminated heaps of clothing and trash strewn around the floor. A bundle in the corner moved. A form rose out of the mess. Cato pounced before the person reached a sitting position. A boot in the figure's chest pushed him back onto a bare dirty mattress concealed beneath the mess. Dull, dark eyes stared in wild eyed terror at Cato's pistol pointed at his head.

Two other men had been asleep in another tiny dank room in the rear. In a sleepy, befuddled, perhaps stoned haze they groped frantically among the piles of clothing and trash strewn around the floor. DeSilva, big and muscular, grabbed one of them by the arm and threw him across the room. When the man hit the wall I thought it'd bring the dilapidated structure down on top of us all.

I dashed any thought of escape by the third with a kick to his chest when he rushed me. The kick sent him sprawling spread eagled onto his back, the wind knocked out of him.

The suspects subdued, handcuffed, and surrounded by constables, Cato, DeSilva and I searched through the mess. We opened all the available windows and doors to let in light and air.

Our search yielded jewelry, most likely stolen, eighteen hundred dollars in EC currency, and another twelve hundred in US dollars. Enough marijuana to sustain a charge of intent to supply. And a thirty-eight caliber revolver and ammunition.

The three men, boys really, none seemed older than twenty, all sporting corn row hairstyles, remained docile and compliant as they were marched down the path to the waiting police jeep.

When we arrived in Port Elizabeth CGV Hairoun had already docked. Zelina waited at the station. As we entered I noticed the surreptitious glances passed between her and Cato.

They greeted each other formally, "Detective McIntosh," Cato said smiling.

"Inspector," she responded. An unmistakable flirtatious twinkle in her eyes.

You go girl! I thought.

I left them together while I gathered my things from the office. After a final briefing with Cato regarding the prisoners, the arrest reports, and identification and cataloging of the evidence found in the shack, Zelina and I departed the station for the waiting cutter.

The noisy bedlam of ferries loading and unloading greeted us at the wharf. The biweekly ferry for Canuoan, Mayreau and Union island had just arrived from Kingstown. The late morning ferry between Bequia and Kingstown loading in preparation for departure. Pink skinned tourists disembarked from a launch shuttling between the wharf and a five story floating monstrosity anchored at the mouth of Admiralty Bay.

A visible police presence on the teeming wharf. The entire Port Elizabeth constabulary by the looks of it, including Constable Johns, and a supplementary contingent from Kingstown. There to shield incoming visitors from petty thieves, pickpockets, and innocent but annoying street kids hawking questionable merchandise and souvenirs.

The constables saluted as I passed through the crowd. The salutes aroused curious, open mouthed stares from the tourists. I wasn't in uniform, and I didn't look local.

"Who's that? Why are they saluting that woman?" I heard whispered as I passed through the crowd. The wide eyed stares grew even larger, the mouths opened even wider, when I boarded the Coast Guard vessel to more stamped boots and salutes from the uniformed crew.

The crew fired up the twin diesels and the cutter backed away from the tumultuous wharf. In a few minutes we'd cleared the congested harbor, cruising at top speed for West Cay.

CHAPTER 9

About the only positive thing to be said for motoring across the sea at twenty five miles per hour is you'll reach your destination faster than on a sailboat. While the sensation of speed can be exhilarating, the bone jarring, teeth rattling jolt whenever the cutter met an oncoming swell, is no match for the gentle graceful glide of a sailboat riding the waves. And the throbbing noise of diesel engines no match for the sea's soothing swish along a sailboat's hull, or the wind whistling in its rigging.

The heavy diesels provided a constant rumbling drone in the background as we sped south for Union Island. The sky south of Bequia had cleared, leaving scattered, low hanging smudgy clouds, and a higher broken layer pierced by shafts of sunlight. To the east the sky remained leaden and dark above a line of squalls marching toward Bequia. Diaphanous curtains of rain hung between the clouds and the sea.

An hour and a half later the cutter eased against the wharf in Clifton. The day already half gone. Lunchtime. The wharf and square empty and quiet as Zelina and I strode to the Clifton Police Station.

Station Sergeant Baptiste the sole occupant of the station when we arrived. Large and heavy set, he sat behind the counter reading an old magazine. When he noticed me his eyebrows converged in a disapproving scowl, and his dark face acquired a mean aspect. As a further sign of his disrespect he neither stood nor offered a salute when I approached the counter. Instead he attempted to stare me down. I held his stare, glaring back with cold ferocity into dark eyes set deep beneath a thick brow. A contest he couldn't win, either by temperament or rank.

He relented. No surprise there. We'd done this dance before. And I knew his type. A mere bully. An overbearing, petulant son of a bitch who derived authority solely from the uniform he wore. He proffered a faux salute I non-the-less accepted. I didn't care about the salute. He needed to know I wouldn't tolerate his usual crap.

Zelina had disappeared into the back of the station during this silent exchange. She returned carrying a dark leather case, like the type commercial pilots use. Packed into the case the basic essentials to process a crime scene. We exited the station together. Neither Baptiste nor I had said a word to each other. Zelina handed me the case.

"Shoh yuh don't want me go wid yuh, Suprintendent?"

"I can handle dis Zelina," I said. "I need yuh to start pulling the immigration forms and photos. He probably flew here directly from Barbados and cleared immigration and customs here. Den head to the wharf and start interviewing de staff. Catch de evening shift on their way over and de day shift coming back."

We departed in opposite directions. I headed to the yacht club in search of a water taxi. I spied Seckie lounging under the awning on his launch.

"Seckie," I called from the dock.

"Suprintendent," jumping to his feet to greet me, his gap-toothed grin in place. "Yuh reach back."

"Still working de case Seckie. I need a ride to PSV."

"No problame. Hop on," he said, hoisting my weekend bag and the crime scene case into the launch. I held on to the shoulder bag and briefcase.

"Do me a favor Seckie. Stop at Wherever first," I asked.

"No problame," he repeated, firing up the mercruiser inboard and shoving off from the dock.

He soon pulled alongside the schooner. Wherever's white gunwale and sparkling red boot stripe complemented her dark blue hull. Stunningly beautiful. She possessed elegant curves, an eight foot bowsprit stretching beyond a sleek sharp bow, and a distinct sexy rake to her wood masts.

"Ahoy de Wheyevah," Seckie hailed, easing the launch gently against Wherever's starboard side.

A head popped through the open coach roof hatch. A wide smile covered the familiar honey hued face. The smile accentuated the chiseled jaw and dimpled chin. His light brown eyes turned even lighter when he moved into the direct sunlight, a dark shade of grey.

Gage.

I hoisted and dumped the weekend bag onto the deck, followed by my briefcase.

"What's up sweetness?" he greeted, leaning over the rail.

I reached up to plant a kiss on his cheek. "I'm gonna be on PSV the rest of the afternoon," I said. "But I'll be back for dinner."

"See you later then," he said, gathering up the bag and briefcase.

Seckie pushed off from Wherever's side, headed for the mouth of Clifton Harbor.

I'd phoned ahead to alert Forester of my arrival. I'd assured him he'd have his cottage back for the weekend as promised, barring unforeseen circumstances. I didn't know how far in advance the cottage had been paid for, or his immediate plans for it. At least I'd be done needing it. I hoped.

Peter Wellington waited by a Mini-Moke when Seckie pulled alongside the PSV dock. He wore his familiar non-expressive face, cracking a small smile when he greeted me. He drove along the winding double tracks through the forested greenery in silence. I had a strange compulsion to break the ice. To engage him in conversation. Instead I allowed the passing scenery to sweep me away.

We crested a ridge overlooking the bluff where Mansfield's cottage lay hidden in the foliage. The view spread out around us in every direction. A three hundred sixty degree panorama of sea, sky and island. It hadn't rained in the southern Grenadines, but all around vibrant color burst from the terrain. Green trees, red hibiscus and bougainvillea, white petunias and lilies, yellow orchids and flamboyants, purple and lavender frangipani, and pink roses and daffodils. As fresh and fragrant as after a spring shower.

The eastern sky had cleared, leaving a brilliant blue sky, and lazy drifting puffy clouds like stretched and torn cotton, casting moving shadows over the restless sea. I finally spoke when Wellington stopped the Moke in front of Mansfield's cottage.

"No one's been inside the cottage since we left it?" I inquired. I noticed the red flag still fluttering atop its bamboo staff.

"No one." Wellington said.

I silently questioned the confidence of his statement, when as though reading my mind he said, "I've had guards posted since you left yesterday."

I didn't see any guards, and again mentally questioned his statement, when a tall, muscular man appeared through the trees at the side of the cottage. Clean shaved head, coal black complexion, he wore dark blue shorts, and a dark blue tee shirt, the PSV logo and 'Security' embroidered over the left breast.

I left both men conversing outside and entered the cottage carrying the crime scene case. I placed the case and my bag on the coffee table, and walked through the rooms again, ordering my thoughts, mapping out how and where to proceed. The cottage appeared as I'd last seen it.

I decided to tackle the bathroom first. And received my first surprise. I didn't find a single fingerprint anywhere in the room. Not on the counter top, the faucets, the shower door, the light switch, or any surface you'd expect a person to touch.

I decided to see if the same held true for the rest of the cottage. It did. No prints. None at all. Not on the inside entrance, table tops, light switches, furniture, sliding French doors, the glass itself, or outdoor surfaces. Nothing. When I'd finished I'd left a patchwork of fingerprint power around the cottage, and not a single print to show for it.

The place had been thoroughly wiped. Why? And by whom?

Next I decided to search the cottage. I tackled the outside sundeck first. I had no idea what I might be looking for, or what I might find. The word 'anomalies' screamed in my head. I searched for the slightest thing out of place. Any disturbance. The soil in a planter; the mortar between the stones, the stone itself.

Inside the cottage I searched cabinets, below counters and through drawers. Behind framed artwork on the stone walls. I removed the covering on the day bed and couch. Searched under the cushions, moved and searched beneath the furniture. I removed the pillow cases and squeezed the pillows. I rolled the corners of the woven carpets. I searched the lamp shades and bases. Nothing. I scrutinized the light switch and outlet plates. No screws disturbed, no scratch marks visible.

I walked into the bedroom. Searched the double bed in the same manner I'd done the daybed and couch in the living room. I lifted the mattress and searched below it. No slits or tears. Nothing hidden beneath it. I checked the lamps, wall switches, outlet covers, the carpets and picture frames as I'd done in the living room. Still nothing. I pulled out the dresser drawers, checked the insides of the dresser, and checked the bottoms of the drawers.

I retrieved the suitcase from the corner where it still lay undisturbed since I'd last seen it. I laid it on the disheveled bed. I searched through it again, feeling around the interior for hidden compartments. Found none. I searched through the clothing I'd dumped on the bed while searching the dresser drawers. I went through each piece of clothing. The hanging clothes included one light linen suit, expensive, a light summer sport jacket, three pairs of khaki slacks, boxer underwear, three polo shirts each a different color, and three short sleeved dress shirts.

I packed the clothing into the suitcase before heading into the bathroom. I checked the cabinets below the sink.

Pulled the towels and linens from the shelves and checked
each. I checked under and around the shelves. I checked the
shower stall and even unscrewed the multi spray nozzle. I
lifted the toilet seat, checked the bowl. Removed the tank lid
and checked inside the tank. Same as the rest of the cottage.
Nothing. Merde!

If not for the clothes, there'd be no evidence Charles
Mansfield had ever set foot in the cottage. No personal items
or toiletries which may contain his DNA. No wallet, no
identification, no passport. As if any trace of his identity had
been deliberately erased.

I called out to Peter Wellington. He'd left me
undisturbed in the cottage. He entered as I peeled off the red
nitrite gloves I'd been wearing. His normally expressionless
face registered a momentary consternation at the condition of
the cottage. Turned impassive again, except for his light blue
eyes. His gaze swept the room in a quick survey.

"I hate to sound like a broken record, but I must ask
again, are you positive no one's been in the cottage since Mr.
Mansfield left for Union Island?"

He didn't seem in the least put out by having to answer
the question again. Rather he appeared pensive. His eyebrows
drew closer, deepening the already deep cleft between his eyes
at the top of his slightly crooked nose. His blue eyes focused
inward. His mouth set in a grim line. His eyes cast a final
glance around the room.

"I can't be one hundred percent certain no one's been
in here since Mr. Mansfield left for Union Island," he said.
"Though it's highly doubtful any of the housekeeping staff
would've entered the cottage. Between the time you left
yesterday, and your arrival today, I've had a guard posted

outside the cottage, but...." He shrugged his shoulders by way of completing the thought.

"Thanks for your candor," I said.

"The place has been wiped," he said, an observation more than a question.

"Why do you think that?"

"The locations you dusted, and there're no prints in the powder."

"Very astute," I said, observing him closely.

"Nothing really," he said. Aware of my continuing gaze he added, "I did a stint with Scotland Yard."

An understatement I'd bet. Probably more than a stint. And maybe more than Scotland Yard. He had a military bearing about him. I mentally filed the observation away.

"I packed Mr. Mansfield's personal belongings, just clothes, in the suitcase." I said. "I'll be taking it with me."

"And you didn't find whatever else you were searching for," he said, again more a statement than a question.

His eyes held mine in a candid and interrogative gaze.

"No," I said, displaying a hint of a smile. He understood, and returned the smile. Aware he'd received all the information I intended giving him.

"You can have the cottage back now," I said instead. I gathered my things. He grabbed the suitcase and crime scene case before I had a chance to. He drove me back to the main building, again in silence.

The restaurant and bar empty of guests as I walked through to the offices in the rear. The staff busy setting tables, arranging furniture, stocking the bar and preparing for the evening. James Forester stood waiting at reception. Dapper in khaki slacks and a light blue summer blazer over a Hawaiian shirt he'd left untucked. He wore tan docksiders and no socks. A roguish handsomeness about him, and a gleeful sparkle in his eyes as he turned to greet me.

"Superintendent," he gushed, taking my hand. "So good to see you again. I trust everything is to your satisfaction?" I had no doubt he'd soon receive a complete report of my activities from his security chief.

When I'd rescued my hand I said "Indeed. I've finished with the cottage and released it."

"And how are your inquiries progressing?" he asked in a more serious and genuinely concerned tone.

"Progressing," I said.

"I understand," he said, returning to his former demeanor. He turned to the receptionist and held out his hand. She placed an eight by ten brown manila envelope in it.

"As requested and promised," he said.

I had the urge to open the envelope and peruse its contents. But knew he'd be offended. He'd cooperated this far, and I figured he didn't want to offend me either. And he undoubtedly didn't want me returning pissed off at him if the contents of the envelope proved less than I'd requested.

"Thank you James," I said, emphasizing the informality of the moment.

"Won't you stay for dinner?" he invited.

"I'm sorry, I can't." I said. "I still have a ton of work to finish. But thank you."

"Then allow me to invite you to the weekend barbecue. You and your friend of course. As my guests."

"Again, I'm not sure of my schedule, but if I can, I'll try to make it. Thanks again."

"I'll look forward to seeing you." A quick glance at his watch. "The day shift will be departing shortly, you can ride back with them, or if you prefer I can have our launch take you across."

"That won't be necessary," I said. "I'll ride back with Seckie."

"Then hopefully I'll see you tomorrow evening," he said, brushing his lips across the back of my hand, bathing me in the kind of smile I'm certain had caused more than a few women to go weak in the knees.

Peter Wellington waited by the palm covered dining tables on the open air terrace. He drove me to the dock where he unloaded the suitcase and crime scene case, and walked them down the dock for me.

"Shouldn't have long to wait," he said, turning to face me. "I see the launch is on the way."

"Well Peter," I said, extending my hand. "Thanks for your help."

"No worries," he said, giving my hand a quick, firm shake. I felt the hard calluses on the inside of his hand at the joints of fingers and palm. Around the knuckles too I noticed. Gage had similar hands. He turned, walked to the end of the dock and boarded the Moke.

Staffers already headed toward the dock, some singly, others in small groups. Seckie had just entered the lagoon, not too far off.

A cruising catamaran had joined two other sailboats anchored in the bay. Across the clear green coral studded water, bright colored sails attached to sunfishes and windsurfers tacked back and forth. One windsurfer having a difficult time. Spending more time alternately attempting to pull the sail upright, falling into the water, and climbing wobbly back onto the board, than any actual windsurfing. A beach attendant would need to fetch him soon.

Closer to shore guests paddled canoes and kayaks. Others had already turned in their water toys for the day, trudging off through the powder soft white sand in various directions. The men bare-chested and clad in colorful board shorts. The women in skimpy bikinis, wispy sarong wraps, and wide brimmed hats.

Seckie stowed the cases and I climbed aboard. I settled into a seat for the fifteen minute ride to Union. I contemplated who to engage in conversation first. Many of the passengers knew me. A few didn't, treating me with the sort of deference they reserved for guests on the island. They'd seen me carrying luggage.

Little chatter aboard as the boat sped across the open water. All on board had had a full day. They'd worked hard, and were visibly tired. Many had their own households to tend to when they arrived home. Conversation remained subdued and hushed.

Word must have spread to the few who didn't know me. They eyed me, their glances furtive, quickly averting their eyes whenever I glanced in their direction. Their manner indicated a different sort of deference.

The decision regarding who to approach first settled for me when a stout, buxom woman in a green print dress, sitting two down from me, leaned forward to speak across the women between us.

"Suprintendent, yuh lookin aftah de guess who dead in de jeep?" she asked.

"Yes," I said. "Did yuh noh im?"

"No. But Shirley ovah dey," indicating a slim, thirtyish woman dressed in tight jeans and a red tee shirt. "Dat is her cottage."

"Shirley?" I said, turning my attention to the young woman. She wanted to glance away. Wanted desperately to become invisible. To be anywhere else but on the boat being questioned by a police superintendent, who moments before she'd assumed to be a guest of the resort. I held my gaze steady on her.

"Yes ma'am," she said finally.

"You tek care of cottage twenty, where de gentleman was staying?"

"Yes ma'am," she said again.

"Did yuh evah see him? Talk wid him?"

"Jus once, when I clean de cottage de Monday. But I nevah tahk wid him. He was ahlways tahkin on de cell phone."

No cell phone had been found.

"When next yuh been in de cottage?" I asked her.

"Toosdey mahnin was de las time. Since den de red flag be out."

"He get food from de kitchen doh," said the woman who'd initiated the conversation. "Freddy bring him lunch Monday and Toosday too."

"Who's Freddy?" I asked.

"Wait staff in de restarant. And he delivah room suhvis."

"What's Freddy family name?"

"Bishop," she said. "Freddy Bishop."

"Anyone see de gentlemahn outside de cottage?" I asked, to no one in particular.

The women in earshot had ceased their own conversations, listening attentively to the back and forth being asked and answered.

"Anyone see him at de beach or de bar? Or anyone see him on Union?

Silence the only response, and shaking heads.

"I remembah de fust time me tek him to Union, he ax me wey he can rent a cyah," Seckie interjected into the silence.

My head swiveled toward him. One of the tiny unknowns nagging at my brain. How had Gooding found Mansfield, or visa-versa?

"And what yuh tell him?" I asked.

"I tell him no cyah rental on Union. But he can fin taxi in de squah."

"Yuh know how he meet up wid Gooding?"

At the mention of Gooding's name I noticed an abrupt turning of heads. Eyes quickly averted, focused on the water rushing by outside the boat. They may've been attempting to hide something. But more likely their reaction stemmed from Gooding being one of them. A neighbor, a friend, a relative even. They knew it'd been his jeep in the ravine. They knew he'd been arrested for a short time. They didn't want to make any more trouble for him.

"No." Seckie said. "He jus say tanks, gemme a tip an leve."

Mon ostie de saint-sacrament de câlice de crisse. Mr. Charles Mansfield had begun to annoy me. I couldn't get a handle on him. Even his identification remained tentative, though in my own mind I remained certain of the ID. Beyond that, the man remained a complete enigma.

At the Clifton dock I found Zelina in a small knot of people waiting to board Seckie's boat for the trip to PSV. Zelina finished her questioning and the group dispersed, climbing down into the boat replacing the resort staff who'd just disembarked.

"Zelina," I called, approaching her. "How it going?"

A drained expression greeted me. The usual spring and bounce gone from her step. Her extra pounds, normally no bother to her, now appeared a burden. She eyed the disembarked off duty PSV staff with weary resignation.

"I already talked with them," I said, observing her evident relief in the lift of her shoulders. "Any beer at de station?"

"Maybe de guys might av sum," she said, perking up but still listless.

"Den le we get some on de way." I said.

My suggestion produced a smile. "I could shoh use a cold one right now," she said.

We paused in the square to purchase four ice cold Hairouns before heading to the station. The shift change in progress when we arrived. Men in different type uniforms loitered in the back. Some wore the black and white of police constables. Some the blue jumpsuit of the fire service. Even a couple of Coast Guardsmen who manned the Union Island Coast Guard Station, consisting of one twenty foot rigid inflatable Boston Whaler. Zelina and I the only women.

As the highest ranking officer, and their commander, the men stamped to attention when I entered. They saluted and assumed a deferential demeanor. Even Baptiste, in the process of handing off to his relief, proffered a smart salute. Zelina's mood abruptly improved, I noticed. The sight of the men displaying deference and respect to a woman produced an immediate uplifting cheer in her.

The police culture had undergone change, albeit at the pace of a glacier. And more women were on the force now. A result of Mike assiduously recruiting and promoting women into positions of authority and command. Zelina herself in line for promotion. She had a shot where none had existed before Mike's arrival as Commissioner. She remained unaware of our private list.

"Oh lard!" she said when we reached her tiny office in the back of the building. She snickered like a schoolgirl having a secret crush. "I jus luv seein dat."

We sat. She behind her desk, me in a straight back wood chair in front of the desk. A window behind her opened outward, allowing a breeze to occasionally waft through the room, aided by a small fan sitting on the corner of her desk. A five drawer metal file cabinet stood in one corner, a few books stacked on top. The cramped room incapable of accommodating any other furniture.

We snapped the caps off a couple of Hairouns, clinked bottles, and each drank a long, slow draught of the cold, thirst quenching liquid.

"So how'd it go today?" I said, resting the beer bottle on her desk.

"Good. And not so good. All de infamachun I get not meking anyting bout dis man any clearer," she said, frustration in her voice.

"I know what yuh mean," I said. "Everything about him is a mystery. So yuh go first."

"First of all, he ahrive Saturday, not Sunday. I couldn't find de immigration forms till I staht lookin through de whole weekend." She pulled a sheaf of papers and a compact disc from her handbag, handing them to me.

"He fly in from Barbados, and de PSV boat tek him over."

"I got his reservation information from PSV, I said. "Haven't looked at it yet."

"Dat's de photos from de immigration camera," she said pointing to the CD. "So den I staht canvasin in de squah. Some people remembah him. He was axing bout rentin a cyah, but everybody tell him no cyah rental on Union. Somehow he meet up wid Gooding. But nobody see weh him went or what him do. Some shop people say he came in de shop. Say he a nice man, tahk nice to dem, but didn't buy anyting. And some say dey see him talking on a cell phone."

"Yes," I said, straightening in my chair. "De maid who cleaned de cottage said she see him talking on a cell phone. But Zelina, we never found a cell phone, or a wallet, a passport, airline ticket. Nothing."

An amused giggle shook her ample chest.

"Glad yuh find it funny."

"Jus how yuh talk funny when yuh get all frustrated or excited. And Lawd yuh cuss like a fisherman," she said, her unsuppressed humor continuing to shake her. "Yuh back an fohth between American an Bequian. Is funny lisning to yuh."

"At least it's not French," I said.

"Sometimes yuh talk dat too. Den me no noh what yuh a say," she said. Her amusement subsiding, she lifted the bottle toward her lips.

"De cottage was wiped clean," I said. "Not a single fingerprint anyweh."

The beer bottle halted halfway to her mouth. "What yuh a say?"

"It was wiped clean. And I don't mean by the maid. Someone, maybe Mansfield himself, didn't want a trace of him found in dat cottage. And I searched it too. Top to bottom. Nothing. If not fe de clothes, nobody would know he was even there." I retrieved my Hairoun from her desk and swallowed a long guzzling swig of the beer.

"So what now?" she asked, finishing the last of her beer.

"You have to interview Gooding again," I said. "Find out how, when, and where he first met Mansfield. But for right now pass me de phone."

She reached across the desk to push the phone closer to me. She watched me as I punched in the numbers.

I said, "Inspector Cato seemed happy to see yuh dis morning."

She blushed. Her mocha complexion turned a reddish brown, like dried blood.

"You gwoin see him?" I teased.

"Why? He say someting to yuh?"

"Crisse. You're like a likkle school girl. No. Jus looked like you two liked each other," I said smiling.

"Chief," I said when the other end answered. Zelina nodded and settled back in her chair. The old metal joints creaked under her weight.

"I have an update but it doesn't amount to much. Doesn't shed any new light on what happened here. But I've been wondering about the autopsy report."

"Received the report from Doctor Gash this morning," he said. "Very thorough. I've emailed you the full report, but here're the highlights."

"Hold on Chief. I'm here with Zelina McIntosh. Let me put you on speaker." When I'd activated the speaker and cradled the handset, I said "Go ahead Chief."

"Nothing we didn't expect," he said. "Multiple blunt force traumas consistent with an automobile accident. She also confirmed advanced atherosclerosis, including significant blockage in three cardiac arteries. It's still possible a coronary might have contributed to the accident. The enzyme studies were inconclusive. A coronary may have happened just prior to the accident, or as a result of the accident. Any number of the injuries would have been fatal, including a crushed area of the right parietal region of his skull, penetrating his brain, and a number of broken ribs which penetrated his lungs. You'll see the anatomical diagrams accompanying the report. We won't have lab results until next week. Right now her findings are the manner of death is accidental, and the cause is multiple blunt force external and internal injuries sustained in an automobile accident."

"Got it Chief," I said.

"I got the feeling she's holding something back. Something bothering her. When I asked her about it she wouldn't elaborate. Kept saying the pattern of skeletal injuries were consistent with an automobile accident. I think something about the autopsy's churning her gut, but she's too much of a scientist to go out on a limb and speculate. Maybe she'll open up to you, maybe in an informal, unofficial setting."

"Think I've got the perfect idea," I said.

"Good. Now What do you guys got down there?"

"Short answer is we got nothing. We haven't been able to develop a timeline of his movements on Union. We know when he arrived from Barbados, when he got to the cottage on PSV. We know he took a couple of trips to Union and when. We have no information on where he went or what he did between the time he obtained the vehicle and the time we found him. We've canvassed PSV staff, and people around Clifton Square. We have witnesses who put him in the cottage on Monday and Tuesday, and witnesses who saw him in Clifton on Tuesday. That's where the trail ends," I said.

"Couple other things though," I interjected. "It appears someone, maybe Mansfield himself, was deliberately trying to conceal his identity. The cottage was wiped clean Chief," I said, pausing for him to digest my words.

"You're sure?" he said.

"Positive. Not a single print in the entire cottage. I also searched it, thoroughly," I emphasized. "I found nothing. No personal items, no ID, passport or airline tickets. Just his clothes."

"Curious," Mike said. "We've sent what we have to Barbados. The US embassy is trying to run down Mr. Mansfield for us."

"We have an immigration photo now too," I said. "And his PSV reservation. They might narrow down the identification."

"Definitely. When can you get those over to me?"

"I'll email them to you tonight."

"Good. What's the second thing?"

"Second thing?"

"You said a couple of things. What else beside the room being wiped?"

"Oh." I said remembering. "A few people we spoke to saw Mansfield on a cell phone. Seemed to be constantly on it. But we haven't found a cell phone anywhere."

"More curious. Okay. Keep me appraised. Good work on the arrest this morning by the way," he said.

"All Inspector Cato Chief. He cracked the case."

"I'll be home on Bequia for the weekend. I'll stop in to see him."

"He'll appreciate that," I said.

After hanging up I immediately placed another call. Zelina's curious gaze observed me as I tapped the keypad. Her eyes widened when I said, "Inspector Cato please." I put the phone on speaker again.

When Cato arrived on the line I said, "Inspector, I'm here with Detective McIntosh on speakerphone," followed by a momentary silence on the line.

"Yes superintendent." And after another pause, "Detective McIntoch."

"Inspector," she said.

I wished they'd drop the formality crap.

"Des," I said. "Let's drop the formalities for now shall we. Give me an update on the arrests from this morning?"

"I finished de repohts," he said. "And I archived dem," indicating I'd be able to access the reports from the police central server.

"We identified some of de other jewlry," he continued. "De three men are now of interest in relation to a series of other crimes on Bequia, Canuoan, and St.Vincent."

"Great job Des," I said. "The Commissioner was pleased to hear how you cracked de case."

"Thank you ma'am," he said after a pause. Zelina had been following the exchange. Her appreciation evident in the brown eyes fixed on me. She knew, as did Cato, and every officer under my command, I gave due credit where and when deserved. Encouraging their best work. Invariably receiving it in return.

"Listen, I need to step away for a moment, stay on the line with Zelina." She glared at me, undisguised suspicion in her large brown eyes.

I stepped to the office door carrying my cell phone. I displayed the contacts list. The phone speed dialed a satellite access code and Gage's number. The call routed through a digital encryption and decryption process I had no interest in understanding. I just knew it worked.

"Hey sweetness," he answered. "What's up?"

"Got a question for you," I said. "I want to invite someone down for the weekend, have her stay over with us."

"No problem." He didn't ask who or why, or anything else. He didn't protest or argue or offer excuses. aware I wouldn't invite anyone aboard who might pose a danger. God I loved that man.

"I'll be done here in about half hour. Can you pick me up at the wharf?"

"I'll be there," he said.

"Love you," I said, disconnecting the call.

Next I dialed the hospital in Kingstown and asked to be put through to Doctor Gash. Her voice pleasantly surprised at my call.

"I just spoke to the Commissioner about your report." I said. "But look, what'd you say to coming down to Union for the weekend? I need you to clarify a few things for me."

"Like what? Maybe I can help you over the phone."

"Best we do it in person," I insisted. "You're welcome to stay on the boat."

"I'd love to," she said, her enthusiasm halted by a hesitant catch in her voice. "But I really couldn't impose on you like that."

"Nonsense," I said. "It's no imposition at all. I'd love to have you, and it'll give us a chance to talk. I'll pick you up at the ferry in Clifton. Oh, bring something nice to wear for Saturday evening."

Before she might pepper me with questions I said, "So see you Saturday," and broke the connection.

When I turned back toward the office Zelina had just cradled the phone, a Cheshire cat grin on her face.

"Yuh bad, yuh noh dat," she said, wagging an accusatory finger in my direction.

The evening shift had departed to assume their posts, leaving the small police station quiet. Zelina and I finished our beers, and prepared to leave the office. She needn't return until Monday morning, unless a criminal incident occurred during the weekend. I remembered to return her camera, waited for her to put away the crime scene case, and tag and log Mansfield's suitcase. We bade good evening to the duty Sergeant and departed the station together, parting ways outside.

CHAPTER 10

Gage waited at the wharf. He sat on the concrete pier, his legs dangling over the side above the bobbing inflatable. He wore old khaki shorts which had seen its share of spilled oil, grease and varnish. And an equally old blue shirt, cut off sleeves exposing the scars on his upper arms. He rose as I approached. His physique still trim and muscular. Though he regularly complained of stiff joints.

Open arms greeted me, enclosing me in a strong secure embrace. He planted a soft tender kiss on my lips.

"You hungry?" he asked.

"Starved," I said, remembering I hadn't eaten since breakfast.

"How about Janti's?"

"Fine. I just need a quick bite. I'm beat."

"We can just head back to Wherever instead. I can whip you up something."

"No. Don't bother yourself. I'll just get a little something and I'll be okay.

"It's never a bother sweetness," he said, but didn't argue further. He jumped down into the dinghy after me, settled onto the aft seat and fired up the outboard.

Janti's Happy Island Bar and Restaurant lay in the shallows on the other side of Clifton Harbor, behind Clifton's outer protective reef. Janti, the proprietor, had built the small artificial island himself, using thousands of discarded conch shells littering Clifton's beaches.

Gage maneuvered the dinghy through the shallow water, raising the outboard as he approached the conch shell seawall capped by concrete. A red and green shack, covered by a roofing of dried palm branches, served as Janti's bar, kitchen, and home.

Not five star or even two star fare, but unique, local, reminding me of the Green Boley on Bequia. Being Friday evening, we expected Janti to be home, preparing for a brisk weekend business given the crowded harbor.

Dusk gathered in the east. To the west, the sky turned orange and raspberry as the sun slid toward the horizon. Gage secured the dinghy and we stepped onto the sand filled interior of the artificial island. Palm trees in front of Janti's shack waved in the gathering evening breeze.

Janti and I had known each other since my promotion to Commander of the Grenadines Division. I'd toured the southern Grenadines, acquainting myself with shop owners, restaurateurs and hoteliers. Assessing public attitudes regarding the police, police effectiveness, and gathering suggestions for improving police services.

Janti and I had also worked together during the whole conch shell beach cleanup episode, an environmental initiative sponsored by Union Island's tourist office. The cleanup had occasionally spawned friction between Janti and a few local fishermen.

We located Janti attending a sizzling, smoking barbecue drum in front of the shack.

"Suprintendent," he greeted me. His pleasure at seeing me genuine. A wide beaming smile on his dark brown face, framed on either side by long braided hair.

"I noh yuh be down heah. Wandahrin when you comin fe visit me. An I see Wheyevah pon she mohrin, so I noh yuh mus come jus now." He turned to Gage. "Skippah Gage. Wha gwoan mahn?"

"All airie Janti," Gage said.

"I have fe watch dem grill heah, jus go fix yuhself a drink."

Janti treated me and Gage like family. He thought nothing of me being inside his home, or behind the bar fixing myself a drink. Or in his kitchen, picking at whatever he had cooking on the stove. When the mood struck, I even filled in as bartender. I decided to stick to beer, having already downed a couple. I opened one for myself, and fixed Gage his usual rum and coke on ice.

Gage had already asked Janti for a plate of barbecued fish by the time I returned outside carrying our drinks. We sat at a white plastic table waiting for our food.

"Who's our guest this weekend," Gage asked, sipping his drink.

"The pathologist Mike assigned to my case. Really interesting woman. Young, but knows her stuff. She's Peace Corps. Anyway I liked her. I kindda thought this might be a good way to get to know her better."

"And?" he said, correctly perceiving I hadn't told him everything. The shoe on the other foot, I thought, recalling my attempts early in our relationship to coax information from him.

"Mike thinks she's holding back. Thinks her gut's telling her something but she's too much of a scientist to speculate. He thought maybe in a less official setting I might get her to open up."

"How's the case going?"

"Frustrating. According to Doctor Gash, manner and cause of death was due to a vehicular accident. But we can't get a handle on the victim. Seem like he, or someone, wanted to keep his identity and whereabouts a secret."

"Possible," he said, his attention turning inward, his mind churning over possibilities, scenarios, contingencies. I'd grown accustomed to and recognized what might occur next. He'd disappear someplace deep in the recesses of his mind. Some distant place and time during which his present seemed suspended. But just for a moment.

It used to scare the bejesus out of me. I'd attempt to snap him out of it. Ask him where he'd gone. Wishing I could reach inside him; see that part of himself he kept hidden. Wanting to drive away the ghosts haunting him. I'd eventually learned to accept it as part of his nature. And over time I'd observed even in his momentary suspended animation, a part of his conscious mind remained attuned to everything occurring around him, like a mental form of passive radar.

"Where'd you go this time?" I asked automatically, not expecting an answer.

"Just remembering something," he said.

Janti approached carrying a tray. He set a plate of barbecued Bonita on the table. The delicious aroma set my stomach growling. He also set down a dish of green vegetables, boiled bananas, and plantains. Gage arranged the plate in the middle of the table, handing me one of two forks Janti had set next to the plates.

I dug into the fish. Perfectly prepared. Seared on the outside, tender and succulent inside. Janti also seasoned it to my liking, using a local hot pepper near scalding to the tongue, giving the fish a rich additional flavor. The plantains added a sweet taste to the palate. The vegetables fresh and crispy. After my first few mouthfuls, I slowed down to my normal pace. Gage picked up the extra fork.

We finished the meal as the sun set. The distant sky had been cloud filled all day, a mixture of low cauliflower shaped cumulus and long undulating stratus. They hung in shaded pink and grey silhouette as the sun perched above the horizon, its lower rim touching the sea. The red sky streaked in amber, and gold.

Later aboard Wherever I shed my clothes. I poured a glass of white wine, and wearing only a long oversized tee shirt joined Gage on the settee. He'd been corresponding with someone on his laptop. I opened my own laptop and put the finishing touches on my day. I typed up my case notes, attaching them to the growing case file on Mr. Charles Mansfield. From the manila envelope I extracted the photocopy of Mansfield's PSV registration provided by James Forester. It listed Mansfield's name and an email address. No billing or mailing address. It also listed his arrival and expected departure dates, and the assigned cottage.

It indicated the nightly rate, one thousand and eighty US dollars. His total room charge amounted to seven thousand five hundred and sixty US dollars. The entire amount, not just a deposit, paid in full by wire transfer. A transaction number appeared on the sheet, and the reservation confirmation and attached email.

I inserted the immigration CD into my laptop's drive and viewed the images of Mansfield clearing Immigration and Customs on Union Island. He'd faced directly at the camera, wearing a nervous expression in closely spaced eyes, narrowed by heavy upper and lower eye lids. Perhaps he'd been aware of being photographed. The face in the image appeared cheerful enough, a weary traveler on the last leg of a long trip. Thin lips around a small mouth parted in a half smile, framed on either side by fleshy cheeks and jowls. An errant wisp of white hair lay across a high forehead.

I studied the image, mentally asking who are you? Why were you here? Who'd you know here, planned to meet here? What kind of work did you do? What about a wife, kids? What happened to all your stuff? I stared. I studied. I questioned. And received no answers. I scanned the PSV photocopies into the laptop, and uploaded it and the time-stamped immigration photos to Mike.

The time stamp! Something off there. I recalled Zelina mentioning Mansfield had arrived on Saturday, not Sunday. The time stamped image confirmed it. As did the photocopy of his immigration entry card. I returned to the photocopies of his PSV reservation. Arrival date Sunday.

He'd arrived a full day before his reservation on PSV.

So where were you all day Saturday, Mr. Mansfield? What were you doing? And where did you stay? Enfant de chienne! Another maudit anomaly!

I downloaded the autopsy report nested in my email account on Gage's secure server. But too tired to concentrate on its multiple pages, forms, and complex language. I closed my laptop. Put everything away. I folded myself against Gage's chest and shoulders. I drifted asleep ensconced in his arms.

CHAPTER 11

I awoke rejuvenated. Climbed topside while Gage prepared breakfast and coffee. A new day. A gorgeous sky. Scattered cotton ball clouds drifted across a brilliant blue expanse.

Clifton Harbor still slept; a somnolent silence broken only by the wind, and the annoying clang of nylon halyards against aluminum masts. Those skippers either too ignorant or inconsiderate to secure them.

More yachts continued arriving in the already crowded harbor. Yachtsmen from Europe and Africa had crossed the Atlantic, the Southern Grenadines their first or second landfall. Others had sailed north from South America, and the Dutch Antilles. Bare boaters from St. Lucia and St. Vincent had passaged south to Union Island. More on the way.

Local fishermen in home built double-enders cast their nets in the shallows. Those seeking deep sea fish already hull down in the distance. Tiny specs of white sail marked their positions.

The aroma of mountain roast coffee and toast drifted into the cockpit from below. Gage emerged through the hatch carrying a loaded tray. He set it on the varnished cockpit table. Coffee, toast, and homemade orange marmalade accompanied by ripe pawpaws cut in half and cleaned. A sweet scented succulent juice oozed from the fleshy fruit.

"When's the last time you swam?" I asked between scoops of pawpaw.

"Here?" The upward thrust of his chin indicating the harbor. "Not since I've been here."

His usual exercise regimen included a long daily swim, five miles or more. On most weekends we also attempted to get in an hour or two of tennis, early in the morning, before the heat rose to an unbearable level.

"Maybe tomorrow," he said. "We'll move Wherever over to PSV."

The drone of twin Pratt and Whitney turbine engines, carried on the wind, reached us in the cockpit. Soon the first of three scheduled flights to Union Island flew into view. A high wing De Havilland Twin Otter in Leeward Island Air Transportation livery. The aircraft passed low over the water, crossing the harbor to establish its approach from the south and west. It dipped its right wing over Ashton to turn final. It landed in a roar of reversed propellers on Union Island's short runway.

We spent the morning sunning on Wherever's foredeck, munching on fruit; dozing off now and then. I'd called PSV to give Forester a heads up on our extra guest. I'd told him I'd pay for her. He rejected any notion of my paying, insisting the extra person also be included as his guest. I didn't argue. At one point I climbed below for my laptop, set up in the shaded cockpit, and read through Eileen's autopsy report.

Dry, factual, to the point. The medical and scientific terminology in certain sections indecipherable. The skeletal diagrams as clinically gruesome as the actual remains. My attention waned. I closed the file and shut the laptop. I didn't want to think about death today.

I recognized my mood. My period due in the next day or two. The timing on schedule. My body attuned to its rhythm, even though it'd changed in character over the years. From the heavy flow and painful cramps of adolescence and my teenage years, to irregularity through the years of birth control pills. And the scares when it'd been occasionally late. Regularity returned when I'd returned to Bequia in my late twenties, discontinued using the pill, and my diet and exercise patterns had changed. Regular like clockwork.

I noted the familiar bloating, the tenderness in my breasts, the spontaneous fatigue, and the morose intrusion on my thoughts of my ticking biological clock.

I heard the ferry before I saw it. Loud Soca music carried on the wind. As it drew closer to Union Island the deep thumping rhythms vibrated the air. The entire vessel like a huge sea borne speaker system. Typical of weekend ferries offering 'excursions' to the Southern Grenadines. Part ferry, part party boat.

I waited until the ferry had almost reached Clifton's wharf before following in the dinghy. The wharf already teeming when I arrived. Waiting relatives and disembarking passengers mingled on the narrow wharf. Music continued to blare from the vessel, background to the loud happy chatter of friends and relatives greeting each other. And young cheerful revelers primed for a weekend of non-stop partying. The staccato stutter of Kawasaki motor bikes rolling off the ferry and down the dock contributed to the din.

Some passengers and folks waiting on the wharf knew me. We exchanged greetings and idle small talk. The LIAT aircraft departed on the next leg of its island itinerary. Its high pitched turbine engines providing additional decibels in the noisome harbor.

A few pale, pink and sunburned tourist faces amid the throng. One of the faces, hidden behind large round Hollywood style sunglasses, belonged to Doctor Eileen Gash. She wore form fitting blue jeans, a lacy summer blouse cinched at the waist, and sandals. She carried a small 'weekender' backpack on her back. I waved and shouted in her direction. She noticed me and navigated her way through the crowd.

Eileen put her hand out as she drew near. Instead I threw my arms around her in a welcoming embrace, producing a small gasp of surprise, greeting her like a longtime friend I hadn't seen in years.

"I'm so glad you came," I said.

"Thanks for inviting me," she said, pushing the sunglasses onto her head where it held her thick auburn hair from her face like a headband, and revealed effervescent blue eyes.

"I was surprised to get your call, and the invitation," she continued. "But by now I guess I'm used to being surprised by you."

"Really?" I said, intrigued and amused.

"When the Commissioner asked me to come down here to look into this case, and to meet the Superintendent in charge, the last thing I expected was a woman. And definitely not a woman who looks like a super model. Then I learn you're a pilot, and you live on your own yacht."

"Actually the yacht belongs to the man in my life," I said.

Her eyes grew wider, her smile broader.

"Yet another surprise," she said. "Although, I guess having your looks that one shouldn't surprise me. You're sure this isn't an imposition," concern replacing the smile. "I could....."

"Stop it girl!" I interrupted. "Let's get out of here." I led her from the wharf to the beach where I'd tethered the dinghy.

"Now I'm here I wish I had more time," she mused aloud, her gaze sweeping the harbor and the variety of anchored yachts. "The ferry returns to St. Vincent early in the morning."

"Don't worry about that," I said, helping her out of the backpack, stowing it in a spot in the dinghy where it'd remain dry.

"Gage and I already talked about it. We'll sail you back to St. Vincent. And if your schedule allows, you can stay as long as you like. Come to think of it," I said, a mischievous lilt in my voice and tilt to my head. "I can clear your schedule. You're assigned to my case exclusively after all."

The smile returned, enhancing the graceful contours of her face; the rounded cheekbones, the dimpled cheeks, round chin, and full lips.

The inflatable skimmed across the water, weaving around and between anchored sailboats. Approaching Wherever Eileen's eyes grew wide. Her mouth opened in silent wonder. Her gaze swept across the schooner, tracing its elegant curves, the sublime sweep of its deck, the height of its masts.

"You live on that?" She remarked in wonder. "Ohmigod."

"Gorgeous isn't she," I said, grinning at her. "Very sweet natured too."

I hooked onto the starboard gate, and hoisted the backpack onto the deck.

"Climb aboard," I coaxed, holding the dinghy against Wherever's side. I followed behind her.

On deck, her wondrous stare returned. Taking in the length of Wherever's white pine deck, its white coach roofs and varnished mahogany trim, and the long questing bowsprit reaching beyond the bow. She turned to gaze at the sunken cockpit and its comfortable fluffed cushions. And the helm, containing the varnished spoked wood wheel and custom designed binnacle and instrument cluster.

"Yo Gage!" I yelled in the direction of the open hatch.

He emerged from below, a wide smile on his lined, rugged face, engaging and welcoming, setting Eileen instantly at ease.

"Welcome aboard," he said in a soft melodious voice, taking her hand in a quick handshake.

"Thanks for having me," she replied, her appraising gaze turning from Gage to me, back to Gage.

"No problem," Gage said. "And please, make yourself completely at home.

"Come on," I said, hoisting her backpack. "Let's get you settled below."

The 'Alice in Wonderland' expression returned when we entered Wherever's open and comfortable interior. The cypress and walnut fittings and mahogany trim warm and inviting. Gage had added bamboo rails, columns, and table legs, giving the interior a tropical touch.

Sunlight flooded the salon from three large windshields at the front of the angled and sloped coach roof, and from curtained windows on either side. Also from portholes along the hull. A pair on the starboard side over the settee, another pair on the port side over the dinette.

I ushered her forward to the starboard guest cabin, identical to the one directly opposite on the port side. Roomy and comfortable. Also well lit. Sunlight streamed through a circular bronze porthole in the hull, and an overhead hatch. Both opened to allow air into the cabin.

The cabin contained a twin size lower bunk, and a smaller top bunk which folded down against the hull when not in use, forming a futon-like back for the lower bunk. A sizable hanging locker had been built into the forward bulkhead. Pull out drawers on the bottom. A flat panel television set mounted on the bulkhead just below the overhead deck. The cabin also contained a small vanity dresser possessing a mirror and drawers. Small reading lamps were mounted on the bulkhead over the bunks, and a telephone intercom mounted next to the lower bunk.

The lower twin bunk could also be folded against the hull, designed to enclose and conceal the smaller top bunk. Folding both bunks away converted the cabin into a spacious cargo hold.

After stowing her backpack I provided a quick guided tour. I showed her the forward shower and head, providing a quick tutorial on how it worked and the dos and don'ts of a marine toilet. I ushered her through the navigation area, port side aft of the salon, showed her the aft stateroom, and the galley on the starboard side aft of the salon.

As we reentered the salon Wherever's diesel rumbled to life.

"What's that?" she asked, startled.

"The engine," I reassured her. "Come on, we're getting ready to move."

"Move?" she asked in surprise. "Where're we going?"

"Just over to PSV," I said. "We've been invited to the barbecue this evening."

"Really," a mixture of surprise, excitement, and a hint of trepidation in her voice. "Is that why you said to bring something nice? I wished you'd told me. Now I'm not sure I brought the right thing to wear."

"You'll be fine," I said, leading her topside.

More than fine. "Gorgeous," I declared when she stepped into the salon later that evening. Exquisite in a knee length, rose-colored and orchid pattern sundress, spaghetti straps and a Grecian neckline. Simple, elegant, perfectly fitting her trim, petite figure. On her feet she wore thong sandals woven from leather straps. Her long auburn hair, parted on the left side and brushed to a silky shine, fell in waves across her shoulders. A delicate gold chain adorned her neck.

"Just one thing missing," I said, remembering an item I'd thrown into my weekend bag while packing. "Hold on a second."

I disappeared into the aft stateroom, returning to hand her a pair of dangling earrings made of small tear shaped stones hanging at the end of a slender white gold chain.

"Perfect," I said when she'd fitted them on each ear.

For myself, I chose another pair of dangling earrings. A dream catcher like design containing small jade stones, matching my full length emerald sundress. Spaghetti straps hung over my shoulders, the breezy sundress cut low and longer in the back, a cinch tie just above the buttocks. I too chose thong sandals, which I intended to shed as soon as my feet hit the sand. On my right wrist I wore an African beaded bracelet. On the left a set of thin silver bangles.

My curled tresses I'd brushed back, the left side pinned behind my ear, the right falling along the side of my face onto my shoulder. The sundress designed to be worn without a bra, I'd decided against underwear too. A practice I'd grown accustomed to physically and socially while living with Gage, who didn't own a single piece of underwear.

He'd dressed simply in a short sleeved silk black batik shirt decorated in a palm tree motif. The shirt tail hung outside faded blue jeans. Flip flops on his feet. He managed to look dapper no matter what he chose to haphazardly throw on. The effect of an innate, intangible, indefinable 'cool factor' he possessed.

An enchanting night greeted us on deck. A half moon bathed the lagoon in a soft diffused light. The scent of lilac, jasmine, frangipani, and wildflowers drifted on the cool evening breeze, amid the aroma of barbecuing food.

Dim romantic lighting glowed from Chinese lanterns strung along the dock, along the paths leading to the main building, and around the barbecue area on the beach. Discordant notes from musical instruments being tuned sounded from a palm covered area where a band had set up.

We headed up the concrete walkway toward the main building. Before reaching it I plucked two bright pink orchids from a bush alongside the path. I handed one to Eileen.

Helped her pin it in her hair just behind the left ear. I pinned the other behind my left ear.

A sprinkling of guests seated on cushioned barstools occupied the gleaming semicircular bar. Dressed in evening casuals. The men in linen khaki or white slacks and polo shirts; the women in sleeveless, spaghetti strapped, mostly backless dresses.

Every head in the bar and dining room swiveled in our direction. Every eye followed our entrance. The men in undisguised admiration. The women feigning an aloof disinterest. But unable to look away. Or take their eyes off Gage.

I noticed Forester across the sparsely occupied dining room. He forged a path straight for us, as though he'd been on the lookout for our arrival, for me in particular. His admiring gaze settled on me and Eileen.

"My dear Superintendent," he greeted, capturing my hand, his smile wide and devilish. His gleaming eyes lecherous, soaking up my presence from head to toe.

"Ravishing," he said, planting a soft kiss on the back of my hand.

His gaze left me momentarily to focus on Eileen, the gleam even brighter, if that were possible. A mixture of admiration and pleasant surprise.

"James Forester," I said, "My friend Doctor Eileen Gash."

"Charmed," he said, touching his lips to the back of Eileen's hand too. He turned to Gage.

"And my very special friend," emphasizing the 'very special' "Nicholas Gage," I said, introducing them. They shook hands, their eyes locked in silent assessment of each other.

"I've heard so much.... " Forester began before pausing. "Actually I've heard absolutely nothing about you, except to know you've managed to corner the market on beauty in these parts. The most beautiful vessel in the region, and the most beautiful woman, women," he corrected himself, a conspiratorial wink aimed at Gage as his glance settled on Eileen.

"Thank you," Gage said, "About Wherever. But I beg to disagree on the second part. In fact it's these ladies who're in complete control of the market."

Forester erupted in a burst of spontaneous laughter. A hearty melodious rumble like a freight train passing through the night.

"Well, you're all welcome as my guests this evening," he said, including Eileen in his smile. "Enjoy the evening, and I will see you again later, yes? Now I must continue to play the host and mingle."

He turned and departed, wandering off among the occupied tables in the dining room, its occupants still glancing in our direction, curious about our little exchange. Gage turned to the bar to get us drinks. The eyes in the room continued to follow us as we moved about.

"How it gwoin Gage?" the uniformed barman greeted him.

"Airie Winston. How's your lovely wife?" Gage asked, dropping the patois, to astonished stares from onlookers at the bar.

"We tink she pregnant agahn."

"Lard man. How much dat mek now?" switching back to patois.

"I stop count," Winston said, a tittering grin on his face.

Our drinks in hand, Gage switching to rum punch for the occasion, Eileen and I a glass of Pinot Gris each, we headed toward the beach where the barbecue and beach bar had been set up. Gage and Eileen conversed like old friends, laughing and joking, immersed in a conversation I paid little attention to.

Instead I'd been swept away by a moment. By the soft soothing sound of rolling surf. By the night breeze brushing my skin. By the pale moon, fragrant night air, sand between my toes and the milky-way sparkling in the heavens above. I savored the moment. Absorbed the entirety of it. A single, fleeting, consummately perfect moment.

The food had been laid out buffet style on a long linen covered table. At the end of the table, off to the side, a red hot sizzling and smoking barbecue pit prepared imported steaks, roast pork, chicken and fish. Gage, Eileen and I moved with the other guests along the table, filling our plates from the variety of dishes. Fresh, locally grown salads, green vegetables, fruit, various preparations of potatoes, yams and cassava. And a variety of seafood, including lobster and crab. From the barbecue pit sliced pot roast, ham, porter house steaks and fish.

Plates piled high we returned to our table on the beach. Eileen observed my plate and smiled. "The surprises just keep coming," she said. "Tell me you're a vegan too."

At first I didn't comprehend her reference. But noting the contents on my plate, and hers, I laughed. "Have to disappoint you this time," I said. "I'm not vegan, or vegetarian. But living in the Grenadines we're a lot closer to the food supply. I tend to stay away from foods if I don't know where they came from. I eat meat occasionally. Not as a regular diet. Goat and chicken mostly. Occasionally beef, but only if it's local and I know where it came from. And lots of fish, fresh from the sea."

"I can't eat the flesh of any creature that was alive at some point only to end up on a dinner plate," she said.

"I can respect that," I said. "How long you been vegan?"

"Since the tenth grade," she said.

Gage listened, interested in our exchange. The only meat on his plate a porterhouse sized Kingfish steak. He also had a helping of lobster salad. We shared the same opinion regarding the source of our food. The fresher the better.

"Ethical, environmental, religious, economic?" He asked.

"I think ethical in the beginning," she said. I saw this TV show about a chicken farm. I was so grossed out I'd get sick at the sight of a piece of chicken. It just grew from there. But I found other reasons over the years. Some environmental, but mainly how healthier my diet was. As a pathologist I see what a meat diet does to a person's insides. Not pretty. But I know what you mean about being close to the food source," she continued. "Even as a vegan I always wished I could grow my own food. I've never been in a place, except maybe here, where it was practical."

"What brought you here anyway?" Gage asked.

"Oh wow," she said, setting her fork aside, sitting back in her chair. "Good question. Big question. I'm not sure I've quite figured it out myself." She leaned forward, forearms on the table, palms facing up and open, fingers bent in a slow wriggle.

"I guess I wasn't satisfied with the trajectory of my life. I'm from a close family, from Long Island, just outside New

York City. All my relatives live within a few blocks of each other. I'd never been anywhere, but I was always smart, ahead of everyone else in school. Everybody said I'd be the one to become someone one day. I don't really know how I became interested in medicine. No one in my family is in the field. But I'd always been fascinated by biology, and anatomy. More the mechanics of it than anything else. Guess that's why I gravitated to pathology. But after all the school, and work, I never really felt satisfied, you know? Like the song I kept thinking 'is that all there is'? Then one day I came across an article in a journal by a doctor who'd just completed two years in Africa with the Peace Corp. Long story short, one thing led to another and voila, here I am."

It'd poured out of her like a clogged pipe finally cleared. Gage and I had listened in rapt fascination. The sudden awareness of our focused attention embarrassed her.

"God. Listen to me going on and on," She said.

"No worries," Gage reassured her. "Sounds like you've been waiting a while to get that off your chest."

"Perhaps," she said. "I don't really have anyone I can talk to about it. My friends and family wouldn't understand. They're more concerned about finding the right guy, starting a family."

"Yeah. Tell me about it," I said, an ample dose of sarcasm laden in my voice.

"Anyway," she said, perking up, her smile back in place. "What about you guys?" she asked, turning to me.

"I was born here," I said. "Lived here until I was four. Then moved to Canada with my family. I guess I felt about the same as you about my life, my career. But I had a place to go to. I always knew I wanted to return. Give something back."

"And what about you Gage?" she said turning to him.

"Just sort of ended up here after I retired," he said, without elaborating. "These islands wield a sort of seductive hold over you after a while. You think you're just passing through, just visiting, and years later you're still here. In my case I met an amazing woman who sorta grounded me. Is anyone ready for another drink?" he segued quickly, indicating our almost empty wine glasses, and subtly changing the direction of our conversation.

"You want to get another plate?" I asked Eileen after he'd left the table.

"God no," she said, giving her plate a little push away from her. "I'm full. And all so fantastic. I've never tasted vegetables prepared like that before. Delicious. But you go ahead if you want. Don't mind me."

"I'm good." I said. "Besides I'm saving space for the chocolate mousse I saw up there."

I noticed Gage returning from the bar, and Forester heading in our direction. Both converged on the table at the same time.

"How is everything?" Forester inquired smiling, ever the gracious host.

"Fantastic as usual James," I said. "Everything is absolutely delicious."

"Excellent," he exclaimed, drawing out the first syllable. "And how are you enjoying our little soiree Doctor?" turning his attention to Eileen.

"Just wonderful," she said. "Thank you."

"Well perhaps a little later, after you've finished your dessert, I might have the pleasure of a dance," he said, ending the sentence as an open question.

"Perhaps," she answered noncommittally. I stifled a laugh in my hands.

In fact I did feel like dancing. Especially after a heavier meal than I'm used to. The band, comprised of a steel drum section, an acoustic, electric and bass guitar section, a keyboardist and drummer, were well into their set. They'd played mostly steel drum heavy calypso while the guests ate, before segueing to lively and danceable reggae and soca. A few couples already on the wood square laid out on the sand as a dance floor.

"Come on," I said, jumping to my feet and grabbing Eileen's hand.

"She rose without hesitation and followed me to the dance area. We didn't dance together, or apart either. We occupied our own tiny space and time, absorbed in the music, moving to the visceral thumping rhythms. Eileen's adept unselfconscious movements a surprise. She moved in flowing harmony to the rocking beat. Her hips, shoulders, arms, and swirling hair free and sensual.

We remained on the dance floor through three or four more songs, difficult to tell. The band blended their selections, segueing seamlessly from one to the other. More dancers had crowded onto the small square. Sweaty and invigorated, we giggled and supported each other as we wobbled like drunken sailors on shore leave back to the table.

I noticed Gage a few paces down the beach in conversation. The person's back to me. But the height and posture resembled Peter Wellington. Dancing had stimulated my appetite for dessert. Eileen too. We headed over to the dessert table.

The band segued again, to slow, soulful ballads. After devouring a wedge of chocolate mousse I grabbed Gage's hand and led him to the dance floor. Not on it. But a short distance off to the side. On the soft sand. I snuggled close, my head on his chest, my arms wrapped around him and his around me. Locked in each other's embrace, bodies pressed close, we swayed to the music. The gentle pressure of his thighs and hips, slight shifts in his weight, guided and led me. I floated on air, unconscious of the powdery sand between my toes.

Gage and I returned to discover Eileen absent from the table. I spotted her at the beach bar, engrossed in a conversation. Unable to discern the man's features in the dim lighting. Gage noticed them too. A fleeting squint of concern in his otherwise impassive expression. In our time together I'd learned to read him well. Something had sparked an interest behind his ever watchful eyes. I also knew the futility of questioning him about it.

The night wore on. We drank, and danced, and talked and laughed. Occasionally striking up conversations among other guests at the bar, or on the dance floor. The men curious about the schooner. The women curious about Gage.

At one point Gage and I strolled away from the festivities, hand in hand along the deserted beach. Pale moonlight danced on the water. We'd kissed. A passionate pantomime of lips and mouths and tongues teasing, tasting. While the rest of the world melted away.

CHAPTER 12

We slept in late Sunday morning. Ambling naked toward the galley, I remembered our guest on board. I threw on an oversized U Penn tee shirt I sometimes slept in and exited the cabin.

Eileen's cabin door remained closed. In the galley I set coffee brewing. Gage entered the galley silently behind me. He wrapped his arms around my waist, a gentle squeeze. His lips brushed the curve of my neck. The touch of his lips in that particularly sensitive spot, and the tickle of his moustache on the nape of my neck sent shivers through my body. The stubble on his chin grazed my skin, providing another layer of sensation.

"Morning sunshine," he whispered in my ear, before departing, as silently as he'd appeared.

Cradling a mug of steaming coffee I climbed topside and settled in the shaded cockpit. A bright day. The sun a blinding silver sphere in a pale blue cloudless sky. The surface of the clear turquoise water sparkled like a bed of tiny diamonds, and in the distance, a lone swimmer cleaved the water where it turned from green to blue.

I'd been scanning the surface through a powerful pair of polarized binoculars when I heard a sound behind me.

Eileen emerged from the hatch in cutoff jeans and a worn
John Hopkins tee shirt, rubbing sleep from her eyes.

"Morning," I greeted her. "Want some breakfast?"

"No thanks. Coffee will be fine."

"Fresh brewed in the galley," I said. "Milk or cream in
the fridge, sugar in the locker above the coffeemaker. Or if you
prefer, honey in the fridge. Help yourself to whatever you
need. Just make yourself at home," I said, returning to my
search.

"What're you looking at?"

"Looking for Gage. He's off on his morning swim, but I
lost track of him a while ago."

"Well how far could he have gone?" she asked, her tone
offering to reassure me.

"He usually does around five miles. Sometimes more."

"You're kidding?" A note of disbelief in her voice.

When I didn't answer, the binoculars still glued to my
face, she said, "Wow, that's a long ways."

"Including out and back," I said.

"Are you worried?" she asked, concern creeping into
her voice.

"No. Not yet. I'm not always around when he takes his
swims. He's used to going off on his own."

She disappeared down the hatch, reemerging a few
minutes later, a mug of coffee cupped in her hands. She
settled in the cockpit and sipped while I continued to search
the water.

"Anything?" she said finally.

"Not yet." I placed the binoculars on the cockpit table
and settled into the plush cushions opposite her.

"Quite a guy," she said. "Older than I expected. Another surprise. Doesn't really say much does he?"

"No," I said, smiling at her. "He's not one to waste words. Kinda tight lipped that way. But you can always be sure he means what he says. One of the things I love about him."

"How'd you guys meet?"

"Through the Commissioner. They became friends when Gage first started showing up around the Grenadines. They're both pilots, both love to sail. They've a lot in common. Only three years apart in age," I said, laughing at the coincidence. "One's like a father, the other my lover."

"I can understand the attraction though," she said. "Even at my age I feel this mysterious magnetism about him, if you don't mind me saying."

I laughed. Experiencing an instant easy camaraderie between us. I'd sensed it the first time we'd met. I'd experienced a similar sensation toward Nora Austin, a reporter Gage and I had met back when Mike had been shot. But confiding in Nora had been out of the question. She'd been a reporter, working on a story, two in fact, involving cases I'd been investigating. But in another time and place, we might have been close friends.

"I don't have anyone I can really share my feelings with about him," I confided. "Not even Mike.... the Commissioner," I said. "I don't have close friends like that at work, or among the expats on the islands. They're involved in their own myopic little worlds I have no interest in. And anyway, none of them provide the intellectual stimulation Gage does."

"Intellectual stimulation. Yeah," she teased, grinning at me.

I laughed again. It came easy with her. "It's true though," I insisted. "He speaks at least seven languages I know of, has an uncanny, almost encyclopedic knowledge of history, biology, chemistry, physics, psychology, you name it. Deep down he has the soul of a philosopher."

"The few conversations we had were definitely interesting, even enlightening," she said. "What kind of work did he do?"

"Foreign service, the State Department." The lie rolled easily off my tongue. At such moments, with someone like Eileen, lying stirred an uneasiness in me. The price I paid to have Gage in my life. I didn't know everything about his past, but enough to understand the stakes.

"Morning ladies." The voice startled us both, even though I'd grown accustomed to Gage's ghostly ability to appear and disappear.

"Hey sailor," I replied, more relieved than I'd expected. "How're the fishies?"

"They said to say hello," he smiled, rising over the aft rail, the water he'd just climbed from glistening on his skin. It ran off his wide shoulders, dribbled through the hairs on his broad chest, down his muscled legs, collecting in a wide pool at his feet.

The effect not lost on Eileen, instantly embarrassed when she caught herself staring. I wondered what she thought of his scars, the mottled spots discernable even against his dark tanned skin. And I wondered, not for the first time, if he possessed such at physique at age fifty-five, how harder, tauter, more powerful he must have been at thirty.

"Close your mouth dear," I said, chuckling. "Now that Aquaman's back why don't we go for a swim?"

"I figure we'll get under way after lunch," Gage said, moving toward the hatch, an unconscious sensual grace in his movements he may not have been aware he possessed.

The water, body temperature and clear when I plunged overboard. Wherever's dark painted underwater surface distinctly visible in the translucent water, like seeing it through glass. Slanted sunlight projected a shadow of her hull against the sandy sea floor.

An exhilarating rush of bubbles flowed through my hair and against my skin as I swam for the surface, toward Eileen's alabaster legs threading water above me. I surfaced beside her, sea water streaming from my face and hair.

"Hey," she said, her face lively and smiling, her arms sweeping ahead and to the sides in a breast stroke motion. "God this is heaven. I didn't do much swimming back home. Mostly the beach was just for lying in the sun in summer. How Gage does five miles? I can't even wrap my mind around that."

"It's his thing," I said. "Like he was born in the ocean. I don't try to keep up."

"And that body. Jesus. He's in better shape than most guys my age. How's he do it?"

"He keeps active," I said, treading water beside her. "Doesn't get to work out much, at least not as much as he used to."

I didn't mention the grueling regimen he'd occasionally put himself through. Not nearly as rigorous or as often as he'd been used to before retiring. And not that he needed to anymore. But he seemed to require it, like food. Sometimes we'd work out and spar together. He'd teach me self-defense and close quarter hand to hand techniques. His speed and agility uncanny. And a little frightening. The number of ways he knew to incapacitate, or kill, using just his hands and fingers.

"Anyway," I said, "Swimming keeps him in shape. I prefer running." I turned over on my back, kicking lightly, my arms spread, keeping me afloat on the surface.

"Me too." She sprayed seawater from her mouth as she spoke. "I try to get in a run most days, and I'll usually run home from the hospital."

"Yeah? What distance?"

"About four miles, and uphill too. I rent a small house up in the Montrose area, close to the botanical gardens."

I noticed Gage moving about the deck. The sun midpoint in the sky. A band of small clouds had formed above the islands, where radiant heat from the land had warmed the moisture laden air. Eileen and I spent a while longer frolicking in the water, swimming and diving below its gleaming surface, savoring the seawater's warm embrace.

Back on deck we toweled off. Eileen threw on a tee shirt over the yellow bikini. We munched on bowls of fruit and salads Gage had prepared. We moved forward to the break between the salon and forecastle coach roofs, where the foremast went through the deck. We sat in the sun, out of Gage's way while he dismantled and stowed the large canvas awning, and made preparations for sailing.

We continued conversing while we ate. Eileen easy to talk to. Intelligent and witty, possessing a tart sense of humor and a maturity beyond her years. I liked her more and more, even after such a short acquaintance. Glad I'd acted on the impulse to invite her. I told her things, feelings, I hadn't with anyone else, except maybe Mike and Gage. But they were men. And I missed having a girlfriend to talk to.

I recognized much of myself in her. Her curious mind, wanting to understand the reasons for things. Not afraid to attempt the new and different. To take a risk. To overcome her shy reticent side. Joining the Peace Corp, moving to live and work in a different place and culture proof of that. She impressed me as adaptable, self-sufficient and self-contained.

She asked me about having a family, about having kids. Whether it might be a possibility at Gage's stage of life. And mine. But the psychologist in me formed the impression her questions sprang from an inner conflict of her own, rather than curiosity about me. She'd chosen an unconventional turn in her life, as I had, and perhaps sought a kindred perspective to validate her own.

"I love kids," I told her. "I really do. It's the parents I can't stand sometimes," I said, laughing together. "So does Gage. He's a natural with kids. They instinctively sense something in him, and gravitate to him like he's a pied piper. And he to them. And these islands are wonderful for raising kids. Vincentians love kids. They crave them and indulge them but don't take any shit from them. Not like the indulgent permissiveness in the States. And every kid is everyone's kid. Child rearing a collective responsibility involving parents, siblings, cousins, aunts, uncles, neighbors, everyone in the community. I have a depressing fear it's changing though," I said, a wistful edge creeping into my voice.

"Anyway, it's not something I dwell on. Despite the constant pressure from family and friends, especially in this environment. Like having kids is the only way to have meaning and fulfillment in my life. I try not to let it influence me. I just don't have any great urge for a family. At least not right now. And I keep telling myself there's still time if I change my mind. But I'd be lying if I said I don't hear the ticking of my biological clock. Seems to get louder every year. Anyway right now I consider myself more than lucky, and completely satisfied, to have found a man who appreciates me for exactly who I am. Who makes no demands of me, and with whom I can be completely myself."

She said nothing. Studied me in silence. Her blue eyes steady on mine, holding my gaze as I spoke. And I hers, catching the tiny, almost imperceptible nod. The small curl of a smile at the corners of her mouth.

Something gained? I wondered. Something resolved perhaps? She didn't say. And I didn't ask.

Gage ambled past heading for the bow, where he pulled the headsails from their bags. He checked the hanks, and sheet knots. He bundled the sail bags and stuffed them down the forecastle hatch. Heading back toward us he removed the ties holding the staysail on its boom, and unsnapped the shackle holding the boom in place.

"Almost ready to go," he said, working at the foremast above us. He hadn't changed, and worked the deck bare-chested, wearing the same blue board shorts he'd swam in. Now sun dried on him.

"Gonna need you soon Jo," he said, tramping off barefoot to the mainmast.

Eileen and I gathered up the bowls from the deck and headed aft. While Gage continued preparing the deck, I inspected and prepared below. Gage had already stowed any items capable of tumbling about the cabins when Wherever lay her side down. I stocked water, soft drinks, beer and fruit in the cockpit cooler.

Eileen stood by the helm observing our activity. "Anything I can do to help?" she asked.

"Done much sailing?" I asked her.

"None," she said, a sheepish grin on her sun reddened face.

"Best thing is to just hang here," I said, smiling at her. "If we need a hand we'll holler."

Gage strolled aft past the cockpit, stood by the aft rail. His right arm rested nonchalantly on the main boom. He gazed along Wherever's deck, at her running rigging, along her untethered booms, up the length of her masts, and down her standing rigging.

His gaze shifted to the water surrounding the schooner. Fixed the positions of other yachts anchored nearby, mentally charting Wherever's departure from the bay. Finally he thrust his face to the wind, checking its direction and speed. I'd done the same moments before, confirming a northeast breeze at about ten to twelve knots.

Satisfied, he headed forward again.

"Got the helm sweets?" he said as he went past. "She'll fall off to port."

"Got it," I acknowledged. I inserted the diesel's ignition key, primed the diesel, ensured the controls were in their proper positions, but didn't start the engine. A true traditionalist when it involved sailing, Gage would use the engine only if absolutely necessary. Conditions were ideal for exiting the bay under sail alone.

He cinched the dinghy tight against Wherever's side. Once under way it'd tow behind. The outboard had already been hoisted and secured to its mounting block on the aft rail.

At the mainmast Gage hoisted the huge triangular mainsail. I ensured the boom swung free and cautioned Eileen to sit and watch her head. The long heavy wood boom lifted from its cradle, swaying back and forth just above our heads. Its slack blocks beat an unholy clamor against the deck. The hoisted mainsail flogged and snapped in the breeze.

Gage headed to the bow. I heard the mechanical grind of the electric windlass winding in the anchor line. I checked over the side, noting the gentle ripple along the hull as Wherever slid forward, shortening up on her anchor. Soon the line turned to chain, and soon after Gage gave the up and down signal. Wherever's bow directly over the anchor.

Her forward momentum plucked the anchor free of the seabed. Her head fell off to port. I spun the spoked wheel in the same direction. She came round, broadside to the wind, sliding sideways through the water. I hauled on the mainsheet, just enough for the sail to catch the breeze and draw. I held the helm over. Wherever's head continued to swing, until she pointed directly between the ketch and catamaran anchored behind us. I hauled again on the mainsheet, cleated it and centered the helm. Wherever passed serenely between the anchored yachts, heading out of the bay.

Clear of the anchorage, Gage hoisted the jib to provide steerage. Wherever felt the new source of power and picked up her head. I gently steered her to a northerly heading, her long bowsprit leading the way. I trimmed the main and jib sheets for the new course.

Busy work for one pair of hands, hauling and cleating the sheets, one and then the other. At times it required both hands, grabbing the wheel in between to keep Wherever on course. Meanwhile Gage hoisted sail after sail. As the steady breeze filled each, Wherever sprang forward with increased vigor. Her pace and rhythm unsteady. But once the hard, busy work had been accomplished, we'd have time to leisurely trim her, stretch her out, and allow her free rein.

Eileen observed the activity in delightful fascination, remaining silent throughout the maneuvers, breaking her silence only as Gage stepped into the cockpit.

"Wow guys!" her beaming face turned to us, her hands clapping in soft applause. "That was awesome." We both returned her smile, infected by her giddy enthusiasm.

Wherever already feeling her head, though still not properly trimmed. Gage grabbed hold of the sheets.

"Bring her up a touch," he said.

I turned the wheel a few spokes to starboard. Gage adjusted the main, foresail, staysail and jib sheets, until each sail stretched and set in perfect curves. The wind blew from just aft of the starboard bow, stronger in the open water away from the sheltered lagoon.

The deck tilted as Wherever heeled. She lowered her curved side deeper into the water, and a remarkable metamorphosis occurred, transforming her into a living, breathing creature of the sea.

Gage and I both glanced over at Eileen, ready to assure her the heel and slope of the deck a normal occurrence. She didn't need our reassurance. She sat on her heels on the high side, legs tucked beneath her, hands clutching the coaming, holding herself in place. Her face pressed to windward, hair streaming like a galloping mare's tail behind her. She gazed at the islands in the distance, and the slow passing swells alongside the schooner's hull.

Gage loved the schooner. As did I. He knew her through and through, as a living organism possessing her own unique type of soul. I hadn't experienced the bond they shared, but I understood the emotion. Sensed her awaken and come alive in my hands, and under my bare feet. Felt her energy, her thrust. Her magical command of her natural element.

Properly trimmed Wherever forged ahead, her long questing bowsprit leading the way. Her sharp bow cleaved the sea like a hot knife through soft butter. The wind sang through her rigging, and water rushed along her sides. Short rolling chop slapped her hull. Nothing large enough to throw her head off course. And given her deep full keel she tracked sweet and true, requiring no more than finger pressure on the wheel.

The islands spread out in every direction around us. Union Island off the stern to port; Palm Island, a small mound poking above the sea, even smaller than Petit St. Vincent, slid by to starboard. Farther off to our right lay the coral reef formations of the Tobago Cays, and ahead on the starboard bow, Mayreau Island.

In the bright afternoon sunlight even the distant islands were visible. Their dark indistinct shapes rose like a mythical humped creature from the sea. Canouan lay seven miles ahead, the tiny islands close to it, Petit Canouan and Savan Island, like smaller humps in the water.

Mustique, twenty miles north, and Bequia, twenty nine miles ahead, both visible. St. Vincent, forty miles north, still out of sight, a distant cloud mass marked its location.

Wherever ran under the freshening breeze at a respectable seven knots, shouldering aside oncoming chop like an offensive tackle clearing a path through a defensive line. We'd make St. Vincent just after nightfall.

Gage lounged in the cockpit nursing a Carib beer, Eileen and I bottled water. We'd settled in for the long leisurely single tack to St. Vincent. Unless the wind shifted, there'd be no need to touch a sheet for the next few hours.

When Gage relieved me at the wheel I turned to Eileen, "How're your sea legs? Want to try a walk forward? I want to show you something."

She gazed at the sloped deck, gauged the placid motion of the schooner, decided to give it a try. I coached her how to use the rail and shrouds to steady herself while walking forward. When we reached the bow I carefully guided her out along the bowsprit's footropes, as far as the forestay turnbuckle. She clung gamely to the stays and guys supporting the footropes, nevertheless enjoying herself. Not one to shy away from new experiences.

Using the bowsprit and forestay for support, we turned, and I showed her how to sit in the hammock-like footropes. We gazed back along the length of the schooner. The curved sails stretched high above the deck, one behind the other, white and resplendent in the bright sun.

"This is my favorite spot," I said. "Hold on tight there," indicating a footrope guy. "Both hands. Now close your eyes for a moment and just feel her motion under you."

"This is so incredible," she said after a moment. "Jolene, I can't thank you and Gage enough for this weekend."

"Our pleasure. Believe me. Look there," I said, pointing down. We turned onto our stomachs, suspended scant feet above the sea. We rose and fell with the bow as it advanced, its cutwater shearing the blue sea into white halves.

Back in the cockpit Gage asked Eileen if she wanted to try her hand at the wheel.

"Really?" Followed by a shy hesitancy. "You sure it's okay. I have no idea what I'm doing."

"We're not going anywhere," I said, chuckling. "And Wherever practically sails herself."

Gage positioned her behind the wheel, guided her hands onto the spokes. He coached her on holding the heading, but more importantly, keeping the sails filled.

"Gentle adjustments on the wheel. Feel what she wants to do, anticipate her, then just small corrections," he tutored.

His hands rested lightly atop hers until she acquired a feel for steering.

"You've got it," he said, relinquishing the helm to her.

Wherever ran off the miles, six every hour, while the sun travelled its inexorable arc across the sky. We chatted and laughed, and embraced the joy of being at sea. The wind brushed through our hair and whistled in the rigging. Occasionally Gage nudged the helm, explaining the finer points of wind, sea, and sail to Eileen.

I steered the conversation around to the case. Eileen reluctant to discuss the details until I reassured her regarding Gage.

"I discuss everything with him," I assured her. "So does the Commissioner. And besides, he has more useful insight into forensics than anyone you'll meet on these islands. I'm mostly curious about your impressions though," I told her. "Stuff you didn't put in the report."

"Except for the lab results, the report is pretty complete," she said.

"I know. I've read it. But it doesn't tell me what you think."

"What I think? How is that relevant?"

"It might provide an insight to get this case moving, because frankly, right now it's completely stalled."

"But you have the manner and cause of death. That's pretty definitive, isn't it?" I had the impression she might not be as convinced as she'd sounded.

"Maybe. Maybe not. I can't tell until all the questions, the loose ends, the little nagging doubts and anomalies are cleared up."

"I'm not sure if I can help. I'm not a criminal medical examiner or a forensic pathologist. My impressions don't mean much."

"What about the stomach contents?" I prodded. "Can they shed any light on where he had his last meal? What his movements or whereabouts might've been prior to death?"

"The stomach contents indicated he'd eaten about two hours prior to death. But we have to wait for the lab results to identify what he ate, and maybe where."

"How about what you do have? Your observations? Tissue samples, x-rays, microscopic examination; anything strike you as odd there?"

"There was something......" She hesitated, recalling the memory, momentarily losing her concentration on the helm. Gage nudged Wherever back on course.

"Sorry," she said needlessly, Gage's attention already shifted elsewhere.

"I'm not sure it means anything though. It's just a subjective impression. And as I said I'm not a forensic expert."

"What?" I prompted.

"His fingers. They showed a fracture pattern consistent with a vehicular accident. But the pattern was inconsistent for both hands. But I guess it all depends on where he had his hands, on the wheel, or somewhere else. I'm just not qualified to form an opinion."

But her words had captured Gage's attention, and interest. He stood next to her.

"Show me," he said, taking her hands and placing them on the wheel in the ten and two o'clock positions.

"Are the injuries consistent with his hands on the wheel like that?" he asked.

She studied her hands on Wherever's wheel, flexed and wriggled her fingers, said "On the left hand yes. On the right no. More like the fingers were forced back."

"Like this?" he asked, taking her right hand in his and gently pushing her fingers back.

"Yeah. The injuries on the left hand were consistent with crushing. And they didn't have this other type of bone and joint injury like the right hand. The other weird thing," she continued, now her reticence had been loosened, "His hands shouldn't have been anywhere near the wheel like that. The reflex is to cover up, like this," she said, demonstrating with her forearms crossed in front of her face like a shield. "The injuries should have looked more defensive, on the forearms, wrists and hands. And if a massive coronary had preceded the accident he'd have been clutching at his chest."

"You're more qualified than you think," Gage said, glancing over at me. Eileen smiled in appreciation of the compliment.

"By the way, who was the guy talking to you at the bar last night? He asked in an offhand manner. "I thought I recognized him from somewhere."

"Which one?" She grinned, recalling the memory of the male attention she'd attracted the night before.

"The guy wearing white slacks, light blue shirt, wavy hair."

"Oh him. Some kind of businessman I gather. Strange accent. Australian maybe. Or South African. Didn't really say much. Kind of a bore actually for such a handsome guy. He seemed more interested in Jolene and the yacht than anything else."

"Was he there with anyone else?" Gage asked.

"Not that I could tell. I did notice he wasn't wearing a ring, and no wife or girlfriend came running over to rescue him from me," her smile wider.

I sensed Gage sniffing at something. I wanted to ask him what. But not the right place or time. He wouldn't say anything around Eileen. He'd had the same concerned expression the night before at the barbecue when he'd first seen Eileen and the man talking at the bar. Last night hadn't been the right time or place to ask either. But his interest convinced me he'd observed something off, some sort of anomaly only he had recognized. I made a mental reminder to ask him at the first opportune chance I had.

"Is there anyone you know who may be able to give you a forensic analysis of the x-rays?" Gage asked her.

She thought for a moment. "I had a professor, an advisor actually, a forensic anthropologist. We still keep in touch. He'd be the best person to show them to."

"Can you ask him to take a look at those x-rays for you?"

"Sure. What should he be looking for?"

"If anything's there he'll know it when he sees it," Gage said.

Bequia lay off the starboard beam. To port, the vast expanse of Caribbean Sea merged into a rose colored sky. The sun a bright gold disk suspended just above the line where sea met sky. The mesmerizing spectacle held our attention, the hues subtly shifting, orange to gold, apricot to raspberry red. The sun slid lower, casting a yellow trail across the blood red sea. With sudden swiftness it dipped below the horizon, leaving a thin crimson sliver in its wake, and a darkening sky lit by a silver moon.

St. Vincent loomed as sprinkled lights in the dark ahead, its southern landmass a nebulous shadow in the pale moonlight. Our destination Indian Bay, east of Kingstown, between Young Island and St. Vincent's southern coast. But we held the heading for Kingstown. We'd need a tack to lay Indian bay.

The shadows grew more distinct as we closed on St. Vincent's coast. The dark landmass acquired shape and form. On our starboard side Rock Fort, a tall rock pinnacle a few yards south of Young Island where an eighteenth century British fort once stood. And Young Island itself, its footpaths and resort facilities brightly lit.

"Let's get ready to come about," Gage said.

Earlier I'd relieved Eileen at the helm. She sat on the high side in the cockpit, gazing out across the dark water at the lights ashore, a serene contemplative expression on her face, her hair streaming in the wind.

"What'd you need me to do," she asked, turning toward the cockpit on hearing Gage's voice.

"We're going to tack, to head in that direction," I explained, pointing toward Young Island. "Move over to this side, and watch your head when the boom swings over."

Gage checked the sheets. He hauled in the slack on the starboard jib sheet, laying two turns on the starboard winch. We needn't touch Wherever's boom rigged sheets until we retrimmed her on the new course. Gage stood by the jib's lee sheet.

"Ready?" he asked me in a soft voice.

"Ready," I replied.

He checked the course ahead. Gazed across the starboard side to check the lay of Young Island. He uncleated the lee sheet, and prepared to unwind it from the winch.

"Come about," he commanded in a low business-as-usual voice.

I spun the wheel right until it reached the stop. Held it hard over. Wherever responded instantly. Her bowsprit swung in a smooth arc as she answered her rudder and changed direction, turning into the wind.

The turn unleashed mayhem on deck. A tremendous clatter as sails spilled their wind, their flogging and flapping sounding like cracking whips. Suddenly slack blocks and running tackle lashed the deck and beat against their hardware. Wherever sounded like she might break apart.

Gage loosened the lee sheet and let it run free as Wherever continued turning, her head swinging through the wind until it blew over her port side. Gage jumped to the starboard side of the cockpit, reeling in the starboard jib sheet hand over hand. The winch drum whirred freely. I centered the helm. A thunderous crack as the main boom whipped to the other side. Tackles snapped taut, sails filled, bellied out and drew. Wherever settled on her new course, gathering speed without missing a beat. The tack flawlessly timed and executed. Gage trimmed the sails for our new course.

Wherever on track for the anchorage between St. Vincent and Young Island.

"That was a tack," I explained to Eileen, who'd watched from her seat in fascinated silence.

"Why'd we do that?" she asked.

"You can't sail directly into the wind," I explained. "And the wind is coming from over there where we need to go," I said, pointing. "To get there we need to have the wind on this side."

"So I guess that's where the expression comes from."

"There you go," I said.

Gage moved forward, shortening sail for the approach. First he lowered the staysail, followed by the foresail. He lashed them to their booms, coiling and securing their halyards and sheets. Wherever slowed, responding to the loss of thrust. She ran sedately toward the anchorage, her heel decreased to a gentle slope of the deck.

Sailboats crowded the anchorage around Indian Bay. Bright illumination from ashore washed out the dim moonlight. Young Island on the right, its colored lights reflected on the water in kaleidoscope patterns. To our left, on the St. Vincent side, the lights of hotels, restaurants, and bars lining Villa beach spilled across the bay. A confused mixture of reggae, soca, and country music reached us, borne on the breeze.

In the middle of the bay lights from anchored yachts also contributed to the illumination, spilling out of open port holes, hatches, and lamp lit cockpits. I counted at least three cruising catamarans, three ketches, a couple of sloops, and an assortment of speedboats. All clustered together between

Young Island's beach and The Lagoon Hotel and Marina, a boat charter base on the St. Vincent side.

Swift currents ran through the cut between St. Vincent and Young Island, changing with the tide. Knowledgeable skippers liked to put out a stern anchor to keep their bows pointing northeast. The unwary and inexperienced woke to their vessels swinging to all points of the compass, dragging their anchors, fouling the lines of other boats nearby, even smashing into them.

Gage selected a spot well behind them, in a clear area just off the Beachcomber Hotel. The area also allowed for an easy unobstructed departure under sail. Wherever coasted toward the spot under mainsail alone. At Gage's signal I put her nose into the wind and simultaneously let the mainsheet run.

Wherever continued ahead under her own momentum, her forward motion dissipating. When she lay still in the water Gage released the brake on the anchor windlass, shattering the quiet as heavy chain rattled over the sprockets. The noise ended as abruptly as it began when rope replaced chain. Gage allowed the line sufficient scope before applying the brake. Wherever fell back until the anchor's flukes dug in and set into the seabed below, pulling her up short. The line rose dripping from the water, stretched taut and straight ahead.

Wherever secure on her anchor, her deck cleared and tidied, her anchor light burning, we headed ashore. We'd decided on dinner at the Beachcomber, the hotel closest to where we'd anchored. And set apart down the beach from the busier strip of waterfront bars and restaurants. We dragged the dinghy up onto the white sand beach fronting the hotel.

The hotel itself set back from the beach, nestled among tall fruit trees and flowering plants.

We walked across the beach to a stone wall rising from the sand, topped by a white picket fence. Concrete steps bordered by purple bougainvillea led from the beach up to the hotel grounds.

The bartender, whose brother ran a dive shop on Bequia, the sole occupant when we entered the bar and dining area.

"Suprintendent," he greeted me, a broad welcoming smile on his face. "Gage mahn. Ow it goin?"

"Fine Peter," I said.

"Airie Peter," Gage responded. "And you?"

"Evryting fine mahn." He said.

"How're Susan and the girls?" I asked. He'd married a Canadian expat he'd met on Bequia. They had two adorable little girls, three and five years old.

"Dem good yuh noh. Growin evry day."

"Peter, this is my friend Eileen. She's working down heah wid de Peace Corp."

"My pleasha Miss Eileen," he said, shaking her hand, including her in his smile.

Eileen and Gage ambled out to the open-air tables while Peter and I conversed further, catching up. I also asked to borrow his bar phone. When he handed it to me I dialed a taxi driver friend I trusted and made arrangements for Eileen's ride home.

"Yuh guys havin dinnah?" Peter asked.

"Yes," I said. "You booked?" I gazed around at the empty bar, and tables.

"Not rite now. Anyway I tell de gurls tek cahe of yuh special."

"Thanks," I said.

"No problame Miss Jo. Wat yuh drinkin?"

"Lemme have two white wines, and a rum and Coke.

"Comin up." He turned to the back of the bar, reaching for the bottles.

"What come in fresh today?" I asked him while he poured the drinks.

"Yellow fin tuna and bluefish."

"Tanks Peter," I said when he'd done pouring and mixing.

I carried the drinks outside to the tables. Gage and Eileen sat at a table close to the rail, overlooking the bay. Eileen laughed at something he'd said. A cool evening breeze rustled through the branches overhead.

"Such service," Gage teased when I arrived bearing the drinks. "And we didn't even have to order." He pulled out a chair next to him.

"Thanks again guys," Eileen said, sampling her wine. "I had a wonderful weekend. And sailing up through the islands. Wow!"

"Yeah. That's what did it for me too," I said, grinning at Gage.

She laughed. "I've done and seen more in the last two days than in the last four months. And I definitely want to learn to sail and do more sailing."

"Any time," Gage said. "Just say the word."

"Don't you ever get out," I asked.

"It's only been four months. The first month I stayed with a host family, getting my bearings, finding a place to stay, getting acclimated. And I've been busy organizing the labs, putting together training and course schedules. I haven't had time to really get to know anyone."

"Well you have an open invitation to my place on Bequia anytime. Just show up whenever you want."

"Thanks."

A young Vincentian woman approached and placed menus on the table.

"What came in fresh today?" Gage asked her.

"Yellow fin tuna and Bluefish," I said before she could answer.

"Then I'll have grilled tuna with rice and peas and fresh house vegetables, whatever you have," he said, ignoring the menu. "You guys ready to order?" Eileen's head buried in the menu pondering a decision.

I reached over and plucked it from her hands. "I got this."

Turning to the waitress I said, "Two callalou soups, cream potato pie, dashine, bananas, plantains, and greens. She wrote everything down on her pad, picked up the menus and disappeared back inside.

"It's so beautiful here," Eileen said, gazing down the slope to the beach, and across the water at the twinkling lights of Young Island. Atop Young Island's peak a lone red light stood vigil, flashing a silent warning to aircraft approaching E.T. Joshua airport at night.

"It used to be a family home," I said; "before they turned it into a hotel."

We chatted while waiting for our food. Two other couples arrived, settling at tables close to ours overlooking the bay. We acknowledged them with polite hellos before returning to our conversation.

When the food arrived the delicious aroma sharpened my appetite. Eileen and I dug into our callalou soup. Gage had ordered a plate sufficient for both of us, anticipating I'd eventually pick at it.

Eileen picked her head up long enough to exclaim, "This is fantastic," referring to the plate of creamed potato pie and plantains. "I've got to learn how to cook this stuff or I'm going to starve or go broke," she joked between mouthfuls.

"Come over to Bequia next weekend," I said. "We'll go shopping. I'll show you what to buy and give you some recipes."

"I'd love that." Then hesitating. Concern clouded her face as her shy side surfaced. "You're sure it won't be an intrusion? I don't want to be in your guy's way."

"Oh, stop that already," I kindly scolded her. "You should know better by now. Like I said, come anytime, make yourself at home. So next weekend okay?"

Her smile signaled her grateful appreciation and acceptance.

"Anyone have any idea of the time? She asked. None of us wore watches.

"Probably around nine," Gage said, staring up into the sky at the moon.

"I suddenly realize I have no idea how I'm getting home," she said, not overly concerned.

"Taken care of," I said. "A friend of mine's going to pick you up and drive you home. You can trust him. He's probably already waiting outside."

"Really? Don't you think we should see if....."

"He'll be fine," I said. "First let's give some serious thought to dessert."

In the hotel yard after dinner, Eileen and I said our farewells. Lots of hugs and 'see you soons' while Gage quietly attended to the fare, paying my friend twice the normal fare to compensate him for waiting.

As the taxi drove away an unexpected forlornness enveloped me. I'd thoroughly enjoyed the weekend in Eileen's company. And longed for more. For her friendship. Eager for the following weekend to arrive.

Later, lying next to Gage in the large cozy aft berth, enclosed in his arms, and on the verge of sleep, I remembered to ask him.

"What did you see?"

"See where?" he mumbled.

"Last night. At the barbeque. When Eileen was talking to that man at the bar. You saw something. You asked her about him when we were sailing."

"He'd been watching you."

I might've laughed it off, dismissing it as a rare display of jealousy. But Gage wasn't the jealous type.

"Everyone was watching us," I rationalized. "That's not so unusual."

He turned to face me. Stared into my eyes. "I'm used to you raising eyebrows," he smiled. "This was different. He was studying you."

"Studying me?" A sudden disquieting tightening in my stomach. Gage didn't form such judgments indiscriminately. He possessed an almost mystical way of reading people.

"As in scouting you. Maybe. Then when I saw him chatting up Eileen. That wasn't a coincidence."

"What makes you think he was interested in me, not Eileen?"

"It's a technique you learn to recognize," he said. "Takes one to know one."

CHAPTER 13

"A body was discovered early dis morning in a Mount Pleasant home," Inspector Cato said over the phone."

I'd returned to Bequia only half an hour before, had changed into fresh clothes, contemplating the day ahead when Inspector Cato had called. Not how I wanted to start my morning, my day, or my week. The first question to spring to mind, "who?" I said aloud.

"Mister Jackson Taylor," Cato said.

"Oh my God." I whispered into the phone. Either Cato hadn't heard it, or chose to ignore it. In any case, my morning just got worse.

"He was found in de bedroom hanging from a rafter in de roof."

"Crisse." I said, again in an undertone.

"Whey are you Suprintendent?"

"Home. Just leaving for the station. I'll meet you at the scene."

Another delicate, high profile case had just landed in my lap. Jackson Taylor a prominent Vincentian who'd spent a lifetime in Vincentian business and politics. A close friend and advisor to the Prime Minister. And a friend of Mike. I had no doubt they'd both take a personal interest in the case, meaning they'd be breathing down my neck.

Before anything else I had a distressing call to place. About to dial the number, my cell phone rang again. The person I'd been about to call.

"I just heard Mike," I said without preamble.

"Good morning to you too. Heard what?"

I'd assumed he'd called about Jackson Taylor. Instead, I still had to break the news of his friend's death.

"I just received a call from Inspector Cato...." I hesitated. No easy way to say it. I just had to get it out. "Jackson Taylor's body was found in his home a short time ago. I'm so sorry Mike."

Silence on the other end. "Mike?" I prompted.

"What happened?" His voice distant, distraught, disconnected.

"I don't have the details yet. I just got the call and I'm heading over there now."

"I'll meet you there. I'm still at home. A Coast Guard Patrol boat is on the way to pick me up. We may need them."

"Mike, you sure...."

"I'm on my way," he interrupted. "I'll meet you there." His tone stiff and surly.

Sacrement, I thought. It'd been selfish of me. A man had died. The friend of my friend. That's where my focus needed to be. But Cato's call had annoyed me, like an intruding nuisance. I didn't need this now. And my period had decided to arrive that morning.

"I'm sorry Mike," I repeated before he broke the connection.

Mount Pleasant sits atop a ridge running like a spine along Bequia. From its height, Mustique and the southern Grenadines are visible on a clear day. It overlooks Admiralty Bay and Port Elizabeth to the west, and the white capped surf of Hope Beach and Ravine Bay to the east.

Mount Pleasant also the ancestral home to blond haired, blue eyed, white complexioned Bequians. Descendants of Scottish workers and white Barbadians who'd settled the heights above Port Elizabeth in the eighteen sixties. Mount Pleasant people had historical last names like Hazel, Wallace, and Ollivierre.

Constable Johns turned right off the main road. The police Toyota 4Runner climbed into the heights above Belmont and the harbor. The steep road wound past lavish foreign owned homes nestled in the wooded hillside. Constructed for their privacy and views.

As a child I remembered Mount Pleasant as forested hillsides and open sloping grasslands swaying in the breeze. The government's desire to raise foreign capital and boost tourism created a substantial selling off of local land to foreign owners and investors. Expansive construction of private homes and rental villas displaced unspoiled tropical greenery and deserted, coconut tree shrouded beaches.

Constable Johns turned into a downward sloping driveway. Another police Toyota already parked there. A light blue Nissan sedan occupied a carport attached to the side of the house, at the end of the driveway.

A two bedroom house built on a stone foundation, topped by a pastel green roof, sat amid lime, lemon, breadfruit and mango trees. Red bougainvillea, and yellow and orange flamboyants contributed vivid color to the small yard surrounding the house. The fruit trees reminded me I needed to pick some lime and ginger leaves for making tea. Generations of Bequia women had used lime and ginger tea during their period. It worked wonders for bloating and cramps, providing an added benefit of a wonderful night's sleep.

A decorative wood railing on either side of five flagstone steps led up to the house. Before heading there I turned to constable Johns.

"De Commissioner is on his way here," I told him. "You secure dis driveway. No one comes down heah, yuh unnerstan?"

"Yes ma'am," He replied, brushing and straightening his ill-fitting uniform as though preparing for an inspection.

At the top of the steps the flagstones continued onto a wide landing leading to the front door, and wrapped around to a verandah on the bay side of the house. The tranquil blue waters of Port Elizabeth and Belmont Bays visible through the trees. A uniformed constable stood at the entrance. He stamped to attention and saluted as I approached.

"Morning Corporal," I acknowledged, as he opened the front door to the house. "The Commissioner will be heah shortly," I said, giving him the heads up. He too commenced brushing and straightening his uniform.

Inspector Cato met me at the front door. "Mahning Suprintendent," his countenance severe and sorrowful. "Dis way ma'am."

He led the way past a large living room. Exposed beams in its high arched ceiling. Book lined shelves built into one wall. A large seascape painting hung in the center of another wall, bordered on either side by decorative wall lamps. Large louvered windows opened on three sides of the room, allowing bright sunlight and a cross breeze into the room.

A wicker couch and matching armchairs containing plush flower patterned cushions were arranged around a polished white pine coffee table. A dining table and chairs stood against the far wall, separated from the kitchen by a counter connecting both rooms.

Passing the kitchen I heard sobbing. Stepping through the arched entrance I noticed a plump middle aged woman sitting at a small table in the center of the room. Her back to the kitchen sink and a wall of modern appliances. Her hands held a rag pressed to her face. Her slumped shoulders and bent back shook as each sob seized her.

"Who is that?" I asked Cato.

"Dat is Mrs. Lewis. De housekeeper for Mr. Taylor. She found de body when she arrived dis morning, and called de poliss."

"Have you spoken to her yet?"

"Jus a likkle. Jus to find out wat time she arrived at de house to find Mr. Taylor, and to make sure she didn't disturb anyting before I arrived. She's been crying since I arrived," he explained.

"Okay," I said. The Commissioner's meeting us here. When he arrives you can follow up with her."

"Yes ma'am."

We headed to the bedroom on the far side of the house. The sight and smell of death greeted me as I entered. I sighed. Two in less than a week.

A large master bedroom. Like the other rooms it had louvered windows, opened halfway, allowing partial daylight into the room. Louvered double doors led out to the covered verandah, and a view of the tree covered landscape sloping toward the harbor. Admiralty Bay visible through the branches.

A king size bed, unmade, stood against the far wall. On the opposite wall a partially opened door led to the master bathroom. A chest high chest of drawers stood next to the entrance. A wristwatch, a couple of rings, wallet, and other personal items strewn across the top. A flat panel television mounted on the wall above the chest of drawers. A walk in closet on the other side of the dresser.

Like other rooms in the house, the bedroom had a high arched ceiling and exposed beams. From one beam, directly over the bed, hung a wood bladed ceiling fan and a coiled mosquito net below the fan.

From another beam, close to the foot of the bed, Jackson Taylor hung suspended from a length of red and blue woven nylon rope. One end had been looped around the ceiling beam, the other tied in a noose around his neck. A straight back wood chair lay on its side below his dangling feet.

The body naked except for boxer shorts, and black socks on his feet. His arms hung stiffly at his sides. The tip of his tongue protruded through slightly opened lips. A trickle of dried blood at the corner of his mouth and chin indicated he might've bitten partially through his tongue. His eyes open, glazed over, lifeless, staring unseeing at some object across the room. His sphincters had loosened, and judging from the odor, his bowel had probably evacuated.

This would be devastating for Mike, I thought.

"Ovah heah, Suprintendent," Cato called, diverting my gaze from the gruesome sight.

He pointed to an open laptop on a small table in a corner of the room. Besides the laptop, the table had a desk lamp, and books and papers strewn across it. It had a center drawer below.

The table sat on an oval carpet of woven straw. I noticed indentations in the carpet, possibly matching the legs of the overturned chair. The table obviously served as a bedroom desk where Taylor worked.

Wearing blue nitrite gloves Cato pressed the return key. The laptop monitor lit up. A Microsoft Word document displayed on the screen. A suicide note.

The Corporal at the front door called. I exited the bedroom and encountered Mike striding down the hall, his face set in grim determination. We entered the bedroom and his eyes studied the scene. His gaze lingered on the sight of his friend hanging from the overhead beam. The blood drained from Mike's face. His pallor turned as ashen as the skin on his friend's lifeless body.

Cato moved to stand at attention and salute. Mike waved it away. "Not the time or place son," he said, not unkindly.

Mike's eyes drew together. The smooth lines on his dark brow deepened. The sorrow on his face unfathomable. And something else. A detached hardness in his eyes I'd never seen before.

He pulled a pair of gloves from Cato's case. He walked slowly around the body, examining it from every angle. He reached out to touch it. The body swung at his touch, accompanied by the sound of stretching rope. Mike steadied the swaying body with both hands.

"Rigor's set in," he observed. "Not full yet. Less than twelve hours since he died I'd estimate. What've you found so far?" he asked no one in particular, glancing from me to Cato.

"I just arrived Chief," I said. "Inspector Cato was first on the scene. He did find this," I said, directing him to the laptop. Mike gazed at the monitor without touching the laptop. He read and reread the note.

"Anything else?" he asked. His manner curt, just shy of abrasive.

"I was about to start photographing," I said. "And I need Inspector Cato to finish interviewing the housekeeper."

"Please see to it Inspector." His tone mollifying, as though aware of his prior abruptness.

"Thank you," he said as Inspector Cato moved toward the door.

Before Cato passed into the hall I said, "Ask the Corporal to look around for a ladder."

"Yes Suprintendent."

I retrieved a Minolta digital camera from Cato's case and busied myself photographing the scene. First the body, from a variety of angles. Then the room. Satisfied I had the shots I needed I switched to examining the room. I checked the doors, particularly the locks and jams. And the window frames and louvers. I checked the surfaces of the bed frame and furniture. I photographed anything I considered of interest.

Mike retrieved a temperature probe from Cato's crime scene case and approached the body. His unease apparent in his hesitant movements.

"I'll do that Chief." I pulled the probe from his grasp.

"Thank you," he said absently.

I pushed the probe firmly into the body, piercing the liver. I noted the reading and pulled it out. I noted the ambient temperature of the room and calculated an approximate time of death.

Mike had been searching through the chest of drawers while I'd worked on the corpse. He worked slowly, absent mindedly, as he searched through the contents of the.drawers.

"I estimate time of death between midnight and one am this morning," I informed him.

"This makes absolutely no sense you know," he said, the remark aimed into empty space.

"How so Chief." My entire being ached for him.

"I just saw him the other night. Friday. After I got home from Kingstown. He'd just got back from New York. We had dinner together." A mournful wistfulness in his voice.

"I mean, you can never tell what's going on in someone's mind. But suicide? Just doesn't track. I'd have noticed something. Not just lately, but before. There was nothing despondent about Jackson."

"Mike," I began hesitantly, "you can't... "

"Don't JJ," he interrupted. "I appreciate what you're trying to do, but believe me when I say something about this doesn't smell right."

"I believe you," I said.

I did. He'd been a cop most of his adult life. His police instincts honed by years of experience. And he had a knack for reading people and situations akin to Gage's.

"So what do we do?" I asked.

"We dig deep and keep digging till we find out what really happened here," he said. "Sorry JJ but this is priority one now."

"Have you spoken to the Prime Minister?" I asked.

"No. Not yet. I tried calling him on the way here but he had a meeting in Parliament. I left word for him to call me. Are you done with the photos?"

"Yeah. Except for some shots up there," I said, pointing to the beam and the rope looped around it. "Where's that damn ladder?"

"See if you can light a fire under them. We need to get Jackson down from there."

Given a little prodding the Corporal eventually located an aluminum extension ladder leaning against a breadfruit tree in the yard. I also checked on Constable Johns, who assured me all remained quiet out front. A couple of vehicles had passed by in the time he'd been out there, but they hadn't been too curious about the police activity and had kept going. No one had tried to stop by the house.

The corporal and I returned to the bedroom carrying the ladder just as Mike completed a call on his cell phone. He turned to us.

"Corporal, please ask the inspector to step in a moment. And keep an eye out front for the ambulance."

"Yes sah," he said, saluting and heading out the door.

Mike and I wrestled the ladder into position next to the body, the top end resting on the beam above. When Cato entered the room Mike issued instructions. He and Cato would lift and hold the body from below, while I cut the rope from above. I climbed almost to the top rung carrying the camera. I shot photos of the rope around the beam, the knots, and the beam itself. And shots looking down at the body.

A white Land Rover, green crosses painted on its sides, its rear compartment gutted and modified to accommodate a stretcher, served as the ambulance on Bequia. Mike had already informed the ambulance crew of the situation. They arrived in the bedroom carrying a folding canvas stretcher and a body bag.

"I'll accompany the remains to Kingstown," Mike said after the body had been zippered into the bag, placed on the stretcher and carried from the room. "You and Cato go over this entire house and yard with a fine tooth comb. Use any resources you need."

"Any Coast Guard vessels in or around Union right now?" I asked.

"Should be. I can check. Why?"

"I could use Zelina McIntosh on this, and some extra hands and eyes," I said.

"You got it. Anything else you need?"

"That'll do it for now Chief."

As he turned to leave I said, "Mike." He turned to face me. "I'm so very sorry."

"Fine tooth comb," he said, turning and striding out the door.

CHAPTER 14

The fine tooth comb turned up nothing. Not that day, or the day after, or the next. The week passed in a daily succession of mounting frustration. By Friday my exasperation reached its peak, increasing my irascibility and snappishness. The onset of my period didn't help. It'd been four days since the discovery of Jackson Taylor's body and we were nowhere.

The Mansfield case also stalled. Taylor's death had diverted my attention, and Barbados appeared to be taking its sweet time getting back to us. I still didn't have a confirmed identification.

"I've never seen him like that Gage," I said, walking toward Friendship Bay where Mike had asked us to meet him. "Like he's put up a wall around himself. But I can tell he's hurting. And he had this scary look in his eyes I've never seen before."

The scent of fresh foliage and damp earth saturated the air. Scrubbed clean by continuous rain showers over the previous two days. The green hillsides, colorful flowers, pastel rooftops, and the lime green surf and dark blue sea; sparkled and shined under a brilliant sun in a bright blue sky.

We approached Mike's house from the narrow gravel road. The back of the house faced the road. The front faced the bay. Set back from the beach, almost at the midpoint of Friendship Bay's crescent shaped shoreline, the house sat on rising terrain, providing a view of the Bay and the southern Grenadines from behind a dense growth of coconut trees lining the beach. Citrus trees filled the yard, the scent of ripe oranges, grapefruits and tangerines borne on the warm breeze.

A stone verandah, bordered by a wood porch railing wrapped around the side and front of the house. The front door, windows, and blue shutters open as Gage and I walked toward the front. The woeful strains of Miles Davis's trumpet drifted from inside.

When we entered Mike greeted us from the kitchen, at the rear of the house. The kitchen level one step higher than the cozy living room. His bearing tired and worn as he stepped down into the living room to join us. Dull eyes sunk inside puffy lids. His usual jovial ebullience absent. I'd witnessed his haggard, grim state only once before, during his recuperation. After he'd been shot. He'd lost weight then. A gaunt shadow of his former self. Now the two hundred pounds on his five foot eleven inch frame appeared an unbearable burden.

"Make yourself comfortable. Fix whatever you need. You know where everything is."

In the privacy of his home no force could stop me from throwing my arms around him. My tight embrace expressed the love, tenderness, and sorrow I'd been unable to display in public. His arms rose, returning the embrace, patting my back. When I released him I gazed deep into his mournful brown eyes, the color of dark rum.

"Thanks, JJ," he said softly.

"You look terrible," I said, not unkindly, smiling at the drawn sorrowful chocolate face. I wiped an errant tear from my eye. A pulse quickening rush of relief when he returned the smile.

"I'm okay. Just been a hard week." He turned to Gage. Without a word Gage too enveloped him in a strong embrace, slapping him affectionately on the back.

"I've seen you looking worse," Gage said, releasing him.

"Don't remind me."

Except for the tired, puffy eyes, Mike's demeanor approached normalcy by the time we'd downed a few beers on his shaded verandah. The conversation light, providing a cheerful boost to his spirits. But eventually he turned the conversation to business.

"I guess by now you've both heard the nasty rumors flying around."

"We know better Mike," I said.

"It's like no one on St. Vincent has anything better to talk about," an exasperated tone in his voice.

"Just small island gossip," I said. "You know how it is. They'll talk about it for awhile and then it'll pass.

"I know that JJ. It's what they're saying that's annoying. About his marriage. Seeing government conspiracies everywhere. Some damn Calypsonian even wrote a song called 'Inside Job' for christsake. It just gets me worked up, and there's not a damn thing I can say about it. Opening my mouth will only add fuel to the fire."

"Gossip loves a mystery," I said. "In the absence of facts and an explanation, people will fill in the empty space with all kinds of nonsense."

"And that's exactly what we have here. A mystery. The autopsy didn't rule out suicide. If anything the findings confirm it. But there're a lot of people, myself included, who think suicide is crap."

Mike's increasing agitation had a distressing effect on me, producing a disquieting discomfort. I wanted to change the conversation from Jackson Taylor and the case but knew it'd be futile.

"You already know we've got nothing," I said, my own frustration bubbling to the surface. "Nothing in the house, the car, the grounds or his movements during that weekend and prior. Nothing to contradict or rule out suicide. Except no one we've interviewed claims he was depressed or despondent. So both of my cases are at a dead end. Douleur dans le cul. Any word from Barbados?"

The question only agitated him further. "Nothing," he growled. "I keep getting the run around. 'The person handling the matter is unavailable. They're pursuing this and that. Taking all appropriate blah blah blah'. I know when I'm being stonewalled," he declared. "I just don't know why."

"Suicide isn't difficult to fake," Gage said, returning from some distant place in his mind. "A talented amateur can pull it off." I wanted to kick him in the chin, but had nothing between us to conceal it.

Mike fixed an interrogative gaze on him; their eyes locked in silent inquiry.

"You suggesting this might have been a hit?"

"I'm not suggesting anything. I'm just saying. The fact there's nothing to indicate otherwise also says something. What about the note? And what else did you find on the laptop?"

"The note doesn't tell us anything forensically," Mike said. "It was created by word processing software. As far as the rest of the computer goes we didn't get anything from it. If Jackson kept any of his work on it, the files aren't there now. And we don't have the expertise here to get anything more from the laptop."

"How soon can you get it stateside?" Gage asked. "Quietly," he added.

A spark of interest flicked in Mike's eyes. "I can get it there in a day, two at the most."

"Then send it to one of your old contacts. Someone you trust. I'll have someone pick it up. If there's anything left on the laptop we'll have it within twenty four hours after it's picked up."

"The sooner the better," Mike said. "The PM is getting pressure from Jackson's friends and relatives to call in Scotland Yard. Especially since they don't believe he committed suicide. I wouldn't put it past some of them to be the ones spreading certain rumors to put pressure on DeFretas."

"That'll really turn this into a circus," Gage observed in a dry tone.

"DeFretas has been able to hold them off because bringing in the Brits now would delay the funeral, which is scheduled for tomorrow, or require exhumation later. It's a fair bet their forensic people will want to reexamine everything."

Turning to me Mike said, "I've been putting together a report on what Jackson's been working on recently JJ. It's incomplete. I still have a bunch of people I need to interview. I'll give you what I've got so far and you can start looking it over. Going back over the last few conversations I had with Jackson, I remembered he'd been more secretive and preoccupied than usual lately. Didn't give it much thought at the time. Much of his work for the PM was sensitive. But nothing I've found so far adds up to suicide. JJ, you and I can fly over and back tomorrow for the funeral."

"You sure you don't mind keeping Eileen company while I'm gone?" I said to Gage.

"Eileen?" Mike interrupted. "Doctor Gash?"

"She's coming over for the weekend. Arriving on the five thirty ferry. Actually," I paused, inspired by a sudden idea which might distract Mike from Jackson Taylor and the case. "Let's have dinner together. And don't you dare say no," I snapped in his direction, jabbing an insistent index finger at him. "It'll do you good to get away from all this for awhile."

"Yes ma'am," he said in mock acquiescence. "Just goes to show who's the boss around here," his smile a welcome relief.

Gage merely shrugged and grinned.

"Jesus," Mike said, returning from the kitchen carrying three more cold Heinekens. With everything else happening I almost forgot. Remember the guy who tried to kill you here in my living room eight months ago?" he said to Gage.

"What about him?" I asked in an anxious tone, the memory springing vividly to the forefront of my mind. Gage standing over the figure prone at his feet, the silenced pistol which had been aimed at Gage's head, the smashed rounds pulled from the kitchen and living room walls. The utter fear and relief. Now the fear returned, constricting my throat as I waited for Mike's response.

"Found dead in the prison toilet two days ago with his throat slit."

Instant relief. "What happened?" I asked.

"Who knows? It's being investigated but we'll probably never know for sure."

"Was it just typical prison violence? Did he have a beef with another prisoner?

"Like I said, who knows? But the timing is suspicious. His case was coming up for a final appeal, and it didn't look good for him. Facing the prospect of life in her Majesty's hell hole, there'd been indications he might want to deal. Maybe someone couldn't afford to have that happen."

"Or tying off that particular loose end took some time to set up." Gage said.

Gage continued to believe the attempt on Mike's life eight months before had been a byproduct of a larger agenda. An as yet unknown, invisible, but continuing menace we needed to remain on alert for. Perhaps lingering paranoia from his old life. But as he liked to say, his paranoia had kept him alive. His conviction had created a bogeyman in my subconscious, and for a second, I'd thought the bogeyman had gotten loose.

But Gage had killed the man the assassin worked for. So if someone had ordered the assassin's death? Who? Did it mean the bogeyman was real, and close?

"Ever find out who he was?" Gage asked, as unconcerned as though discussing the weather.

"Never really got a handle on him," Mike said. "We charged him as Ramon Ortega, the name he used to enter the country. Turned out to be one of a dozen aliases he'd used all over South and Central America. The authorities in Columbia,

Mexico, Panama, the DEA, all had files on him, under different names. Apparently he worked for a bunch of different groups over the years, which led some to believe he was a freelancer for hire. Others think someone was pulling his strings, but no one knows for sure."

The sun slipped lower in the sky. Still a couple of hours from setting. I didn't want to miss Eileen's Ferry.

As though he'd read my mind Mike settled into his chair and said, "There's another matter I've wanted to update both of you on."

His eyebrows drew together and contemplative lines etched his forehead as he gathered his thoughts, his usual habit prior to launching into a briefing. His earlier despondency shelved, at least for the time being. His manner the assured, confident commander once more.

"That conversation we had some months back while sailing down from St. Lucia. Consolidating the gains on the force, preparing it for maybe tough times ahead and a new Commissioner," his inflection sounding like a question. "I've been working it day and night since then. You've probably heard talk, seen the news, and the police grapevine has been buzzing more than usual. I've discussed bits and pieces with both of you over the past few months, but I want to get you both up to speed on everything that's happening. Get your insights on what I've done so far."

He paused, marshalling his thoughts again before continuing. "The PM, who as you know is also Minister of National Security, signed off on all this. But even he isn't aware of the rationale behind it. To him it's just good politics, especially with an election coming up. I convinced him to appoint a couple of emeritus consultants to put a public face other than mine on the whole scheme. Make it look like independent recommendations for reforming and modernizing the force. It gives me political cover and helps me get around the bureaucratic bullshit. Anyway, here's what I've been able to get done so far."

"Personnel," Mike said, raising his thumb like a hitch hiker. "I've placed key people in key positions, using promotions based on merit rather than favoritism or cronyism. Thanks for your help by the way JJ," he said, gazing directly at me. "Your lists were spot on. Keep that going. We still need to keep a lookout for that kind of talent. We've been able to make major improvements in the Special Services Unit, and we've created a Major Crimes Unit and a Narcotics Unit staffed by reliable dedicated people who will make a difference."

"We've been able to increase salaries, and increase training and educational allowances, especially for advanced degrees overseas in law, criminology, forensics, psychology and management. We've extended paid paternity and maternity leave to police men and women, and arranged hundred per cent mortgages at the State-owned Bank. Taken together it's nothing compared to the amount of money narco traffickers can throw at us, but that's the reality anywhere."

"The Rapid Response Unit is still a huge pain in my ass," frustration evident in his voice. "Given the proper leadership and training the unit could be the key to this whole thing. But it's rotten to the core. They've lost the confidence and support of the public who see the unit as nothing more than armed thugs. People call them the 'black shirts'. And the unit is a ripe target for narco corruption rather than a shield against it. Plus they have access to automatic weapons. I wish I could dismantle the whole damn unit," he mused aloud.

"Did I just say that out loud? You didn't hear me say that."

Gage and I just smiled.

"We've established an independent Police Oversight Board. But that's just a political sop to get more money from parliament. It may or may not amount to anything."

"Anyway, recruitment and training," he continued, raising his index finger. "We've raised the educational standards for eligibility and instituted psychological assessments. We've also increased the size of the force. By the way Gage, the help I got from your guys in designing the training program was invaluable. And the contacts they provided in the States for in-service guest training really paid off. I only wish I could thank them again in person."

"Not necessary," Gage assured him.

"We're installing modern telecommunications facilities and equipment" he said, holding up a third finger. "We're upgrading our labs and brought in outside expertise in pathology and forensics until we can train up our own people."

"Of primary importance," holding up a fourth, the ring finger, "the Coast Guard. They're our first line of defense. We're expanded and upgraded the fleet with fast new Rigid Hull Inflatable patrol boats and high speed interceptors. We've expanded the facilities at Calliaqua, including two advanced coastal surveillance radar systems we recently acquired and installed to supplement the radar site on the Leeward side. And most important, basic and advanced training of Coast Guard personnel both here in the region and abroad. I've been promoting key people into leadership positions there too. Lieutenant Commander David Pompey, the new Coast Guard Commander is starting to really turn the service around."

"Mike," I interrupted. "The other day on Union the thought occurred to me we need to provide more opportunity and incentive for women to go into the Coast Guard. We have what, something like a hundred and twenty women on the force, and very few of them in the Coast Guard."

"The opportunity is there JJ, and we can provide the incentive. But we'd still have to get around the cultural bias, not just of the men, but the women too."

"That can be overcome if they see it as a viable career choice," I said.

"Well if you're up for another challenge," he smiled at me, already aware of the answer.

"Finally," he said, holding up the fifth finger, his pinky. "Our relationships in the Regional Security System, CARICOM, Interpol, and our law enforcement counterparts in the US, UK, Canada, and Europe. I've been working those relationships hard. I speak their language. And thanks to Gage here, JJ you and I enjoy a certain degree of celebrity I can leverage to our advantage."

He turned to face Gage. "The item you just happened," emphasizing the 'happened' "to get off Ramirez and out of Antigua provided a mother lode of intelligence on cartel finances, banking, shipping routes, payoffs, real estate and business holdings. The works. Even when a few million dollars vanished from one of the accounts," leveling a piercing, suspicious stare at Gage, "The Feds didn't pay it much attention. Too giddy with everything they had and the networks they were able to shut down."

"Quite a legacy," Gage said. "And when you're no longer Commissioner?"

"If it truely is a legacy it'll survive. At least that's the plan. And to some extent it'll depend on who's the next commissioner. I know who my choice would be, but I can't show my hand."

"Deputy Commissioner Huggins?" I said, nodding my agreement. "He'd be the best choice."

"Actually my first and best choice would be you," Mike said, his gaze steady on my face.

I stared back at him. Shocked. And amazed. And caught completely by surprise. The thought had never occurred to me. I'd never imagined myself remaining on the force without Mike there. But as Commissioner of Police.

"You can't be serious," I said. "It'll never happen."

"It'd take some doing," he said, his gaze still leveled at me. "But it can be arranged."

Not a joke. Not pulling my leg. His dark brown eyes conveyed his conviction, and his seriousness.

"The police part I can handle," I said, accepting the preposterous premise. "But Vincentian politics is another matter. Not sure I'd want to be mixed up in that."

And yet, I thought, Commissioner of Police of the Royal St. Vincent and the Grenadines Police Force.

"You'd be better at it than you realize. Anyway it's food for thought," he said, shelving the subject and moving on.

We decided to dine close to home. None of us in the mood for the crowds we'd invariably encounter in the better known establishments around the harbor. Most of them frequented by seasonal visiting 'yachties'. The harbor had grown into a veritable forest of masts.

After settling Eileen at home, she, Gage and I waited at De Reef. I'd missed her, not cognizant of just how much until she'd walked off the ferry. We'd greeted each other like life-long girlfriends.

Another delightful tropical night. A cool breeze blew through De Reef's open sided bar and restaurant, ruffling the coconut branches outside. The surf rumbled onto the beach with a roar, withdrawing with a sigh. The bay bathed in the silvery glow of an almost full moon. The heavy bass rhythms of reggae music poured at low volume from hidden speakers.

"This place is terrific," Eileen said, scanning her surroundings, sipping from a colorful rum and fruit concoction through a straw. "And the food smells great."

"The kitchen here is fantastic," I concurred. "But this isn't where we're eating."

"Really? So where're we going?" her joyful enthusiasm infectious.

"Where the food is just as terrific, but the atmosphere a bit more secluded and quiet. We just have to wait for....and here he is," I said, rising to greet Mike as he approached the stone wall where we sat. I discreetly planted a kiss on his cheek.

"Commissioner," Eileen said, surprised and formal as Mike shook her hand. We hadn't told her there'd be another joining us for dinner, much less the Commissioner of Police.

"Please Doctor," Mike said, a charming smile directed at her. "This is a social occasion, and you've apparently been adopted by my two closest friends, so it's Mike."

"Only if you drop the Doctor," she said. "I'm Eileen. Don't you find it weird how people use 'Doctor' like it's their first name?"

"I always thought it kinda weird too," I said. "But I'm sorta impatient with sanctimonious people who love to stand on ceremony and take themselves too seriously."

"Me too," she said, scrunching her nose as if she'd caught a whiff of something foul.

"Let's continue this over food," I said. "I'm starving."

We departed De Reef and strolled along the moon lit road in the direction of my house. Three turnoffs before mine, at the edge of the village, we exited the road and climbed a stone path into the darkness above. The path bordered by a thick growth of short trees and flowering plants. The night air lightly perfumed. Lilac and jasmine. I led the way holding a flashlight aimed ahead. Gage held another, bringing up the rear.

A house stood in a clearing ahead. Its outdoor lights shaded and muted, creating a cozy intimate atmosphere on the open sided verandah. We entered the small moonlit yard and climbed the steps onto the verandah.

Grace, affectionately called Gracie by family and friends, emerged from the house to greet us. Short, trim, fortyish, we'd been friends since childhood. Her beckoning, impish smile greeted us. Lively brown eyes stared out from a deeply tanned fawn colored face framed by natural rust colored hair. Gracie's family owned and operated De Reef, where you'd find her most days. But she also operated the small, intimate 'Grace's Hideaway' restaurant out of her home.

I hugged her in greeting, a kiss on both cheeks. So did Gage. She turned to Mike and hugged him.

"So sorry about Mistah Taylor," she said in a soft silky voice.

I introduced Eileen. "So appy to meet yuh," she said, shaking Eileen's hand.

"Come. Sit." She motioned us over to a table at the corner of the white porch rail. The spot provided a view of Lower Bay and the congested harbor in the distance. We ordered drinks. Rum and Coke for the guys, white wine for me and Eileen.

I'd called earlier to reserve a table and ask Grace what she'd planned for dinner, considering Eileen's dietary preference. Grace's Hideaway accommodated only four tables, and had no menu. On the four evenings a week she operated the home cooked restaurant Grace usually prepared just one or two different dishes accompanied by an assortment of sides. She'd assured me Eileen wouldn't be a problem. She'd whip up something special.

Jazmine, Gracie's nineteen year old daughter, delivered the drinks to the table. I jumped from my chair, almost spilling the drinks she carried. My greeting a high pitched delighted shriek. We hugged each other in a tight embrace after she'd set the drinks on the table.

Slim and pretty, she possessed her mother's looks, light coloring, long naturally curly hair, and doe-like eyes. Jazmine had been born deaf, and our hands and fingers signed rapidly as we greeted each other.

Gage, who also signed, of course he did, asked Jazmine for a basket of fried plantain chips and bread for the table. He also teased her about boyfriends, which produced a blush and girlish giggle.

"You never cease surprising me," Eileen said, when I sat down. "You know sign language?"

"Get used to it," Mike said chuckling. "I've known her for years and she still manages to surprise me."

"Yeah, she's like that," Gage concurred, smiling at me.

"Gracie and I've been friends forever," I explained to Eileen. "When Jazmine was born and we realized she was deaf, Grace considered sending her to a school for the deaf on St. Vincent. The only one in existence at the time. But it meant being separated from her, so Grace and I both started learning sign language and teaching Jazmine. It wasn't until an American started a school for disabled kids here on Bequia that Jazmine began consistently learning to sign. But I continued learning sign back home, becoming more proficient. During summer and winter breaks from school I'd teach Grace and Jazmine. Then when Jazmine was old enough Grace sent her to school in Barbados where she finished our equivalent of high school and community college."

"She's gorgeous," Eileen said.

"Isn't she? Ordinarily she'd probably have a couple of kids by now, married or not. But Gracie and I've been very protective. And Jazmine's still trying to decide about college."

"And how did you learn to sign?" Eileen asked turning to Gage.

"I found it handy from time to time," he said. Gage also read lips, a fact I'd only recently learned, and Eileen didn't need to know.

"At the risk of being rude by bringing up work," Mike said, addressing Eileen and quickly moving the topic away from Gage, "I want to thank you for your help with these cases, and the work you're doing improving our pathology labs."

"It's why I'm here. How're the cases going anyway?"

"Dead ended and cold as a frozen turkey," I said. "And that's the last we'll speak of work."

Jazmine arrived carrying a bowl of fried plantain chips and a basket of sweet bread and butter.

"I don't know if this is work or not," Eileen said, trying a plantain chip. "Maybe I'm just naïve, but it seems there's a lot more crime here than I'd imagined. I didn't expect to handle so many crime related corpses. You should have requested a forensic pathologist."

"We accept what we can get and make do," Mike said. "People like to believe small tropical islands like these are crime free paradises. It's how we advertise and promote ourselves. But crime and criminal behavior are universal. It's just a matter of degree. And how it's handled. Tourists aren't around long enough to get to know a culture. And they're deliberately insulated from the uglier aspects of a society. You're closer to it than most. You see the bodies."

"The islands are changing," I told her, a wistful note in my voice. Mike and Gage hadn't known St. Vincent and the Grenadines as I had, as a child, before tourism and development emerged as the primary economic drivers, irrevocably altering the islands' way of life.

"We have the double whammy of tourism and development, and crime escalates as well," I said. "Plus these islands happen to be located in the middle of the supply chain for drugs and guns."

"The irony is," Mike said, "for a region which doesn't produce a single firearm, or a single gram of cocaine, we're awash in both. And our justice system is clogged with drug-related crimes and criminals, and increasingly violent gun related crimes."

"But isn't development a positive thing for the islands?" Eileen asked.

"Don't get me started," I said. "I'm more than a little biased when it comes to that topic."

The arrival of food interrupted us. Mike and Eileen had split pea soup. Gage and I each a hot bowl of 'boil-in', a fish soup concoction containing flour dumplings, green bananas, hot pepper, vegetables and anything else lying around the kitchen which needed to be used before it spoiled.

"I grew up on these islands," I said after a few spoonfuls of the delicious spicy hot broth, carefully separating fish bones in my mouth. "They were uncrowded and unspoiled back then. Lots of empty land you'd just wander into, picking fruit to eat on the spot, maybe loading a handful to take home. Living in harmony with the land and sea. I'm a little nostalgic for those days I admit, and I'm not totally against all development. But it's like growing up. You lose a certain happy innocence."

"Depends, don't you think?" Eileen said. "I mean wouldn't someone who grew up poor and deprived think the loss of innocence a fair trade for a better life?"

"Perhaps," I said. "But I wouldn't characterize the lifestyle before development as poor, or deprived. A wholesome quality of life existed, a tradition, an ethos, and a self-sufficiency that's being replaced by dependency. I wouldn't characterize that as a better life. Development has its good and bad aspects. But the rampant short sighted development taking place here isn't the good kind."

"Like what?"

"Like the amount of local land moving into foreign hands. Land has always been a family tradition on Bequia, passed down from generation to generation. Now the land's being bought up by foreign owners at prices locals can't afford, and with lease terms and tax and duty concessions locals can't obtain.

"Not to mention how the land is developed. Exclusive resorts deny access to areas locals have traditionally used. Especially the beaches. The resorts encourage this isolation by creating segregated enclaves, affording little or no interaction between guests and the local population. It fosters hostility against tourists. We have a nasty situation brewing right now between local residents and the resort on Canuoan.

"And besides the social impact there's also the environmental impact. We might protect an environmentally sensitive area, like the Tobago Cays. But for every one area like that, there are others, like the Canuoan and Mayreau marinas which have significant negative environmental impacts. The goal of course, building resorts, marinas, the new airport, is to attract and accommodate more tourists. But no one's taking into account that high-volume tourism is itself a problem. There's a physical threshold, and these islands are being forced to deal with more than their size or infrastructure can handle.

"And whether all that additional tourist revenue is actually benefiting the local population is an open question. Most of the money goes offshore. The local population receives a disproportionately small share of the benefits in low paying tourist related service jobs. It exacerbates a social inequality which didn't exist before. Vincentians are the friendliest most generous people you'll ever meet, but there's a growing resentment percolating just below the surface."

"So tell me how you really feel," Eileen said, smiling.

"I warned you not to get me started."

"Another irony," Mike said, "Is few visitors realize or appreciate the strain they put on the very unspoilt beauty they came to enjoy in the first place. Or they don't care. Most come and leave without a thought beyond their own comfort. And we're left to deal with the consequences. I saw the same thing happen in the Florida Keys. When the popularity of Key West grew, big money moved in and the local population got priced out. More people turned to running drugs and other crime. There'd been a time you could walk the length of Key West along the beach. Before the hotels and condos fenced in their portion of beachfront. Now you can't get to a beach unless you have access through a hotel or condo."

"Development should be about people," I said. "Making their lives better. Improving their standard of living. Unfortunately that's not what I see happening here. And it depresses me."

"What are your impressions so far?" Mike asked Eileen. "You've been here long enough to get over the culture shock, but not long enough to be totally acclimated yet."

"I'm not sure I'm over the culture shock. This is so different from anything I've ever done, or anyplace I've ever been. It's just so gorgeous here. The weather, the towns and villages. The Islands. And the people. They're the most generous, kind, friendly people I've ever met. Which makes the other side of it, the crime and all, that more incomprehensible."

The second course arrived. Fresh red snapper for Mike, curry chicken for Gage. A small helping of jerk chicken for me. Grace had prepared a dish of seasoned broiled breadfruit and rice and peas for Eileen. Side dishes included boiled bananas,sweet plantains, and green salad.

"Hmm," Eileen moaned after a few bites. "Did I mention the food? Amazing. Being vegan was the main thing I worried about before coming here. I did some research on the internet of local foods. But I'd never heard of some of the fruits and vegetables I read about online."

"Speaking of which," I said. "Gage is taking you shopping tomorrow. Mike and I have to attend Jackson Taylor's funeral in Kingstown."

She ceased chewing, glancing quickly between me and Gage.

"No worries," I reassured her, amused by her shy awkwardness. "He's a terrific cook. Better than I am, and I was taught by a Vincentian mother. He can show you everything you need. And we'll have all of Sunday to spend together."

"You know, we can do it another time. There's no need for Gage to disrupt his day just to......"

"No disruption," Gage said. "I have to go to the market anyway. I'm making Sunday dinner for you ladies."

"Which reminds me, what time does the first ferry leave on Monday morning? She asked.

"Don't worry about the ferry," Mike assured her. "You can hitch a ride with me on the Coast Guard cutter Monday morning. Be at the wharf at eight am."

"Wow. That'd be great. Thanks. You know the other thing I love here is the pace," she said. The shy awkward moment behind her she resumed the earlier conversation.

"Everything is slowed down. You guys actually stop working and take time out for lunch. And tea in the afternoon, even though I've never seen anybody actually drinking tea. It takes some getting used to."

"Oh, there're still a few who take their afternoon tea time seriously," Mike said smiling.

In no hurry or need to depart after dinner, apparently we were Grace's only guests for the evening, we spent pleasant hours in Grace's and Jazmine's company. After clearing the table Grace set out cold beers and a chilled bottle of wine. We sat and talked and drank and laughed the night away. Gage, Mike and Grace talked politics and the prospects of DeFretas winning another term in the next elections, which appeared slim. Eileen and Jazmine enjoyed a growing acquaintance while I translated.

Later, in the wee hours of the morning, Gage and I lay entwined in bed. A gentle breeze wafted through the open windows, ruffling the lace curtains and mosquito netting. Lying against him, the heat of his naked body warming mine, inhaling his natural scent, running my fingers through the wispy hairs carpeting his chest, caressing his scars; I wanted him with a deep burning desire. To feel his weight on me. His fullness deep inside me.

It'd have to wait for a more opportune time. My menses not a hindrance for either of us. But I had a guest sleeping over, and I wasn't normally the quiet type. Gage consistently capable of unleashing the primal, uninhibited full throated woman in me.

Instead I whispered quietly next to him, "Exactly how wealthy are you?"

"I always knew you only wanted me for my money," he whispered back.

"I've known you to spontaneously do things that must cost a lot of money. I've seen you use resources and money you're able to tap whenever you want. Doesn't make any difference to me my love. Just curious is all. Where'd all the missing Ramirez millions go?"

"What makes you think I know anything about it?"

"What Mike said earlier. He thinks you had something to do with it and so do I."

"It went to a victim's fund," he said.

I lifted my head from his shoulder to stare at him in the dark. Unable to read the face shadowed by soft moonlight filtering into the room.

"A victim's fund?" I laughed. Convinced he'd been making a joke. The eyes staring back into mine not joking eyes. "You're kidding....right?" I asked anyway.

"A very select completely anonymous victim's fund," he said without further elaboration.

"And you talk about me being full of surprises." I laid my head on his chest. Listened to the soft dull thumping of his heart. "You're the guy Gage," I whispered. An expression he'd heard me use often. One I'm sure he didn't fully understand. But it summed up all the wonderful things he meant to me.

"I love you," I said, closing my eyes, wishing I could skip Saturday altogether and fast forward directly to Sunday.

CHAPTER 15

Sundays are special on Bequia. A day of rest and relaxation. A family day, when aunts, uncles, cousins, siblings, grannies and pappies gather for family meals, attend church, and head to the beaches for the weekly 'sea bath'.

The sun already past its zenith, heading into early afternoon. But its blinding brightness and radiant heat still a potent presence. De Reef alive. Families and Sunday revelers eating, drinking, playing table tennis, cards, dominos, and dancing to thumping soca rhythms.

The beach dominated by children skipping and scampering across the sand. They ran in every direction, and frolicked at the water's edge. Adolescent girls sat docilely in the sand as mothers, aunts, grannies or older female siblings ministered to their hair, pulling out braids, brushing, re-braiding, or fixing a new style for the week. Toddlers romped in a tidal pool created by surf spilling over a low rock formation along the beach.

The expat community also in attendance. A mixture of Americans, Canadians, British, Australians; other nationalities who'd made the Grenadines their home. Some retirees. Others who'd settled and married locals. Couples raising children born on Bequia or St. Vincent. A few single moms. Divorcees who'd found refuge and created new lives. And yacht owners who made a living providing charter services.

A handful of tourists lay sunning on beach towels. The tumultuous happy family mayhem around them provoking curious bewilderment.

Eileen and I lay in a quiet spot set off from De Reef, close to the road. An area occupied by Lower Bay's fishermen. Their home built Bequia fishing boats pulled up on the sand off to our left, shaded by thick manchineel trees festooned in fishing nets hung to dry. A group of fishermen sat in the sand weaving and repairing their nets.

Eileen lay face up to the sun, stretched out on a floral beach towel. A yellow bikini swim suit displayed her admirable petite form, the trim figure, toned arms and legs, flat firm stomach, and round proportional breasts. She wore large sunglasses covering her eyes as the rest of her baked in the sun.

"How was the funeral?" She asked after a long, shared silence. I'd thought she'd fallen asleep.

"Prolonged agony," I said. "I hate funerals. Almost as much as I hate weddings. At least a wedding has a reception afterwards which is pretty much a party. They held the service at the Anglican Cathedral. The Archbishop of St. Vincent and the Grenadines officiated. The Prime Minister gave the eulogy. Pretty big funeral. Taylor had lots of friends in and out of government. And there were dignitaries from CARICOM countries. He'd had an accomplished life. He was buried in the Anglican cemetery next to the cathedral. Then Mike and I had to make the obligatory rounds in our official capacity. Couldn't wait for it to end."

"I can understand funerals, but you really hate weddings?"

"I keep getting wedding invitations from back home. Girlfriends from high school, or college, and graduate school. I'm glad I'm down here so I have an excuse for not attending."

"Why?"

"Dunno. Guess I'm still rebelling against conventional notions of womanhood. The whole wifey mother role still a raw nerve. Should've outgrown it by now, since I really don't care anymore. But took me a while to get over it."

"I know what you mean. Back home it seems all the girls I knew growing up are getting married and having babies. It's the normal thing to do. I didn't question it until I'd been away at school. And the weird thing is, even being away, having a career, I still felt like I was heading down the same road. Like it was inevitable, you know? Having my mother's voice inside my head saying now I'd gotten my education, started my career, it was time to settle down, think about a family. It's what they all expected. Coming here was one way of getting off that merry go round. Anyway, what'd you mean by getting over it?"

"Other people's expectations. Especially because of how I look."

"You mean because you're drop dead gorgeous."

"See. The way even you said it is loaded with preconceived ideas. I've been getting that shit all my life."

"I guess so. Maybe. I just mean, I remember what it was like in high school. Trying to fit in. And I wasn't one of the pretty girls."

"Are you kidding? Have you looked in a mirror? You're gorgeous my friend. And that figure of yours is to die for."

"But I never thought so. I was sorta geeky in high school and college. Anyway I'm not your kind of gorgeous."

"I had my share of teenage anxieties in high school. Believe me. Which adolescent doesn't? I had problems fitting in too. Only my problem was different."

"How?"

"I'd always been sought after by the popular kids, the in crowd, and of course the guys. Especially the jocks. But I gradually figured out they weren't really interested in me. They wanted me in their clique, or club, or as their friend because hanging out with me made them seem cool. And ever since I can remember I'd always heard, 'oh you're so adorable'; 'oh you're so pretty'; 'you should be in commercials'; your mom should take you to an agency'; 'you should be a model'. I grew up thinking that crap was normal, you know? Until I realized all these expectations other people had of me was only because of how I looked, and sometimes based on selfish ulterior motives, like in high school. It had nothing to do with who I was as a person or what I wanted. Let's just say I developed trust issues. And it cured me of ever wanting to be a joiner."

Eileen laughed. A soft cooing sound like a night owl. "It's hard enough trying to figure out guys without adding that into the mix," she said.

"Tell me about it. And it didn't end in high school. The same crap at University, Grad school, at work. I couldn't escape the notion that a woman's looks is both a weapon and her only real currency. Guys thinking they had an open invitation to hit on me. And I got so infuriated when men, and some women too by the way, assumed anything I achieved happened only because I look the way the I do, or because I'm black, or that I must have slept with someone to get ahead. Mon Crisse I really hate that."

"So how'd you manage to get over it?"

"Get over what?" I asked, forgetting how the conversation had started.

"You know? The thing about your looks?"

"I decided it wasn't my problem. But theirs. That the power rested with me, to be whoever and whatever I wanted, and damn whatever other people thought or expected."

"Hard thing to do. How'd you manage it?"

"My family, I guess. I sorta have the same willfulness as my mother. When she makes up her mind to do something, she just goes right ahead and does it. Regardless of what anyone might think, or say. My dad is more conventional, but he has this adventurous spirit. It gets the better of him sometimes," I said, chuckling at the hilarious predicaments he'd landed himself and his family in over the years. But they'd been adventures we'd shared as a family, like the Swiss Family Robinson. And I wouldn't have missed them for the world. And if it hadn't been for that spirit, taking off on a whim to come to St. Vincent and Grenadines, and falling in love with a local girl, I wouldn't be here today.

"Anyway I learned from them how to be comfortable with myself and my choices. And growing up with two brothers," those memories also provoking a chuckle. "Mon Dieu. Around them I learned to be fearless. I was kind of a tom boy growing up. Seems like I've always wanted to do the kinds of things men do."

"How come you speak, or at least curse French?"

"Grew up in Montreal. My dad's French Canadian, from Dutch ancestry."

"And your mom?"

"Vincentian. They met when my dad was here on a training project funded by the Canadian Government. Sorta like you."

"I was scared shitless about coming here," she confessed. "Especially as the time to actually leave got closer. It sounded great and all in the abstract, but I kept asking myself if I was doing the right thing. If it was really what I wanted to do, or if I was just being restless and silly. Now I'm here I can't imagine what I'd been so afraid of."

She rolled onto her stomach, exposing her back to the sun. We'd applied sunscreen before leaving the house. I noted the brown freckles dotting her shoulders.

"Anyone serious, before Gage?" she asked.

"One. I was really in love with him too. Always thought he was the one, you know."

"So what happened?"

The question normal, innocuous even, eliciting a smile as it occurred to me how easy it'd been for her to ask. And my corresponding comfort level in responding. My natural ease around her, relating my story. Revealing innermost thoughts I'd be reluctant to share with anyone else after so short an acquaintance.

"Our paths just diverged. We were sweethearts since freshman year at University in Montreal. I went to the States for grad school and he went to the University of Ottawa to study business. We kept up the relationship. Distance wasn't our problem. He wanted a conventional life, a corporate career, the wife and kids. And I'd just come to terms with the realization I didn't. I didn't want a conventional lifestyle. I wanted to do special things, to wake up to constant surprises."

"So you became a cop," she said in a casual deadpan voice.

I erupted in full-throated laughter. When I tried to speak, her succinct dry take on the arcane turn my life had taken produced another wave of convulsive hilarity. Tears welled in my eyes.

"Oh girl...." I tried between spasms; "you....have....no idea."

"I didn't mean anything........"

"No. No. Of course you didn't. It's just......." The words smothered by another bout of laughter.

My laughter subsided in small gasping exhalations. "Oh, you're funny, I swear," I said sitting up, gazing across the beach.

The scene hadn't changed much. Different swimmers in the water. Two bikini clad blond tourists sunning on a square floating platform moored off the beach. Half a football field distance beyond the float Wherever nodded on her mooring. The tide had turned, coming in, and had swung Wherever's head seaward. Her davit equipped stern and bold transom lettering now faced us.

"What's it like being a cop on the islands?" Eileen asked. "I guess you wouldn't be doing it if didn't matter to you."

"It's fulfilling and satisfying work. At least for me it is. And it surprised me how much I was able to use my psychology background. Wasn't always like that though. Don't know what the hell I was thinking when I first joined. Seemed like the right thing at the time," I said as a painful memory, deeply buried and suppressed, threatened to percolate into my consciousness.

"I realized later it'd been an impulsive and naïve decision. Found myself trapped inside a patriarchal misogynistic boys club unable to accomplish what I'd set out to do by joining up. Until Mike came along it looked like the biggest mistake of my life. Mike had been appointed to turn the police into a modern professional force. And his arrival was the turning point for me too. He provided the opportunity to do meaningful work, and accomplish what I'd initially set out to do.

"Which was that?"

Her question stirred the memory. Although I'd long since come to terms with it, I hadn't reached a point where I wanted to talk about it.

"Demolishing the old boy's club. Tossing the rotten apples off the force, or better yet in jail. Creating a sense of community service in its place. How the hell I ever thought I'd manage that on my own is still a mystery. As I said, impulsive and naïve. But soon after getting here Mike realized he and I were on the same wavelength, had the same goals, and we developed an effective partnership. Of course everyone assumed we had to be sleeping together since he put me in charge of special projects, and gave me more responsibility and authority through promotions.

"Must've been tough earning respect with all that."

"Didn't bother me. Like I said I'd learned how to handle that nonsense. The respect was slow in coming. But once people appreciated how I led, and understood I wouldn't tolerate their bullshit it got better. A few years later Gage showed up. Before I knew it, and despite everything I did to resist it, I fell in love with him."

"Where is he by the way? She asked. "I was sure he'd meet us on the beach at some point."

"He's around someplace. Maybe behind De Reef fixing rum coconuts. Or across the street watching the cricket game. Maybe playing in it. How'd it go yesterday by the way?"

She rolled over, sat up to face me, her eyes hidden behind the big sunglasses.

"Terrific," she said in a gush of enthusiasm. "Shopping at the market was amazing. The fruit and vegetable stalls. I couldn't believe the variety. Gage showed me the vegetables and roots to look for at the market in Kingstown, how to pick them, pronounce the names. Those I'll have to practice. And the whole bargaining thing. So much fun. He got stuff for the house and Wherever. After we dropped everything off he took me on a tour of Bequia. Over to Industry, up to Mount Pleasant and down to Hope beach. We had lunch in Friendship Bay and he showed me Mike's house. Then we rode over to Paget Farm. And everyone we met were so great. At first I thought it'd be kinda awkward, you know? I mean, I didn't want him to feel he had to entertain me, or babysit me. But we had such a fantastic time. He's so easy and comfortable to be around."

I smiled at her excitable, happy recollection. I'd had no doubt she'd be able to relax, be herself, and enjoy Gage's company.

"He's got this aura about him." She said. "Something you can't quite put your finger on, you know? Well of course you know," grinning at me. "Not sure what it is exactly. Like danger. Not the 'bad boy' kind of danger. He just makes you feel comfortable and safe when you're around him."

"Very perceptive," I said, careful to keep the conversation from veering off in an unwanted direction. Conversation, even sharing private thoughts, came easily with her. But some topics remained off limits. Gage specifically.

"He has a way with people like that," I said. "Actually he may already be back at the house. He did say he was making dinner tonight."

"And he cooks too. Is there anything he doesn't do?"

"I'll let you know if I ever find out what it is," I said, chuckling. "Anyway you're in for a treat. You ready for a swim?"

"Sure."

We waded into the cool surf; a soothing balm to the sun's scorching heat. The sandy bottom fell off steeply beneath us a few yards from the beach. I dove beneath a curling incoming swell. It broke above me, its powerful undertow tugging me farther from shore.

I surfaced next to Eileen. Her hair a dark silk carpet floating behind her. Together we stroked for the moored platform. Alongside, we held onto it as it bobbed like a cork in the water. The blonds still sunning on its surface.

"How about a cold beer?" I asked, spilling salty sea water from my mouth.

"Sounds like a plan."

Slow steady strokes carried us to the swim ladder hanging from Wherever's transom. We climbed over her aft rail onto the deck, depositing puddles of sea water at our feet. I motioned Eileen to wait while I climbed into the cockpit, opened a watertight compartment housing the VHF and internal intercom. On the intercom dial pad a tiny red LEDblinked. Gage had armed the alarm. I lifted the intercom handset from its cradle and punched in the disarm code on the keypad. The LED winked out and remained off.

I thumbed in a second combination on the keypad. Heard the locking bolts on the main hatch disengage. Gage had installed the remote controlled lock after an intruder had disabled an external keypad lock attached to the hatch. The intruder hadn't been aware of the alarm, which had alerted Gage and probably saved his life.

I pushed back the sliding top of the hatch, opened the hatch doors, and climbed down the companionway into the cabin.

I returned carrying two towels and two cold Heinekens. I popped the caps using a bottle opener hanging by a lanyard on the binnacle. Handed one to Eileen. We settled in the shaded cockpit under the awning, gazing out at the beach.

"You know the stuff we were talking about the other night at dinner? she said, halfway through her beer. "The crime and all. And the changes. It really is a shame, in a place so idyllic."

"You know, when I was laughing back there on the beach about being a cop. You know what's even more absurd? The fact I carry a weapon for work. Like cops in the States. That was inconceivable just a few years ago."

"Well, I have to say I admire you. And I thought I was adventurous."

"I admire you. Believe me. Picking up and coming here the way you did. Defying convention. That takes guts. And what you're doing here is important. It'll make a difference."

"What happens now with your two cases?"

"A coroner's inquest has been scheduled for Jackson Taylor. We'll present our findings, including your pathology report, to a magistrate. A judicial determination will be made about manner and cause of death, and whether there are grounds for presenting a case to the Director of Public Prosecutions. That's how the process works here. Right now the evidence points to death by suicide, even if no one believes it. But absent evidence to the contrary, that's how the magistrate will rule."

"And Mansfield?"

"His inquest hasn't been scheduled yet, pending confirmation of the identification, and your final report. For some reason we're getting the runaround from the U.S. embassy on Barbados. The evidence points to death as a result of a vehicular accident. But something's hinky about that case too. Gage smells something rotten too, and he's got a pretty good nose for stuff like this.

"Gage? Really?

"Yeah. He had some investigative experience in the foreign service," I lied. "Have you heard back from your friend yet on Mansfield's x-rays?" switching the focus from Gage.

"Not yet. I plan to call him when I get back tomorrow. And I'll check on the progress of the lab. The test results should be ready by now."

"Well there isn't anything new in either case to change the determination regarding manner and cause of death. At this point I need some sort of breakthrough. Something to shed new light on both cases. Just have to keep shaking the trees. But there's no way to know when, or even if, anything might fall off."

"So what do you do?"

"Move on to the next case. Unfortunately crime doesn't stop."

The break in the Mansfield case blindsided me the next day.

CHAPTER 16

Monday dawned amid drenching rain showers. By midday the sky cleared. The sun blazed in a bright blue sky smeared by wisps of high altitude clouds. I sat at an outdoor table at the Frangipani, close to the seawall. The surf a scant few paces behind me.

I'd just finished half of a tuna salad sandwich, sipping an ice cold glass of bitter lemon, aware of a figure hovering by my table.

Medium height, maybe five foot ten, a hundred and fifty pounds, solidly built. His lips parted in an amused half smile, exposing a perfect line of ivory teeth. His hair close-cropped, military style. But most startling, his eyes, grey-green, like ripe avocados. At odds with his olive brown complexion. And direct, like Gage's, accustomed to measuring everyone and everything.

They held me enthralled, and I finally appreciated the startled reaction people had to meeting me for the first time. The hazel coloring of my eyes a normal feature I seldom gave conscious thought. And not uncommon around the Caribbean. But to most Americans astonishing in someone of my complexion.

"Wow," he said. His eyes widening. His head jerked backward in a double take as if a fly had landed on the tip of his nose.

"Articulate," I said. My gaze steady on his remarkable eyes. "Can I help you?"

Instead of answering he pulled a chair and sat opposite me at the table, the bemused grin on his face unchanged.

"I thought he was just pulling my leg, but he wasn't kidding," his smile grew even wider. His voice a soft baritone. His accent American, without any discernable regional inflection.

"I have no idea what you're talking about and I didn't invite you to sit."

"But you would have," he said, his smile transforming into a self-assured grin.

Merde. One of those. I thought. I decided to leave rather than get into a thing with an obvious jerk.

"Well, you have yourself a good day. If you'll excuse me," I said, preparing to stand and leave the table.

"Superintendent," he said, freezing me in mid motion. "I'm actually here to see you."

I settled back into the wood armchair. On the verge of asking him his business when my cell phone rang.

"Ahh, that's probably it now," he said.

What the hell is he talking about? Mike's number on the display.

"Excuse me, I have to take this," I said, grateful for the interruption.

"Yes Chief."

"Now I know why Barbados was giving me the runaround," his voice raised and agitated. "Just got a call from the FBI liaison at the embassy. Some damned special agent is on the way here. They've made a request for him to meet you to discuss the Mansfield case. Dammed FBI is involved."

While Mike spoke my gaze rested on the stranger's face. He smiled and nodded. The entire episode a big amusement to him.

"Actually Chief I think he's already here."

"What?" The barked word made me jerk the phone from my ear. "Give him the goddamn phone." We both heard the shouted command. I handed the stranger my phone.

He put it to his ear, before moving it away to protect his eardrum. I couldn't hear every word Mike said, but as his voice rose and fell in volume a few came through loud and clear. Including, "Who the damn FBI think they are;" "Proper protocol to check in;" "No damn jurisdiction;" "Your ass in her majesty's jail so fast...."

The stranger's bemused expression remained unchanged. He listened and nodded and responded politely with "yes sirs," "no sirs," and "I understand sirs," at appropriate places. He returned the phone at the end of Mike's tirade. Despite myself I smiled.

"Damn FBI," I heard as I put the phone to my ear.

"I'm back Chief."

"Sorry you got blindsided like that JJ. Listen, you're gonna have to handle this guy. Cooperate as best you can, but don't take any crap from him. I'm gonna give you know who a heads up after I hang up with you. Then let me know what the hell's going on."

"Will do Chief." And he clicked off.

"So, that went well," the stranger said.

I stuck my hand across the table. "Superintendent Johanssen," I said. "And you are?"

"FBI Special Agent Forde," he said, shaking my hand in a firm grip.

"Well we're way beyond protocol already, but why don't you indulge me with your credentials anyway."

He flashed his incandescent smile and extracted a bifold ID case from the side pocket of his slacks. He opened it and placed it on the table. I lifted it and examined the picture ID matching the face opposite me, and the small gold badge shaped like a shield bearing the carved eagle and U.S. Department of Justice seal.

"Well FBI Special Agent Owen Forde, why'd you break protocol and not check in with the senior police authority before coming here to see me?"

"Too much waiting around. It's been a long trip getting here, and I'm already way behind on this case as it is. I just wanted to get where I needed to be, see who I needed to see. And truth is I'm not real big on protocol."

I allowed the remark to sink in. It informed me he might be an unconventional talent. Or an arrogant pain in the ass.

"Would you care for half a tuna salad sandwich?" I offered, pushing my plate toward him. "I'm finished. And maybe something to drink?"

"Sounds good. Came straight from New York. Haven't given much thought to food until now. What's that you're drinking?" he asked, hefting the half sandwich and biting into it.

"Bitter lemon." I said.

"Sounds good."

I motioned to the bartender for two more bitter lemons.

"Wow. This is good," he said, chewing and examining the sandwich.

"Fresh tuna," I said. "Caught this morning."

The bitter lemons arrived. I allowed him time to savor the sandwich and swallow a few gulps of his drink in silence before speaking again.

"Sure you won't have something else? The way you snorted that down you must be really hungry."

"It'll do for now," he said, wiping his mouth on a paper napkin.

"What'd you mean before about some guy pulling your leg?" I asked.

The smile again. "I stopped by the station first. Desk sergeant said you were here having lunch. So I said I'd try to catch you here and asked him who to look for. He gets a big grin on his face and says: 'look fa de pretiess womahn in de place'," Forde said in a close imitation of Lucenti.

I smiled. "Pretty good imitation," I said.

"He wasn't kidding," he repeated.

"So FBI Special Agent Owen Forde. What exactly can I do for you?"

"Well first you can drop the Special Agent formality. It's Owen," flashing the smile. The combined effect of his mesmerizing eyes and enchanting smile capable of charming the white off rice.

"I hoped you'd show me where Mansfield was staying and where he met his demise."

"I'm afraid you're a little late. There's nothing left of the accident scene and I very much doubt the resort will allow you into the cottage. It's probably been rented out to other guests."

"Then that just leaves you and your case file."

My turn to pour on the charm. I matched his smile.

"That depends Special Agent Owen. How about a little quid pro quo? For example, why was the embassy stonewalling us and what is the FBI's interest in this case?"

His smile remained fixed in place, but a subtle shift occurred in his piercing green eyes. A growing awareness he'd be dealing with more than a pretty face. His direct stare, and faint furrows across his brow, conveyed a decision in the making. Scenarios posed and discarded, game plan adjusted, thoughts processed; questions resolved.

"First off the Embassy wasn't stonewalling you," a more serious tone in his voice. "They genuinely didn't know anything. They weren't able to find any information on your corpse using their normal channels. Wow, this is nice," he broke off, examining the bitter lemon bottle. "I can tell eating and drinking is going to be a pleasurable experience around here. Among other things," the compelling avocado eyes leveled at me.

Crisse! I thought.

"Anyway they asked the FBI liaison for help. He sent the particulars and description to DC. That immediately set off alarm bells."

"Alarms?"

Now I clearly noticed the conflict behind his eyes. But he'd already made the decision to disclose his information.

"Charles Mansfield is an alias. His real name is Arnold Greene, and he was about to be indicted by the Justice Department on federal charges of money laundering, fraud, and a bunch of other SEC irregularities."

He'd detonated a bomb. And he knew it. The smile returned. Not the charm the pants off you smile of before, but a 'how's them apples' kind of smirk.

"Your turn," he said, his eyes locked on mine.

Still shell shocked I held my tongue. At a complete loss for words. And wary of saying the wrong thing. He waited, anticipating a reciprocal exchange of information. I had to disappoint him.

"We'll have to pick this up later," I said.

A sudden change in demeanor, like a chameleon changing color. The cheerful, easy-going charm replaced by a hard-edged, surly determination.

So he could be that too, I thought. Good to know.

"What happened to quid pro quo?" he snapped.

"What you've just told me puts an entirely new light on my report," I said. "I have to rethink some things and get back to you." A stall, but not altogether untrue. I needed to talk to Mike. And to Gage.

"Where are you staying?" I asked.

"Here, I believe. But I haven't checked in yet. I went straight to the station from the airport looking for you. I left my bag there."

"Then Owen," I said, deliberately using his first name, cranking up the charm. "Why don't you get settled and let's meet for dinner this evening. Say seven o'clock?" I'd made a snap decision, which produced an unsettling discomfort, like I'd overlooked something important. But also convinced I'd called the correct play.

It mollified him, if not by much. The smile returned, lacking the casual charm of before.

"It's a date," he said, a new wariness in the guacamole eyes.

I walked him back to the police station. Remained in his company while he retrieved his travel bag, and watched as he retraced his steps through the harbor to the Frangipani.

In my office I called Mike and Gage. Informed them of Special Agent Forde's bombshell regarding Mansfield. And my dinner appointment later in the evening. I spent the remainder of the day secluded in my office, attempting to place the new information in perspective. Fit it into what I already knew.

From the office I headed directly to De Reef. The expansive open sided room empty except for three men sitting at the bar drinking beers. They lived in Lower Bay and I recognized them. Gage had said he'd meet me at the bar. I didn't see him. I stood at the end of the bar, close to the concrete walkway leading onto the beach. I gazed out at Wherever bobbing on her mooring. Wondered if Gage might still be aboard. But noticed the dinghy pulled up onto the beach.

"You weren't followed," a soft voice said behind me.

As accustomed as I'd grown to his stealthy silence; his startling ability to materialize out of nowhere; my heart still froze. My stomach leapt to my throat, and my breath caught in mid inhalation before recognition sank in.

"Merde," I hissed. "I wish you wouldn't do that." When I'd regained control of my breathing I said in a peevish voice, "I know I wasn't followed. I checked."

"Let's go," he said.

Aboard Wherever I recovered my equanimity. I kissed him on the lips. We sat at the dinette while he auto dialed the satellite access code and Mike's cell number. He set the cell phone on the table between us.

Mike's voice answered on the third ring. "Here's what we got," he said in a business-like manner without preamble. "Our boy's got quite a resume. Been with the Bureau six years. Ex-marine, like his father, a career officer who spent most of his time in Europe attached to NATO forces. Married a Belgian."

"That explains it," I whispered.

"What's that?"

"Nothing Chief. Continue."

"Got a law degree while in the marines, specializing in international law. Spent some time with JAG, and also force recon in the Gulf in ninety one, and a tour in Iraq in oh three. A major when he joined the Bureau. Stayed in the marines as a reservist. Word is he's a force to be reckoned with. And the dad's politically connected. My guy says he's a bit of a maverick. Likes to color outside the lines. Impatient with bureaucracy. But he's broke some major cases in the short time he's been with the Bureau. And he's been moved around more than most agents, like he's being groomed for higher office in the Justice Department. He's currently with the white collar unit working out of the New York Field Office. My contact didn't know anything about Mansfield aka Greene. Hadn't heard about an investigation, much less a pending indictment. Apparently the whole thing is very hush-hush, highly compartmentalized."

"I have someone checking into it," Gage said. "Should have something by tonight or tomorrow. Should have more on Forde too."

"Good. Don't mind telling you this is giving me a migraine. I don't like the turn it's taking. And on top of Jackson's death. Couldn't come at a worse time."

"Speaking of which," Gage interjected. "My guy picked up the laptop. We'll have something in the next day or so."

"Thanks Gage," Mike said. "The case has everyone's knickers in a twist. I've been talking to everyone in Jackson's close circle. Had a long talk with Marlene, his wife. Still coming up empty. You have a chance to go over the material I sent you JJ?"

"A little Chief. Nothing popped out at first glance."

"Same here. And I've been pouring over it all week. Okay, lemme know if you come up with anything. Now, this meeting with Special Agent Forde?"

"Yeah."

"You sure about this dinner?"

"Call it instinct. Or intuition. I just think I'll be able to get him talking more in that kind of setting."

"How you want to play it?"

"Straight. I promised him a quid pro quo. Give him what we've got. God knows it's not much. And his information may help to make sense of the whole thing."

"Okay. I trust your instincts JJ. Lemme know how that goes too. Anything else?"

"Can't think of anything else right now," I said.

"Talk with you later then," he said, and disconnected the call.

The conversation had set my mind churning. Until Forde's appearance I'd considered Mansfield's - still not used to the idea of Greene - death an accident accompanied by nagging, frustrating questions. Since Forde's bombshell my thoughts had turned almost exclusively to the possibility he'd killed himself, or been deliberately killed. But I still couldn't rule out a heart attack.

"You get anything off those immigration photos I gave you?" I asked Gage. "Your guy from PSV in there?"

"No. But it's possible he didn't clear immigration and customs through any airport. Might've been arranged privately."

"What make you think that?"

"He has a cabin cruiser. Probably chartered. He probably entered by sea."

"How do you know that?"

"Saw it anchored in the cove down from his cottage. Did a quick recon of the cottage too."

"Christ Gage. When did you manage to do all that?"

"Sunday before we left PSV. I swam around the point to the beach down from his cottage. He was there so I didn't get inside. Got a good look around though. And at the cabin cruiser."

"Now that you mention it I remember seeing a cabin cruiser both times I drove across the island. How do you know it's his?" Aware the moment the words left my mouth it'd been a silly question.

"It's his," he said.

"Who do you think this guy is?"

"Don't know. But I know what he is."

"What does that mean?"

"Some kind of operative," he said, his eyes leveled at me. "Maybe a spook. Maybe something else. Moves like a Springbok."

"What the hell's a Springbok?"

"South African. Trained in the military or intelligence services. Maybe both. Probably a free-lancer for hire."

"You can tell all that from just looking at him?"

"He has certain tells, acquired by how he was trained, where, and by whom. They're like accents. They're distinctive. Like Wellington, the PSV security guy. Ex SAS. Most people aren't even aware they have them."

I searched his eyes, questioning. Not concerning the accuracy of his statement. Rather I contemplated the kind of world he used to inhabit. The where and the how enabling him to recognize people in such a fashion. Predators. Like himself. Like he used to be. The words he'd spoken in Villa sprang into my thoughts, 'it takes one to know one'.

"What would they call you?" I asked.

"I got rid of any tells."

"How?" Anticipating an evasion or no response at all.

Instead, to my surprise, "By mimicking other people's tells. Took me a while to master it. But eventually I could make a kill look like whoever I wanted it to. The Russians, Chinese, Israelis, CIA, anybody really."

"Jesus Gage."

"Yeah," a somber, almost penitent resignation in his voice.

"You think this guy has something to do with Mansfield, ah, Greene?"

"Dunno. He may just be on vacation in a private secluded place. Just coming off a job maybe. The way he's set up is classic tradecraft. But his interest in you, and Eileen. Maybe he's just being careful. Nothing more than keeping tabs on the environment maybe. Still, there've been a couple of mysterious deaths and he's in the vicinity. I don't believe in coincidence."

"You've said. What do we do about it?" I asked.

"Watch the watcher," he said, observing me closely as I activated my cell phone and dialed a number. His phrasing had stirred an elusive memory.

"This is Superintendent of Police Johanssen. Connect me to the morgue please."

"Eileen. Glad I caught you. Listen, did you find any discrepancies in Mansfield's time of death. Anything that didn't jibe with the time on the broken wristwatch?"

"Actually yes," she said. "I was just about to call you too. Lab results finally came in, indicating a massive coronary. That was the cause of death. And it occurred prior to the accident. The enzyme studies indicate at least a half hour before."

"Crisse. Eileen you sure?"

"If the lab didn't screw up, which from reading the report I don't believe they did, I'm positive."

"So he couldn't have been driving the Jeep?"

"No. And take a look through the photographs again. I just went through them and saw no evidence of arterial spray anywhere on the Jeep. His blood pooled from the lacerated flesh postmortem."

"That's great work Eileen. Thanks"

"One more thing," she said. "I spoke with my forensic anthropology advisor. He'd seen those types of phalangeal injuries before. He said they're associated with forceful pulling, twisting, or wrenching of the fingers. They're not crushing or blunt force injuries.

"Oh my God. He's sure about that?"

"Positive. The injuries are distinctive."

"Thanks again Eileen."

"Glad I can help. How's it going?"

"Remember I told you how sometimes you need a freak breakthrough in a case?"

"Yeah."

"I think you just broke this case wide open." I said.

After hanging up I turned to find Gage staring at me. A Cheshire cat grin on his face. The predatory expression gone from his eyes.

"What?"

"You're an excellent detective, you know that?"

I smiled at him in turn. Reached over to kiss him on the mouth.

"Well what I first considered an accident, then a suicide, is now most definitely murder."

The grin slipped from his face.

"What did Eileen tell you?"

I related Eileen's side of the conversation.

"He was questioned before he died," he said, a statement more than a question.

"The injuries to his fingers," I said.

"Yeah."

"I'm thinking that too. And that trauma probably caused the heart attack," I said.

"This is a whole new ballgame now love. You need to be careful."

"What're you going to do?" I asked, recognizing the predatory glare returning to his eyes. And aware that in protecting Mike and me he wouldn't hesitate to kill.

"I'm gonna watch your back," he said, his smile sly, lacking humor.

"I gotta get going," I said, glancing at my watch. "I need to get ready for my meeting with Agent Forde."

"Okay. Hang here a bit." He headed up the companionway and out the hatch. After a few minutes he called down.

"Let's go."

He held a powerful Leupold spotter's scope to his right eye, scanning the beach and surroundings when I climbed through the hatch. I climbed down into the waiting dinghy. On the beach we parted after a short kiss.

"Time to be extra careful," he said, his face inches from mine, his eyes staring into mine.

I nodded.

CHAPTER 17

Forde waited at the Frangipani's outdoor bar. He occupied a barstool at the far end, his gaze directed toward Port Elizabeth. Perhaps expecting me to approach from the harbor. I'd entered from the Belmont side, at the opposite end of the bar from where he sat. It provided me a few moments to observe him before making my presence known.

He'd dressed in casual tan slacks and a powder blue short sleeved dress shirt, unbuttoned halfway down his chest. And the same brown leather loafers he'd worn earlier, this time minus the socks.

Turning toward the bar he noticed me. His frank admiring gaze flowed over me, rising from my sandal clad feet to my forehead. A subtle but none-the-less full undressing.

I'd dressed deliberately for the occasion. Neither too flirty or festive, nor too businesslike or staid. I wore black light weight denim slacks, a purple chiffon off the shoulder blouse cinched at the waist and flared over the hips. A hint of eye shadow my only makeup. My jewelry a small heart-shaped piece of scrimshaw on a thin black velvet chocker, and gold hoop earrings.

He rose from the barstool to greet me, his smile welcoming, his eyes inviting.

No thanks, I thought, returning his smile.

"What can I get you to drink?" He asked, motioning to the bartender.

"Evening Suprintendent," the barkeep said, ambling over to our end of the bar.

"Evening Ron. A bitter lemon with a twist please."

He eyed me. His gaze shifted to Forde.

"Not drinking?" Forde said when Ron moved out of earshot. "Don't tell me you're on duty."

"As a matter of fact I am. Aren't you?"

"Trying not to be," he said. The smile dazzling and mischievous. The face freshly shaved. The two day stubble I'd noticed earlier on his defined jaw and narrow chin now gone.

We carried our drinks to a table on the covered outdoor patio, out of earshot of other diners. Mostly guests at the hotel. I'd chosen a time before the yachite rush later in the evening.The rhythmic splash and sigh of surf rolling across the beach provided a soothing background sound. And a cool evening breeze ruffled the palms and frangipani bushes lining the walkway. The subtle fragrance of frangipani flowers perfumed the air.

Lights from anchored yachts crowding the harbor twinkled in the dark like swarming fireflies. In the distance, the lights of a recently arrived floating resort shone like a small city.

"I'd ask what a girl like you etcetera etcetera," Forde said, "But that'd be a bit too cliché for me. And my guess is it'd be for you too."

"That'd be a good guess. And it'd also be disappointing."

"And if I said you look absolutely stunning."

"Better. But I'd say you were probably tired and hungry and in need of something to eat."

"Witty as well," he said, the smile a permanent fixture on his face.

"You don't want to find out," I said.

"Then tell me what's good to eat around here."

"Everything. What do you feel like?" Aware I'd stepped into a potential verbal trap as the words crossed my lips.

His smile widened, but he gallantly didn't take the shot. Maybe it would've been too cliché.

He ordered the fish special which included soup, dessert and coffee. He asked them to forgo the soup. I ordered a small conch platter and a salad.

"Quite a shocker you dropped on me earlier," I said, steering the conversation to the purpose of our dinner.

"Sorry. Shouldn't have sprung it on you like that."

"No you're not. You were looking for a reaction. Mine told you exactly what you needed to know about what I know."

"Not bad for a small island detective."

"So what else can you tell me about Mr. Mansfield... ah... Greene?"

"Actually, I believe it's your turn Superintendent. Nice try though."

"Okay. What we have is an American tourist staying at a private resort who pretty much kept to himself. Three days after he arrives he obtains a vehicle from a local Union Island resident and goes for a drive at night, on a deserted mountain road. The next morning the vehicle is found halfway down a ravine. His body is found in it. He had no wallet, no ID, passport, return airline tickets, or any other identifying documents on his person, or anywhere in his cottage. That's about it."

"That's it?" Irritation and disappointment in his tone. The smile disappeared and the hardness I'd observed earlier returned to the eyes scrutinizing me.

"You have a laptop?" I asked him.

"Yeah. Brought one with me."

I retrieved a thumb drive from my pocket. It contained an edited version of the case file. But not the final autopsy report from Eileen. Or the notes regarding our conversation. In truth I hadn't yet updated my own case file, except in my head.

"This is the case file," I said, passing it across the table to him.

He studied the small thumb drive sitting on the table, as though it presented some unseen danger. After a few moments he picked it up, held it between his thumb and forefinger, studied it some more. His gaze left the drive, his eyes refocused on me. In them I read doubt, mistrust, and maybe a small measure of acceptance.

"It's all there," I said. "Case notes, autopsy report, photographs."

The smile returned. His forefinger idly tapped the drive.

"Why do I still get the feeling you're holding out on me?"

"You're FBI," I said. "Occupational hazard I guess. I'm not holding anything back," I lied. "But after what you told me today I'm beginning to think this might be a suicide by vehicle. It'd explain a number of anomalies."

He emitted a soft chuckling sound.

"What?"

"Interesting word choice. Anomalies." Forde's remark recalled my conversation with Gage regarding tells.

"Your turn," I said, as an ambrosial aroma enveloped our table. Our food arrived, halting further conversation. We arranged the various dishes around us before settling down to eat. The first forkful of curry smothered conch created a taste bud bacchanalia in my mouth. Forde's facial expressions reflected his own palatine pleasure. We ate slowly, savoring each mouthful.

"You mentioned suicide," he said, "How real a possibility is that? In your expert opinion as a psychologist I mean." He leveled an inquiring gaze at me. His piercing eyes interrogative. A small smirk-like curl at the corner of his mouth as he observed whatever micro expression had betrayed my reaction.

No surprise he'd checked up on me. Instead my reaction had been to his deliberately informing me he knew more about me than I thought he did. An interrogator's trick to keep me guessing and off balance when responding to his questions. Wondering how much he actually knew. Perhaps enough to catch me in a lie. I often used the technique myself against suspects.

I smiled. So he wanted to play. "You did your homework," I said after swallowing and washing down another mouthful.

"After this afternoon I figured it was a good idea."

"I'm flattered. Didn't think I'd have that effect on a force recon marine lawyer turned FBI agent." He hid his reaction well. But not before I'd noticed the micro-second twitch around the eyes.

"Touché," he smiled.

I returned the smile. On even ground again.

"To answer your question. Suicide is very possible. But it's difficult to form a conclusion without knowing anything about the man. The probability increases depending on the type of person he was. His personality type. His state of mind. How fragile his ego? What kind of sentence he was facing if convicted? What he stood to lose? How would his ego cope with that? All of which I have no clue about," I said.

He'd finished eating. His plate empty. Not even scraps. From hunger or delicious delight I couldn't say. He wiped his mouth on a red linen napkin. His extraordinary eyes studied me, possessing the decision making expression I'd observed when we'd first met.

"He was looking at a lot of time," he said. "Hard time too. Not the country club time most white collar types get. He was facing charges under both RICO and National Security statutes. I can't discuss the specific charges." Holding up his hands defensively he quickly added, "Sorry. A lot about this case is classified."

I didn't protest or push it. Gage would undoubtedly breach that wall anyway.

"He'd known for a while a grand jury was hearing the case. His lawyers even put out a few feelers to the Justice Department about the possibility of a deal. They were waiting on the indictment."

"Who the hell was this guy?" I exclaimed softly.

The arrival of our waitress interrupted him. She wrote our desert order on her pad before clearing the table. Forde asked for coffee, no desert. I also ordered coffee and a slice of the Frangipani's signature lime pie.

"He was the CEO of an international investment banking firm," Forde continued after the waitress departed. "Small, very private and low key, but controlling Billions in funds and assets around the globe. Probably more than the national budgets of these small island nations around here. The firm specialized in acquisitions and development funding in third world and developing countries. A lot like these islands actually."

The information set my head buzzing. Synapses fired in my brain, connecting words and memories, thoughts and patterns not yet consciously recognizable. Something swimming into focus. Just out of reach.

Dessert arrived. I love any kind of lime pie. Key lime, lemon meringue, lime cheesecake. Chocolate a distant second where my taste buds are concerned. The slice of pie on the plate before me had a smooth green lime filling on a shortbread crust, topped by soft fluffy meringue. Delicious doesn't describe it. Words can't describe it. If heaven had a taste this would be it.

Forde asked, "What was it like growing up in the Islands and Montreal?"

"What was it like growing up a marine brat all over Europe?" I asked in turn.

I'd surprised him again, possessing knowledge of his biography he didn't think I'd have. Not surprised he knew mine. He was FBI after all. And the U.S. embassy in Barbados kept itself well informed.

The initial tingling delight of creamed lime subsiding I said, "It may have been a heart attack," deflecting his personal question, and the magnetic allure of his flirtatious eyes and captivating smile.

"Say again."

"It's in the preliminary autopsy report I gave you," I said. "He had advanced atherosclerosis and indications are he may have suffered a massive heart attack which may've precipitated the accident. Or the other way around. The plunge into the ravine precipitating the coronary. Can't rule it out until we get the final results back from the lab," I lied.

"So it still could be a suicide?"

I nodded. And decided to take a chance. "Or another possibility," I said, my gaze focused on his face, peering into his eyes. "Can you think of anyone who would want to kill him?"

A slight narrowing of his eyes, and a shift in focus, from flirtatious to cautious.

"Why do you ask that?"

"Just covering the bases," I said, holding his stare, maintaining a neutral tone. "You said the charges against him were RICO and national security. Maybe he crossed somebody he shouldn't have. Or if he was looking to make a deal as you said maybe someone didn't want him telling what he knew."

"You have any evidence indicating he might've been murdered?"

Now for the tricky part. Forde undoubtedly a skilled interrogator. The penetrating green eyes staring into mine capable of spotting the lie.

I held his stare. Not blinking. Not glancing away "I've given you the case file. You tell me. You have more insight into his background and what's going on than I do."

His eyes searched mine. Uncertainty registering in his.

"You didn't answer my question," he persisted.

"Because I don't have any answers," I said. "Just a lot of questions."

The return of his smile dissolved the mounting tension between us. I didn't believe for a moment my responses had satisfied him. But he probably realized he'd get nowhere on his present course, deciding instead to tack. He leaned back in his seat, spread his arms, laid his hands on the table palms down in a gesture of surrender.

"I have to admit to being put at a disadvantage," he said.

"What do you mean?

"You. I'd expected to meet a local official, perhaps with a small island mentality. In any case a pushover I could handle. Instead I get you. Not only gorgeous but smart, tough, and cagey too."

The make-or-break moment behind us my attention returned to my pie, carefully marshalling the remaining bites. Uncomfortable with the personal tack he'd taken, but needing to keep the topic off Mansfield, at least for a while. And needing to keep Forde on my side.

"Probably got it from your parents. I know I did," he said.

"What're you talking about?"

"That strength and confidence. Independence. That sense of knowing exactly who you are. A strong sense of your identity. Not what anyone else expects you to be."

I lifted my gaze from the pie. My attention refocused on him. His observations not obtained from any file.

I smiled. "Very perceptive," I said.

"Not all that difficult really. We share something in common," he said.

"And what would that be?"

"We're both from a multicultural family?"

The corners of my mouth curled into a tiny smile. "Thanks," I said.

"For what?"

"For not using that meaningless term 'interracial.'"

He laughed. The sound soft and mellow, an embellishment of his smile. "See. Something else we agree on. We don't identify ourselves by that typically American perspective. America's obsession and its curse. Everything viewed and processed through a racial lens."

"I gather you had a different experience."

"Probably similar to yours, growing up outside the U.S. You no doubt know I grew up mostly in Europe. Marine brat like you said. Moved around a lot, which provided a perspective you don't get growing up in the States. And since my dad was an officer with a family we lived off base wherever we were. My mom insisted on it. Didn't want us confined to the insularity of a U.S. base. Made sure we were immersed in the communities and cultures we lived in. Race was never an issue. Being American and having a military dad more of an issue frankly."

I placed the last bite of pie in my mouth. My tongue smooched it against my upper palette. His eyes studied me in a vaguely different manner as he drained the last of his coffee.

"Was never an issue for me either, I said. "Outside the States you don't find America's persistent preoccupation with race. A meaningless concept really. My friends just figured I was whatever they were. My black friends saw me as black, my white friends as white, my Canadian friends as Canadian; my Vincentian friends as Vincentian. Kindda cool too, going from

Tourtiere and Poutine one moment to Breadfruit and salt-fish the next. As normal as changing clothes."

He laughed again. I appreciated the pleasant sound of it. The unrestrained spontaneity of it. And his easygoing, quick to laugh manner.

"You retained dual citizenship. Vincentian mother." A statement rather than a question. Both of us reconciled to the fact we'd studied the other's biography. "That what brought you back here?"

"Partially," I said.

"Must be quite a woman."

"What's this sudden interest in my mom?"

"Helps me fill in the blanks," he smiled.

"Maybe if you told me about yours," I said, an unmistakable challenge in my tone.

"Shy. But not unsociable. Fierce when it comes to her kids," he said without hesitation or reservation.

"Kids? You have siblings?"

"A sister," he said. "A lot like you actually. You'd both take an instant liking to each other. Anyway mom doesn't have a race conscious bone in her body. Like you and probably your mother, she considers the concept a relic of the eighteenth century, best left back there. It meant nothing to her when she and my dad met, fell in love. When she encountered racial attitudes in the States, the persistent, pervasive preoccupation with it, she just saw it as a bewildering silliness. Anyway by the time we returned to the States she'd already instilled her values in her kids."

"You're right. Sounds like my mom," I said. My turn to reciprocate. "They'd probably like each other. My mom's headstrong. Knows what she wants and doesn't let anything stand in her way. She taught me and my two brothers that strength. She came from privilege. My maternal grandparents were upper class professionals on St. Vincent. A mix of African, Carib-Indian, and some Scottish blood in there somewhere too. Her parents didn't object to her marrying a white French Canadian. More a class thing, which trumps race here in the islands. Something Americans on both sides of the ethnic divide can't understand."

"Different histories," he said. "Other than the common event of getting dragged out of Africa, people in the Caribbean developed a different racial logic from the one defining America. And with seventy or more nationalities running through their blood, and absent the victimology of Jim Crow, they're gotten over the legacy of slavery both black and white Americans still obsess over."

"You have an appreciation for Caribbean history and culture I didn't expect," I said.

"Although born and raised in the States my dad came from Caribbean roots," he said. "Different perspective. And you're correct. Most Americans don't understand it at all."

We'd finished our coffee and dessert, but neither of us made a move to leave the table. He sat back in his chair, relaxed. More relaxed than I'd seen him since our first encounter. His eyes absorbed the atmosphere. His demeanor at ease.

"Why the FBI?" I asked. "You had a promising career in the military. Didn't want to follow in dad's footsteps?" I'd made the remark lightly. Instantly aware I'd hit a raw nerve as his eyes narrowed and the smile slipped.

"I'm sorry. I didn't mean....."

"No need," he interrupted. The smile back in place. "My family and I are close. I'm proud of both my parents. It just seemed a better way for me to serve."

The psychologist in me detected an underlying issue in the father son dynamic despite what he'd said. I let it go.

"The Attorney General's chair someday?" I said instead.

His smile grew wider, parting his lips. He said nothing to confirm or deny that ambition.

"What about you?" he said instead. "Left a promising practice to come here. Commissioner of Police of this tropical paradise in your future perhaps?"

"Not hardly," I said automatically, before the memory of Mike's incredulous proposal sprang into my conscious mind. "Just wanted to do something meaningful. Give something back which might make a difference. The migration of brains and talent is usually in the other direction."

His eyes held mine in their mesmerizing grip. The tug of his easy magnetic charm a palpable presence, drawing me in. I'd enjoyed his company and our conversation. But that's as far as it was going to go. And he must've concluded by now the evening wouldn't end with me in his bed. No matter how compelling his charm.

When I rose to bid him goodnight he offered to see me safely home.

"Sweet. But unnecessary," I said. I planned to meet Gage for a nightcap just down the beach at the Green Boley. From there we'd dinghy over to Lower Bay.

"Tomorrow after you've had a chance to look over the case file, call me," I offered. "I should be in the office all day."

In the morning I planned putting the puzzle together. I had more pieces now. But too many still missing.

CHAPTER 18

The following morning, December sixteenth, heralded the first day of 'Nine Mornings. The main road into Port Elizabeth unusually busy and festive. Young people in bright costumes darted along the road, heading home. Older folks lingered by the open doors and manicured flower beds of the Anglican Church. The sharp bong of its bell reverberated in the misty morning air. In empty lots on both sides of the road makeshift bandstands and stalls had been left in place for the next eight days of festivities.

The origins of 'Nine Mornings' lost in obscurity. Some say it derived from the Catholic Church's 'novena' tradition nine days before Christmas. Others say it has its roots in an African ritual brought to the Caribbean by slaves. Neither theory explains the celebration's absence from other Caribbean islands. Nine Mornings unique to St. Vincent and the Grenadines. It's celebrations a particular point of pride for Vincentians.

My main concern as I entered the station, a concern shared by Station Sergeant Lucenti, the festival's impact on our meager resources. Bequia already besieged by tourists. Two unresolved deaths to close. Across St. Vincent and the Grenadines twelve unsolved homicides which would probably carry over into the New Year. And now the Nine Mornings festivities. Normally a peaceful joyous celebration. But accompanied by its share of public drunk and disorderliness, public nuisances, and other petty offenses. Absenteeism, sick calls, and sleeping on the job Lucenti's primary worry as the days wore on toward Christmas. Especially among younger constables, who tended to celebrate through the night and into the next day in a practice known as 'round de clock'.

"How's the morning going?" I asked Lucenti after he'd saluted and bid me good morning.

"No worries as yet. But is jus de first day."

The Mansfield case uppermost in my mind as I entered my office. An offhand remark by Gage the night before, and a restorative night's sleep, had spawned an idea. A belief in a connection between the two cases. No indication such a connection existed. My conviction nothing more than a gut reaction, an intuitive leap. Accompanied by a disconsolate logic. Discovering the connection, if it existed, a near impossible task. And while both murders, assuming Taylor had also been murdered, had occurred in my jurisdiction, the motives apparently lay elsewhere, perhaps beyond my reach. And therefore perhaps the killer too.

I passed routine matters into Inspector Cato's capable hands. I sat in my office, the door closed. The open windows permitted a cross breeze and noises from the wharf and street below to enter.

I spent a few minutes sorting and organizing. Before long hard copies of reports, handwritten notes, and the physical evidence, sparse as it was, everything I had on both cases, lay in sorted piles across my desk. The case files open on my laptop.

I tackled Mike's notes first. He'd paper clipped a two page itemized summary to three larger documents. Reports authored by Jackson Taylor prior to his death. Bold, underlined lettering at the top of the summary read: WHAT TAYLOR WAS WORKING ON.

The first document was a report on financial contributions to St. Vincent and the Grenadines in the wake of recent hurricane damage. According to Mike's summary the report detailed sources of funds, amounts, and, pledges of contributions not yet received. The report estimated hurricane damage and relief costs totaling one hundred million EC dollars.

In the second document Taylor had provided an analysis of St. Vincent's offshore financial services sector; land sales to foreigners; foreign investments and development projects; and issues concerning unemployment and poverty, public policy and planning, and crime and corruption.

The final document a twenty page report entitled TOURISM AND DEVELOPMENT IN ST. VINCENT AND THE GRENADINES. In his summary Mike suggested the report had been prepared primarily as a political document for the PM, even if it also contained important policy implications.

I decided to read the full report. My dismay increased as I flipped the pages. The report, in impersonal, clinical, black and white statistical detail, confirmed my worst fears, and put to rest any notion my feelings toward development in St. Vincent and the Grenadines might merely be a nostalgic emotional over-reaction. Taylor appeared neutral and objective throughout the report. Careful to omit personal opinions on the issues. After all, he'd been a businessman who'd spent half his career attracting foreign currency and capital into St. Vincent and the Grenadines.

And Mike had been correct. The report read like a political document. Talking points for an election campaign. It charted the growth of total foreign investment, tourism development as it affected employment, the growth in available hotel rooms, and tourism income and expenditures as a percentage of Gross Domestic Product. It listed a number of development projects completed, or underway, including their costs, and expected contribution to the local economy. But Taylor also raised troubling issues in his report. Whether an attempt to include recommendations for policy planning, or to identify potential political landmines, he didn't make clear.

He highlighted shortcomings in control, supervision and regulation of the Offshore Financial Services Industry. The inflationary impact on land values. Ineffective monitoring and enforcement of the provisions required under the Aliens Landholding license system, and lack of a strategic policy and planning system for development, allowing development to proceed on an ad hoc basis in response to the needs of developers and investors, rather than the state and its citizens.

He also included environmental concerns, particularly the impact of tourism related construction in coastal areas. He cited depletion of critical eco-systems affecting coastal fishing and fisheries. Increased coastal erosion due to beach sand mining for construction. Poor engineering in the construction of marinas, jetties, and other structures along shorelines, and deterioration in shoreline water quality as a result of inadequate planning, engineering, and construction of facilities for collection and disposal of solid and liquid waste.

The problem of solid and liquid waste will only become more severe, he noted, given the increasing number of beach front resort facilities and number of yachts using St. Vincent's coastal waters.

At the end of the report Taylor addressed crime and corruption. His concern the negative impact crime had on foreign investment and tourism development. Not only on St. Vincent and the Grenadines, but the region as a whole. He referenced a United Nations report entitled "Threat of Narco-Trafficking in the Americas." The UN report indicated an increase in the overall murder rate in the region, much of it related to narco-trafficking. The report estimated 20 percent of the cocaine destined for North America travelled through the Caribbean, and predicted this would likely increase, given the islands' location, and their large coastlines and territorial waters relative to their law enforcement capabilities and resources.

The report's findings nothing I hadn't already been aware of, given my vantage point on the police force. The statistics the report detailed in dry analytical bureaucratese, I encountered in tragic human reality.

Mike had also provided a photocopy of a lined notepad page. Dark lines on the photocopy indicated where the page had once been crumpled up. The page contained three groups of seemingly meaningless numbers and letters. Maybe some sort of shorthand notation Taylor had used. I put it aside for the time being.

Next I turned to the autopsy reports. The dry clinical findings reduced Taylor and Mansfield to laboratory specimens and courtroom exhibits. My mind recalled the macabre death scenes. Jackson Taylor's lifeless body hanging from the overhead beam. Mansfield's mangled body trapped in the wrecked vehicle. The sights and scents indelibly impressed in my memory.

I paid particular attention to the x-rays of Mansfield's hands, and the peculiar injuries evident on the fingers of his right hand, absent from the left. Twisted, pulled and snapped, Eileen's friend had concluded, strengthening my conviction Mansfield had been questioned in a very painful manner prior to his death. Perhaps by the same person who'd placed him in the jeep and sent it over the cliff. Maybe the person he'd planned to meet. The unanswered questions lead me full circle. The evidence supporting such a supposition and pointing to a suspect lay beyond the shores of St. Vincent and the Grenadines.

No obvious connection to Taylor. Except perhaps for Taylor's laptop, now somewhere in the States in the possession of one of Gage's many mysterious contacts.

I reviewed the physical evidence gathered from Taylor's house. The rope, a common type of nylon yacht braid, similar to others found among boating equipment stored in a space beneath the carport.

I reached for the photographs of the knots forming the noose, and around the overhead beam. I laid the photos aside, reminding myself to take them home with me. I wanted Gage to examine them, recalling our conversation regarding tells. Maybe the knots might tell him something. I smiled at my unintended pun.

Taylor's cell phone had been missing. We'd never found it. Like Mansfield's. Coincidence? I didn't think so. At least we had Jackson's number. We'd called it. The call went straight to voicemail. And we hadn't been able to get a GPS ping on the phone. Turned off maybe. But more likely destroyed.

We'd obtained his voice mail and text message accounts but found nothing enlightening there either. We'd obtained his home and cell phone records, and traced the numbers to friends, relatives and colleagues. In the two weeks prior to his death he'd received six calls from phone numbers traced to unidentified phones. Probably prepaid cell phones. Intriguing, but no help. Just more questions. He hadn't made or received any calls on the night of his death.

The other piece of evidence, the suicide note found on the laptop, had been short and uninformative. It simply read 'I'm sorry. Please forgive me.' What he'd been sorry for and needed forgiveness for a mystery. The note told me nothing. Or did it?

I retrieved the printed note from the pile on my desk. I stared at it through the sealed plastic evidence envelope. The psychologist in me contemplated the note, and the subject of suicide.

Suicide notes are actually rare, about one in four suicides leave behind any last words. Nearly half of all suicides are impetuous acts, committed within minutes of the ideation of killing oneself. And nearly ninety-five percent of all suicides are preceded by some form of mental illness or mood disorder. There'd been no evidence of either in Jackson Taylor.

Suicide notes rarely give a reason for why the person wanted to die. The notes usually vague and apologetic, like Taylor's. And genuine suicide notes contain a stereotypic quality. A typical feature being detailed directions on how to dispose of the body, and the disposition of financial and other family matters.

In the absence of other psychological factors, I questioned the authenticity of Taylor's note. But nothing I'd examined shed any new light on his death, or suggested a connection to Mansfield.

I turned to my laptop, navigated to the emailed file on Mansfield-Greene provided by another of Gage's contacts. A knock sounded on my office door.

"Yes," I called. My attention focused on the laptop's monitor.

Sergeant Lucenti opened the door and stepped in. "Dat gentleman from yestiday heah to see yuh Suprintentend."

My mind still absorbed in the material I'd been reading, only half listening, Lucenti's announcement required a moment to penetrate.

"Dat gentleman is from de FBI," I informed Lucenti. His indifference indicating he already knew, or didn't care. "Show him up," I said, closing the laptop.

"Ma'am," he said, withdrawing and turning for the stairs.

Moments later he ushered Special Agent Forde into my office. I asked Lucenti to close the office door on his way out.

I offered Forde a seat, but he remained standing, wandering the small office, studying the framed pictures, certificates, and awards hanging on the walls.

"Not too shabby," he said, pausing at the open window overlooking the harbor road and the wharf.

"Perks of rank," I said.

"Superintendent? What does that mean exactly? Same as in the UK?" He turned from the window, leveling his green eyed gaze and incandescent smile on me.

"Probably. A few small variations maybe. It means I command the Grenadines Division of the Royal St. Vincent and the Grenadines Police Force. Thirteen islands, 6 police stations, and two dozen police men and women. I also head the CID in the Grenadines, and hold the equivalent rank of Lieutenant Commander in the Coast Guard. We've done a lot of modernizing, modeled on U.S. law enforcement. But we've kept many of the British traditions, including the rank structure and protocols. But you didn't come here to discuss the Police Force. And you could have called."

"Actually I came to give you this." He extracted a folded sheet of paper from a back pocket and handed it to me.

"After our conversation last evening, which I thoroughly enjoyed by the way," He said, pausing and smiling. An expression of pleasant self-reflection on his face. "I don't usually talk about myself like that. Especially with someone I've just met. Most people can't relate. With you it just sort of flowed out."

"Me either. I sorta felt the same way."

"I was hoping for a repeat," he said, a twinkle in his eyes.

"Perhaps, " I said.

"Anyway I requested a psychological profile on Greene. I don't know how accurate it is or how much good it'll do. It was cobbled together from interviews with his lawyers, staff, and prosecution witnesses."

I unfolded the sheet and quickly scanned it.

"Thanks," I said, dropping the sheet onto the pile on my desk. I didn't mention I no longer considered Greene's death a suicide.

"The Greene case?" he asked, his gaze wandering across the assortment of papers and evidence covering my desk, as though quickly cataloging each item. Glad I'd closed the laptop before he'd entered.

"One of them," I said.

"Jackson Taylor?"

"You're well informed Special Agent Forde."

"Came up in my Barbados briefing," he said. "Apparently he was an important figure in these parts. So where do you go from here?" he asked. "On the Greene case, I mean?"

"I've got nothing further to go on. I'm going to review everything we have, make sure I've dotted all the 'I's and crossed all the 'T's, and prepare my report for the coroner's inquest."

"When will that be?"

"Probably not until after the new year. Things pretty much close down around here from now through the holidays."

"Have anything to do with the racket got me out of bed so early this morning? Must have started around four am."

"Get used to it," I smiled at him. "It's called Nine Mornings. A uniquely Vincentian celebration occurring every morning, starting around four am, from now until Christmas day."

"For real? When do you people do any work?"

"It usually breaks up around seven each morning so people can get to work. Although some people party all day and night. Like I said, everything pretty much slows down if not stops altogether between now and the New Year. People wake up before dawn and take to the streets. Some dressed in Christmas costumes. Some attend church services, some head for the beach. There's music and dancing. Performances by drama groups, dance groups, steel bands, even the Police band. There're games and competitions. A particular village may have a special traditional thing of their own they do. Then on Christmas Eve morning there's a huge steel band 'jump up'. What you'd call a street party. Kinda wonderful really. Creates a festive spirit leading up to Christmas day. Like window dressings, street decorations, public Christmas trees, and sleigh rides in the States. Think you might stick around?" I asked.

"Don't know. I'm at loose ends for now. I'm on this Greene case until it's closed. We're still trying to run down how he managed to slip our net and get down here. And what he was really doing here. Making a run for it maybe? And why come all the way here just to kill himself? He could've done that at home. Anyway, maybe I'll head back home, work it from that end. I can put in an official request for your coroner's report and the findings of the inquest. Or you can just do me a big favor. One law enforcement officer to another," he said, his radiant smile beaming at me.

I smiled in turn, a slight nod acknowledging his request.

"Sounds like a plan. As long as we maintain our quid pro quo. I want the answers to those questions myself," I said. "And I'm not sure I'm going to find them down here."

"Oh, I'm not so sure of that," he said.

My reaction a questioning tilt of my head.

His smile broadened to a grin. A conspiratorial twinkle in his lively green eyes.

"Received a strange report from my office this morning," he said. "Seems there was a breach in the Bureau's firewall."

"Really?" I said. "How could something like that happen at the FBI? Did they find out who did it?"

"No. But whoever did it has to be very good to hack the FBI." His eyes grew more mischievous. "Funny thing though, the hacker was only interested in the Greene case. And the hack occurred the day after I arrived here."

"Quite a coincidence," I said.

"Maybe. Or maybe you're more resourceful than I gave you credit for Superintendent." Without missing a beat he segued to: "You free for dinner again, perhaps?"

"As of right now I can't say. I'm swamped and not making any plans. Take a rain check?"

"It'll have to do for now," he said, turning toward the door.

Following Forde's departure I returned to the laptop. Forde's comments created the impression he hadn't bought into the Greene suicide hypothesis. Though for reasons privy to the FBI which he hadn't shared.

The day wore on. I hadn't eaten. The growling in my stomach, the noise from the street, ferries arriving and departing, the nagging questions and numbing monotony of the numerous reports, turned into distractions. I caught myself staring absently at the same words of the same line of the same paragraph of the same page. A jumble of printed letters without coherence.

The ringing cell phone jarred me from my mental stupor . Mike's number on the display. He wanted to meet. At home in Friendship Bay. Unusual for Mike to return home to Bequia during the week. But not uncommon. His Friendship Bay home provided the privacy to discuss police matters away from the gossipy corridors of police headquarters. It also permitted Gage's presence.

When we met later in the evening Mike appeared preoccupied and broody. His eyes hollow and sunk behind puffy lids, as if he hadn't slept in days. His mood similar to the days immediately following Jackson's death. Instead of sitting he paced the verandah.

"What's going on Mike?" Gage asked, beating me to the question.

Mike leaned against the verandah rail, facing us, his hands pressed flat on top of the blue railing cap.

"That's the problem," he said, his brooding gaze sweeping over both of us. "I don't know what's going on. But I'm damned sure something is. People aren't leveling with me. Including the PM. And the more I dig the more I'm convinced something's going on. I just don't know what."

"Jackson Taylor was having an affair," Gage said in the silence. A statement. Mike neither shocked nor surprised.

"I gather." He said. "Though he never spoke to me about it. I caught hints during my conversations with Marlene. She didn't say it outright, but that's the impression I got from things she said. How do you know about it?"

"The laptop," Gage said.

The comment captured Mike's interest. And mine.

"What else did your guy find?" Mike asked.

"The contents of the computer were deliberately erased," Gage said. "My guy was able to trace the deletions to a couple of hours before Taylor died. But whoever did it, could even have been Taylor himself, didn't completely wipe out everything. Could've done it by reformatting or destroying the hard drive, but then you wouldn't be able to type and leave a suicide note on it."

"I'm questioning the note anyway," I said, producing a further spark of interest in Mike's eyes.

"How come?"

"It doesn't contain the typical features associated with a suicide note. The shortness suggests an impetuous act. But those types of suicides are almost never accompanied by a note. And I haven't found anything in Taylor's personality to suggest impetuousness, or anything in his recent behavior to suggest depression or despondency."

"Depression and despondency no," Mike said. "But something was bothering him. Everyone I've spoken to said he seemed more stressed lately, on edge, and more secretive. And constantly preoccupied. I noticed it too when we had dinner the weekend before his death."

"Think it could've been the affair?" I asked.

"I don't think so," Mike said. "From what I gather it'd been going on for a long time. And Marlene seemed okay with it. Apparently the marriage existed in name only."

"At least a couple of years," Gage said.

"How'd you figure a couple of years?" Mike asked him. "Thought you said the contents had been erased."

"My guy retrieved a couple of email addresses. Hacked the servers and found emails going back two years with a Gloria Meeks of New York City."

"Jackson had just returned from New York the weekend he and I had dinner. And Marlene said he'd been spending more time in New York and DC. Makes sense, the World Bank, IMF, USAID, have their headquarters in DC and offices in New York. Did you get a physical address or phone number in New York for this Gloria Meeks?" Mike asked.

"Five fifty West Eighty-Eighth Street, apartment four."

A memory flashed in my brain like a blinding spotlight. I sprang from the wicker armchair and ran into Mike's living room. Rummaged in my briefcase and returned to the verandah to a pair of perplexed stares. I studied the plastic enclosed sheet of paper in my hand, the photocopy of the crumpled note Mike had included among Taylor's materials. The second set of numbers and letters scrawled in Taylor's handwriting read 550W88#4.

"Look at the second set of numbers," I said, handing the sheet to Mike.

He stared at it. Stared at me. Shifted his stare to Gage. Mike handed him the sheet.

"That was in the materials you sent me on Taylor. Where'd you get it Mike?"

"From Madelyn. She found it crumpled up with some stuff Jackson left at the house in Miami the last time he was there. She has no idea what it means. Though she figured it might have something to do with the other woman."

"She was right," Gage said. "This second set of numbers definitely fits the New York address. And from the looks of it the first set may also be an address. But the third set doesn't follow the same pattern. It's something else. Maybe a telephone number. Or account number."

"Can we track it down?" I asked.

"Possibly," Mike said. "But I'm beginning to get nervous asking questions about Jackson. The deeper I dig the more people begin distancing themselves. And the PM is downright skittish. He's not leveling with me. Even avoiding me lately. When I try reaching him I get the Permanent Secretary or Attorney General instead. And I get the definite feeling the AG's trying to steer this investigation."

"Steer it how? Where?" I asked.

"Toward suicide. And a quick resolution."

"My guy can try to crack the other set of numbers." Gage said. "We can keep this strictly between the three of us."

"You said your guy retrieved a couple of email addresses. What was the other one?" Mike asked.

"Another of Taylor's accounts. Mostly routine and business correspondence. He kept it separate from the account he used for Gloria Meeks. We should have the dump from it soon. As for the physical laptop itself, your people found no prints on it. My guy didn't either. So what happened to Taylor's prints after he typed the note?"

"You're already convinced this was murder, aren't you?" Mike said, an inquiring gaze locked on Gage.

"So do I," I said.

Mike's gaze switched to me. I shot a quick glance at Gage. If he didn't mention the man on PSV I wouldn't either. I'd follow his lead as far as that item was concerned.

"I also think it's connected to the Mansfield-Greene murder," I said.

Mike sprang off the railing. "What? How?"

"Don't know yet. I'm still looking. Right now it's just a gut feeling."

"Keep trusting that gut," Gage said, his gaze resting on me. "My guy came up with a couple of interesting connections. The case against Mansfield aka Greene was developed out of the Ramirez information. It's why the FBI's playing it so close to the vest."

Mike, who'd resumed casually leaning on the railing, bounced off it again. I sat up straight in the armchair. The bogeyman surfaced in my mind.

"The FBI identified Greene's firm while following a trail of money and subsidiaries in the Ramirez material. The firm is a privately held corporation with equity financing and holdings around the globe. Hotels, resort properties, manufacturing, oil leases, even cruise lines. The Feds were seeking indictments against Greene on multiple counts of money laundering, accounting fraud, conspiracy, and making false statements and filings. But the corporation is a subsidiary, hidden behind a wall of companies the Feds haven't been able to crack. It extends beyond Ramirez's drug operations. Ramirez may have been just another client. Looks like Greene and Equity International Group were moving money by acquiring overseas properties."

"Do you have the address?" I asked, a spark of excitement rising in me.

"Thought of that when you made the connection to the other address. Doesn't match the numbers. Greene's offices are in the financial district. His home address doesn't match either."

Would've been too easy, I thought, disappointed.

"Your guy dig up any other connections?" Mike asked, his attention riveted on Gage.

"This just came in," Gage said, retrieving his cell phone. He powered it up and accessed something on it before handing it to me. "This file was on the laptop."

The small rectangular screen displayed a document divided into three vertical columns. Each column contained a list. The first column a list of five names I didn't recognize. The middle column a list I did. Argyle airport, Buccament Bay, Canouan Resort, Clair Hall Boatyard, and the initials SVGNB, CDB and ECCB. The first four the names of multimillion dollar development projects in St. Vincent and the Grenadines. SVGNB referred to the St. Vincent and the Grenadines National Bank. CDB the Caribbean Development Bank. And ECCB the Eastern Caribbean Central bank, which regulated all monetary matters in the Eastern Caribbean. The ECCB also regulated all domestic commercial banks in St. Vincent and the Grenadines.

The final column contained a list of six company or corporate names. Five were unfamiliar to me. One, halfway down the list, jumped at me like a startled cat. Equity International Group. Greene's firm.

An involuntary gasp escaped my lips. Mike's eyes narrowed at my reaction. I handed him the cell phone. The screen hidden in his cupped hands, his eyes scanned it. He read the lists. Finally he drew a deep breath, releasing it in a soft slow sigh.

"Either of you know what that means?" Gage asked.

Mike nodded. "One thing it means is JJ's gut was correct. Did he find anything else?" The question directed at Gage.

"There's more. Still working on it. But my guy wanted to get this to me right away."

Mike returned the phone to Gage. "It also means this investigation is dead in the water," he said, voicing the fear haunting me all morning.

"How so," Gage asked.

"The answers to what that list means, and how it connects to the deaths of Greene and Jackson, are in New York and St. Kitts. Under ordinary circumstances it'd be difficult getting authorization for such a trip with the little we have to go on. Given the type of reactions I've been getting lately, especially from the PM and the AG, it's never going to happen."

"We said we were keeping this just between the three of us," Gage said. "Getting authorization would just alert people we don't want alerted."

Mike and I both stared at him.

"Gage, arranging something like that takes resources....."

"I can arrange it," he said, interrupting Mike. "Not a problem."

My head swiveled between them like a spectator at a tennis match.

"We'd be operating outside our jurisdiction, outside official channels, without official sanction," Mike argued.

"Been there, done that," Gage said.

"No doubt you have. But this is not one of......"

"I've been thinking of visiting home for Christmas," I said to no one in particular.

"JJ....." Mike began.

"We could stop in New York to do some Christmas shopping and make a stop in St. Kitts on the way back," I continued, as though I hadn't heard him.

"And what will that accomplish?" Mike said. "Even if we find what we're looking for, if these were hired hits we probably won't be able to pin it on anyone."

"We'll have the answers Mike," I said. "Even if we can't put away the guy who did it," I glanced at Gage, the silent question passing between us. The Springbok guy on PSV?

Mike's brow furrowed in thought. He pushed himself off the railing. Paced back and forth on the verandah before arriving at a decision.

"Okay," he acquiesced. "But I'll handle St. Kitts. I have a contact there whose discretion I trust. The problem will be getting there without alerting anyone."

"A simple misdirect." Gage said. "Fly me and Jo to wherever we'll be catching our flight north then take a little unscheduled side trip to St. Kitts. Should give you enough time to meet your contact."

"You really want to do this?" Mike asked, his eyes leveled at me, penetrating, questioning. And concerned.

I glanced at Gage. Read the reassurance in his eyes, the slight nod of his head. I nodded at Mike.

"Gotta see this through Mike. These men were murdered in our back yard. I think Special Agent Forde is beginning to smell a rat too."

"Why? What's he got?" Mike asked.

"Nothing. At least nothing he's told me. But he's got a lot of unanswered questions. And my impression is once he's on the scent of something he's not going to let go of it easily."

"So what's he gonna do?"

"Probably head back Stateside. Work it from there. We promised to stay in touch and maintain our quid pro quo."

"Could be useful," Gage said. And it's better if he's not poking around in our yard."

"He also told me they detected the hack. Your guy got away clean but they know someone accessed the Greene files."

Mike turned to Gage. Their eyes locked in silent communication.

"Don't worry about her," Gage said. "Just watch your back while we're gone. There's a guy staying on PSV you need to keep an eye on."

CHAPTER 19

A week later, Christmas Eve, the Gulfstream IV sailed serenely through the thin air at forty one thousand feet. Two hours out of Martinique, where Mike had dropped us off in the Seneca. Gage hadn't divulged the details of his travel arrangements, and it'd surprised me when we'd headed not for the commercial terminal, but toward a dull grey executive jet waiting on the general aviation tarmac.

Gage had fallen asleep on a plush blue leather couch. The young copilot strode through the cabin to inform me the pilot wanted a word. When I entered the cockpit, Monk's wide welcoming smile greeted me. Another surprise. The last person I'd expected to see on the tarmac in Martinique. I hadn't seen him since we'd first met, when Gage had arranged a medivac flight after Mike had been shot. At the time Mike had needed urgent medical treatment, and wouldn't have survived the wait for a Government sponsored airlift to a hospital in the states. The next morning Monk had arrived, courtesy of Gage, and airlifted Mike to Miami.

"Figured you might like a change of view," he said. His grey eyes, under a full head of snow white hair, glinted at me in the sunlit cockpit.

"Definitely," I said, stepping over the switch studded Radio Management Panel between the cockpit seats, settling into the copilot's seat. I scanned the panel, glancing at the six CRT screens displaying digital flight instruments, flight status, engine status, navigational information and weather.

The sky outside pale blue. The ocean below a deeper indistinct blue. The sleek metal tube transporting us seemingly suspended in midair, motionless, but racing across the earth at close to the speed of sound.

"How's our guy doing back there?" Monk asked.

"Fast asleep," I said.

"Yep. His usual posture when he's not in the cockpit."

"I was glad to see you," I said. "A little surprised. Although Gage is always so full of surprises I should be used to it by now."

"That's Raul for you," he said grinning.

"Why do you call him Raul? And why does he call you Monk? Your name's John right?"

"Search me sugar," he chuckled. "I haven't a clue. Names just seemed to fit the first time we met. Turned into a habit I guess."

"You've known each other a long time I gather."

"We go back a ways," he said noncommittally, as tight lipped as Gage.

I searched his friendly face. Observed the same impenetrable quality in his eyes as Gage had. The same dual capacity for caring and death. So much I still didn't know about Gage's past. I'd grown beyond needing to know, or wanting to know. I knew all I needed to love him. But whenever I met a person from his past, the handful he called brothers, like Monk, or Max and Mendez who'd guarded Mike after he'd been shot, my curiosity resurfaced.

"Anyway, I'm glad I have a chance to thank you in person for helping Mike. Last time we met things were kinda rushed. You and Gage saved his life. And now this. You must owe him a lot?" A leading question, hoping for a further insight into Gage's past.

He laughed out loud, a boisterous short staccato sound, like the tat-tat-tat of a machine gun. "Sweetheart you have no idea. Truth is we've pulled each other's asses out of the fire so often we've both lost count. Anyway this is practically his bird."

"His bird?" I exclaimed.

"Yeah. He had a little operation going, back when your friend got shot. He set it up so I was able to acquire this baby. Add it to the fleet.

"Repayment of a debt," I said softly to myself, recalling the exact words Gage had spoken in Antigua at the end of the Ramirez affair.

"Something like that," Monk said. I hadn't thought he'd heard me.

So here we were flying in the private jet once owned by the drug kingpin Eduardo Alonzo Ramirez. A jet reported lost and believed to have crashed in the Caribbean Sea. A smile crossed my face and a soft chuckle escaped my lips, turning to quiet laughter as the full irony of the situation sank in.

"Hope it was something I said," Monk remarked when my laughter subsided.

"Just another Gage surprise," I said.

"You know the phrase 'a riddle wrapped in a mystery inside an enigma?' Our friend back there is the living embodiment of it. The real deal. The most empathetic, protective, soulful person I know, though he doesn't show it. And also the most dangerous, deadliest bastard I know."

He turned to face me. Held my attention in his deep searching stare. "But you know that, right?"

I nodded.

"Then it's all you need to know."

I nodded again, turning away to gaze outside at the infinite sky.

We landed at Saint-Hubert Airport outside Montreal, a forty minute drive to my Parent's home in Auteuil on Laval Island, close to the Mille Iles River. The entry formalities informal, private and polite. The documents Monk had handed Gage when we'd departed Martinique passed inspection on first glance. They identified Gage as John Anderson, an American industrialist who'd been vacationing in the Caribbean. A friend who'd offered me a ride home on his private jet. I travelled under my own identity, using my Canadian passport.

Spending Christmas at home an unexpected treat. I hadn't thought I'd make it home for the holidays. My parents' holiday cheer buoyed by my unexpected presence. In typical Caribbean fashion mom had cooked enough to feed a battalion. The aroma of Vincentian, Canadian and Dutch traditional Christmas dishes permeated the house. Accompanied by mom's inevitable urgings to "have some more honey, you need to put sum flesh pon dem bones." I devoured enough tourtière, Banketstaaf, Kerststol and rum cake to last me through the next year.

A highlight of the visit spending time with my brother Danny. Three years older than me, an attorney in Montreal, married, the only sibling who'd stayed close to home. And mom's best hope for grandchildren any time soon. Our oldest brother Alex, a successful journalist, maintained a busy travel schedule which kept him single. On assignment overseas as usual and unable to make it home for the holidays. We all gathered around Dad's computer to exchange holiday greetings with him via Skype.

Me the baby sister. Would always be no matter my age. Gage's and my arrangement, as mom and dad phrased it, not exactly a harbinger of grandchildren. My parents had met Gage during previous visits to Bequia, growing to accept him over time. My evident happiness their only concern.

The day after Christmas, Boxing Day to us Canadians and West Indians, in the Gulfstream again, winging our way south for the United States. We landed at Republic Airport on Long Island, arriving in the evening. The suburban airport, thirty miles east of Manhattan, sleepy and quiet.

The entry formalities into the States as quick, and more importantly as private, as our entry into Canada. The aircraft registered to a legitimate charter company. And Monk had filed the required pilot and passenger manifests using the Customs and Border Protection's Electronic Passenger Information System. The bored immigration and customs official, who I gathered would rather be home on the evening after Christmas, checked our passports against his printed copy of the manifest, sent his canine companion through the cabin sniffing our baggage, and bade us Merry Christmas, Happy New Year and welcome to New York.

A maroon Ford Taurus had been left for us in the short term parking lot. It had a keyless touchpad entry on the driver's door. Gage opened the door and popped the trunk.

Before loading our luggage, he retrieved a brown leather attaché case from a concealed compartment between the trunk and rear seats. The hidden compartment contained a second aluminum case he didn't disturb. The attaché case had two triple digit combination locks. Gage entered the combination and the latches sprang open. The vehicle's ignition key had been clipped to a file pocket on the inside of the attaché's lid. A large bulky manila envelope lay in the bottom compartment.

We exited the airport onto route 110, connecting to the Long Island Expressway. In silence I observed the scenery rushing by outside. The Expressway a rushing river of ubiquitous suburban SUVs, minivans, and the barreling mega-tonnage of long haul tractor trailers. The bright lights of commercial and residential communities lay beyond the Expressway behind tall sound barriers.

I'd been to New York on a number of occasions when I'd lived in Philadelphia, a two hour drive away. By New York I meant Manhattan. The city's boroughs and outlying suburbs still as foreign to me as any tourist. Names on the large green highway signs passing overhead held no meaning.

We merged onto a route named the Brooklyn Queens Expressway. An involuntary surge of excitement bubbled inside me as the dazzling Manhattan skyline rose into view across the East River.

"Which hotel you have us in," I asked, breaking a long silence.

"No hotels," Gage said. "Too many things to sign. Too much of a paper trail. And too many cameras."

"No hotel? So where're we staying?"

"My place."

"Your place?"

"I have a place in the village," he said

"Of course you do," I chuckled. "One of the many new things I learn about you every day."

"Isn't that what being together is all about? Learning about one another?" Turning to smile at me. "Plus, if you know everything about a person where's the mystery, the surprises?"

"Nice try my love, but what you're referring to doesn't usually mean secretive."

"My secrets protect people I care about."

"I know," I said.

Only the second time we'd travelled beyond the Caribbean region together. The first being Mike's airlift to Miami. Both experiences provided a succession of surprises. Private air travel for one. All miraculously accomplished by a couple of phone calls.

Crossing the Williamsburg Bridge, the East River a wide dark ribbon below, and the brightness of Manhattan drawing closer, an ominous realization occurred to me.

"Gage?"

The concern in my voice momentarily diverted his attention from the road. He turned to face me.

"What?" he asked, his gaze shifting back to the road.

"I just realized. This is a risk for you isn't it? Your being here in the States?"

"Not if we're careful."

"I didn't think of it before, with the excitement of Christmas at home and everything. And not being used to this cloak and dagger stuff. But it just occurred to me this is dangerous for you, isn't it?"

"If I thought my being here might put you in any danger I'd never have agreed to this operation." His voice hard and sincere, and characteristically calm. "I'd never put you in that kind of danger."

I accepted his calm reassurance without reservation. Those traits, so much a part of him, a deep abiding condition at the center of his being, had the effect of always making me feel safe.

"We got in clean. We'll stay that way and leave that way. And I have an exit contingency at the first sign of trouble."

Another sudden revelation occurred to me. My previous concern replaced by a new, cherished closeness. Not as a lover, but a partner. Sharing a side of him I hadn't been part of before. A side I'd often imagined in my silent wondering. I rejoiced in the sensation. The unspoken but undeniable partnership conveyed by his choice of words, 'operation', 'exit contingency'. Innocuous yet momentous words. Implying an unspoken partnership. A new dimension to our relationship.

We'd arrived in Manhattan. Gage navigated the wide avenues and narrow side streets as though he'd never been away from the city. I recognized my surroundings as we traversed the east village and the environs of New York University. I'd attended many seminars, and given lectures at NYU.

On East Tenth Street, just off Broadway, Gage pulled off the street, turning onto the sidewalk in front of a four story red brick building. The car's headlights illuminated a steel roll top door to the right of the building's front stoop. He pulled a set of keys from his pocket, a small remote control attached to the key ring. He pressed a button on the remote. The steel door rolled up. Interior fluorescent lights flickered on as Gage drove into an underground basement garage.

He parked and we exited the car. Gage's posture stooped and stiff after a day of sitting for prolonged periods. He stretched, winching as he straightened up. We retrieved our luggage and both cases from the trunk before heading to a freight sized elevator.

Gage inserted a key from the ring into a lock on the outside of the elevator, unlocking bifurcated upper and lower doors. He pushed the lower door down, level with the floor, and pushed the upper door above our heads. Inside the oversized elevator he closed the doors and inserted another key into a panel above a set of numbered buttons. He twisted the key all the way to the left, then all the way to the right, and punched in a combination on the buttons. The freight elevator jerked from its resting position and ascended.

When the elevator stopped Gage opened the doors and we stepped into a short passageway as wide as the elevator. The passageway ended at a heavy, solid wood door. Gage inserted the same key he'd used in the elevator into a keyhole on the door. Again he turned it left and then right. A small panel on the wall popped open to reveal a keypad. He punched in another combination and the heavy door slid open.

I stepped into a cavernous loft sized space. Red brick walls, shiny hardwood flooring and a high cathedral ceiling. Muted lighting spilled from floor and table lamps spaced around the room, revealing a spacious sitting area close to the door we'd entered. A large white leather sofa and matching armchairs surrounded a beige throw carpet and a sturdy glass topped coffee table. The sofa faced a functioning fireplace beneath a black marble mantel. A large mirror in a filigreed bronze frame hung above the mantel.

I stared at my surroundings in jaw dropping astonishment. The comfortable but understated furnishings. The large curtained bay windows overlooking the deserted street. The oil paintings hung on the red brick walls, and the oak paneled double doors of the main entrance at the opposite end.

"This is yours?" I asked incredulously, heading toward the kitchen at the far end of the room. The kitchen area open and spacious. Two large double sinks between stainless steel appliances against the wall. A long bar-like island, surrounded by high backed cushioned bar stools, separated the kitchen from a polished ovoid dining table and chairs. A brick wall separated the kitchen from the front entrance and cantilevered staircase. On the kitchen side of the wall hung a wood rack containing an assortment of shiny pots, pans, cooking utensils, and long stemmed glasses.

"Yours too," Gage said.

"But when're you ever here? Who looks after this place? It looks lived in. And the fridge is even stocked," I said, opening the large shiny double refrigerator freezer and perusing the fresh groceries filling it.

"A family manages the building for me. They keep the apartment ready to be occupied at any time. And stock it when they get word someone's coming to use it. There's an apartment below this floor where the family lives. And on the first floor a large studio space we rent out. I believe a modern dance company currently has it."

"What's above this floor?"

"Three bedrooms and bathrooms."

"Gage, how many other places like this do you have?"

"A brownstone uptown in Columbia Heights. And a warehouse in Long Island City. A couple of places in Miami. Another warehouse in LA. A couple of places in Paris and London, Bangkok. Hong Kong. Thailand. A few other places."

I listened to his list in stunned silence.

"You've got to be kidding?" An automatic response, aware he wasn't.

"There were more, but I unloaded a lot of them when I quit working."

Too flabbergasted to inquire further, I continued to stare in wonder at my surroundings. And deep down I already had the answers. I didn't need to ask.

Instead I said, "Well show me where to put our things, and I need to get out of these clothes."

"Now that's the best idea I've heard all day," wrapping me in his arms.

"Back your main, sailor," I said, smiling. "Right now I need a bath."

He laughed as he led me up the oak cantilevered staircase to the floor above. The staircase ended in a long hallway spanning the length of the building. More paintings on the walls, seascapes and square-rigged sailing ships. A closed door on my right, another farther down the hall. On my left, halfway along the hall, an antique table stood next to closed double doors. A fresh bouquet of red roses, yellow marigolds, and white tulips sprouted from a glass vase in the center of the table.

Gage pushed open the double door and led me into the master bedroom. Another jaw-dropping experience. The suite occupied the entire front section of the building. Its tall curtained windows provided the same street view as the floor below. Against the wall at the far end of the room stood a king size four poster bed of classic American design, minus the cornice and canopy. The head posts taller than the foot posts, all elaborately carved and topped by finials.

In the middle of the room a sitting area similar to the one below. A plush wide couch and two armchairs faced another fireplace. A door at the opposite end of the room led to a full bathroom, separate tub, shower, and his and her sinks.

"Well Mr. Gage," I said, completing my inspection. "All I can say is this is much better than any hotel."

He smiled, reached for me and pulled me close against him. He kissed me lightly on the mouth. I returned the kiss, a primal desire rising within me. My knees turned spongy. I gently pushed back from him.

"Right now I'm heading for that spa sized bathtub in there," I said.

"You'll find everything you need," he said, his eyes searching mine in his characteristic see-right-through-me manner. "Enjoy," he said releasing me.

I did find everything I needed. As though the items had been provided specifically for me. Lavender scented bath beads and soap. Natural shampoo. Even scented candles. The overall effect a sense of home.

I lit four candles and placed them around the tub. Started the tub filling while I undressed and brushed out my hair. The tub ready, I climbed into the sudsy warm water and turned on the massage jets. The pulsing hot water soothed and relaxed my tensed muscles. I lay back, closed my eyes. Allowed the spa to work its magic.

Not sure how long I remained in the bath. Time not a pressing concern. I'd lost any sense of its passage while luxuriating in the huge tub. I climbed out, dried off, and donned a white terry robe made of soft Egyptian cotton. I brushed out my wet hair, opened the tub drain and blew out the candles.

Gage had a small fire burning in the fireplace. The dried logs snapped and crackled, and a warm cherry red glow spread across the dimly lit room. Gage lounged on the couch, bare feet up on the coffee table, his laptop open across his knees. I pulled the folds of the soft robe closer around me and joined him on the couch, facing the fire, my legs tucked beneath me.

He closed the laptop and laid it on an end table next to the couch. Two long stemmed glasses of red wine sat on the table. A partially decanted bottle of an expensive Pinot Noir vintage sat in a stand next to the table. He handed me one of the glasses.

"Do you miss it?" I asked. "All of this?" I said, an inclusive wave of my arm indicating the room.

"Not for a second," he said.

"How could you not?"

"This, all the other places, they're not real homes. Just a transient place to stay or hide or operate from. Tools of the trade. Like multiple IDs and weapons. Part and parcel of the hiding, the stalking, living in the shadows. The violence and betrayals. None of it permanent. Until Wherever I've never had a place that was truly a home. And having you, nothing else matters."

I searched his eyes. Read the sincerity in them. Heard the anguished pain of a life he'd left behind. I leaned in toward him. Touched my lips to his. The taste of him called for more. I pressed my mouth against his, opening it, and my tongue probed inside, meeting his, rolling it around mine. Desire rose in me, like a spark fanned into a tiny flame.

I reached across him to place my glass on the table. I took his, sipped without swallowing. My mouth pressed his mouth open again, and I squirted the berry tasting liquid into his. I set his glass on the table next to mine.

He ran his fingers through my damp hair, stroking my scalp, and the back of my neck. He twirled long strands of my hair around his fingers. I reached for the belt buckle at his waist. Unbuckled it. Grasped the button and zipper of his jeans and unfastened them. Unbuttoned his shirt, opening it, pushing the material wide to expose his broad, hairy chest.

His right hand cupped the back of my neck, pressing our mouths together. His left hand untied the knotted belt and opened opened the robe. His lips moved to the tip of my nose, to my closed eyelids, to my cheeks, down the side of my neck. His lips everywhere, caressing my bare skin, sending shivers along my spine.

He bent and kissed the tops of my breasts. His tongue brushed a nipple, circled it. He blew gently on it. First one, then the other. Goosebumps sprouted in the areolas. The nipples turned to hardened nubs. I moaned and pressed his face against the sensitive flesh.

Nineteen days into my cycle I calculated. Past ovulation and on the low odds end of possible fertilization. But we still needed to be careful. So far we had been, and maybe a little lucky. We only used non-hormonal birth control methods.

"Fertile waters sailor," I whispered, while I still possessed a modicum of control, using our private code for the stages of my cycle.

"Your choice," he whispered back, as always. The freedom to choose motherhood entirely under my control. My faith, trust and confidence he'd avoid an accident, take no chances without my permission, never betrayed.

He shifted position on the couch. His hands pushed the robe from my shoulders and he pushed me into a reclining position. He straightened my legs, and his lips resumed their roaming journey across my body. He kissed my stomach, moved lower to my navel, his facile tongue rimming the shallow indentation.

The spark grew to a flame. An intense heat swept through me. My thighs parted as he kissed and nibbled his way lower. Lips brushed my inner thighs. His one day stubble grazed the flesh, increasing the tingling sensations. His tongue flicked at the crease between my legs and groin. Moving closer. Exquisitely, excruciatingly closer. Until his lips touched the most intimate of places, turning the flame to a blaze. His tongue parted the soft velvet lips. Ran up and down its sides; found the opening; pushed inside; thrusting in and out like a soft prehensile penis.

A flash of white blinding light behind my closed eyes when his lips brushed against the hardened sensitive nub, turning my insides to jelly. I gasped. My pelvis writhed in involuntary motion, arching against his warm wet mouth. His mouth enclosed the tiny pearl, suckling, pulling, gentle at first then harder as I bucked against him; my fingers entwined in his hair, pulling his head hard against me.

A finger probed inside, then two, flicking, rubbing the inner walls, thrusting in and out in rhythm to my bucking while he simultaneously licked and tasted, tugged and suckled, turning the blaze into a roaring runaway conflagration, possessing a life of its own, uncontrollable. His thumb found my sphinctered orifice, pressed against it. A flaming flicker shot up my spine, and a seismic convulsion shattered my senses. And another, as the fingers inside me rubbed the magic spot, releasing a raging flood of hot, blazing, liquid delight. My breath rushed from my lungs in a ragged cry, more animal than human. And the world dissolved behind my eyes in multiple convulsions.

I wrapped my arms around him. I pulled him close and held him tight. I pressed my mouth to his and tasted myself. I ran a finger along his spine. I kissed his hairy chest. A gentle nip on a nipple grasped between my front teeth. Delighted in the small shudder it sent through his body. My hands roamed his shoulders, his chest, his back, gently caressing the mottled scars as my mouth moved lower.

I sat up, pushing him onto his back. I kissed his navel as he had mine. Felt his stiff arousal pressed against me, and the raw animalistic power building inside him. I had a deep primal desire to possess it. Make it my own. Still suffused by the warm glow inside me I reached for him. Grasped his hardness in my palm, caressed it; kissed it; my tongue flicking at the swollen head, circling it, tasting it. I enclosed it in the wet heat of my mouth, my lips stroking it. My tongue slid along the smooth underside, taking him deep, until the scrotal sack cupped in my hand clenched. I massaged it lightly, as my closed lips moved up and down the stiff saliva slick shaft, alternating between soft and slow, hard and fast; my tongue circling the sensitive head when I reached the top.

A soft moan escaped his lips as I sucked him deeper, the swollen head tickling my throat. His loins clenched in my palm and his breathing quickened as my throat massaged the sensitive glans, as I softly squeezed his balls, as a finger traced a line below his scrotum and a fingernail pricked his anus. He tensed and shuddered. The combined effect of his erupting shaft pulsing in my mouth and the salty sweet taste on my tongue produced a rippling spasm of my own. I sucked his juice like nectar from a flower until his shudders subsided.

Pure desire still filled us both. We merged in a wild thrusting dance, moving as one, our sweat slick skin sliding against each other. The passionate fire grew again, rising from the center of my being. I clung to him. My fingers dug into the flesh on his back. Faster and faster. Deeper and deeper. Frantic. Wanton. I heard my voice from some distant place. A deep animalistic grunting, rising in volume, reaching a crescendo as a convulsion shook me, rebounded, and hit me again with greater force, shattering my insides into blissful oblivion.

We moved to the bed. Made love again. And again. Until we'd exhausted our desire and ourselves. We sagged against each other, sated and spent. Wrapped in the safety of his arms I succumbed to sleep's peaceful embrace.

CHAPTER 20

I awoke from the best night's sleep I can remember. Perhaps the result of travel fatigue. Or sexually fueled endorphin overload. Or the enrapturing arms I'd fallen asleep in. Or maybe just the scrumptiously comfortable bed. Sunlight streamed through the tall windows, flooding the room in a bright warm glow, like the glow inside me.

After I'd showered and dressed I headed downstairs to be greeted by coffee, eggs, toast and fruit laid out on the table. Gage at the sink washing a skillet. I sidled up behind him, wrapped my arms around his waist. He turned to face me. I pressed my mouth against his, flicking my tongue against his. He tasted like Colgate toothpaste.

"Morning," I said.

"Morning to you. How'd you sleep?"

"Best sleep I've had anywhere. Except maybe on Wherever."

I moved to the table and fixed a cup of coffee.

"When do we see Gloria Meeks?" I asked, biting into a heaping of eggs on toast and sipping the hot brew.

"After we do our homework."

He retrieved the leather attaché case from the island and joined me at the table. The aluminum case had vanished after our arrival the night before. He opened the attaché case. The large brown manila envelope still there. He removed it. Also in the case, hidden beneath the envelope, two nine milliliter Glock 19s three extra magazines for each, and two cell phones.

I lifted one of the Glocks from the case. slid the weapon from the soft middle-of-the-back concealed holster and hefted it, turning it over in my hand. Similar to the weapon I carried every day on the job. Its heft and feel familiar, like a comfortably worn-in pair of shoes.

"I requested Glocks because you're already familiar with it," Gage said.

The case also contained two bi-fold identification wallets. I held them up and flipped them open. One displayed a photo ID of me, the other of Gage. They identified us as FBI Special Agents.

"How did you get a photo ID of me and my signature?"

"Took a photo of your Vincentian ID. Those IDs are solid. The agents are real and under deep cover. We're got a solid backstop if anyone checks our IDs."

"I wonder what Special Agent Forde would think about this," I mused aloud, examining the small gold shield, an eagle with spread wings at the top. My finger traced the raised lettering, 'Federal Bureau of Investigation, U.S. Department of Justice'. In the center a figure held a sword in one hand, the scales of justice in the other.

While I'd been examining the IDs Gage had opened the envelope. He spread the contents across the table. A dozen eight by ten photographs of Gloria Meeks. Entering and exiting her apartment building. Standing outside an office building. Entering the United Nations. Walking on a

Manhattan street. Sitting at a restaurant table. A stapled sheaf of papers catalogued her movements, providing dates, places, and times.

I selected a close-up headshot of her as she walked along a busy Manhattan street. A handsome woman. Grey streaks in her short dark brown hair. Delicate lines around her mouth and neck bestowed a distinguished mature appearance. The image captured an intense intelligence in her eyes.

Two other pages, stapled to a three by five headshot, detailed her background. I read her biography. Born and raised in Washington DC. Sixty years old. Never been married. But attached to various men at one time or another in her life. Some of the men well known in certain financial and political circles. Some not as much. She'd attended Cornell University. Bachelor's degree in Political Science. Received her Master's in Business Administration from the Harvard Business School, and had been a Rhodes Scholar at New College, Oxford, where she received her Doctorate. She spoke fluent French.

Smart lady , I thought, studying her photograph again.

Never interested in politics, she'd spent a career in international finance and development. Currently an executive at the International Monetary Fund. According to the notes the odds on favorite to be the first female head of the IMF. I placed the biography on the table and perused the piles Gage had laid out.

"Where did all this come from?" I asked him.

"Ever since we decided to head to New York I've had someone watching her. We'll have to figure the best time to approach her. When she's relaxed and receptive, not stressed, or hurried. And something in all this," a sweep of his hand indicating the pile, "Might provide the hook to get her talking."

"And this," he said," picking up another sheaf of pages, "Is the rest of what was on Taylor's laptop."

He handed me the pages. Notes of a personal, informal investigation Taylor had been conducting, beyond the reports he'd presented to the Prime Minister. No apparent chronological order or sequence to the printed pages.

The notes covered five development projects on St. Vincent and the Grenadines. The ones listed in the document we'd first seen on Bequia. The first page concerned the St. Clare Marina and Shipyard project, which Taylor had coupled to the Union Island Resorts Project. Both projects involved the same developer, an Italian businessman named Maurizio Allegretti, and his construction company Cabrinaro Marine Fabrikant. Ice cold fingers clutched at my heart upon reading the final paragraph.

Fifty million dollar (US) loan to developer guaranteed by SVG. Additional fifteen million dollars (EC) provided by SVG National Bank under pressure from PM. Regulatory procedures circumvented. Political interference. Relevant cabinet officials unaware of details. Construction Company a shell.

"Merde!" I exclaimed. "No wonder the PM was skittish."

"What're you talking about?"

"Read this," I said, handing Gage the first page.

I continued reading. The second page contained notes on the Argyle Airport project. At an estimated cost of six hundred million EC dollars, the most expensive project in St. Vincent's history. The Airport expected to attract over a million passengers a year. Taylor's notations indicated he'd been tracking the sources of funding. He'd listed a number of countries and financial entities investing in the project, including two he highlighted, Omniworld Financial, which I didn't recognize, and Equity International Group, which I did. Greene's company.

"Crisse."

"Now what?" Gage asked.

"Check out the firm lining up investors and underwriting the Airport project." I handed him the page.

Each of the next three pages concerned the development of Canuoan Island, and two other large resort projects nearing completion on St. Vincent. Again Taylor appeared to be tracking the investment capital behind those projects.

"This is huge Gage," I said when I'd finished reading. "And Greene's company keeps popping up in Taylor's notes. There're a couple of other companies he highlighted we need to track down too."

"Take a look at this," Gage said, handing me a stack of pages.

"What am I looking at?"

"The dump from Taylor's other email account. And a rundown of the names and corporations from Taylor's list."

None of the individual's names familiar to me. They existed in a different universe from the one I inhabited. According to the sketchy bios Gage's contact had provided, all were financial types involved in international finance. The same for the corporations. International finance firms. Two of the individuals listed also named as directors of two of the corporations.

I glimpsed a tiny gold nugget buried in the mass of raw data. Taylor had contacted two of the listed names by cell phone. Emails to one of them followed, a Henry Lowell, head of The Lowell Group, a privately held international Equity firm like Greene's Equity International Group. The emails short and cryptic. Taylor attempting to arrange a meeting. The home address listed for Henry Lowell, Seven Forty Park Avenue.

"Gage," I said in rising excitement.

"I know," he said. "But it's not a match. He extracted the photocopy of Taylor's photocopied note from the pile and passed it to me. The top row read 740P71E71#21.

"The 740P could be Seven Forty Park Avenue," I said.

"Possibly. And the #21 probably an apartment number. But what do the other numbers mean? In any case we need to talk to this Henry Lowell too. But we need to contact Mike before approaching him. And before you interview Gloria Meeks."

"What do you mean before I interview her? Aren't you going to be there too?"

"Not when you meet her, no. But I'll be close. And there're some protocols we need to go over before you meet her."

"You think that's really necessary?"

"She's being watched."

"Yes. By you."

"And someone else."

"What. Who?"

"Don't know yet. Working on it. The surveillance is long range and fairly loose. Like someone just wants to keep tabs on her. Her office is covered too. And we have to assume they're listening to her phones, maybe inside her apartment and office."

"So how do we handle it?"

"We'll go over the protocols later. Right now let's call Mike."

Gage set his cell phone on speaker, placed it on the table and dialed.

"Hey guys. How's winter treating you?" Mike said when he answered.

"Ha. Ha. Funny guy," Gage responded. "How was sunny St. Kitts?"

Silence.

Finally, when he spoke, "It's a fucking mess, and I've only seen the tip of the iceberg." A somber heaviness laced his voice, as though he bore the weight of the world on his back. Gage and I exchanged a concerned glance.

"The potential scandal is huge. Disastrous. Likely bring down the government," Mike said. Gage and I exchanged glances again.

Switching gears Mike asked, "Have you interviewed the woman yet?"

"Not yet," Gage told him. "We've just been going over her file. Trying to determine the best way to approach her, and pin down the information we need from her. I think you better fill us in Mike."

"It involves the National Bank," Mike said. "The bank is owned by the government of St. Vincent and the Grenadines, and it's on the verge of collapse. The government's been using it as a personal piggy bank and owes over a hundred million EC dollars in loans. The government is about to default on the loans. When it does the bank will collapse."

"Typical banking and financial stuff," Gage said. "Where's the scandal and how does Taylor figure into it?"

"On the surface it seems like simple financial mismanagement. But according to my contact there've been a number of financial shenanigans and irregularities. Enough to raise eyebrows in St. Kitts and spark a quiet investigation. The bank's hemorrhaging money like a severed artery. It's lost millions on some questionable transactions, personally backed by the Prime Minister. My contact doesn't know what Taylor's role was in all this, but they believe he was making his own discreet inquiries."

"Was he aware of the ECCB investigation?" I asked.

"Don't know for sure. But I wouldn't doubt it. He was pretty well tuned in over there. Another thing," Mike continued. "There's a whisper going around Taylor was also exploring the possibility of the government divesting ownership of the bank. ECCB would have to approve such a sale. Apparently Taylor was feeling out the Caribbean Development Bank about a loan to the government to pay off its debt prior to a sale. You get anything more from the laptop?"

"That's why we called," I said. "We were just going over the material. And it doesn't look good for Defretas here either Mike."

I passed on the information I'd read.

"Dammit. God Dammit," Mike swore when I'd finished. "Any other connection between Jackson and Greene other than the name of Greene's company?"

"None," I said. "But we did find a connection to a couple of other names on the list. They showed up in the call records from Taylor cell phone. One of them, a Henry Lowell, also showed up in the emails from Taylor's other account. But his company isn't on Taylor's list. We want to speak with him too."

"Any ideas yet why those names, and those corporations? The significance of the lists?"

"Not completely," I said. "Except Taylor was definitely investigating the projects on the list, and the banks would figure into it since he was following the money. Mike, it may have led him to something that got him killed."

Another silence. This entire case had been hard on Mike.

"Any idea what?" His voice hollow and distant.

"No. But the documents we have from his laptop seem incomplete to me. More like an outline, and preliminary notes. Like you said, just the surface. There doesn't seem to be any follow-up. At least not on the laptop. Wouldn't he have been more thorough?"

"Definitely," Mike said. "Jackson was a stickler for detail. Just read any of his reports."

"My guy thinks the third set of numbers may be a password, or some sort of decryption key," Gage said. "But he doesn't know for what. Anyone showing any interest in your trip to St. Kitts?"

"Nothing so far. I think we got lucky with the timing. Everything's pretty much shut down for the holidays. Both on St. Kitts and back here. I met my friend at his home. I was in and out in a matter of hours."

"Sounds good," Gage remarked.

"Anything else?" Mike asked.

"Just one Mike," I said. "A lot of what Taylor dug up he didn't get from public records. So who were his sources? And he must have had more than we have here."

"Good question. We need to track down his source. And Jackson wouldn't just settle for a fanciful conspiracy theory. I'm positive he'd have backed up his conclusions with evidentiary documentation. We need to find that too. I'll keep an ear to the ground here."

"We'll run down the leads on this end," Gage said. Call us if you come up with anything."

"You do the same. By the way Gage, that guy staying on PSV, flew outta here right after you guys left."

"I know," Gage said. I turned to him in surprise.

"You know?" Mike similarly surprised.

"I've been keeping an eye on him too," Gage said.

"How?" Mike asked.

"Not relevant," Gage said. But I recalled the PSV barbecue, Gage and another man I thought might be Wellington deep in conversation on the beach.

After disconnecting, Gage and I returned to the subject of Gloria Meeks. We decided I'd meet Gloria Meeks at her home the following day, Sunday afternoon. The surveillance indicated she'd go out for a late morning Sunday brunch on Broadway, after which she'd return home with the Sunday New York Times. She'd spend the rest of the day in. Perhaps the most opportune time to approach her.

"What do we do about the surveillance?" I asked Gage.

"We'll need a distraction," he mused aloud. "Something to occupy their attention without disclosing our presence. At least not yet. Not until we know more about them. Who they are and what they're after. If they have eyes and ears inside the apartment it's a safe bet they're using wireless transmitters. Maybe remotely activated. They might even be using her landline phone, or cell phone, remotely activating the microphones to listen in. We need to jam any signals going into or out of the apartment while you're there."

Merde. A straightforward visit and interview had turned into a potentially dangerous situation.

CHAPTER 21

Five-story brownstones lined both sides of the quiet street between West End Avenue and Riverside Drive. Cars parked end to end along both sides. The trees had surrendered their leaves to winter, standing like stick figure sentinels guarding the street.

I approached the stoop of Gloria Meeks's building, halfway down the block. The building's features familiar from studying the surveillance photos, its reddish brownstone façade, tall bay windows overlooking the street, brown L-shaped cement stoop and steps, and black metal railing and gate enclosing the street level apartment.

Not many pedestrians on the street. The few out and about walked briskly to avoid a bracing wind blowing from the Hudson River. A young couple holding hands strolled toward West End Avenue. A middle aged man bundled in a heavy coat and scarf, wearing a wool cap and gloves, patiently walked a skittering corgi on a leach.

Gage nowhere to be seen. He'd said he'd be close. But he remained invisible.

I climbed the steps and opened a heavy wood door recessed beneath the arched brick entrance at the top of the stoop. I stepped into a small square vestibule and faced an inner set of locked doors. Tall glass panels in both sets of doors provided a view into the building's first floor and out onto the street. On one side of the small enclosure mailboxes had been built into the wall. A card slot above each mailbox contained the occupant's name. Next to it a small white button.

I noted the closed circuit surveillance camera. Reached into my handbag and activated the frequency jamming device Gage had mysteriously procured the previous evening.

When I pressed the call button nothing happened. We'd followed Gloria Meeks from the café on Broadway. Knew she'd returned home. She either hadn't heard the bell, it wasn't working, or she intended to ignore it. I waited a few minutes. Ready to push the button again a metallic voice rasped from a wall mounted speaker.

"Yes. May I help you?"

"Miz Meeks," I called. "I wonder if you can spare a few moments to see me. I was a friend of Jackson Taylor."

Silence. I wondered if she'd refuse to see me. She hadn't refused. Or accepted either. She hadn't said anything. I pictured her in the apartment studying my image on a monitor. Following a prolonged interval a loud buzz sounded from the inner door. I pushed on the door and it opened.

I entered a well-lit hallway, red brick walls on either side. An apartment door stood at the end of the hall. On my right a staircase bordered by a dark redwood banister led to the upper floors.

When I reached the fourth floor her apartment door stood open. Gloria Meeks stood in the doorway waiting for me. She wore dark casual slacks, and a loose, colorful print blouse highlighted by bright red material around the collar, sleeve cuffs and hem. A long string of African beads hung around her neck and down the front of her blouse.

She studied me as I approached. Close up and personal she appeared more striking than in the photographs. She possessed an indefinable presence. The architecture of her face still strong, despite the lines drawn by the passage of years. Her stern visage held me at bay. Alert brown eyes held me captive. My immediate impression, like peering into a volcanic crater, placid on the surface, deep and fiery below.

I extended my right hand. "Thank you for seeing me," I said.

She accepted my hand. Her handshake soft but firm.

"How do you know Jackson?" Still standing at the door. She hadn't invited me in. Her vigilant eyes continued to study me, conveying an adeptness for reading people. I decided any attempt to bullshit her would be a losing strategy.

"I knew him through Mike Daniels," I said.

"Yes." She nodded. "He spoke of Commissioner Daniels often."

"Miz Meeks I want to be completely honest with you because I need your help. I'm a Superintendent with the St. Vincent and the Grenadines Police Force. I'm trying to find out what happened to Jackson Taylor."

Thin eyebrows rose. Discerning eyes searched mine. She appeared to be weighing a decision.

"Please come in," she said finally, stepping aside and ushering me into the apartment.

I entered a short hallway. Framed photographs hung on beige colored walls. A small hallway table stood against the wall just inside the door. On it an empty flower vase, and a pair of matching hand painted ceramic bowls.

"Please, let me take your coat."

"Thank you," I said, shrugging off the long black wool overcoat and removing the pale blue cashmere scarf around my neck. I handed both to her. She opened a door to a narrow hallway closet and hung them inside.

The hallway opened into a large, bright airy room. The plaster walls painted beige like the hallway. The far end of the room ended in a red brick wall, providing contrasting color to the room. Two tall windows allowed sunlight to flood the room. The windows flanked a grey fabric sofa, burgundy throw pillows piled across it. Sheer lace curtains, bordered by heavy burgundy drapes matching the throw pillows hung in each window.

Gloria Meeks led me to a brown leather sofa against the adjacent wall, arranged perpendicular to the grey one against the brick wall between the windows.

"Would you care for coffee, or tea?"

"Ah, coffee, please. If it won't be any trouble."

She headed behind a counter separating the kitchen from the sitting room, and a small dining area containing a black topped dining table. Four high backed grey cushioned dining chairs surrounded the table. A tall crystal vase containing long stemmed white and red flowers sat in the middle of the table.

I rose from the couch while waiting. I scanned the framed photographs hanging on the walls. A bookcase covered the opposite wall. Amid the books lining the shelves, smaller framed photographs. I walked over and scanned those too. All the photographs, on the walls, on the shelves, showed her in distant parts of the world. In primitive villages. On farms. In front of schools or clinics. In the photographs children or official looking men surrounded her. In a few photographs she stood next to former U.S. presidents, European Prime Ministers, and US Secretaries of State. No family photos. No husband. No children.

She returned carrying a loaded tray. A coffee urn, two cups on saucers, a small decanter of cream and a sugar bowl. She set the tray on the coffee table in front of the sofas. She sat on the grey sofa and poured the coffee. I resumed my seat on the brown leather one.

"You have a very remarkable life," I said. Mike had taught me to conduct interviews like a conversation. Especially when the subjects weren't suspects, the objective to obtain information.

Her eyes met mine. In hers a discerning perceptiveness, as though searching for hidden meanings behind my words. She pondered for a moment.

"It's been fulfilling," She said.

"Any regrets?"

She smiled, as though she'd read my thoughts and had been anticipating the question.

"You mean a family, children?"

She had read my thoughts. Her life, no husband, children, a family of her own; struck a personal chord in me.

"Yes," I stammered, thrown by her perceptiveness. But also appreciative of her forthrightness, welcoming it. Glad I'd decided to be straight with her.

"None," She said. "But why don't we talk about why you're here? I must say I'm a bit surprised a member of the St. Vincent Police Force would come all this way to New York to see me."

"Miz Meeks....."

"Gloria, Please," she interrupted.

"Miz...Gloria. Do you believe Jackson Taylor capable of suicide?"

"My dear, anyone is capable of suicide I suppose. If you're asking if I think he killed himself. The answer is no."

"I don't believe he did either. It's the reason I came all this way."

She smiled, as though acknowledging her appreciation for my own forthrightness. The inquisitive eyes studying me since my arrival acquired a different aspect, as though seeing something else for the first time.

"I take it you're investigating his death?"

"Yes I am. It's my case."

We sipped our coffee. Her eyes focused on the wall behind me, as if reliving the moments captured in the photographs. The light streaming through the windows behind her highlighted her hair and the back of her head, creating a halo like effect.

"Jackson was a very special man," she said. "I knew he was married of course. And I don't usually conduct relationships with married men. But their marriage was over in all but name only. Had been for quite some time. And Jackson was around only infrequently. It worked for us for some reason. And I cared deeply for him, even if it might not have been what a true romantic might describe as love. He was a brilliant man. And I shall miss him."

She possessed a precise manner of speaking. Her words thoughtfully chosen, her diction preternaturally proper.

"I couldn't attend his funeral of course. Not my place really. But at some point I hope to visit his grave. Say my farewell."

"When did you see him last?"

"The day he flew back to St. Vincent."

"How did he seem when you were last together?"

"If you mean depressed or despondent, nothing like that. If anything I'd say he was frightened."

"Frightened?" Her word choice alarmed me. "Do you know why? Had he been threatened in any way?"

"That I don't know. He'd been consumed with some sort of project the last few months. I attributed his anxiety to fear it might not conclude as successfully as he desired. Normally that wasn't his nature. But I gather the stakes were fairly high."

"Do you know what project he'd been working on?"

"Not specifically. We tried not to talk shop when we were together. We were each other's escape from our workaday world."

I opened my handbag, extracted two folded sheets of paper and a photograph.

"Do you happen to know what these numbers might mean? The second notation apparently refers to your address." I handed her the sheet.

She studied it for a moment. "Well if the second notation represents an address, the first appears to also. The third is different, and I have no idea what it means."

Quick, I thought. Definitely a mind for numbers.

"If I'm not mistaken this is Jackson's handwriting," she said.

"Yes. The note was found among his things." I didn't mention Jackson's wife.

She continued to study the photocopied note and her eyes narrowed. Age lines appeared across her brow and formed crow's feet between her eyes at the top of her nose. Perhaps grief I reflected. Taylor's handwriting a tangible reminder of him.

Instead she said. "You know, this may refer to Seven Forty Park Avenue."

On the verge of informing her it didn't quite fit, she continued. "Most people don't know the building also carries the address Seventy One East Seventy First Street."

My heart skipped a beat.

"Quite a famous building actually," she said. "Among the most expensive in Manhattan. John D. Rockefeller, Jr. kept an apartment there. If I'm not mistaken Jacqueline Kennedy Onassis had an apartment there at one time too."

A desperate internal struggle to contain my excitement.

"What about this?" I asked, handing her the other sheet. Do you recognize any of the names in the first or third columns?"

Her gaze rose to meet mine. Had she detected the slight tremor in my voice? In the hand holding the papers?

"The names are familiar in the financial world," she said. "I've met a few of them on occasion. But I do not know them personally. The third column contains the names of corporations involved in international financing, banking, contractual negotiations, that sort of thing. Some have approached us in the past regarding underwriting various development projects. What is the significance of these?"

"Jackson Taylor was interested in them," I said without elaborating. "Do you recognize the man in this photograph?" I handed her the photograph of Arnold Greene aka Charles Mansfield.

"No. I've never seen that person before," she said handing back the photograph.

"What about Arnold Greene. Does the name mean anything to you?"

"I know the name. He heads one of the corporations on the list you showed me. Equities International Group I think it is. I know who he is, but I don't personally know the man. I've never met him. Actually Jackson also asked me if I knew him. He seemed keen to arrange a meeting with him."

The internal struggle continued to rage. The ability to contain my growing excitement proving more difficult as the connection between Taylor and Greene drew closer to reality.

"Do you know if they actually met?" I asked, practically holding my breath.

"That I do not know."

My disappointment palpable. I hid its expression from my voice, and my face.

"I've been going through documents Mr. Taylor had on his computer," I managed in an even tone. "They appear to be connected to this project you mentioned. But they seem incomplete, preliminary. Do you know if he kept any files, or notes, or any of his work anywhere else besides his laptop computer?"

Her gaze sought mine again. Her eyes held mine in a searching stare, again conveying the impression of reaching for a decision; attempting to make up her mind about something. Perhaps regarding me.

"What do you hope to accomplish by this investigation?" She asked me. Her stare boring into mine.

"I want to know what happened, and why he died," I said.

"You don't believe he killed himself, therefore you must think someone killed him." Not a question.

"I believe so, yes."

"How long will you be staying in New York?"

"Not long. Maybe another day or two."

"Is there a way for me to reach you?"

"Yes." I reached into my handbag for a pen and a notepad. I wrote down the number of the prepaid phone Gage had provided. I handed it her. She studied it.

"This is a local number," she said.

"Yes."

She nodded. "I will call you tomorrow."

The interview appeared over. She didn't exactly say so, or say anything at all. But I had the distinct impression we'd arrived at a conclusion. I didn't want to push her, and I'd run out of questions to ask anyway. We sat silently observing each other until I rose from the sofa.

"Thank you for taking the time," I said. "You've been really helpful, and I look forward to hearing from you."

"I thank you, my dear, for your diligence. And for caring."

She walked me to the front door. In the hallway she handed me my coat and scarf before opening the door. We shook hands.

Before leaving I said, "Thank you again. Please accept my condolences. I'm very sorry for you loss."

She smiled. Her gaze followed me to the staircase before closing the door.

On the front stoop of Gloria Meeks' building I switched off the jammer. Late afternoon. The sky had turned a drab grey. Dark, heavy clouds moved in from the west, obscuring the descending sun. More activity on the street. Residents of the block hurried along the sidewalk in the focused obsessive manner typical of New York pedestrians. A blue and white NYPD patrol car, its rooftop beacons flashing, sat at the end of the block. Another at the corner on Riverside Drive.

The temperature noticeably colder than when I'd arrived. I wrapped the scarf around my neck, and buttoned and belted the long overcoat. I pulled a pair of black lamb skin gloves from my handbag and tugged them on. I continued scanning the street, and the people moving about. No one appeared particularly interested in me.

The prepaid cell phone hadn't rung. Gage would've called should anything be amiss. Still out of sight somewhere. I'd been instructed to walk two blocks east to Broadway and head south to a restaurant at Eighty Fourth Street. He'd meet me there if everything appeared okay. If not he'd call, and I'd follow the protocols I'd assiduously studied over the past day and night.

I crossed the wide divided thoroughfare to the restaurant located on the east side of Broadway. The atmosphere inside warm and inviting. The room decorated in cherry red, from the buttoned leather seating to the lamp shades on the tables. And quiet. Soft muted music in the background. Early yet for dinner. Only a few of the tables occupied.

A host in a suit and tie greeted me. I informed him I'd be expecting someone and he invited me to wait at the bar, located on a balcony overlooking the dining room. A few male eyes followed me as I headed up the staircase. I shook off my overcoat and removed the scarf, hanging them over the back of the barstool. My handbag I placed next to me on the bar. Its weight a reminder of the Glock nestled in the bottom.

Only two other patrons at the bar, two guys. They eyed me curiously, between glances at a hockey game playing on a pair of overhead flat screens. The bartender approached and I ordered a Manhattan. My homage to the city.

The bar provided an unobstructed view of the entrance. I'd been nursing my drink for about ten minutes when Gage entered. His eyes dissected the room in his usual manner. When his gaze rose to survey the balcony he noticed me. A slight nod the only acknowledgement. He headed up the stairs.

We met at the bar, a quick kiss in greeting. The guys at the other end of the bar unable to conceal their disappointment. The bartender returned and Gage ordered a Rum Collins.

"How'd it go?" He asked after his cocktail arrived and the bartender departed.

"Really well. And the best thing, Lowell's address actually does match the numbers on Taylor's note."

"How?"

"Gloria told me the building actually has two addresses. Seventy Forty Park Avenue and Seventy One East Seventy First Street. He combined the two addresses. She's quite a woman Gage. Smart. Perceptive. Parhaps a touch lonely too."

"She have anything else useful?"

"One thing. She said Taylor was 'keen', her word, to meet Greene. For a second I thought she'd make the connection between Taylor and Greene. But she didn't know if they'd actually met. Then toward the end, when I asked her if Taylor kept any of his work anywhere else besides his laptop, I got the impression she was holding back. She asked me for my number and said she'd call me."

"What do you think it means?"

"Dunno. She's very careful and thoughtful in the way she speaks and makes decisions. Maybe I didn't completely gain her trust. Or maybe she needs more time to think about whatever it is she knows. I couldn't tell. How'd it go on your end?"

"Two man team in a white panel van parked at the end of the block. They had more pressing matters to deal with at the time."

"The cops?" I said, remembering the patrol cars at the end of the block. He nodded. I smiled and asked, "What do you want to do now?"

"There's still a couple hours of daylight left. Let's take a look at the other address."

We hailed a cab outside the restaurant. Gage provided the driver a destination. The cab turned east on Eighty Sixth Street and we traversed Central Park. The cab pulled to the corner at Madison and Seventy First Street. Gage pushed a twenty dollar bill through the payment slot and told the driver to keep the change. We exited the cab and headed arm in arm across the avenue.

A Gothic brownstone cathedral dominated the northeast corner. Its entrance façade occupied half the block on Madison Avenue, and its side extended halfway down Seventy First Street. From one corner of the magnificent building a tall spire rose into the sky. One of the things I loved about New York City. The marvelous juxtaposition of old existing alongside the new. The stunning contrasts, at once grandiose and simple, cosmopolitan and parochial. And the fascinating diversity of people and neighborhoods.

Toward the end of the block we approached the seventeen story luxury apartment building. Its imposing mass dominated the corner, like the church at the other end. Perfect bookends at either end of the block. One old, one new. Denuded trees bordered the canopied entrance on Seventy First Street.

We strolled past, like any other couple on the street. Crossed on the green light to the east side of Park Avenue. We ambled north, pausing to gaze at the limestone sheathed building, its fluted art deco base, and polished granite entrance. A green canopy covered the front entrance, topped by finials and flanked by more bare trees. The building's address carved into a granite slab above the entrance.

I gazed up at its height, noted the balcony railings on the upper floors, the cartouches, and the elegant columned entrances.

"What do you think?" I asked.

"Heavy hitters with heavy security," Gage said. "And probably very discreet, very closed mouth staff. We need to think of some other options."

We continued walking. We crossed Park Avenue again at Seventy Second Street. Christmas lights adorned the trees lining a center island dividing the avenue. The lights had just switched on, producing a festive holiday display as far as the eye could see.

We walked west to Fifth Avenue. Crossed to the Central Park side and headed south. Dusk closed in on the city, darkness arriving early as a result of daylight saving time, and increasing clouds. The air cold, but we'd dressed for warmth, and walking held the chill at bay.

We strolled hand in hand. Silent for the most part. Absorbed in the scenery and our own thoughts. Another thing I'd loved about the city, walking its streets. Manhattan a true pedestrian city. Its sidewalks pedestrian highways containing fascinating sights and sounds. Always something new to see. No matter how often you travelled the route, or how well you knew the neighborhood, something new might await around the corner. Something unusual, offbeat. A colorful character or unexpected happening. And the city acquired an entirely different intensity at night, morphing into a gloriously lit landscape possessing a nocturnal vivacity of its own. A city that never sleeps.

The sidewalk grew more crowded as we neared Fifty Ninth Street. A small crowd had gathered around a huge Hanukkah Menorah erected in the plaza between the opulent Pierre and Plaza Hotels. The entire scene - the oversized Menorah, the hotels' gilded facades festively decorated for the season, the horse drawn carriages parked around the plaza - quintessential New York.

We continued south along Fifth Avenue into the commercial area, passing Salvation Army carolers and bell ringing Santas on every other corner. We joined other sidewalk spectators lingering in front of elaborate Christmas window displays, virtual winter wonderlands created behind the storefront glass of FAO Schwartz, Bergdorf Goodman, and Cartier.

In the middle of the block between Fiftieth and Forty Ninth Streets we turned into a promenade of channel gardens between two soaring office buildings. The Pedestrian plaza a festive celebration of holiday decorations and lights. Lights hung from eight foot tall winged angels on either side of the central channel, their long lit trumpets pointed at the sky.

At the end of the promenade, above the gilt bronze Prometheus statue, Rockefeller Center's Christmas tree stood six stories tall, adorned by thirty thousand lights. Below the tree, in a bright, white ice oval, ice skaters cavorted. Young and old, singles and couples, kids in bright colored garb bundled against the cold; all gliding across the ice to Christmas music emanating from a hidden source.

I leaned against Gage, squeezed his arm.

"It's wonderful." I said. "Especially being here with you."

He smiled, and kissed me lightly on my lips.

We lingered a while longer, observing the skaters, gazing in wonder at the enormous tree, absorbing the festive atmosphere surrounding us. We strolled along Forty Ninth Street to Sixth Avenue, known officially as Avenue of the Americas, but no real New Yorker called it that.

Office buildings lined both sides of the avenue. Lights shimmered in their tall towers reaching into the inky sky. A block farther north neon signs and a scrolling marquee announced the location of Radio City Music Hall.

"That's it," Gage said.

"What?"

"Lowell's office building," indicating a soaring office Tower directly before us on the opposite side of the avenue.

I thought we'd been strolling aimlessly, taking in the nighttime Christmas sights. At least I had. Gage had evidently chosen our direction more deliberately, wrenching me back to the purpose of our presence in New York. But the city at

Christmas time, at night, Gage's arm around me, had worked its magic. Had already cast its spell.

Not ready to break the spell just yet.

CHAPTER 22

Gage and I sat at the kitchen island drinking coffee, mapping out our day. After scouting both locations Gage decided Lowell's office our best approach. A few phone calls and a plausible cover story provided Lowell's schedule. We'd catch him at his office.

"What if he refuses to see us," I asked.

"He won't. We're federal agents. The problem will be getting to his floor without security in the lobby alerting them. They've enhanced security in those buildings since nine-eleven." Gage studied schematics of the building on his laptop, particularly its lobby, entrances, and exits.

The morning had dawned murky grey under an overcast sky. And colder. Gage remarked it might snow. He'd dressed in a dark blue gabardine suit, a white dress shirt and striped blue tie. He wore a tan greatcoat and a brown scarf. A fashion I'd never seen on him before. And yet natural. As if he wore a suit every day. It surprised and amused me at the same time. He'd dressed to blend in. An upper management type. Invisible among other New Yorkers similarly dressed in daytime business attire.

I'd also donned a suit hanging among the wardrobe provided in the closets. All my size. All my style.

Characteristically thorough Mr. Gage. I'd chosen a dark blue pant suit accompanied by a white cashmere turtle neck, white scarf, and the same heavy wool overcoat I'd worn the day before.

We arrived at the corporate stretch of Sixth Avenue between Rockefeller Center and Radio City Music Hall. The wide avenue like a river bed at the bottom of a steep canyon. Streams of humanity flowed along banks. Farther out a rushing river of traffic surged in a cacophonous tide.

We headed for a fifty-four story building fronted by a landscaped plaza and a large fountain pool at the entrance. The fountains turned off to accommodate automobile sized cherry red Christmas ornaments erected in the pool.

We entered the high ceilinged, marble walled, marble floored Lobby. Ornately decorated and furnished. A large Christmas tree stood at one side of the lobby. A wreath the size of a hot tub hung against one wall. A mural covered the immense ceiling.

Gage paid particular attention to a small Garden Park visible through tall glass walls at the other end of the lobby. The area contained seating, food kiosks, and a two-story wall over which water cascaded in an artificial waterfall. He strode confidently to the main security desk, approaching the far end of the counter from the side, rather than directly in front to avoid direct exposure to the security cameras. I followed in his footsteps.

"We need an escort to the fortieth floor," he said, discreetly displaying his FBI identification to one of the dark suited security officers. "And it'd be in everyone's interest if we were not announced," his voice soft yet commanding.

After inspecting the ID the man moved from behind the counter and instructed us to follow him. He led us across the lobby to the building's bank of elevators. Again Gage chose a path out of the direct line of the lobby's cameras. The elevators stood behind a cordon of waist high glass barriers, accessed through turnstiles. The security guard swiped his access card and entered through the turnstile. He swiped it again for me, and for Gage.

In the elevators we'd be unable to avoid the cameras. Gage had coached me on how to angle my head down and away, preventing the cameras from obtaining full on face shots usable by facial recognition software.

The Lowell Group occupied the entire fortieth floor of the skyscraper. The high speed elevator launched us upward, producing the sensation of leaving my stomach in the lobby.

The elevator slowed, stopped, and opened onto a wide corridor. More marble walls and floors. Floor to ceiling windows provided a vertigo inducing view of Sixth Avenue below. Above, dark grey clouds close enough to touch.

The guard escorted us to a reception desk of polished glass and chrome. Behind it sat a twenty-something receptionist possessing cover girl features and a practiced smile. She wore a slim telephone earpiece and mike tucked behind her left ear. Her gaze rose as we approached. Noticing the security guard accompanying us a shadow of concern fractured the smile.

"May I help you?" she asked, the smile struggling to remain in place. Gage showed her the ID, again holding it discreetly below the reception counter so as not to alarm other staffers moving to and fro behind the reception desk.

"We need a few moments with Mr. Lowell," Gage said.

She punched a button on her console and spoke into the mike next to her cheek. An exchange followed, in which Gage insisted on seeing Mr. Lowell. We needed only a few moments of his time, Gage pressed, threatening that a short quiet interview was preferable to the alternative. The receptionist asked us to wait, her smile returning as though aimed at unseen photographers.

Moments later another woman, older, dressed in an expensive, tailored business suit strode down the hall and approached us. She halted in front of Gage.

He again presented his ID and introduced us. "And you are?"

"I'm Mr. Lowell's executive assistant. May I ask what this is about Agent Burke?"

"You may, but it really is a confidential matter between me and Mr. Lowell."

She pondered a moment before inviting us to follow her. Lowell's office occupied a corner suite overlooking Sixth Avenue and Fiftieth Street. The executive assistant ushered us into a carpeted conference room, separated from the corridor by a glass wall. Floor to ceiling windows lined the opposite side of the room, providing views of the street far below. The pedestrians ant like. The vehicles match box toys.

A long, polished mahogany table occupied the center of the room, surrounded by plush burgundy leather armchairs. The walls at both ends of the room paneled in mahogany, matching the table. One wall contained a built-in sideboard and cabinets. On the other, recessed bookshelves on either side of a window sized impressionist oil painting. Closed doors at both ends of the room.

The door in the wall closest to us opened. A brief glimpse of a large office and dark furnishings before the man entering the conference room closed the door. I recognized him from his internet bio. Henry Lowell. Tall and trim for his age. Immaculately dressed in a custom dark blue pinstriped suit. Italian or Saville Row I guessed. Beneath the suit jacket a micro striped dark blue dress shirt, white collar, rose colored silk tie, and gold collar pin. His overall appearance sharp, crisp and distinguished.

Fifty six years old according to his bio. Same age as Gage. Slicked back silver hair, a George Hamilton tan, and strong, handsome features. A discernable presence when he entered the room.

He shook our hands and greeted us in an open welcoming manner.

"What can I do for my government today, Agent....?" his smile revealing a row of perfectly straight perfectly white teeth.

"Special Agent Burke," Gage said. "And this is Special Agent Berrigan. We just need a bit of information you might be able to help us with.

"Certainly, certainly," he said, offering us seats on either side of the conference table. He reserved the chair at the head of the table for himself.

"Can I offer you something? Coffee? Tea?"

"No thank you," Gage said.

An almost imperceptible nod dismissed the assistant, who'd remained hovering in the background.

"So how may I help you?" he said after she'd exited the room.

Gage gestured to me, and I took over. Lowell's gaze lingered now we were directly engaged. His blue eyes held the familiar speculative glint I'd grown to recognize. At least his eyes held mine. His gaze didn't stray to my chest or attempt to undress me.

"What can you tell us about Arnold Greene?" I asked.

His eyes lost their playfulness. Abruptly focused, and intent, shifting rapidly between me and Gage.

"I've heard rumors..." hesitating, not sure of his footing. "Something about an investigation."

"That isn't our interest here," I said. "What can you tell us about him?"

"Nothing you probably don't already know yourselves. We travel in the same business and social circles," he said, his accent Boston Brahmin.

"Did he ever mention a Jackson Taylor to you?"

"Jackson," he smiled. "Dear fellow. As far as I know they'd never met until recently. I happened to introduce them," he said.

"How exactly did that come about?" I asked. A herculean effort to contain the erupting excitement inside me.

"I received a call from Jackson. He said he was working on a project Arnold might be of assistance in, and would I arrange an introduction. He knew Arnold and I moved in the same circles."

"And how did you arrange it?" The struggle to contain my excitement continuing.

"My wife was hosting a charity event at our apartment. I knew Arnold would be there. I invited Jackson."

Connection achieved. A giddy tingling swept through me.

"Did Mr. Taylor happen to mention the project he was working on?"

"No he didn't. I presume it had something to do with St. Vincent and the Grenadines. That's a small island nation in the Eastern Caribbean," he explained pedantically. I tried not to smile.

"That's where Jackson's from. Doing magnificent work down there. He's very dedicated. Driven sometimes."

"After you introduced them did Mr. Greene ever mention Mr. Taylor or what they might've been working on?"

"No. I haven't seen Arnold since that night. In light of some of the things I've been hearing, I can understand why."

Gage and I exchanged a glance. He had nothing further to ask.

"Well Mr. Lowell," Gage said, pushing his chair from the table and standing. "We appreciate your time."

Gage stuck his hand out. Lowell, clearly surprised at the abrupt end to the interview, stood, grasped and shook it.

"That's it?" he said. "I wish I could have been more helpful."

"On the contrary. You were very helpful. Thank you for your time." I said. He grasped my offered hand and shook it, holding it a bit longer than necessary.

Back on earth on Sixth Avenue Gage whipped off his tie and opened his collar. My lips parted in an amused smile.

"We've got the connection," I said. "They did know each other."

"Good gut. You were correct. Now we have to figure out what it means."

"Greene-Mansfield was supposedly meeting someone on Union Island. What if it was Taylor? What if that's what got him killed? Got them both killed?"

"Possible," Gage said. "But you've still got a piece missing."

"I know. Motive. And who ordered the hit?"

An unfamiliar obnoxious sound emanated from my handbag. The sound penetrated my thoughts, and I remembered the prepaid phone Gage had given me. When I answered it a voice on the other end said, "Superintendent Johanssen?" Gloria Meeks' voice.

"Yes."

"This is Gloria Meeks. I wonder if you might meet me downtown, by the United Nations building."

I cupped the phone in my palm and whispered to Gage.

"It's Gloria Meeks. She wants me to meet her. How long to get down to the UN?"

"Tell her you'll be there in fifteen minutes."

I told her so.

"Very well. I'll meet you on the northwest corner of Forty Fourth Street and First Avenue in fifteen minutes, in front of the Chase bank. I shall not wait if you are late."

Gage hailed a cab on Fiftieth Street. We piled in. The cab continued east to Second Avenue before turning south. Vehicles filled the Avenue from curb to curb, moving in a pulsing ebb and surge like blood corpuscles coursing through the City's arteries.

Gage instructed the driver to pull up on the east side of Second Avenue at Forty Fifth Street. We exited the cab and parted after a brief kiss. I headed down Forty Fifth toward First Avenue. Gage headed toward Forty Fourth.

He had a thing about Gloria Meeks, especially after learning she'd been under surveillance. He figured any danger might come from that quarter. The circle around Greene might also be covered he'd explained, including surveillance by the FBI. But we hadn't gone close to anyone in Greene's circle. And the FBI wasn't investigating Jackson Taylor. They had no need to cover his circle. It meant whoever had Gloria Meeks under surveillance knew of her connection to Taylor. Maybe the people responsible for his death.

During the cab ride he'd again repeated the protocols, substituting midtown locations which provided similar advantages to the upper eastside ones he'd chosen around Gloria Meeks's apartment.

I turned into the long block between Second and First Avenues. Walking briskly I kept pace amid the pedestrian traffic, but timed myself not to arrive too early or too late. The surrounding buildings all part of the United Nations community. Many bore brass plaques announcing the offices of this or that mission to the UN. The UN building housed Gloria Meeks' agency, but she also had an office on Forty Fourth Street. I passed the high rise towers and sprawling plaza of the Millennium UN Plaza Hotel. The plaza stretched across the block to Forty Fourth Street, its flagpoles bearing the national flags of member nations.

When I turned the corner at First Avenue the United Nations Complex itself lay before me across the wide divided avenue. The swift flowing East River gun metal grey in the background. A tall glass skyscraper sat on the corner of Forty Fourth Street. Its glass frame flared at the bottom, forming a glass canopy above the sidewalk. The front entrance also glass, a large Chase Bank sign visible through the glass above the double doors.

Exactly twelve minutes since Gloria Meeks' call. I waited at the entrance. Gage nowhere in sight. The bank's swinging glass doors in constant motion as people entered and exited the Bank.

"Superintendent," a soft voice called from the doorway. Gloria Meeks stood inside the entrance, immaculate in a tailored grey skirt suit and white silk blouse buttoned to her neck. Over them she wore a tan calf length fur collared overcoat. She motioned me inside.

Her intense inquiring gaze held mine.

"Jackson gave me something for safekeeping," she said in her forthright manner. No preamble or small talk. "I've kept it here in a safety deposit box. I was unsure what to do with it after Jackson died, until my conversation with you. I've decided it might be best for you to have it."

Her eyes remained fixed on mine while she spoke, as though seeking confirmation she'd reached the correct decision. She pulled two large bulky manila envelopes from her handbag and held them out to me.

"Do you know what it is?" I asked.

"Jackson never said, and I never looked," she said.

"What would you have me do with these?" Unconsciously imitating her diction.

"Whatever you think best, my dear. I believe I can trust you."

"Thank you," I said, staring at the envelopes, accepting them from her tentatively, as though they contained some kind of explosive. I had no doubt they did. I folded them lengthwise and stuffed both into my handbag.

When our gaze met again she smiled. "Be very careful my dear. And good luck," she said. "And if you need anything further, please do not hesitate to contact me." She handed me a folded slip of paper. I opened it to read her numbers written there. Home, office, and cell.

We parted on the sidewalk in front of the bank. She strode across the avenue toward the UN building. I headed up Forty Fifth Street.

The sidewalk uncrowded, but the sparse pedestrian traffic bustled along in the focused frantic manner characteristic of New Yorkers. Like columns of ants following different scent trails. And yet a certain logical order existed in the chaotic bustle. Walkers kept to the right, like drivers on the streets, maintaining a steady, unobstructed flow. The system occasionally broke down, producing a pedestrian traffic jam, usually the result of out-of-towners pausing to mill about and gawk. Knowledge of the pattern useful when tailing someone. Or conversely, spotting a tail.

I had an acute sensation of being followed. My imagination perhaps. An amped up paranoia produced by the mysterious envelopes burning a hole in my bag. Perhaps they contained the reason Greene and Taylor had been killed. Meaning someone wouldn't hesitate to kill again to obtain them. And now I had them.

Reassured by Gage's presence, somewhere on the street, watching my back. But hoping my anxiety and paranoia were unfounded.

I used the reflective surfaces of the buildings and vehicles along the sidewalk to monitor the pedestrian pattern behind me. I didn't notice anyone breaking the pattern. Unable to shake the ominous sensation either. I slowed, reached into my bag for the cell phone. My fingers brushed against the Glock in a subconscious affirmation of security. I rearranged the grip's position for easy access, wishing it rode in a holster on my hip instead.

I used the excuse of dialing to check behind me. Noticed a man halfway down the block slow his pace and change direction to cross the street. Uncertain if his change of direction had been normal or not. He hurried along the opposite sidewalk, attention focused ahead, moving ahead of me. I continued toward Second Avenue, speed dialing the preprogrammed number as I walked.

"At the risk of sounding paranoid," I said when Gage answered, "I can't shake the feeling I'm being tailed."

"That's because you're being tailed," he answered calmly. Too damn calm for the jolt his words sent up my spine.

"Two man team. One just crossed to the opposite side of the street, the other far enough behind to make him difficult to spot. Probable a car too, waiting on Second Avenue in case you take a cab."

"What do I do?"

Silence. I moved the phone from my ear to check the display. Reassured myself we hadn't been disconnected.

"Gage."

"Change of plan," he said. "This may be turning into a snatch."

"What the hell does that mean?" My anxiety growing.

"The guy who crossed the street just crossed back, ahead of you. The one behind is moving up. And a town car just turned into the street pacing you."

"Gage....."

"Not to worry my love. Just do exactly as I tell you. Don't stop for anything, no matter what happens. Get to Second Avenue and grab the first cab you can get. Follow the protocol."

"Gage...." Unable to vocalize more than his name. My pulse quickened, racing. Rising anxiety and fear constricted my throat, stifling my words.

"Got you covered Jo. Just keep walking. Don't turn around. Don't pay any attention to the guy coming toward you.

As he said this I recognized the man moving along the sidewalk in my direction. The man I'd noticed earlier crossing the street. His eyes focused ahead. Not paying any particular attention to me or anyone else on the sidewalk.

Offices on my left. Not sure of Gage's position. He wanted me to keep heading toward Second Avenue. Toward the man heading in my direction.

I clutched the phone to my left ear. My right hand went into my bag. Touched the grip of the Glock nestled there. Every impulse in my body screamed for me to do something. To take action to protect myself. I fought the impulse. Put my trust in Gage.

My heart pounded in my chest as the distance between me and the man closed. A commotion behind me. The natural instinct to stop, turn and look.

"Keep moving Jo. Don't stop," said Gage's voice in my ear as the man shifted direction to intercept me. A flash of concern clouded the man's face, momentarily distracting his attention to the unknown commotion behind me.

He fell forward, onto his knees, as though tripped by something on the sidewalk. Both hands gripped his right knee, held at an odd angle. He made no sounds, but his face bore the unmistakable signs of painful agony. And then I noticed the red stream seeping through the fingers clutching his knee. I hadn't heard a shot.

I lifted my gaze from the fallen man. Scanned the sidewalk ahead as I continued walking. I skirted the writhing man on the pavement as though nothing had happened. Noticed a tan trench coat clad figure crossing the street ahead, a cell phone pressed to his ear.

A few pedestrians slowed, gawking at the stricken man. Unaware of exactly what had happened. Others simply detoured around the scene, like water flowing around a rock.

I continued moving. I reached Second Avenue and hailed a cab. Before entering the cab I glanced down the block. A small knot of people surrounded the man. Farther down the block a similar knot surrounded another man desperately attempting to wave off the Samaritans and hobble to a waiting black town car.

Still clutching the phone to my ear as the cab entered the downtown traffic stream I said, "What the hell was that?"

"One team neutralized but you may not be out of the woods yet. They may have a backup team on the Avenue."

As he said it I shifted in the seat to gaze out the taxi's rear window.

"So what now?"

"Follow the protocol. Get to Grand Central Terminal. Lose the tail and go to ground until you hear from me. I'll sweep your trail. Call me when you get there." The click in my ear indicated he'd disconnected.

Another wave of anxiety welled up inside me. I didn't relish breaking contact. Even for a short time. Gage's voice on the phone my lifeline. And just as abruptly a calm confidence replaced the anxiety and fear. Gage had anticipated this scenario. Had been prepared for it. His actions had saved me and cleared my path. Still out there watching my back, literally. Doing the thing he did better than anyone.

I mentally ran through the protocol and planned my moves for Grand Central Terminal. We'd discussed two scenarios. Get in and get out before anyone had a chance to take up positions at the entrances and exits. They'd need a few bodies to cover them all. Or head for the subways and take the first one leaving the station. It'd depend on how close they were when I entered the station. They'd want to get in as soon as I did. And they'd need to stay close to not lose me in the crowd.

I had a vague recollection of the Terminal's interior. I'd been inside a number of times to take Metro-North trains to Westchester. But it'd been years ago, and apart from its iconic features, I didn't remember much about the details.

I checked the cab's meter a block from the Forty Second Street entrance. I pressed a bill covering the fare and tip into the slot, telling the driver to keep the change. I maintained a watch out the rear window, but in the swarm of traffic I couldn't be sure if anyone had been following the cab.

I speed dialed Gage as the driver pulled up to the bustling entrance. I exited the cab before it ceased moving.

CHAPTER 23

"I'm at the terminal," I said when Gage answered. "I don't remember much about the layout."

"I'll talk you through it," he said.

As we talked I moved into the crowd, scanning the wide street outside the entrance. A pedestrian stream flowed along the sidewalk. A crush of vehicles, most of them yellow, ebbed in both directions along Forty Second Street. A rumbling rush overhead on the Park Avenue overpass.

I saw it. A black town car similar to the one on Forty Fifty street pulled up. Three men scampered out. Headed toward the terminal. They hadn't seen me. I relayed this information to Gage as I dashed inside.

I passed through an interior archway and another set of doors. The marble floored passageway sloped downward into the belly of the terminal. I moved toward the main concourse, weaving a path through the crowd streaming in the opposite direction.

In the immense Beaux Arts main concourse I slowed, orienting myself. A gigantic American flag hung below the celestial mural adorning the vast vaulted ceiling. Large melon-shaped chandeliers hung below it. Directly ahead, the famously recognizable four-sided brass clock stood atop an electronic information booth. To my right and left, arched entrances led to the east and west sides of the terminal. Retail shops and restaurants lined the passageways. Stairs led to restaurants lining balconies overlooking the concourse. A constant stream of people entered and exited the restaurants. Others loitered on the balcony. Great arched windows provided natural light. Not much sunlight penetrating the grey overcast outside.

"I'm in the main concourse," I said into the phone, resuming my pace.

"Keep to your right. Stay away from the center of the concourse. Head east to the passageway for the Lexington Avenue subway."

The crowd in the main concourse hadn't yet reached the tumultuous rush hour crush. But adequate for my purposes. I moved quickly. Purposefully. Inconspicuously. Merely another commuter rushing to catch my train. I resisted the urge to glance over my shoulder. My recent anxiety forgotten. My faith in Gage unshakable.

The public address system announced arrival and departure information for the platforms and tracks in and out of the terminal. I twisted and weaved through the crowd, remaining close to the old ticket booths. I slipped into a passageway behind the stairs leading to the east balcony. The sign on the marble archway read "Lexington Passage."

"I'm in the passage," I told Gage, rushing past a variety of retail stores lining either side of the marble passageway.

"Okay. You've got two guys on the inside. You're maybe three minutes ahead of them. The driver went around to Vanderbilt. And there's a third moving around to Lexington.

Come out the Lexington Avenue exit. I'm already in position to sweep your trail."

At another place and time I might've considered the jargon amusing. But I appreciated the seriousness of my situation. And the stakes. Two men already dead. And I'd become a target.

I merged into the pedestrian flow moving north on Lexington Avenue. An acute sensation of having a target painted on my back. I focused on the protocol. Exfiltrating the immediate area. Changing direction. Locating a place to lay low. Waiting for Gage to contact me.

I turned right on Forty Fourth and quickly covered the long block. Turned left onto Third Avenue. On my left, halfway along the block, a storefront sported a green façade and a green canopy over the entrance. The sign above the canopy read "Blarney Stone". Cafeteria style tables and a long bar visible through the front glass. A dozen or so customers eating and drinking inside.

I entered. The establishment a combination deli, restaurant, dive bar and Irish pub.

The green décor continued inside, including the walls, tables and floor. Like a never ending St. Patrick's Day celebration. The clientele noticeably blue collar types, and mostly male. Multiple pairs of eyes followed me as I headed to the far end of the bar. Oldies music from the fifties played in the background.

I selected a barstool at the far end of the bar, facing the door and front glass, providing a view of the sidewalk. I ordered a roast beef sandwich on whole wheat, and coffee. I ate at the bar. The men along the bar eyed me. Some surreptitiously, some openly. I returned the smiles in a pleasant but uninviting manner, my demeanor cop-like. Their figuring me for a cop worked to my advantage.

A couple bites of my sandwich remained when the cell phone rang.

"You're clear," Gage said when I answered.

"Good to hear," I said, genuine relief in my voice.

"I'll pick you up outside in five minutes." Didn't surprise me he'd known my location without my having to tell him.

We disconnected and I called the bartender over for the check. I dropped a twenty dollar bill on the bar top for the surprisingly small tab, and headed toward the entrance. In five minutes a Crown Victoria yellow cab pulled to the curb. The rear door opened. Gage sat in the rear seat waiting. I strode across the sidewalk and slid onto the seat next to him. The cab joined the northbound traffic flow as soon as the door closed.

"Merde." I said, settling in beside Gage.

"You okay?"

"Yeah. Who do you think those men were?"

"Later. You handled that well."

"Did you have any doubt?"

"Not for a second. What did she give you?"

"Two packages. She said Jack....." about to say the name when Gage's arched eyebrow reminded me where we were, and of the cabdriver sitting within earshot of our conversation.

"They were given to her for safe keeping," I said instead.

"Any idea what's in them?"

"None. And she didn't know."

"Doesn't matter." His gaze distant. And contemplative.

"What?" I asked.

He leaned toward me, his voice almost a whisper.

"She's in danger. Your meeting her. Her passing something to you. Makes her more important now to whoever's been watching her. They'll want to find out what she gave you. What she knows. Even if she doesn't know anything."

"Sacre Crisse. Gage, we have to warn her."

"Probably won't accomplish much."

He reached into an inside breast pocket and pulled out his cell phone. Not the prepaid phone, but his personal cell, the sat capable encrypted phone. He selected a contact and sent a text.

"What're you doing?"

"Getting her some protection until I can come up with something more permanent."

The taxi turned left, heading west. And left again at Fifth Avenue, heading downtown. The drive progressed in silence. I gazed through the taxi's glass at the passing scenes. The ebb and flow of Manhattan life. During a break in texting Gage reached over and held my hand in his. An affectionate squeeze. I turned to him. Gazed at the hard set of his face, the steely impenetrability of his eyes. Like gazing into the core of a hurricane, calm and peaceful in the center, a violent maelstrom around the edges. An expression I'd observed before. And never fully comprehended. Now I understood its genesis.

Approaching Thirty Fourth Street Gage instructed the driver to turn right. "Drop us at Macy's," he told the driver.

I didn't question him, or inform him I wasn't in the mood for shopping.

The light changed to green. The cab surged through the sprawling intersection formed by the convergence of Broadway, Sixth Avenue and Thirty Fourth Street. It pulled to the corner next to the iconic eight story department store. Noise and color assailed us as we stepped from the taxi onto the sidewalk. People and traffic; an amorphous mass, possessing an avid kinetic energy.

The pedestrian stream on the sidewalk parted and flowed around us. Gage used the opportunity to check our rear. He lingered in front of a large display window enclosing a scene from the Christmas film 'Miracle on 34th Street'.

"You think we still have a tail?" I asked.

"Just being careful."

"You were expecting it, weren't you? Ever since we contacted Gloria Meeks. How'd you know?"

"I didn't. But when the probability exists, you have to assume it'll happen. It's how you stay alive."

We passed through the store's main entrance on Broadway, encountering a bewildering array of glass counters and displays. Bags, belts, jewelry, cosmetics and other merchandise. Immediately clear we weren't there to shop. Gage held my hand in a firm grip as we navigated the throng of stop and go shoppers, bypassing the scented perfume section, the women's fashions and the men's section. And all the other sections. Abruptly shifting direction. Mingling among the shoppers. Checking our rear in the mirrored surfaces, shined glass, and polished chrome within the store.

The store spanned the entire city block. We exited on Seventh Avenue. Merged into the teeming anonymous crowds

along the sidewalk. A yellow river flowed south, branching off
into smaller streams in front of Penn Station and Madison
Square Garden.

Gage waved over a passing cab. A yellow minivan
pulled to the curb. It rejoined the flow after we'd settled into
its rear seats. The taxi deposited us at Fifth Avenue and Tenth.
We walked east along Tenth, on the opposite side of the street
from Gage's building, both of us scanning the street, the
pedestrians, the parked cars. Nearing Broadway we crossed
East Tenth and approached the building.

The front door at the top of the stoop opened into a
small vestibule. Two doors on either side. The door on the left
led to the first floor studio and second floor apartment. The
door on the right, which Gage unlocked, led to the third and
fourth floor duplex.

The emotional roller coaster left me physically drained.
Glad to be back in the warm apartment. I stripped off the
overcoat and scarf. Hung them in the front closet by the door.
Desperate to shed the constricting suit. And I needed to use
the head.

In the bathroom the oversized tub beckoned. I longed
to indulge in a warm soothing bath. My desire overwhelmed
by a more omnipresent curiosity to explore the envelopes. And
my belief they contained the answers I'd been searching for.

I changed and returned to the kitchen. Gage gearing up
to go out again. He'd changed into black slacks, a black
turtleneck, and a black leather long coat. The aluminum case
mysteriously present on the counter, next to my handbag.

"You're going out." Not a question.

"Can't leave Gloria Meeks hanging out there. I have to
get her clear of this."

"You have a plan?"

"The beginnings of one maybe."

"Any idea yet who the people are watching her? And who tried to intercept me?"

"The plates from the van and the car trace to a security company based here in New York. Probably hired help, but I need to pay them a visit to find out who hired them. Before they move on Meeks, or come at you again."

"And you think they will?"

"We have to assume so. We also have to assume they know who you are, and why you're here. And they know Gloria Meeks gave you something. They don't know how to find you, and until today whether or not you're working alone. That's probably why the attempted snatch on the street. A huge risk in daylight with witnesses around. Right now they're probably busy trying to reacquire you."

"And they'll keep trying until they do?"

"Those envelopes are probably the reason two people are already dead. Maybe others we don't know about. I don't intend for Gloria Meeks to join that list. And we have to assume whoever's behind this will eventually track us down. We need to be super alert from here on. You keep the alarms and security monitors on while I'm out. And from now until this is over you wear the vest. I noticed you packed it."

I didn't protest or press the issue. Like it or not, the investigation had entered a realm familiar to him. And I had no qualms accepting his part in it. Or the harnessed lethality I'd perceived when we'd first met. It no longer frightened me. I'd long ago accepted it, by accepting him. All of him.

I contemplated accompanying him. Recognized the folly the moment the thought materialized. A product of my own anxiety for him. My safety an unnecessary complication. A distraction which might compromise what he needed to do. Protecting Gloria Meeks his primary concern. My primary concern, discovering who had killed Jackson Taylor and Alfred Greene, and why.

"You be safe," I said, planting a long tender kiss on his lips before releasing him into the night.

CHAPTER 24

I fixed myself a cup of coffee from the fresh pot Gage had brewed. I retrieved the bulky envelopes and settled into the comfortable couch in front of the fireplace. Gage had set a small crackling fire in the fireplace. I used the remote to switch on a large flat panel television and selected the closed circuit channel as Gage had shown me. Eight squares appeared on the screen, each an image from a closed circuit security camera. One square showed an empty basement garage.

I opened both envelopes and poured their contents onto the coffee table. A sheaf of papers, maybe two dozen in total, spilled across the table. Memos, letters, financial reports, lists of accounts and holdings, copies of emails. One letter in particular, bearing the familiar government seal and letterhead of St. Vincent and the Grenadines captured my attention. An ice cold stricture clutched my chest as I read its contents.

The letter was a response to an inquiry regarding the granting of Vincentian citizenship and a diplomatic passport to Alfred Greene. The letter affirmed the possibility of such an arrangement.

Greene seeking asylum and diplomatic immunity made sense, considering the charges he faced in the U.S. But why St. Vincent? Did he have something of particular interest to trade? Or perhaps he intended to simply buy citizenship. Not uncommon, though primarily used to facilitate foreign ownership of property and businesses in St. Vincent and the Grenadines. Inappropriate at best. Corrupt and possibly illegal at worst.

Sacrement!

One of the envelopes contained a pair of sixteen gigabyte thumb drives. I plugged one into the laptop. The drive opened automatically, presenting a blank screen on the laptop's monitor, a flashing colon in the upper left corner. I opened the computer's hierarchy of library folders. It listed the drive. But I couldn't access it.

Son of a bitch. Enfant de chienne. Disappointment and frustration grabbed hold until I remembered Taylor's note. I sprang from the couch to find Taylor's file among the pile on the dining table. I rifled through the file for the photocopied page of addresses and the unknown notation. I placed the cursor next to the flashing colon, entered the numbers letters and punctuation symbols as they appeared in the note.

A string of files blossomed across the screen. All MP3 audio files, named by dates. I inserted the second drive and opened it using the same decryption key. A list of word document files, some named by company. Corporations Taylor had listed in his other notes.

I returned to the first drive and opened an audio file named 'Report affidavit'.

"My name is Jackson Taylor," said a deep basso profundo from the laptop's speakers. Jackson Taylor's voice.

I'd heard it often on Vincentian radio and television. Its vibrant, resonant quality a stark contrast to the lifeless corpse embedded in my memory.

"I'm a consultant and advisor to the government of St. Vincent and the Grenadines," the recording continued. "This recording, along with accompanying recordings and documents, is my affidavit outlining the results of an investigation I undertook three months ago. I hereby affirm the statements and allegations contained herein are true, as evidenced by documentation wherever possible."

A pause. Unidentified ambient sounds in the background. A tantalizing curiosity gripped me. Did I truly have the answers right here in front of me?

"On September fifth of this year," the voice continued, "Prime Minister Defretas asked me to undertake two assignments on his behalf. The first involved a report on development projects in St. Vincent and the Grenadines, and their positive impact on the local economy and population. I inferred from our conversation the report might be instrumental in showcasing the Government's accomplishments in the next election campaign."

"The second assignment involved exploring the feasibility of liquidating the government's ownership interest in the St. Vincent National Bank. The Government is in debt to the bank to the tune of several hundred million Eastern Caribbean dollars, and is in danger of defaulting on the loans. Such an event will precipitate the bank's collapse. The Prime Minister wished advice on how liquidating the government's interest and privatizing the bank might be structured. He also wanted me to identify potential buyers. He wished the inquiry to be kept strictly confidential, so as not to cause rumors and a panicked run on the bank by depositors. A reasonable and prudent precaution. However, in light of my recent discoveries, he may have had other reasons for secrecy."

Another pause. Taylor spoke in the accented English of a Vincentian who'd lived and been educated abroad. He didn't exhibit the pedantic verbosity and polysyllabic conceit of many educated Caribbean speakers and writers. A characteristic compelling the use ten words where two would suffice. Instead Taylor's language was thankfully economical and concise.

His recorded voice continued. "I approached both requests as separate, unrelated tasks. While gathering data for the report on development, I decided to also examine negative impacts surrounding the issue. If the report might be used in an election campaign, having foreknowledge of information the opposition might use against the Prime Minister and Party seemed a prudent precautionary exercise.

"I discovered a widespread pattern of apparent mismanagement and lax oversight. Although politically problematic, these were manageable. However, the deeper I investigated, the more these lapses acquired the appearance of actual malfeasance, misconduct, and outright corruption, reaching as high as the Cabinet. I discovered a pattern of investments in local development projects from suspicious sources. And a suspicious pattern of funds transfers resembling schemes most often used in money laundering. Furthermore, investment capital transferred to St. Vincent and the Grenadines by a number of offshore corporations and individuals, appeared to be aimed at manipulating the local economy and the government.

"I uncovered a number of fraudulent schemes involving development projects in St. Vincent and the Grenadines. Among them the Claire Hall Boat Yard project, the Union Island Marina project, and the Canuoan Resort and Marina project. Furthermore, two of the corporate entities involved in these development projects also surfaced in my inquiries regarding the National Bank. The two tasks I'd undertaken were not as separate or unrelated as I'd originally believed. And the suspicious activities I'd uncovered in the first I also found present in the second.

"I presented my reports to Prime Minister Defretas in early November. I did not include my suspicions or concerns in either report, or inform him directly. I also did not inform him of my intention to pursue my investigations further.

"On November tenth of this year I travelled to New York in an attempt to speak with certain individuals at companies I'd identified in my inquiry. Through a mutual acquaintance I arranged an introduction to one such individual, a Mr. Arnold Greene, the Chief Executive Officer of Equity International Group, an international investment firm involved with the development projects I named earlier.

"When we were introduced I informed Mr. Greene of my reason for wanting to meet him. He indicated he may have information helpful to my inquiry, and we set an appointment to meet privately later in the week. At that subsequent meeting, Mr. Greene claimed to have insider knowledge of criminal activities involving St. Vincent and the Grenadines, and officials within the Government. He insisted I relay a proposal to my government. He'd agree to tell us everything he knew in exchange for Vincentian citizenship and a diplomatic passport.

"I was shocked by this request, and considered his proposal preposterous. I told him so. He ended the meeting, informing me it would be our last if his proposal was rejected. I therefore considered it our last meeting, and made arrangements to contact other individuals on my list. Nevertheless I sent his request to Attorney General Gaymes by Diplomatic currier.

"A few days later I received an official communiqué from Attorney General Gaymes relayed through the New York embassy, instructing me to meet Mr. Greene, and hand him an accompanying sealed envelope. After which I was to cease all further contact and communication with Mr. Greene.

"I disregarded these instructions. I opened the envelope which contained a letter from the Attorney General affirming Mr. Greene's deal. Not in exchange for information, but for his silence. I was shocked and appalled. I considered taking the matter to the Prime Minister directly, but upon reflection, I realized the improprieties I'd uncovered reached into the Prime Minister's office, since he also holds the portfolio of Ministry of Finance. Under the circumstances I did not know who to trust. The circumstances represented a level of corruption I'd never imagined.

"I photocopied the Attorney General's letter, and prepared an altered copy for my next meeting with Mr. Greene. In our subsequent meetings I led Greene to believe I was an emissary of the Vincentian government. As such I recorded our meetings and the information he provided, with Greene's knowledge and consent. In fact he spoke quite openly and candidly, believing his information would secure his deal for diplomatic immunity. He revealed a complex conspiracy perpetrated against St. Vincent and the Grenadines, with known and unwitting complicity by senior government officials.

"The implications for the current government are devastating. And I find myself in a compromised position. I have not told anyone, particularly the Prime Minister, of my investigation and findings. I face a choice between competing loyalties to my lifelong friend and party, or my country. To choose the former will make me complicit in a criminal conspiracy and cover up."

The recording ended. I sat. My mouth open. The fireplace flickered in the background. The recording reverberated in my brain. I'd struck the mother lode. And it filled me with dread.

"Sacre bumbo claat," I breathed aloud, digesting the calamitous implications. Not the least of which had been two murders. That we knew of.

I rose from the couch and fixed another cup of coffee. Returning to the couch I opened the next audio file in the sequence. Taylor's voice again, providing the date, time and location of the recording.

"As agreed, you'll tell me everything you know. I'm also going to record our conversations," Taylor's voice said.

"As long as there's an actual agreement I have no objection," another voice responded. "Otherwise no. But I presume you wouldn't have called, and we wouldn't be meeting again if my terms hadn't been accepted."

A scratching sound on the recording, like a sheet of paper unfolding. "This is what you requested," Taylor's voice said. The voices fell silent. Muted background sounds filled the empty space on the recording.

"I believe we may proceed," the other voice said.

I assumed the other voice belonged to Arnold Greene. Higher pitched than Taylor's, possessing a smooth swarmy quality, like a used car salesman. Difficult to conceive both were dead while listening to their voices.

"First," Taylor said, "Explain your involvement and how you have knowledge of these events."

"About five years ago my firm was on the verge of going under. I'd been looking for investors, but almost everyone I met either wanted to buy the firm outright, or weren't interested. And I didn't want to sell. At the eleventh hour an investor approached me and we reached an agreement. I didn't know it at the time, but he was the devil and I had sold my soul."

"Who was the investor?"

"To this day I don't know."

"How can that be?"

"I dealt with the investor's board and management team. The deal handled by a reputable law firm. Everything was in order. I never met the principal. It happens sometimes. A silent investor who wants his holdings to remain anonymous. And it was profitable. Business picked up. Larger deals came my way. My clientele grew. And I expanded in the international arena. I didn't look too hard behind the curtain. And when I did, it was too late. By then all my dealings with the investor company was handled through a man I knew only as the Director. He handled the operational details for transactions my firm, among others, were involved in. He referred the clients, and handled most of the negotiations. Most of the time the deals were completed prior to my involvement. I'd be brought in as a principal funder, or an underwriter. Usually in partnership with other firms. And the money just kept pouring in."

"Did you ever find out a name, or anything else about this Director?"

"No. And after a time it became clear to me I shouldn't try. He preferred operating in the background. And he'd take extraordinary steps to keep it that way. He'd have his security coterie collect cell phones, electronic devices and disable security cameras before a meeting. The meetings usually took place outside my offices, in a secured location, and I'd never know when or where a meeting would take place until a few minutes before."

"Do you have any photographs of him?"

"Are you kidding?"

"A description then. What he looks like. And where he might be reached?"

"He has a way of looking at you, like the dead black eyes of a shark before it rips into you. Except his eyes are blue, but just as empty and unfeeling as a shark's. A smile like a shark's too. If the open jaws of a shark can be called a smile. A scar on his temple, next to his left eye."

Background noises on this recording too. A distant mournful sound, like fog horns in the distance.

"Now everything's unraveling. For some reason the FBI has taken notice and is tracking my firm's transactions. Maybe funds passed through an account they had flagged. I dunno. And I have little control over that. Funds go where they're needed. I don't control the accounts clients use or where. Anyway I got wind of the FBI and SEC investigation. That's when I took a close look behind the curtain. I'd had my suspicions before that, but turned a blind eye. But whoever is behind this is very well protected. The corporate veil impossible to crack. It's vast and global. A constellation of companies. A river of money flowing in and out of thousands of accounts. Soon after the FBI launched their investigation funds began disappearing from various accounts. Many of them controlled by my firm. The trail stopped at my front door so the FBI is targeting me. You're one of my narrowing options to stay out of prison."

"What do you know about the St. Vincent National Bank?" Taylor asked.

"It was brought to my attention by the Director. Apparently the bank is ripe for takeover. At the time I didn't understand why they'd be interested in such an asset. A small island bank. But as it turned out they'd already picked up one bank in the Caribbean. The one in Antigua formally owned by Mark Sanford. Remember that episode? They'd been undermining the Vincentian bank for some time, making it difficult for your government to maintain control and driving down both its attractiveness and its price. You ever heard of Benjamin Adams?" the voice asked.

"No I haven't," Taylor said.

"About four months ago Benjamin Adams arrived in St.Vincent claiming to be a foreign investor. He was listed as a Director of American Investment Trust, which was in fact a registered Off Shore Company in St. Vincent. Anyway Benjamin Adams opened an account at the National Bank with a check for half a million dollars drawn on a New York Investment account. The Bank cleared the check and began making payments from the account for checks Adams wrote, ignoring their normal six week waiting period for foreign checks. A cabinet official was paid to pressure the bank to forego its normal procedures. The check Adams deposited turned out to be bogus, and the bank paid out a half million dollars it hadn't collected before it discovered the deposit was fraudulent. Of course Benjamin Adams left right after completing the transactions. It was a scam perpetrated against the bank to weaken it, and at the same time clean some dirty funds."

"How in the world can something like that be kept quiet?"

"The government appoints the bank's directors and controls what goes on inside the bank. It'll eventually come out though. Someone might finally get up the nerve to blow the whistle. Or it'll be leaked in a further attempt to undermine the bank, or the government. It's a delicate game. Timing is everything. And that wasn't the only scam."

"Like the Clair Hall Marina project?" Taylor said.

"One of them," the other voice said. "But we'll have to get into that another time. I have an appointment to get to. I'll call you to set up another meeting."

The recording ended.

Oh my God, I thought, light-headed. My assessment of the packages when Gloria Meeks had handed them to me proved correct. Their contents incendiary and explosive. Powerful enough to destroy Defretas's government. And anyone who threatened to expose it. I'd found the motive. And proceeding further required extreme caution.

The person I suspected of killing both men remained out of reach. Not a shred of evidence to connect the man on PSV to either murder. And anyway he'd been hired to carry out the murders. Had made the kills look like an accident and a suicide. I had no idea who'd hired him. And my suspect pool had expanded to include the top tier of the Vincentian government.

I needed advise. I needed to talk to Gage. And Mike. It'd be especially hard for Mike. He considered the Prime Minister a friend.

I decided to examine the Word document files. Taylor had named one 'meetings'. I opened it. It listed dates, times and locations of his meetings with Greene. The dates corresponded to the audio files. The final entry incomplete. My breath caught in my throat as I read it.

'Final meeting', it read. 'To be scheduled. Location St. Vincent and the Grenadines.'

I closed the file. I opened another named 'Corporations'. It contained a list of companies, board members, vital statistics, and their relationships to each other. A headache inducing document requiring a session all by itself. And probably a forensic accountant. I closed it after noting the corporations Taylor had listed in his earlier notes also appeared on this list.

Next I opened a file titled 'National Bank'. It detailed the bank account opened by Benjamin Adams, accompanied by scanned copies of cancelled checks. One check for two hundred thousand US dollars to a company named Woodbridge Management. Another in the amount of one hundred thousand to an Arco Consultants. And one hundred twenty thousand to a third company.

I reopened the 'Corporations' file and compared the payment recipients to the list. The recipients among the corporations Taylor had listed.

I returned to the payments. Ten thousand U.S dollars had been paid to the Vincentian law firm of the Attorney

General; thirty thousand to the bank account of the Attorney General's wife, and forty thousand to a Colin Small, a permanent secretary in the Finance Ministry.

Taylor had included a scanned copy of the Central Bank letter informing National Bank of the fraudulent check. How Taylor had obtained the bank records he never explained. But Taylor had documented everything Greene had told him. I reopened Taylor's meeting list, noting the date referencing the National Bank. Scrolled to the corresponding audio file and opened it.

"Tell me about the takeover of the National Bank," Taylor asked.

"Still in the works. You may still have time to quash it. A consortium has been put together, based in the Caribbean, to make an offer on the bank. The consortium is underwritten by a couple of other corporations. All reputable. The consortium won't mind assuming the debt. The objective is to control the bank."

"Do you know the name of the Consortium or the companies behind it?"

"No. But I'd guess it'll be recently formed. Probably have offices in the region. Antigua or St. Kitts. Maybe St. Lucia. The bank is going on the market. That's inevitable. And I'm not sure even the most thorough due diligence will spot anything. The consortium will have solid financials and the firms involved outstanding reputations."

"What I still don't understand is the purpose behind all this." Taylor's asked. "There is more money behind this than can be recouped. It seems to be about more than just money."

"From my perspective it looks like the classic moves prior to a hostile takeover. Only we're not talking about a company here, but a small nation. The principle's the same though. And these are sharks you're dealing with. This particular one a great white. Why they need to control a small country is anyone's guess. I have no knowledge of their endgame. But use your imagination. I'm sure you can come up with a dozen good reasons, particularly given its location."

"Do you recognize any of the companies on this list?" Taylor asked.

"For all intents and purposes they're the same company. They're all connected, either through their board members, their ownership, or their subsidiaries. Good luck trying to identify who actually controls them."

The recording ended. I'd lost all sense of time. The fire little more than red glowing embers. Mounds of snow clung to the window sills. White fluffy flakes fell past the glass panes.

I piled on another log and stoked the fire back to a blaze. Fixed a fresh pot of coffee. Back on the couch I chose another audio file. I wanted to hear Greene's account of the Clair Hall project.

"You said you'd tell me about the Clair Hall project," Taylor's voice after the customary introduction of date, time and location.

"Another scam," Greene's voice said. "It further weakened the bank and sank the government further into debt. Not to mention filled the pockets of certain individuals."

"How was it accomplished?" Taylor asked.

"An Italian company, Cabrinaro Marine Fabrikant, was bought by an Italian businessman named Maurizio Allegretti. The deal financed by my firm and Emirates Financial Group International, a firm based in Qatar. We also underwrote the project. At least on paper. No funds were ever transferred to

Cabrinaro Marine. At least not for the projects. But a lot of cash was washed through the company."

"The proposal was to build a Marina and boatyard facility at Clair Hall on St. Vincent, and a Marina on Union Island. Local officials were paid to suspend normal procedures and fast track the projects. In all, twelve and a half million U.S. dollars was taken out of the country. And again, both the National Bank and your government absorbed the losses."

In another recording Taylor asked Greene how he'd come by all his information. Did he have another inside source and could Taylor speak directly with him?

"There is no source," Greene said on the recording. "I'm putting this together by following the money and from inside knowledge of these companies and the deals. Many underwritten by my firm and others. But all these other companies, as I've said, are one and the same. Once you know that, you're able to see the pattern."

I opened more files. But only scanned them. Overwhelmed. And exhausted. The gist similar. Some scams; some actual investments. Aimed at gobbling up large chunks of St. Vincent and the Grenadines, reaching across every sector of the economy and across the government.

Greene had been correct. Sharks.

CHAPTER 25

I awoke on the couch. Bright daylight streamed through the tall windows. The sky outside a clear and brilliant blue. I didn't recall falling asleep, or when. Only a vague memory of Gage spreading a blanket over me.

I glanced at the littered coffee table and headed upstairs. The bed hadn't been slept in. I heard the shower through the open bathroom door. I entered and used the toilet.

"Morning sunshine," Gage said from behind the shower's glass enclosure.

"When did you get back?" I said, stripping off my clothes, dropping them on the bathroom floor.

"Couple of hours ago."

I slid the glass door open. Gage stood beneath a steaming shower spray. Water sluiced off his brown skin. His face and neck and the portions of his arms and legs exposed to the tropical sun two shades darker than the rest of his toffe huedbody.

I joined him in the shower. He drew me under the hot spray, activating the shower head on the opposite wall. Water rained on us from both sides of the enclosure, plastering my hair against my face. Gage pressed a button on the liquid soap dispenser affixed to the wall. His hands ran over my body, lathering my skin in lavender scented body soap. My soap. He'd thought of everything.

"How'd your evening go?"

"Subcontractors like I thought. Hired by another security outfit called the Phoenix Group. Legwork and passive surveillance only. Until they saw Gloria handing you the package and got orders to intercept you. They weren't prepared for that. Moved too quickly and they were sloppy. Exposed themselves. Not to mention innocent bystanders on the street. Anyway they got the message loud and clear. It's being sent up the chain. She should be safe from now on. I have someone keeping an eye on her just in case. How'd you make out?"

"It's all there. Taylor gave us everything except the who."

His hands massaged my breasts, smothering them in soapy suds. He pinched the nipples between slippery fingers. A soft moan escaped my lips.

"It was eerie. Hearing their voices," a throatiness in my voice. "Like interviewing ghosts from beyond the grave."

"How bad?"

"Bad. It's going to destroy Defretas' government. And now they're all suspects too. But my feeling is this isn't local, and goes way beyond government corruption."

"How so?"

"It's all being orchestrated from outside. And....." I hesitated. Ever since the Ramirez affair and Gage's ominous warning, I'd harbored a secret fear. A fear I hadn't verbalized to anyone, not even Gage. Now the specter of my secret bogeyman rose to the forefront of my thoughts.

"Remember after the Ramirez thing you told me and Mike you didn't think it was over?"

"Yeah."

"What did you mean?"

He hesitated. His hands paused on my hips. His eyes peered deep into mine. He'd never told me the whole story regarding Carlson, the man who'd tried to kill Mike. And who Gage had killed on Antigua.

"Something Carlson said to me," he said finally. "About someone else behind him pulling the strings. Someone worse than Ramirez. But he may've been trying to stall, to play me."

"I think that's who I'm seeing in all this," I said. I told him about my bogeyman.

He pressed more soap onto his hands. Resumed rubbing me, lathering my back. A finger ran down the length of my spine. I arched against him. His slippery hands moved downward, cupping and squeezing the supple flesh of my rear cheeks.

A hand slid to the front, moving across my sensitized mound. Slippery fingers combed through the wet curly hair. Moved lower. Between my legs. His lips kissed the curve of my neck, sending a shockwave of sensation through my body. I shuddered against him.

My mouth found his; my tongue exploring. The hot shower pelted us as I thrust my tongue deeper into his mouth. Magical fingers stroked and probed the lips between my legs, pushing inside, rubbing against the inner walls. Prickly sensations tickled my nerve endings, spreading, growing; travelling from my groin to every region of my body. Wave upon wave. A building intensity as his fingers pushed in and out. The sweet friction lifted me onto my toes, consuming me as I surrendered to his unselfish desire to give me pleasure. For its own sake. Without need of reciprocity.

His slippery thumb slid upward, parting the covering over the hardened sensitive nub, rubbing it from its base to its head, pressing against it, sending an explosive eruption of liquid fire surging through me. The shock of it drove the breath from my lungs. Drove all thought from my mind. My body shook and quivered against his; leaving me limp.

Later, sipping coffee at the kitchen island, I related everything I'd learned from Taylor's recordings and documents. Gage listened in silence, without interruption, absorbing it all behind analytical eyes.

"I need to brief Mike too," I said. Gage merely nodded.

We set up the secure call between Gage's and Mike's cell phones as before. When Mike answered I said, "Happy birthday Mike." His fifty ninth birthday had been the day before.

"Cheers buddy. Many happy returns," Gage added. "We'll hoist one over here for you."

"Thanks guys. Now what've you got for me?" Mike not the sentimental type regarding birthdays, or most other holidays for that matter. Except for Christmas, and his children's birthdays. Fussing over his birthday appeared to only embarrass him.

I wished I had another excuse to delay, but I didn't. I relayed the contents of Taylor's envelopes, encapsulating the documents and recordings. Mike listened, as Gage had, without interruption.

"That's it then," he said at the conclusion of my recitation. His voice hollow, distant, devoid of emotion. "We're all thinking these were contract killings, right?"

"Looks that way," I said.

"And we'll probably never find the contractor or the person who ordered it."

I sought Gage's eyes, a beseeching stare in mine. Before I asked, he nodded.

"Actually Mike," I said. "This confirms something Gage has been thinking for a while. He thinks the contractor was the guy on PSV."

Silence from the phone.

"And we think the person behind all this may be someone Carlson warned Gage about before Gage......you know," I said, filling the silence.

"Still doesn't tell us who that person is or how to find him." Mike said. "And right now our immediate problem is what to do with this information. It might blow up in our faces if it's not handled properly. Not to mention destroy the country."

"I have an idea might help with both situations," Gage said.

"Am I gonna like this idea?" Mike said.

"I think we can exploit Jo's relationship with the FBI."

"What relationship with the FBI?" I asked.

"JJ has a relationship with the FBI?" Mike said through the phone.

"We turn the material over to Agent Forde. It gives them what they need to pursue and maybe wrap up the Greene investigation. And in exchange we get whatever their forensic accountants come up with. I'll have people working on it too. But the Justice Department knows how to do this, and they have the resources."

"And what about the second part, our immediate problem?" Mike asked.

"We let the information come from the FBI. That way our fingerprints aren't on it. We steer them toward the Governor General maybe, or someone like that."

"And how do we get the FBI to play ball?" Mike asked.

"That's up to Jo."

"Me. How am I supposed to make all that happen?"

"Through Agent Forde. He's your asset," Gage said. His eyes drilling into mine.

"Gage, I'm not sure about this....." Mike's voice hesitant and concerned.

"You're already half way there," Gage said to me, ignoring Mike and staring steadily into my eyes. "You just have to build on that. You can do this. Make this happen. But the decision is entirely up to you."

Silence in the room. Mike silent over the phone. My mind wandered. Grasped again in the glow of a special connection to Gage. A connection having nothing to do with our romantic relationship. A connection to the side of him I hadn't been part of before. Until this case. Until this trip to New York; working beside him in the field, as a partner.

"I want to do it Mike," I said. "It's the best option we have right now. Unless you have a better idea." My tone sharper than I'd intended. Sounding too close to insubordination, which Mike my boss didn't deserve. And unfair to Mike, my friend.

"I always knew spending so much time around that guy was a bad influence," he said. "Awright. I'll go along with it. But you guys be careful you hear me. You come home safe."

"So how do I do this?" I asked Gage after we'd disconnected the call.

The corners of his mouth curled ever so slightly. His eyes softened to the same extent, containing a mischievous glint. Enough to elicit a smile of my own.

"Pleasant surprise," Owen Forde said. "Not that I'm complaining. I'm glad you called," his tone indicating genuine pleasure at hearing my voice. "Wish I'd stayed in your neck of the woods. Could use some tropical sun about now."

"I know what you mean," I said.

"I doubt that, you don't have to trudge through a foot of snow."

"Actually, that's what I wanted to talk to you about."

"What, about snow?"

I laughed. "No." I said, "About our quid pro quo."

"What about it?"

"Where are you?" I asked instead.

"In New York. We think we've located the guy who provided the fake ID for Greene."

"Well so am I. And I have something that might help you close the Greene case."

"What do you mean so are you?"

"I'm in New York. And we need to meet," projecting I hoped, the right amount of apprehension in my voice. Enough to set the hook. If I read Forde correctly chivalry might be the right bait to get him to bite.

"Where are you?" he asked.

"I'm staying with a friend. But we can't meet here. And I'd prefer not to meet at the FBI, or even let them know we're meeting. At least not yet. You'll understand when you hear what I have for you."

"Okay. When?"

"As soon as possible."

A pause. His silence unnerving. I hoped I hadn't overplayed my hand. But confident he wouldn't pass up an opportunity to see me again. Business or not.

"How about an hour?" He said. "Manhattan Public Library. I'll meet you at the front entrance on Fifth Avenue."

"Make it two hours." I said.

"See you then."

An hour and fifty minutes later I climbed the snow covered steps of the New York Public Library, paying careful attention to my footing. The previous night's snowfall had melted during the day, turning to slush and ice as the temperature fell.

A risk being out in the open. The sensation of having a target on my back returned. My senses tuned to high alert, subjecting everyone and everything around me to a vigilant scan. I wore my vest. Gage out there too. Somewhere close. Invisible as usual, but his presence palpable.

Forde waited beneath one of the columned archways of the entrance portico. His huge smile greeted me, followed by a gentle hug and a light kiss on each cheek in the European manner.

"Look at you all bundled up," he grinned pleasantly at me. "Such a gorgeous bundle too."

"Not so bad yourself," I said, smiling back at him. He wore a tan trench coat, unbelted and open, revealing casual business attire beneath. A grey suit, light blue oxford shirt and striped blue tie. The colors enhanced the green of his eyes.

We passed through a revolving door into the cavernous white marble interior and arched vaulted ceilings. Another

Beaux-Arts design like Grand Central. We crossed to one of the grand stairways and climbed the marble steps to the second floor.

Forde halted at a locked door in an ornate hallway spanning the width of the building. He produced a keycard from his pocket and unlocked the door. We entered a large unoccupied room containing work tables and chairs. Racks of wide drawers against the walls.

Forde pulled out a chair for me at one of the tables. But the room's grandeur occupied my attention. Captivated by the gilded, elaborately decorated arched ceiling; the hanging chandeliers; the oil paintings on the walls. And the huge arched windows allowing natural light into the room.

"One of the research rooms the FBI has access to," Forde said, noticing my wandering gaze. "I believe this is the map room," glancing around the room before resettling a curious gaze on me.

I sat in the offered chair, my mind refocusing on the business at hand. I assumed the demeanor required for the role I had to perform.

"You okay?" he asked. Concern in his voice and the questioning green eyes.

Success, I smiled secretly inside. I nodded, using just enough reticence to convince him I might not be entirely okay.

"So what brings you to New York?" His eyes held mine in an interrogatory stare.

"I went home to Montreal for Christmas," I said. "Figured I might tie up a few loose ends before heading back to Bequia. In particular, I wanted to speak with one other person who was close to Jackson Taylor. That person lives here in New York. Turns out Taylor left a package for

safekeeping. The person gave the package to me. And now...."
I hesitated, feigning an uncertainty and anxiety he couldn't
mistake.

"The package contains information I can't handle on
my own. It's the reason both Greene and Taylor were killed.
And I don't know who I can trust. I thought of you."

"I'm flattered. But what makes you think you can trust
me?"

"Don't know that I can. But you're an outsider. You're
FBI. And I just have a feeling about you, is all."

"Where's this package?"

"Before we get to that, I need to know a few things," I
said.

His eyes assumed the hard edge I'd observed on
Bequia. They searched mine in the lie detector manner astute
interrogators possessed.

"Like what for instance?" He leaned back in the chair,
his gaze still fixed on me, but withdrawing, spatially and
symbolically. I hoped it'd only be temporary.

"Where did you get the information that put the FBI
onto Greene?" I asked. I already knew the answer. The
question an opening gambit if I hoped to achieve the objective
of our meeting.

He remained silent. But the expression in his eyes
familiar, his brain pondering a decision. He leaned forward,
forearms resting on the table between us. His intense eyes
drilled into mine, as though peering into my soul.

"Assistant Director Quinn, head of our CID." He said,
cracking a small smile.

"And he's read into this information and its source?"

"That's classified," he said.

"Does that mean you don't know, or you won't tell me?"

He only smiled.

"Is Director Quinn running your investigation on Greene?"

"He isn't directly supervising the investigation, but he's in the loop."

"Can you get to him directly?"

"Why would I want to do that?"

"Because the fewer people who know the contents of the package the better."

A shift in his eyes, from wary skepticism to occupational curiosity.

"He'll just refer me to the supervising agent in charge," he said after a moment.

"Not if you tell him the information comes from the same source as the Ramirez material," I said, closely observing his reaction.

I'd hit the target. Received the reaction I'd aimed for. Forde obviously knew the source of the information on Greene, if not the details.

"How do you know about Ramirez?" the hard edge back in his eyes, and voice.

"Ramirez was my case. The data you guys are working with came from me."

His eyes registered genuine surprise. To his credit, his face remained impassive. He broke eye contact, his attention turning inward, ruminating, probably matching what I'd told him against what he knew. When his eyes met mine again they viewed me a different light. A grin spread across his face.

"Damn. That was you? No one ever mentions any names. But it makes sense. Do you know in certain circles of the Bureau they talk about you like a celebrity?"

My response a suitably self-deprecating smile.

"Needless to say, you'll get the AD's attention. Anything else?"

"Yes," I said. "The information in the package can destroy St. Vincent. It has to be handled with extreme discretion. For yours and his eyes only. At least for now. And I'll deal only with you and him."

"Superintendent," using my title for the first time. "You can't ask us to sit on vital information...."

"No. No. Nothing like that," I interrupted. "It's just that the Bureau is in a better position to handle this material. You have access to certain channels and resources I don't."

He snickered at the suggestion. "It's your backyard, your jurisdiction. You know the players, where to go, who to see, how things work. And I happen to know you're more resourceful than you let on. What can we do you can't?"

"Both Greene and Taylor were contract hits," I said. "The assassin is probably already outside our jurisdiction. And everything points to a conspiracy from outside St. Vincent. You'll understand after you've gone through the material."

He pushed back from the table again, scrutinizing me. The skeptical gaze returned.

"Why do I get the feeling I'm being played here? Like you're setting up the FBI to do your dirty work for you?"

I fought to remain calm. To curb the autonomic tendency to tap dance around the suggestion. To prevaricate at this critical juncture. I didn't underestimate his ability as an experienced observer and interrogator.

"That may be the practical outcome," I said. "But it doesn't change the reality of what I've told you, or the position I'm in. I need your help," delivered in an emphatic tone, and a dash of anxious distress. "Like I said, you'll understand when you go through the material."

We lapsed into another silence. Held by each other's stare. A plaintive plea in mine. I maintained the silence. Pushing might overplay my hand. He needed to come the rest of the way on his own.

"Who was Taylor's contact here in New York?" he asked.

"Not relevant," I said. "And there's one final thing."

He smiled. "Of course there is," accompanied by an overdramatized sigh. "Let's hear it."

"Our quid pro quo. I want to close out my cases. I give you the goods on Greene. You keep me in the loop on whatever you find."

"Fine by me. But I can't make any guarantees for the Bureau."

"That's why I have to see your AD Quinn."

He leaned toward me. "In any case you've got me. I'll get you to him. Where is this package?"

The final hurdle. Gage and I had agreed to hold onto the package until we had everyone on board. And certain we'd be placing the evidence in the proper hands. I'd hand over Taylor's materials and personally brief Forde and his Assistant Director, putting the final pieces of our plan in place to expose the conspiracy in the manner we intended. But I couldn't meet Forde empty handed. I'd need to give him enough to set the hook and get the ball rolling. Confident my performance had won him over I reached into the overcoat's pocket and retrieved a thumb drive.

"This is a copy of Jackson Taylor's recorded affidavit. It's enough to get your AD on board. Taylor explains his investigation and his connection to Greene."

"And the rest? This can't be everything you have."

I provided a verbal synopsis of the rest. Forde's mouth and lips pursed in a whistle, but made no sound.

"Now you understand why this has to be handled carefully Owen," I said. "I trust you, but I can't hand over Taylor's information to the Bureau without certain guarantees."

"How do I contact you?" he asked.

I gave him the number of the prepaid phone. "I just bought it to use here," I explained. "I don't get service here in the states with my regular carrier." He had no need to know about my phone's satellite capability.

"Well if there's nothing else, I need to get this to AD Quinn ASAP," he said, pocketing the thumb drive. "I'll be in touch."

"Thank you," I said, my voice measured to express relieved gratitude.

We parted on the sidewalk in front of the library. Forde crossed Fifth Avenue to a parked black SUV. I watched it pull away into downtown traffic. Following Gage's protocol I headed west on Forty First Street, past Bryant Park, shrouded in winter white. The snow and slush covering the sidewalk trampled into a passable path by pedestrian foot traffic.

At forty First and Sixth Avenue I sensed a presence close behind me. My heart raced. Adrenaline rushed into my bloodstream. I turned, prepared for a confrontation.

"Sounds like he's in," Gage said.

"Don't do that." I said, my pounding heart gradually subsiding. Aware my words had no effect on so natural a part of his being. Asking him to stop appearing and disappearing like a ghost tantamount to asking him to stop breathing.

"You heard okay?" I said

"Loud and clear."

So what now?"

"We wait."

CHAPTER 26

The Black GMC sped north along Sixth Avenue, wending its way through the maze of traffic like a sheepdog through a wayward flock. In Manhattan no one paid attention to lane markings. Drivers aggressively headed for the empty space in search of driving room. Along the busy streets preparations already underway for the annual New Year's ball dropping celebration.

Forde had called me that morning. Despite my confidence I'd spent the previous day on pins and needles awaiting his call. Certain the gambit had worked. But anxious nevertheless. Gage had passed the intervening hours as though he hadn't a care in the world. Patience and waiting a natural part of his being. He'd spent much of the time on his cell phone, or laptop, checking on all the pieces, he'd explained without elaboration.

Forde had picked me up in the village for an afternoon meeting with Assistant Director Quinn at an uptown apartment the FBI used as a safehouse. But first he needed to run down a lead on the forger who'd provided the documents to Greene.

"We're sure we've identified the guy but he's still in the wind," Forde explained. "We have surveillance set up on his place but he hasn't showed. We just got a second location for him. Hope you don't mind. This shouldn't take long. I just need to check it out before the lead gets cold. And it may be nothing anyway."

I didn't mind. I had a vested interest in the case too, even though the forger concerned me only peripherally. But it'd connect another dot and cross another T in closing my file on Greene.

We entered Central Park where Sixth Avenue ended at Central Park South. Continued north along a winding road under a canopy of leafless tree branches. Heading deeper into the Park we passed horse drawn carriages carrying tourists snuggled under lap blankets. We stopped for a red light next to a closed boathouse at one end of a partially frozen lake.

The scenery passing outside the tinted windows of the SUV another world. Part of the city and yet apart. A pastoral oasis in the midst of steel and concrete. Covered beneath a white blanket of fresh snow. Serene, like a Norman Rockwell winter landscape.

The road skirted the east side of a reservoir. Joggers loped around its two and a half mile perimeter. Past the great meadows the road wound like a coiled snake northward toward the Harlem Meer. We exited the north end of the park into Harlem.

I'd been uptown to Harlem only twice during my visits to New York City. Both times I'd passed through to and from Columbia University. The Harlem passing outside the SUV different from the one I remembered, undergoing a revitalizing renaissance. Reinventing and transforming itself as it'd done many times before in its storied history. Yet still maintaining a distinctive character and culture, like other New

York neighborhoods, linked by history, family, religion, music, cuisine and ethnicity.

We drove north on Seventh Avenue, officially Adam Clayton Powell Junior Boulevard. But like Avenue of the Americas, no New Yorker called it that. The sidewalks, even in the crisp winter cold, a bustling Agora of Senegalese cloth merchants, Nation of Islam stalls, and vendors hawking bootleg DVDs, self-published books, dashikis, posters, incense, vials of perfume and oils, musical instruments and ethnic tchotchkes.

Forde turned left onto 131st Street, slowing to check the building numbers.

"Looking for One Twenty-Eight," he said.

We passed it two thirds of the way up the block, on our right. A five story brownstone apartment building in a row of brownstones. The building swathed in construction scaffolding, undergoing renovation like many other buildings in Harlem's gentrified neighborhoods. The brownstone brick and flagstone steps pressure washed and gleaming. New window fixtures faced the street and in the hardwood double door entrance.

Forde parked on the opposite side of the street. He scanned the front of the building before exiting the SUV. I disembarked on the street side.

"Where'd you think you're going?"

"Coming with you."

"No you're not," delivered in a paternalistically protective tone.

"I'm not staying out here by myself. Besides you might need backup."

The don't-argue-with-me determination in my eyes halted any further protest. He acquiesced, using words to the effect of my strictly being an observer and staying out of the way.

I hardly heard him. Alarm bells flooded my brain.

I had no idea why. I scanned the street. Deserted except for a white panel van parked in front of the building. 'Matthews Construction' stenciled on the side and back. A workman in white overalls busy loading tools and equipment into the back of the van.

We approached the newly renovated front entrance. The workman, white, close cropped black hair and dark aviator glasses, stepped aside to allow us through. The entrance doors held open by a ladder.

Alarms still blared in my head. Forde strode unconcerned into the building's ground floor lobby. Newly painted walls, ceiling, and ceramic tiled floor. Our conversation on the street stifled the urge to voice my concern. A concern lacking any tangible basis. Difficult to explain. A gut feeling only.

I'd observed something out of place. An anomaly. No idea what I'd actually seen. Wishing for Gage at my side instead of Forde. But reassured by the knowledge he'd be close. Our coms active. The microphone activated on my cell transmitting to his earbud.

Forde and I climbed the stairway to the top floor. Our footsteps echoed through the empty landings and hallways. No tenants in the building yet. We exited into a narrow hallway. Apartments on both sides. A maintenance man halfway up a ladder in the middle of the hallway. His attention focused on an overhead light fixture.

"Owen," I said as Forde approached the door we wanted. He turned to face me.

"Careful," I said. "Something doesn't feel right here."

He smiled. More like a condescending smirk. I ignored it. The clanging bells in my brain had been joined by screeching sirens and blaring klaxons as his tapping knuckles pushed the door inward. It'd been left ajar.

Forde turned to face me again. This time concern and a respectful acknowledgment in the sparkling green eyes. He reached beneath his suit jacket for the holstered weapon on his hip.

Time to pay attention to the insanity roaring in my brain. I'd seen something. Before we'd entered the building. And again once we were inside, in the hallway. Unrecognized anomalies had been piling up in my subconscious brain, still eluding my conscious mind.

Something odd about the maintenance man on the ladder. Something about shoes. I turned toward the hallway. In time to see the maintenance man advancing rapidly toward us, a silenced pistol in his right hand.

"Gun." I yelled at Forde, kicking an empty mop bucket resting near the wall, propelling it into the maintenance man's chins. The bucket not only empty, but dry. No mop. The maintenance man working on a light fixture carried no tools. Spotless shiny black shoes beneath equally spotless coverall cuffs. The accumulated anomalies registered in a flood.

The bucket slowed his advance, almost tripping him. I rushed toward him while Forde moved to cover the man. Instead the door to the apartment jerked open. A figure in the doorway smashed Forde's arm against the jam.

Forde's reaction, lightning fast. He spun into the doorway to confront the new threat. The man in the doorway reacted just as swiftly. He blocked Forde's gun arm and drove a solid punch into Forde's side. The blow spun Forde farther into the apartment, out of my sight line. Forde's service weapon fell to the floor inside the doorway.

No time to help him. The maintenance man already regaining his balance. I moved in on him. Grabbed the wrist holding the gun, hoisting it high and away from me. I spun under his raised arm and pivoted, twisting his arm behind him in the process. I continued twisting, until his palm opened and the weapon fell from his hand. I used my right foot to send it sliding down the hall as his right leg lashed out behind him.

I'd seen the kick coming. Raised my forearm in time to block it. But the force pushed me back, loosening my grip on his wrist.

He turned. Came for me. The bulk nestled at the small of my back suddenly conspicuous. But no time to un-holster the Glock before my assailant closed the gap. Gage's hand to hand coaching sprang to the forefront of my brain. A handgun next to useless in close quarters he'd instructed. His other admonition to strike fast, use lethal force. End it quickly and decisively.

I needed to get to Forde.

I allowed the man to close and grab me from the front before propelling my knee into his groin. Driving it into him with every pound of force at my command. The weight of my body behind it. Hot air exploded from him onto my face. His eyes rolled upward, the white sclera alone visible between narrowing eyelids. My right elbow pistoned into his throat as he sucked for air, producing a strangled gasp. His hands no longer concerned with me or his genitals. Instead he clawed at his throat in a desperate, scratching, futile attempt to clear his crushed windpipe choking for air. He collapsed onto the floor in front of me.

I tugged the Glock from its holster and rushed through the door. It'd only been seconds. Forde locked in a savage struggle, throwing and parrying blows. My eyes instantly registered they'd both lost their weapons, and a small living room, darkened by drawn drapes, wood floor, red drop cloth in front of a white armchair and wood work bench.

No clean shot. Both men twisted and turned in and out of my gun sights. The odds of hitting Forde too high to risk the shot. I advanced into the room, angling for a cleaner shot.

Forde hit the man in the face, tried to follow up but the guy blocked the blow. When Forde attempted to move in close his assailant rammed a knee into Forde's exposed side. Followed by a straight arm combination to Forde's chest. Forde staggered, but didn't fall. He moved in again, still attempting to get close, searching for a handhold. Any opening.

Aware of my presence the man batted away Forde's arms and pushed him back, disengaging for an instant to swing at my arm holding the Glock. The weapon thrown off target he moved in. A short stiff fingered jab speared the soft flesh on the underside of my arm, close to my elbow and funny bone. A paralyzing jolt ran along my arm, from my fingers to my shoulders, forcing my hand open. The Glock flew to the floor at the same instant recognition flooded my brain. The man from PSV.

Using the same arm, now bent, his elbow advanced toward the side of my head with ferocious velocity.

I saw it coming, twisted my face away, but couldn't avoid the blow. It caught me on the back of the head instead, propelling me against a wall.

The instant he'd engaged me Forde charged, landing a blow to the assassin's face as I crashed into the wall. He'd seen Forde coming. Had spun away from Forde's punch as it connected, taking the force out of it. Used it to continue his spin. Halfway through the turn he raised his right knee and extended his leg, providing even more impetus to his spin, twirling like a dancer performing a pirouette. At the completion of the arc his heel impacted Forde's jaw. The reverse round house kick snapped Forde's head to the side. Blood sprayed from his mouth. The kick lifted Forde off his feet and he crashed onto the floor. Unmoving.

I witnessed the final moments of the fight in a foggy haze. And knew I had to move. Had to do something if I hoped to survive. I glanced at Forde's still form.

The assassin turned to me. His undivided attention focused on me now. He moved closer. A murderous calm in his eyes. A malevolent smirk around his lips. His nose bent, crooked; a tendril of blood leaked from one nostril, ran along his chin, dripped onto his shirt. Another trickle flowed from the corner of his mouth and from a split on his lower lip.

Crunched against the wall, my hand concealed from his view, I reached into my pocket for the switchblade. Held it hidden in my palm.

He reached out for me. Grabbed me by the front of my coat and pulled me to my feet. His astute hearing caught the sound of the blade snapping into place. He twisted away at the same instant I thrust upward. Instead of his midsection the blade caught him on the outside of his left thigh. It sank to the hilt.

He didn't howl or scream. Instead, a loud hissing intake of breath through clenched teeth. Like an asp before it strikes. His left hand closed over mine, squeezing it hard in a vice like grip, preventing me from pulling out the blade and stabbing again. His thumb dug into the webbed flesh between my thumb and forefinger, stimulating the nerves, forcing my hand open. He pried my hand away from the switchblade.

His free hand a clenched fist converging on my face with horrifying speed. I'd expected it, the final incapacitating blow. I raised my left arm and turned away a split second before the blow connected. Instead of my face it brushed the side of my head, behind my left ear, its force blunted by the partial block and my turning away. Still, a blinding white light exploded behind my eyes, blotting out my vision, blotting out my hearing. Blotting out everything. Short circuiting my brain. I spun, falling. A long slow fall through space and time, like in a dream.

I crashed onto something. The work table maybe. It disintegrated beneath me. Sharp stabbing pains like jolts of electricity flashed up my side and through my body, jumpstarting my senses like a defibrillator. My vision returned.

He moved away from me. Drew the knife from his thigh. Held it up to watch his blood drip from the red stained blade. He limped across the room in search of his weapon. I searched the floor for one too. I needed a weapon. No match for him. The assassin too fast. Too well trained.

I had to move, or die. Had to reach the Glock lying on the floor. Had to move.

My vision clearer. But my arms and legs encased in lead. Had to move. I focused all my will, all my strength, all my concentration into moving my arms and legs. Move or die.

He found his weapon. Stooped to pick it up.

Had to move. Had to reach the Glock.

He straightened, favoring the injured leg. Hefted the weapon.

Move now! My mind screamed. I'd turned onto my stomach, in a crawling position. Didn't remember doing it. His back to me. Turning.

Move now! The single thought my entire universe. On the cusp of passing out. Ready to give in to the pain.

Move! Screamed my brain.

I leapt through the air, hand outstretched. An explosion of pain upon landing, like I'd fallen onto a bed of red hot nails. My hand closed around the Glock's grip. I rolled over, sat up, the wall against my back. Lifted the weapon in a two handed grip, pointing in the direction I'd last seen him.

Found him. Lined him up in the pistol's sights. His silenced weapon held out in front of him. Aimed directly at me.

We'd acquired our targets at the same instant. I stared at the eyes behind the weapon pointed at me. He stared into mine. Time stood still. My finger curled, squeezing down on the trigger as a movement registered at the edge of my peripheral vision. His eyes told me he'd seen it too. But except for the momentary flicker they remained fixed on me. his aim unwavering.

Three weapons discharged simultaneously. The sharp pop-pop of the Glock reverberated around the room, drowning out any other sounds. In time distorted slow motion

I watched three rounds impact the assassin, push him backward. Shock, surprise, disbelief, registered in his eyes.

A simultaneous impact on my chest, like a solid punch, the hot pressure spreading outward like ripples from a stone thrown into a pond. The pressure dissipated, leaving behind a dull burning sensation.

The assassin fell backward onto the floor.

I sat in a daze. Braced against the wall at my back. Gasped for breath. The Glock still pointed at the empty space where the assassin had stood. My ears rang from the gunshots and the blows to my head. Certain I'd been hit. Not sure how bad. Still alive and conscious for the moment. Not sure for how much longer.

The figure in the shadows approached. Gage. A silenced gun held at his side. Tall, his movement languid, moving out of the dark shadows. Black wavy hair, a deep tan, electric blue eyes.

Not Gage.

Arms like lead weights swung to line up the Glock. The approaching figure raised his arm. I stared at the hole at the end of the cylindrical suppressor attached to his weapon.

"That wouldn't be wise. I'd have to shoot you. Preferably not to kill. Though certainly more painful. I couldn't allow him to kill you. His chin gestured toward the dead assassin. "It wasn't his assignment. At least not yet. In any event he'd outlived his usefulness, unlike you. You and I still have a great deal to discuss."

He moved closer. Stood directly over me. A menacing curl of his lips passed for a smile. Accentuated by a jagged scar next to his left eye. Icy blue eyes appraised me like a circling shark.

The Director. The man Greene had described to Taylor.

I followed his movements in a surreal haze. He pried the Glock from my grip. Stepped over to Forde's prone body, removed dark gloves from his left hand and checked for a pulse. He moved over to the assassin, checked the inert body.

"Quite fortuitous actually. We'd prepared all this for your FBI friend here. Hoping to use him to draw you into the open. Only to have both of you show up together."

He returned to stand before me. "Though a bit messier than we anticipated. You both put up quite a fight," he said, his smile like a shark's jaws opening. "Quite impressive you were able to get the best of him. He was supposed to be amongst the best. But all that is done. Here we are, and you will tell me everything you know about Jackson Taylor, Alfred Greene, and exactly what was given to you by Gloria Meeks. Also it seems you had some unorthodox help here in New York. I need to know who that person is." His voice neutral, emotionless, as though conducting a routine business meeting.

My vision swam in and out, seeing doubles. Two of him stood before me. No. Not doubles. A ghost, materializing from the shadows.

"No." I managed in a groan.

The Director's cold blue eyes held mine in a blank stare. I stared back at them. Held them fixed on me.

"I assure you, you will."

"He... the Director." An effort to force the words out.

His emotionless eyes flickered. A brief uncertainty in the blank stare. Followed by a sudden realization. I hadn't been speaking to him.

He spun. The arm holding the pistol outstretched. Already too late. Gage had moved, shifting position in the blink of an eye, as though supernaturally teleported from one spot to another.

My dazed senses registered a dull thud. The Director's body spasmed and stiffened. His mouth fell open. A grimace, half formed, froze on his face. The blow forced the air from his body in an explosive "Aieep".

He stood frozen, like a Madame Tussaud wax figure. Only his eyes exhibited any sign of life. Blank no longer. His fear manifestly present as they moved frantically side to side, up and down, attempting to comprehend what had happened to him. Gage remained out of his field of vision, and removed the silenced weapon from the outstretched, immobile hand.

A while later, it might've been moments, in my brain time continued to crawl, the Director's eyes rolled upward, his knees sagged, and he crumpled like a rag doll. Gage caught him under the armpits before he hit the wood floor.

I wanted to cry. Too amped up for tears. When the rapid infusion of adrenaline subsided the tremors began. Slowly at first. Then more violently. Strong arms closed around me. Held me tight. Soft whispers in my ear.

The convulsive shakes eased. Conscious awareness returned, like a ship emerging from a dense fog. Gage! His arms around me. Strong. Secure. Safe. I never wanted to leave their embrace.

"One in the hall," I managed in a scratchy voice, sounding like a stranger to my own ears.

"Not a factor," he said.

"One out front," I said, vaguely remembering the crisp clean coverall and brown loafers which had originally triggered my alarms.

"Taken care of. How're you?"

He'd been running a quick but thorough examination I realized. Checking my head, the side of my face, my torso, particularly my ribs, and my extremities. I still had difficulty speaking, my breath rasping in and out. A dull pressure on my chest.

"Think I've been shot," I managed. "How bad?"

He held a small object before my eyes. A miniature metallic mushroom. Dawning comprehension. I'd forgotten I'd worn the vest.

I nodded, forcing a smile. He released me. Moved to check on Forde.

"He'll be okay. But he's going to need orthodontic surgery." He returned to my side carrying Forde's cell phone. "I'll call it in. The Bureau will be here soon," he said, searching the contact list on Forde's phone.

"Let me," I said, straining to get the words out. "You can't be here....Feds mustn't find you here."

"I'm not going to leave you like........"

"You have to go," summoning the strength to put force in my voice.

Anguished brown eyes stared into mine. An expression I'd seen only once before, the night Mike had been shot. A raging conflict apparent in those normally inscrutable, unfathomable eyes as a succession of raw emotions flickered behind them. Indecision. Love. Guilt. Rage.

"No. I won't........"

"Go." The single word emphatic, requiring exerted effort. An alien sound to my ears. "I won't be responsible for exposing you. I'll be okay right? You checked me over. I'm okay right?" My eyes searched his. Something he wasn't telling me about my injuries? How bad?

The hard eyes softened. A smile around his lips. Unambiguous, tender, reassuring. His love manifested in his eyes, in his smile. Enduring and abiding. Even in my battered state my heart soared.

"You'll be fine," he said.

He retrieved the Director's weapon and wiped it thoroughly using the unconscious man's blue blazer. He pressed the weapon into the dead assassin's hands. Returning to me he handed me the weapon.

"Here, grip this like you've fired it."

He removed it from my grip and placed it on the floor, close to the door.

"Remember the trajectories," he said as he expertly worked the scene. "Your got hold of his second weapon and your first shot came from over there," he said, indicating the position the Director had fired from. You crawled over to Forde to check his condition. You thought the shooter was down but he came at you again. You used the Glock lying on the floor and shot him again. They won't be able to trace it. Probably assume it came off the assassin since they won't be able to trace the other weapons either."He plucked the holster at my back from my belt.

I nodded. "I've been around you long enough to know how to tell the story. Now get the hell outta here."

"You ready?"

I nodded again.

"We're still on coms. And I'll be close."

He scrolled to the New York Field Office's number on Forde's contact list, pressed the call icon. He handed me the phone. I groaned out my mayday call to the dispatcher while Gage performed a final survey of the scene.

He knelt beside me. Checked me over a final time. He lifted my eyelids and checked my eyes. He lifted my wrist and checked my pulse.

"Physically you'll be fine," he said, folding me in his arms again. A soft gentle kiss on my mouth. He hoisted the limp Director onto his shoulder in a fireman carry.

"What're you gonna do with him?" I groaned.

"He's gonna answer some questions," he said.

Gage exited the apartment as silently as he'd entered.

CHAPTER 27

Somnolent silence greeted me on the ward. The hiss of elevator doors closing behind me the only sound. A nurse's station faced the elevators, flanked on either side by empty tiled hallways and glass enclosed recovery rooms. Three duty nurses sat behind the waist high counter, one on the phone, one perusing a patient chart, the other typing date into a computer.

Forde's room indicated by the presence of two uniformed NYPD officers stationed outside the sliding glass door. The officers barred my entry until I explained I was Forde's partner. I used my Vincentian police ID, but they only glanced at it, accepting the fresh welts and bruises on my face, and the sling on my arm as my ID.

I tiptoed into the room. My quiet entrance unnecessary. Forde lay awake on an adjustable hospital bed, wired to silent machines monitoring his vital signs. A clear fluid dripped from an intravenous bag into a needle in his arm. Groggy, medicated eyes followed my approach to the bed. They might've been smiling. His heavily wired and braced jaw incapable of performing the act.

"That's a new smile I haven't seen before. Bet all the women love it."

He indicated a pad and pen on a rollaway tray table next to the bed. I handed them to him.

"Only hurts when I laugh," he wrote, drawing a smiley face at the end of the sentence.

"How you doing?"

The pen scratched across the pad. "Good, considering." More scratching. "How you?"

"Good." I said. "They kept me overnight for observation. Possible concussion and all that."

The pen scratched again. "Owe you my life."

"You can buy me dinner," I said, smiling into green eyes dulled by medication.

He drew another smiley face. Larger. "Thanks," written next to it.

"Don't mention it."

"What happened?" he wrote.

"Your people haven't spoken to you?"

"Not much. Surgery. Sedatives. Debrief when I'm up to it," he wrote.

"Had mine with AD Quinn. Seems getting hold of Jackson Taylor's materials spooked whoever was behind the killings. They had Taylor's contact under surveillance. Saw the contact hand me the package. And they knew you were working the Greene case. Kept tabs on you. When they spotted us together, probably at the library, they probably figured they had to move fast. Determine what we knew. They set a trap for you. Set you up through the forger. According to Quinn NYPD found his body in the trunk of an abandoned car. They just got lucky when both of us showed up together in Harlem. Or not. We being together didn't work out too well for them."

"Who's them?" he wrote.

"Your people identified the shooter as Harry Flynn. South African. Interpol believes they can tie him to a dozen or so hits. We know he was in the Grenadines when Greene and Taylor were killed. As to who contracted him, there's nothing right now, but your guys may find a lead in Taylor's material. Quinn's set up a small select task force."

The exertion appeared to be tiring him. Probably the meds too. His eyelids drooped. Manipulating the pad and pen a noticeable effort. I took them from him and placed my hand on his shoulder.

"I'm heading back to Bequia tomorrow. But I'll keep in touch. I'll call to see how you're doing. You take care of yourself and get well. We'll talk soon."

I leaned over him and kissed him gently on his forehead.

CHAPTER 28

A new year. The gulfstream banked above Manhattan, climbing out of Teterboro New Jersey. The blue Atlantic Ocean on the left, the packed high rises of Manhattan and the urban sprawl of surrounding boroughs on the right.

Gage had been pensive and distant since the encounter in Harlem. Not his usual taciturn silence. Instead a withdrawn brooding miasma surrounded him like a thick fog. He sat in the plush leather armchair, gazing absently through the jet's oval window.

My injuries on the mend. Not much to speak of. Mostly contusions and bruising from the blows I'd sustained. No concussion. No internal damage. The welts had shrunk, leaving splotchy areas of mottled purple and dark red on my arms, legs and torso. And a conspicuous plumb colored area over my right cheekbone extending below my ear.

Physically I'd be fine. Psychologically I'd require more time. Death's close encounter had left a deep impression. But like my physical bruising it'd heal, leaving no lasting scar. The other thing a different matter. I'd killed a man. Had taken a life. All be it to save my own. That scar I'd bear for the rest of my life. And the memory. The death denying details of his face as his life dissolved in his eyes. But Gage my primary concern at the moment.

The emotions eating at him required healing too. Those emotions a new paradigm for him. Its landscape unfamiliar. An unaccustomed vulnerability for which he'd never required a defense before. My being okay insufficient to overcome the debilitating doubts ailing him.

I unlatched the seat belt and leaned forward in my seat, close to him. I reached for his hands. Held them in mine. Gazed into his impenetrable, resolute eyes. They contained a sadness so profound my heart ached.

"You have nothing to blame yourself for my love," I said.

"You were almost killed. I should never have put you in that situation."

"You didn't. I put myself in that situation."

"Should have gotten to you sooner,"

"Don't see how. The whole thing lasted less than five minutes. And the important thing is you did get there. You were there when you needed to be. Or we wouldn't have gotten the Director. And you saved me. It was your voice in my head, the skills you taught me, the vest you gave me, all those things got me through it. You saved my life."

"I don't know how to handle this. Never had to before," a perplexed tone in his voice, reflected in the brooding eyes. Confusion and indecision also new to him. But the confession, voiced aloud, a good sign. A plea for help only I could provide.

"I know. But this is your life now. I'll teach you how to handle it. The same way you're teaching me. And the first lesson my love, I'm a police officer. An investigative detective. Risk comes with the territory. I freely choose those risks. You don't make those choices for me. And you can't protect me from them. Every step I took in this investigation was my choice. I'd have pursued the case wherever it led, with or without you. But I'm glad you were with me. Working this op with you meant more to me than you can know. And knowing you always have my back. But having my back is not the same as having to protect me. Do you understand the difference?"

A barely perceptible shift in the brooding eyes. A spark of understanding, eclipsing the cold dullness present moments before. But not entirely. His emotional turmoil still evident behind them.

And in his anguished voice. "Jo, if I'd lost you.... "I can't......"

"Yes you can. Just as I can. The joy of having you in my life is worth the risk of knowing one day you might have to disappear. I've had to come to terms with that. With who you are. All of you. I'm not someone you're responsible for. I'm someone you take the risk of having in your life, because it's worth the risk. You can't have the rose without risking the thorns. Or as my mother would say 'when you wahn swim in de river yuh have fe plunge in de watah fuss'."

His eyes softened. The corners of his mouth curled into a tight little smile which didn't completely extinguish the dour mood holding him like an anchor stuck in a muddy sea bottom. But sufficient for the time being. A start. I squeezed his hands in mine. Reached over and kissed him on his lips.

I sat back in the plush leather armchair. "I keep forgetting to ask you what you did with the Director?" I said, changing the subject.

"He's in good hands. Let's just say he's a Christmas gift that'll keep on giving," a mischievous smile brightened his face and lifted his mood another notch.

I gazed out the window. Caught a last glimpse of Manhattan before it disappeared from view. Leaving one island headed for another. The one below what it has always been. A fascinating place. Enchanting, exciting; pulsing with life. A place of glittering character. Whimsical, fanciful and dangerous. The city which never sleeps. And yet an island which for me at least, was no substitute for the idyllic solitude of a Grenadines beach.

Happy to be heading home.

About the author

A native New Yorker, Michael W. Smart spent eight years sailing around the Eastern Caribbean. Deadeye is the second novel in the Bequia Mysteries, which draws on his intimate knowledge of the islands, its people, and his sailing adventures in the Caribbean.

Thank you for reading my novel. If you enjoyed it please take a moment to leave a review where you purchased it and spread the word to your friends. Thank you. Fair winds and following seas.

Preview Book 3, the final chapter in the opening trilogy of the
Bequia Mystery Series

Commissioner of Police Mike Daniels copes with the political
fallout resulting from the scandals uncovered by
Superintendent Jolene Johanssen, while he investigates the
murder of an undercover constable, and completes the task of
cleaning up the police force before a new Prime Minister
replaces him as Commissioner of Police. Corrupt cops and
politicians, and two murders, lead Mike, Jolene and Gage to
the man behind the conspiracy, and a climatic showdown to
save St. Vincent and the Grenadines.

CHAPTER 1

I awoke to the cackling cries of roosters. My mind clear and refreshed. The phantom ache of my wounds no longer a waking presence.

The fresh fruity scent of a brand new day greeted my short trudge up the steep road from Friendship Bay. The sky held the promise of a bright cloudless day, the last lingering lentils of puffy white fading as the cerulean blue sky paled beneath the rising sun.

The day also promised another mind-numbing medley of meetings. My tedious daily routine since the recent scandals and their aftermath. I'd soon be immersed in the dread I'd fallen asleep to. No longer a nebulous worry, it'd coalesced into solid form. Whole and substantial. As dangerous as a cobra poised to strike.

And I'd soon be unemployed. My second retirement. The first had occurred twelve years earlier, prior to relocating to the Grenadines from Florida. Unlike the first retirement this one promised to be acrimonious, accompanied by a foreboding sense of a job left unfinished.

I feared for the future of the Royal St. Vincent and the Grenadines Police Force. Questioned if I'd achieved any real impact. Contributed to a lasting difference. And beyond that, I also feared for the future of these islands I now called home.

St. Vincent and the Grenadines remained under siege. Though the public remained unaware of it. We'd barely dodged the last bullet, aimed at a takeover and control of the Island Nation by a foreign entity. But we hadn't come through it unscathed.

The Attorney General had been forced to resign. And soon after Prime Minister DeFretas followed, the only viable option to prevent a complete collapse of the government. Arturo Bacchus, number two in the party leadership, had assumed the office of Prime Minister until an early general election could be called. The party held a scant one seat majority in parliament. The opposition party appeared poised to win a landslide at the polls. And I'd be out of a job sooner than I'd expected.

The threat, although exposed, remained. A foreign Bogeyman – Superintendent Jolene Johanssen's description for the nameless, faceless enemy – still out there. Still possessing designs on St. Vincent and the Grenadines. We'd uncovered his operation. And his possible motive, given St. Vincent's strategic geographic location. But not who.

At the main road I flagged a dollar van heading into Port Elizabeth. Drowsy smiles and Mahnin Commisshunah" greeted me as I hopped into the back, one buttock on the edge of the wood seat. The van as usual overloaded to meet the first early morning ferry headed to Kingstown. The van's passengers packed into the back. Each hairpin turn squeezed the crush of bodies together.

Normally I'd have police transport, including a Coast Guard Cutter for the trip across to St. Vincent. Normally I returned home only on weekends, staying at my rental residence in Kingstown during the week to avoid a daily commute.

But sometimes I needed to get away. Needed the solace of my own space; the respite of personal time. My reason for returning home to Bequia the night before.

The van unloaded its passengers on the main road facing the crowded, bustling wharf. Passengers and vehicles swarmed around a red and white ferry tied alongside the wharf, like bees around a hive. Cars, vans, small trucks and motor bikes mounted its stern ramp lowered onto the dock.

Gazing out across the tranquil harbor, brightening as the sun peeked above Bequia's highland, I glimpsed the Coast Guard Vessel "Chatham Bay," a twenty four foot fiberglass Boston Whaler normally based on St. Vincent. Accompanied by the sixteen foot skiff, SVG 12, based in Bequia. They headed toward the dry dock at the Hamilton Marina, the rigid inflatable Whaler towing a small fishing boat.

Turning back to the van I asked the driver to drop me in Hamilton instead. The road through the harbor passed the spot where I'd been found, shot and dying, a little over a year before. I'd crawled through the debris strewn yard between the marina and supermarket to get to the road, my life blood flowing from three bullet wounds. An involuntary constriction squeezed my chest and my pulse quickened as the van drove past the spot.

A year and a half later I still have no memory of the events immediately following being shot. Of how I made it to the road.

At the Hamilton Marina dock I encountered an unexpected surprise. Superintendent Jolene Johanssen and two CID detectives disembarked from the Boston Whaler.

Disheveled and preoccupied, she nevertheless projected a striking presence among the men on the dock. Tall, gorgeous in a natural, earthy manner, brilliant and determined, she evoked an intense familial pride. The kind I felt for my own daughter. In many ways I treated her like a daughter.

"An early morning I see," I said in greeting.

"Morning Chief." She and her contingent of police and Coast Guard personnel came to attention and saluted, Jolene's less formal than the others.

"As you were," I said to the gathered group. "What's this?" My question directed at her.

"Some fishermen spotted that fishing boat washed up on Petit Nevis. They went to check it out and found a body on board. Dead at least two days. I summoned the Coast Guard and Detectives Cato and DeSilva. We processed the scene. I had the Coast Guard tow the boat in for further processing and called Calliaqua for a cutter to transport the body"

"Any identification?"

"No ID on him," she said. "Decomp is pronounced, and sea birds have been at the remains. Not a pretty sight Chief. Just this in his pocket."

She held up a clear plastic evidence bag containing a few coins, some paper currency, and an odd shaped bronze medallion the size of a silver dollar.

The breath rushed from my body. Like I'd been punched in the gut. My senses reeled. My knees turned weak and spongy. A vertiginous wooziness clouded my vision.

"Chief! You OK?" The grip of Jolene's arm on mine. Her voice reaching me as though from a great distance. My eyes refocused on her face.

"You look like you've just seen a ghost or something."

"I need to see the body," I said.

Concern filled the hazel eyes staring back at me, and etched delicate lines across her mocha toned brow. The arm she'd placed around mine tried to hold me back. Or maybe up.

I moved toward the covered bundle lying in the Boston Whaler.

Her eyes, and the eyes of the detail, followed my movements as I knelt next to the body. I turned back a corner of the canvas tarp covering it. Stared down at it. I lifted a side of the tarp, revealing the corpse's right arm and hand.

"Will someone please hand me a pair of gloves."

I didn't see who the outstretched hand holding the blue nitrite gloves belonged to. My gaze fixed on the corpse before me. I lifted the corpse's right hand. A ring embedded in the blackened swollen flesh of his fourth finger bore the same design as the medallion. The dizzying sensation returned. Not due to the sight of the lifeless, decomposing body. I'd seen many, too many, and worse, in a long law enforcement career. But the body lying beneath the tarp had been one of my own.

I'd lost colleagues before too. Felled in the line of duty. A hard thing to witness. A terrible burden to bear. Especially when your decisions and orders had placed them in harm's way.

I needed a plausible excuse for my initial reaction. I needed to resume a professional, detached demeanor. No one other than myself knew of this constable's existence. I needed it to remain so for a little while longer.

On the dock I drew Jolene aside. Her earlier concern dissipating, replaced by a knowing curiosity. She knew me too well, and possessed a keen perceptiveness. Another of her remarkable traits.

"I want you in charge of this case," I said. The sharp edge in my voice only increased her curiosity.

"Inform the Coast Guard vessel coming for the body I'll ride over with them. But I'll be back home tonight. Let's meet at my place around eight. I'll want as much on this case as you can put together by then. So you need to get a move on."

I perceived the questions forming, many of them, but turned away before she had a chance to voice them. Not the time or place.

"Oh," I said turning back to face her. "Bring Gage."

A glossary of nautical and aviation terms used in the
Bequia Mysteries

Abeam - A relative bearing perpendicular to the sides of a vessel or off the wingtip of an aircraft.

Abeam the Runway – Indicates the runway is directly perpendicular to the right or left side of the aircraft.

Aboard - On or in a vessel or aircraft.

Adrift - Afloat and unattached in any way to the shore or seabed, but not under way. Also refers to any gear not fastened down or put away properly.

Aft - Towards the stern (rear) of a vessel or aircraft.

Aground - Resting on or touching the sea bottom (usually involuntarily).

Ahead - Forward of a vessel's bow or aircraft's nose.

Ahoy - A shout to draw attention. Term used to hail another vessel.

Air Data Computer (ADC) – An instrument which displays information on the surrounding atmosphere and the aircraft's flight through it, such as pressure altitude, outside air temperature, airspeed, and aircraft attitude.

Aileron – A control surface attached to the outer trailing edge of an aircraft's wings allowing the aircraft to bank.

Alee - To leeward. Referring to the lee side (away from the wind) of a vessel.

Aloft- In the rigging of a sailing ship. Above the ship's uppermost solid structure; overhead or high above. An aircraft at altitude. High altitude winds.

Alongside - By the side of a vessel or pier.

Amidships (or midships) – At the middle of a vessel.

Anchor – A metal hook or plough-like object designed to dig into the seabed and hold a vessel in place. Attached to the vessel by a line or chain. A sea anchor is used to prevent or slow a vessel's drift at sea.

Anchor/Mooring buoy- A small floating buoy secured by a line to an anchor or mooring to indicate position of the anchor or mooring.

Anchor Chain - Chain connecting the vessel to the anchor. (See Ground Tackle)

Anchor Light – A white light displayed by a vessel at anchor usually from the tallest masthead. Anchor Rode - The anchor line, rope or cable connecting the anchor chain to the vessel. (See Ground Tackle)

Anchor Watch – An electronic instrument (GPS) or crewmen assigned to monitor the ship while anchored or moored, to ensure the anchor is holding and the vessel is not drifting. Most marine GPS units have an Anchor Watch Alarm capability.

Anchorage - A suitable area for a vessel to anchor. A harbor or port.

Anchors Aweigh – An anchor pulled clear of the bottom.

Aport - To port. Referring to the port (left) side of the vessel.

Apparent Wind - The combination of the true wind and the headwind caused by a vessel's forward motion.

Approach Charts – An aviation chart displaying instrument approach information such as holding fixes and procedures, approach and missed approach procedures, in addition to the plan and profile views of various instrument procedures. Other information on approach charts include obstacle location and clearance height; navigational aid frequencies and identifiers; transition altitudes and levels;

airfield elevation; approach, tower, ground and ATIS radio frequencies; the location of outer, middle and inner markers; approach fixes and missed approach points; minimum safe descent altitudes; final approach course; decision height/altitude, and other airport information.

Approach Control – Air traffic controllers assigned to the approach segment of a given airport who provide directional guidance (vectors) to the final approach course.

Approach Segments - The parts of an instrument approach to an airport: arrival, initial approach, intermediate approach, final approach and missed approach segments.

Area traffic Control Center – Air traffic controllers responsible for large areas of enroute airspace, as opposed to approach, departure, tower and ground controllers.

Ashore - On the beach, shore, or land, as opposed to being aboard or on board).

Astarboard – Referring to the starboard (right) side of the vessel.

Astern – Referring to the stern (rear) of a vessel.

ATIS (Automated Terminal Information Service) - A continuous broadcast of recorded airport information updated hourly including active runways, arrival and departure procedures in use, weather, radio frequencies and other safety information.

ATR - A twin-engine turboprop regional transport aircraft used by many regional airlines in the Eastern Caribbean.

Attitude - An aircraft's position in flight relative to the three axes: pitch, roll and yaw.

Auto-flight System (AFS) - The combination of autopilot, autothrottle /autothrust, flight director, and autoland systems used to control flight through an aircraft's Flight Management System (FMS)

Autoland - An autopilot function which enables a "hands-off" automatic landing.

Autopilot (AP) - An automated computerized system which enables an aircraft to pilot itself.

Autothrottle (ATHR) - A computerized engine power control system enabling an aircraft to automatically adjust its power settings in different flight configurations.

Backstays - Lines or cables from the stern of a vessel to the masthead to support the masts. Part of the vessel's standing rigging.

Backtrack – To taxi on a runway in the opposite direction used for landing or takeoff.

Bank - A large area of elevated sea floor. The angle at which an aircraft is inclined about its longitudinal axis, used mostly during a turn.

Bareboat Charter – To hire or charter a vessel without a crew or provisions.

Base Leg - Part of the standard airport circuit an aircraft completes when landing. The aircraft parallels the runway on a downwind leg and turns to a base leg perpendicular to the runway before turning to the final landing leg. Referred to as "turning base".

Beam - The width of a vessel at the widest point, or a point alongside the vessel at the midpoint of its length (abeam).

Beam Ends - The sides of a vessel. "On her beam ends" may mean the vessel is literally on its side and possibly about to capsize. More often the phrase means the vessel is listing 45 degrees or more.

Beam Reach – A point of sail with the wind directly over the vessel's beam.

Bear down or bear away - Turn away from the wind. Also fall off.

Beat or Beating - Sailing as close as possible in the direction from which the wind is blowing.

Becalmed – A sailing vessel unable to sail due to lack of wind.

Belay - To secure a line around a fitting, cleat or belaying pin. Belaying Pins - Short movable iron bars or hard wood to which running rigging may be secured.

Berth (navigation) – Safe distance to be kept by a vessel from another vessel or an obstruction, hence the phrase, "to give a wide berth."

Berth (sleeping) - A bed or sleeping accommodation on a vessel.

Berth (vessel) - A dock, slip, or mooring area provided for vessels to tie up or moor.

Bilge - The compartment at the bottom of a vessel's interior hull. The lowest area of a vessel's interior.

Bimini Top - Canvas top covering the cockpit of a vessel, usually supported by a metal frame.

Binnacle - The stand on which the vessel's compass is mounted.

Bitt or Bitts - A post or posts mounted on the vessel's bow for fastening ropes or cables.

Bitter End - The last part or loose end of a rope, cable or chain.

Block - A pulley or set of pulleys.

Boarding Ladder - A portable flight of steps down a vessel's side or over the stern.

Boat-hook - A pole with a hook on the end, used to reach into the water to catch buoys or other floating objects.

Bobstay – A cable or chain which supports the bowsprit from below, counteracting the upward pull of the forestay.

Bollard - A stout vertical pillar on a dock or pier around which dock lines are made fast.

Booby hatch - A sliding hatch or cover.

Boom – A spar to which the foot (bottom) of a sail is attached.

Boom vang - A line which applies downward tension on a boom, countering the upward tension of the sail. The boom vang anchors the boom and allows control of the sail shape.

Boomkin (Bumpkin) - A spar, similar to a bowsprit, but projecting from the stern to extend the backstay or mizzen sheets.

Boot Stripe (Boot Top) - A painted stripe along a vessel's hull at the design waterline.

Bow - The front of a vessel.

Bowline - A type of knot, producing a strong loop of a fixed size.

Bowsprit - A spar projecting from the bow used to extend the forestay forward allowing the headsail to be set further forward.

Brightwork - Exposed varnished wood or polished metal on a vessel.

Britten Norman Islander – A twin engine light utility aircraft manufactured by the Britten-Norman company in the UK in the 1960's and still used by some regional airlines in the Caribbean for its STOL characteristics.

Broach - When a sailing vessel is forced by wind, sea, or too much sail into a sudden sharp turn which may lead to a capsize. The sudden change in direction is called broaching-to.

Broad Reach – A point of sail with the wind between the beam and stern, or 'on the quarter'.

Broken (BKN): A meteorological terms indicating cloud cover between 50% and 90% of the sky.

Bugs (Speed, Heading, Altitude) - Small plastic markers on analog instruments, or dials for digital displays, which are set at critical airspeeds, altitudes or headings during takeoff, climb and descent. When autopilot is engaged it automatically pursues the bug setting.

Bulkhead - An upright, watertight, load-bearing wall within the hull of a vessel or separating compartments on an aircraft.

Bulwark - The extension of the vessel's side above deck level.

Buoy - A floating object of defined shape and color used as an aid to navigation. A floating object indicating the position of an anchor or mooring.

Burgee - A small flag, typically triangular, flown from the masthead to indicate yacht-club membership.

Cabin - An enclosed room inside a vessel or aircraft.

Cabin Altitude (Pressure) - the artificially maintained atmospheric pressure inside an aircraft during high altitude flight, approximately 6,000- 8,000 feet inside the cabin.

Cabin Sole - The cabin floor, also referred to as an interior or lower deck.

Cable - A thick rope or bundle of spun wire.

Calibrated Airspeed (CAS) - The indicated airspeed (IAS) of an aircraft corrected for airspeed instrument errors.

Call-out – Verbal readout of flight data by a co-pilot or automated synthetic voice.

Capsize - When a vessel lists too far and rolls over, exposing the keel, often resulting in sinking.

Cardinal Points- Refers to the four main points of the compass: north, south, east and west.

Careening - Tilting a ship on its side, usually when beached, to clean or repair the hull below the water line.

CAT III Conditions - When visibility is very poor and aircraft require ILS automation for take-off and landing.

CAT IIIC - The crew, aircraft and airport are qualified and equipped to land in CAT III Conditions of 0 feet longitudinal visibility and a Decision Height of 0 feet.

Catamaran - A vessel with two hulls.

CAVOK - Ceiling and Visibility OK, spoken by pilots as "CAV-O-KAY".

Chafing - Wear on a line or sail caused by constant rubbing against another surface.

Chafing Gear - Material applied to a line or spar to prevent or reduce chafing.

Chain Locker - A space in the forward part of the ship containing the anchor chain and rode, typically behind the bow in front of the foremost bulkhead.

Checklist - A series of checks which are performed and confirmed during specific phases of a flight.

Chine - The angle formed where the sides and bottom of a vessel join. Soft chine is when the two surfaces join at a shallow angle, and hard chine is when they join at a steep angle.

Chocks - Rubber or wooden blocks placed against an aircraft's tires to prevent the aircraft from rolling while parked.

Circuit Breaker - An electrical safety device on vessels and aircraft which opens a circuit in case of current overload. On vessels the CB panel is located with or in close proximity to the main electrical panel. In large jet aircraft circuit breakers are located on the cockpit overhead panel, and at the bottom of the instrument panel on smaller aircraft like Mike Daniel's Piper Seneca.

Clean Up- To retract an aircraft's flaps, gear, slats and other exterior devices which may affect aerodynamics and speed.

Clew - The forward corner of a sail attached to the deck or forward end of a boom.

Close Aboard - In close proximity to another vessel.

Close-hauled – A vessel sailing as close to the wind as possible, referred to as beating.

Close Reach – A point of sail with the wind between the bow and beam.

Clear (CLR) – A meteorological term indicating a clear sky with no clouds.

Clearance (Cleared) - Authorization from air traffic control to proceed as requested or instructed.

Coach- roof – A cabin roof higher than the main deck.

Coaming - The edge of a hatch, cockpit or skylight raised above the deck to keep out water.

Cockpit - The area on deck containing helm and other vessel controls. Compartment from which a pilot operates an aircraft.

Companionway - A ladder leading from an entrance hatch to cabins below deck.

Compass – Navigational instrument indicating the direction of the vessel in relation to the Earth's geographical or magnetic poles.

Control Tower - An air traffic control facility located at an airport.

Controlled Airspace - Airspace of defined dimensions within which air traffic control is exercised and mandatory for aircraft flying through it.

Crabbing - Flying with drift due to crosswind.

Crossfeed - A valve which allows an aircraft's engines to obtain fuel from any of the available fuel tanks. A crossfeed also allows transfer of fuel from one tank to another.

Crosswind - A wind blowing at an angle to an aircraft's flight path, not necessarily perpendicular, which is a direct crosswind.

Dash 8 - A twin engine turboprop regional transport aircraft manufactured by De Havilland Canada (now Bombardier).

Davit – A paired set of cranes used to hoist, lower and hold a dinghy in place, usually affixed to the stern of a sailing vessel.

Dead Ahead - Directly ahead in front of the vessel.

Dead In The Water - Not moving; used only when a vessel is afloat and neither tied up nor anchored.

Dead Reckoning – To navigate without the aid of precision instruments or celestial observation where current position is estimated based on time and distance travelled from a know fix.

Deadeye - A wood block with holes (but no pulleys) which is spliced to a shroud. Used to adjust the tension in the standing rigging of a sailing vessel by lacing a lanyard from the deck through the holes. Performs the same job as a turnbuckle.

Deadlight - A strong shutter fitted over a porthole or other opening and closed in bad weather.

Deadrise - The design angle between the keel and vertical rise of the hull as measured from the horizontal.

Deadwood – The structural reinforcement of the aft portion of a vessel's hull between the keel and sternpost.

Decision Altitude (DA) - The altitude at which a pilot must decide to land or go around.

Decision Height (DH) - The height above the ground as displayed on a radio altimeter at which a pilot must decide to land or go around.

Deck - The top surface of a vessel. An interior floor below the top deck (See Cabin sole).

Deck Hand - A person (crew) performing tasks which aid in sailing and maintenance of the vessel.

Decks Awash – When the deck of a vessel is partially or wholly submerged.

Dinghy - A small inflatable or rigid hull boat carried or towed as a transport tender for the vessel. May be rowed, powered by an outboard motor, and some types can be rigged for sailing.

Displacement – The volume (weight) of water displaced by a vessel's immersed hull. Exactly equivalent to the vessel's weight.

Displacement hull - A hull designed to travel through the water, rather than planning over it.

Distance Measuring Equipment (DME) - A radio transmitter located on the ground which provides distance information for aircraft. Though still used its been mostly replaced by GPS.

Dock – A pier or wharf which a vessel can tie up to. Also maneuvering a vessel against a pier or wharf to tie up.

Dockyard - A facility where ships or boats are built and repaired. Dockyard is usually associated with vessel maintenance and repairs, while shipyard is usually associated with vessel construction.

Dodger - A hood with a clear plastic section to prevent wind and spray from entering the cockpit. Functions like a windshield.

Double Ender – A boat with its stern shaped like the bow enabling it to move forward or backward equally well.

Downwind Leg – Part of the standard airport circuit an aircraft completes when landing. On the downwind leg the aircraft parallels the runway before turning onto the base leg perpendicular to the runway.

Draft -The depth of a vessel's keel below the waterline.

EGT (Exhaust Gas Temperature) - Indicated by a gauge in the cockpit. EGT is a principal engine performance parameter monitored during flight.

Elevator – A part of an aircraft's horizontal tail section which controls pitch.

Empennage - the tail section of an aircraft, consisting of the fin, tailplane or elevator, and the part of the fuselage to which they are attached.

Endurance - The time an aircraft can fly without refueling.

Engine Room – The space containing the vessel's engine, batteries and other machinery like a generator.

Engine Run-up - Operating an aircraft's engine on the ground over its full power range. Usually conducted following repair and prior to takeoff.

Ensign - The principal flag or banner flown at a vessel's stern to indicate its nationality.

ETOPS (Extended Twin Operations) - The term for long distance twin-engine operation over the ocean, desert or arctic regions where there is no suitable airport within 60 minutes of flight in case of an emergency. Referred to by pilots as "Engines Turning Or Passengers Swimming".

Fairlead - A ring, hook or other device used to keep a line or chain running in the correct direction or to prevent it chafing or fouling.

Fall- The part of the tackle or line a crewman hauls on.

Fall Off - To steer away from the direction of the wind. Also to bear away, bear off or put the head down. The opposite of pointing up or heading up.

Fast – Secure, as in tied or held securely.

Fathom – A unit of length equal to 6 feet (1.8 m). Particularly used to measure depth.

Feet Per Minute (FPM) - A unit of measurement indicating an aircraft's rate of climb or descent.

Fender - An air or foam filled bumper used to protect the sides of a vessel from rubbing against a dock or another vessel tied alongside. Used tires are most often used on locally owned boats in the Grenadines.

Fetch - The distance across water the wind or waves have traveled. Also to reach a navigational mark without having to tack.

Final Approach Fix (FAF) – A navigational reference point from which an aircraft begins its final approach to an airport. The beginning of the final approach segment.

Final Leg (On Final) – Part of the standard airport circuit an aircraft completes when landing. The aircraft turns onto the final leg inbound for landing from the base leg, referred to as "turning final" or "on final".

Fitting-out – The interior construction of a vessel after the hull has been completed and launched.

Fix - A radio transmitted beacon or GPS coordinates indicating an aircraft is in a specified position, either an enroute waypoint, or a point from which to begin an initial approach (IAF) or final approach (FAF).

Fixed Base Operator (FBO) - An airport operator serving General Aviation aircraft.

Flare – A nose-up pitch movement to slow an aircraft just prior to touchdown.

Flight Deck - Compartment from which the crew operates an aircraft. Also cockpit, flight compartment, or control cabin.

Flight Plan - Specified information relating to the whole or portion of an intended flight.

Flight Management System (FMS) – An onboard computerized system using preprogrammed route data and flight instrument data to interface with an aircraft's Automatic Flight Control System (AFCS) and Electronic Flight Instrument System (EFIS) allowing automated flight.

Fluke - The wedge-shaped part of an anchor's arms which dig into the sea bottom.

Following Sea – Waves or tide moving in the same direction as the vessel.

Foot – The lower edge of a sail. The bottom of a mast.

Fore/forward - Towards the bow (front) of the vessel.

Forecastle – The area (usually a cabin or locker) at the forward end of the vessel just aft of the bow.

Forefoot - The lower part of the stem (bow) of the vessel.

Foresail - The headsail on a sloop. The sail directly ahead of the mainsail on a schooner.

Forestays – Lines or cables from the bow or bowsprit of the vessel to the masthead to support the mast. Part of the vessel's 'standing' rigging.

Frame - A transverse structural member which provides the hull's shape and strength.

Freeboard - The height of a ship's hull measured from the waterline to the highest gunwale.

Furl - To roll or gather a sail against its mast or spar.

Fuselage - The main body of an aircraft excluding wings, tail, landing gear, etc.

G-IV – A twin engine jet aircraft designed and built by Gulfstream Aerospace for private and business use.

G-V – Larger and improved version of the G-IV with a longer range.

Gaff – On a Gaff rigged vessel the upper spars (a short boom) which hoists and stretches the upper edge of the four sided Gaff sail.

Gaff Rigged – A vessel rigged to use a four-sided fore-and-aft sail with the sail's upper edge supported by a spar or gaff which extends aft from the mast.

Galley - The kitchen on a vessel or aircraft.

Gear - The landing and ground operation apparatus on an aircraft, including the wheels, tires, struts and other mechanisms connected to them.

General Aviation Pilot - A pilot who flies for pleasure, business or hire.

General Aviation Terminal – Airport terminal serving private, business and leisure aircraft.

Genoa (Genny or Jib) - A large triangular sail flown at the front of the vessel from the forestay. Referred to as the pulling sail since it functions in the same manner as an airplane wing.

Gibe or Gybe - To change from one tack to the other by turning a sailing vessel's stern rather than its bow through the wind. Also known by the historical term 'wearing' or 'to wear'.

Glareshield – A cockpit panel above the main instrument panels and below the windshield in an aircraft to protect the instruments and prevent reflected glare.

Glide Path - The flight path of an aircraft during landing approach to a runway.

Glideslope - A cockpit instrument depicting an aircraft's glide path during an instrument landing.

Global Positioning System (GPS)- A satellite based navigation system providing continuous worldwide coverage of position and time on the ground, at sea, and in the air.

Global Navigation Satellite System (GNSS) - A GPS based instrument Landing System which combines satellite and local data to provide accurate navigational positioning for landing.

Go-around - Pulling up and flying to a hold position or reentering the airport traffic pattern after discontinuing an approach to landing.

Grounding - When a vessel while afloat touches the seabed or goes 'aground'. A vessel hard aground is stuck in the sea floor.

Ground effect - the increased lift an aircraft's wings generate close to the ground. When landing ground effect may cause the aircraft to 'float' and delay touchdown. On takeoff ground effect allows level flight just above the ground in order to accelerate to a safe climb airspeed. Especially useful when taking off from a short runway.

Ground Tackle - All the parts of the anchor system including the anchor, anchor chain, anchor rode and shackles.

Gunwale – The top edge of the hull or Bulwark.

Halyard - A line used to raise a sail. Also refers to any line used to raise any object aloft, like a flag, pennant or spar.

Hangar – Building for garaging aircraft on the ground.

Hank - A fastener attached to the luff of the headsail which then attaches the headsail to the forestay. The hanks slides along the forestay as the headsail is raised.

Hatch - An opening or entrance in a vessel's deck providing access to the vessel's interior. The cover or door to the opening is also called a hatch.

Hauling Wind - Pointing the vessel in the direction of the wind.

Hawsepipe, Hawsehole or Hawse – A shaft or hole in the side of a vessel's bow, bulwark or stern through which the anchor chain or dock lines pass.

Haze - Fine dust particles causing the sky to appear unclear and reducing visibility.

Head - The forwardmost or uppermost part of a vessel. The forwardmost or uppermost part of any individual part of the vessel, e.g., the masthead, beakhead, stemhead, etc. The top corner of a triangular sail. The toilet on a vessel.

Heading – The direction in which a vessel is sailing or an aircraft is flying as indicated on a magnetic or electronic compass, and distinct from the directional track of the vessel or aircraft.

Header - A change in wind direction which forces the helmsman to steer further away from the current course or requiring a tack. The opposite of a lift.

Headsail - Any sail flown in front of the most forward mast. Usually attached to the forestay.

Head Sea – A sea in which the waves are directly opposing the forward progress of the vessel.

Headwind - A wind blowing in a direction opposite to an aircraft's flight path and affecting the aircraft's speed over the ground (SOG). The opposite of a tailwind.

Heave - A vessel's up-and-down (pitching) motion in a seaway.

Heel/Heeling - The lean of a sailing vessel onto its side caused by the wind's force on the sails. Also measured by the angle the deck is tilted sideways from horizontal.

Helm – The Vessel's steering mechanism connecting the wheel in the cockpit to the rudder.

High Frequency (HF) – Radio frequencies in the 3 to 30 MHz range used for aeronautical and marine communication beyond VHF (Very High Frequency) range. HF is not affected by the line of sight limitations of VHF, but are susceptible to atmospheric conditions including ionization by solar flares.

High Intensity Runway Lighting (HIRL) - Airport runway lighting where the brightness can be adjusted by the Tower depending on atmospheric conditions and time of day.

Hitch - A knot used to tie a rope or line to a fixed object.

Hold - An interior space in a vessel used for storing cargo. A circular flight pattern around a specified fix flown by an aircraft waiting to descend and land (Holding Pattern).

Horizontal stabilizer – The horizontal tail section of an aircraft's empennage which articulates up and down to control the aircraft's pitch. Also referred to as the tailplane or elevator. It can be trimmed by a control in the cockpit to reduce the aerodynamic pressure on the tail which the pilot feels as resistance on the control yolk.

Hounds - Attachments on the masts for connecting stays and shrouds and to support topmasts.

Hull - The shell and framework of the flotation part of a vessel.

Hypoxia - An inadequate amount of oxygen reaching the brain which occurs in an unpressurized aircraft cabin above 10,000 feet, requiring the use of supplemental oxygen.

Indicated Airspeed (IAS) - The relative speed of an aircraft through the surrounding air as displayed on an airspeed indicator in the cockpit.

Inertial Navigation System (INS) - A self-contained computerized navigation system using laser gyroscopes and accelerometers to sense an aircraft's movement and velocity around all three axis and calculate its precise position without external references.

In Irons - When the bow of a sailboat is pointed directly into the wind and the vessel is unable to maneuver.

Initial Approach Fix (IAF) - The point from which the initial segment of an ILS approach begins.

Iron wind/Iron Jenny – Using a sailing vessel's engine.

Instrument Approach Procedure (IAP) - The procedure for a specified ILS approach at an airport.

Instrument Landing System (ILS) - A system using radio signals to guide an aircraft down to the runway in poor weather conditions. The system depicts a Localizer for horizontal guidance and a Glide Sloop for vertical guidance on cockpit instruments.

Instrument Meteorological Conditions (IMC) - Weather conditions (cloud, fog, rain etc.) making it impossible to fly by outside visual references (VMC). The pilot has to fly solely by reference to the aircraft's instruments (IFR).

Jenny (Genoa or Jib) - A triangular headsail flown at the front of the vessel.

Jeppesen Charts – Aviation charts manufactured by the Jeppesen Sanderson Company used by pilots worldwide.

Jib (Genoa) - A triangular headsail flown at the front of the vessel.

Keel - The central structural foundation of a vessel's hull. The vessel's 'backbone'.

Ketch - A two-masted sailboat with the aft mast (the mizzen) shorter than the main mast and stepped (mounted) closer to the stern.

Knot - A unit of speed: 1 nautical mile (1.8520 km; 1.1508 mi) per hour.

Landing Distance Available (LDA) - The actual length of runway which can be used for landing and roll-out.

Lanyard - A rope or line which ties something off or from which something is suspended.

Lay – The direction (relative bearing) of a designated mark in relation to a vessel's course.

Lazarette - A small stowage locker on deck, usually toward the aft end of a vessel. Also seat lockers in the cockpit.

Leading Edge - The forward edge of an aircraft's wing, engine blades, tail fin and stabilizers.

Lee - The side of a vessel or island away from the wind.

Lee Shore - A shore downwind (to the lee) of a vessel. A vessel which cannot sail well to windward risks being blown onto a lee shore and grounded or smashed against a rocky coast.

Leech - The aft or trailing edge of a sail. The leeward edge of a spinnaker.

Leeward - In the opposite direction from which the wind is blowing.

Leeway - The amount a vessel is blown sideways by the wind.

Length Overall (LOA) - The maximum length of a vessel's hull measured parallel to the waterline, including any overhanging ends which extend beyond the bow and stern. In sailing vessels this might include the bowsprit, boomkin, or stern swim platform.

Liferaft - An inflatable, covered raft, used in the event of a vessel being abandoned.

Lift – A change in wind direction enabling a close hauled sailboat to steer up from its current course to a more favorable one. The opposite of a header.

Line - The nautical term for the cordage or ropes used on a vessel. A line may have a specific name specifying its use, such as main or jib halyards, or main and jib sheets.

Luff - The forward edge of a sail.

Luffing - When a sailing vessel is steered too close to the wind causing insufficiently filled sails to flap. The luff of the sail begins to flap first.

Mach Number – Commonly used to express a jet aircraft's airspeed, measured as a ratio to the speed of sound.

Main Deck - The uppermost continuous deck extending from bow to stern.

Mainmast - The tallest mast on the vessel on which the mainsail is hoisted.

Mainsheet (See Sheets) – A tackle line attacked to the main boom used to controls the trim of the mainsail by controlling the angle of the boom. The downward tension on this line also affects the shape of the mainsail, sometimes aided by a boom vang.

Making Way - A vessel moving under its own power.

Marconi Rig – A fore-and-aft sail rig using triangular sails, as opposed to square rigged or gaff rigged. Also call the Bermuda Rig.

Marlinspike - A tool used in rope work such as unlaying rope for splicing, untying knots, or forming a makeshift handle.

Mast - A vertical pole on a sailing vessel which supports sails.

Maximum Landing Weight - The weight at which specific aircraft can land without risking structural damage.

Maximum Takeoff Weight - The weight at which specific aircraft can take off without risking takeoff and climb performance.

METAR - A weather report from an airport or other ground weather station used by pilots during flight planning, enroute, and approaching the destination.

Minimum Approach Speed - The minimum speed at which a specific aircraft can safely maintain flight in the approach to landing configuration (flaps, slats and gear extended).

Minimum Descent Altitude (MDA) - The altitude in the terminal area (around an airport) below which no aircraft must descend unless it is on its approach path. At some airports the MDA may be different in different directions depending on terrain.

Missed Approach - When a aircraft aborts its landing approach usually due to low visibility or a runway obstacle and performs a go around.

Nautical Mile - A unit of distance corresponding to one minute of arc of latitude. 1,852 meters; approximately 6,076 feet; 1.1508 mile.

Navigation Display (ND) - In an aircraft cockpit equipped with LCD panel screens navigational data is digitally displayed on a screen in front of the pilot next to the Primary Flight Display (PFD) screen.

Navigation Lights – Required on marine vessels and aircraft to avoid collision by indicating position, relative angle and direction of travel. The location and type of lighting is specified by international law to include lights visible on both sides of a vessel or aircraft - red on the port side or wingtip, green on the starboard side or wingtip; and a white light visible from the rear of the vessel or aircraft. Aircraft also use high intensity flashing or rotating strobe lights.

NOTAM (Notice to Airmen) - A printout providing information regarding changes to aeronautical facilities, services, procedures or hazards used during flight planning.

Outhaul - A line used to tension the foot of a sail along the boom.

Outer Marker – A radio beacon used for ILS approaches positioned 4 to 7 miles from the runway threshold and aligned with the runway centerline. The outermost of three beacons including a middle marker and inner marker.

Painter - A rope attached to the bow of a dinghy used for towing or tethering the dinghy.

Phosphorescence – A bright blue-green luminosity in a vessel's wake seen at night, caused by the bioluminescence of marine organisms disturbed by the vessel's passage.

Pilot Flying (PF) - The pilot actually doing the hands-on flying of the aircraft at a given moment.

Pilot In Command - The pilot in command of the aircraft, not necessarily the pilot flying.

Pilot Report (PIREP) – Updates of weather or other flight conditions provided by pilots when they encounter them enroute or during approach and landing.

Pitch - A vessel's motion in a seaway in which the bow and stern rise and fall repetitively (See heave). The nose up or down attitude of an aircraft in flight.

Plane - To skim over the water at high speed rather than push through it.

Point Up - To change the direction of a sailboat so it is heading more upwind. To steer toward windward. Also called heading up. The opposite of falling off.

Points Of Sail - The course sailed in relation to wind direction. Close hauled (sailing as close into the wind as possible); Close reach (wind between the bow and beam); Beam reach (wind on the beam and the vessel perpendicular to the wind); Broad reach (wind on the quarter between the beam and stern); Running, sailing downwind with the wind behind.

Port - The left side of a vessel or aircraft when facing forward.

Port Tack – Sailing with the wind blowing from the port side of the vessel. Must give way to vessels on starboard tack.

Porthole or port - An opening or window in a vessel's side for admitting light and air, fitted with thick glass, and often a hinged metal cover.

Precision Approach Path Indicator (PAPI) - A series of flashing lights leading to the runway threshold providing pilots with a visual approach reference.

Radio Management Panel (RMP) - A control panel located on the center pedestal between the two pilot seats where the pilots tune and manage the aircraft's communications radios including VHF, HF and satellite up and down links. On smaller general aviation aircraft like Mike Daniels' Piper Seneca the radios are usually located in the center of the instrument panel.

Reaching – Any point of sail from about 60° to about 160° off the wind including close reaching, beam reaching and broad reaching.

Reefing - Temporarily reducing sail area in strong or gusty wind conditions by reducing the amount of exposed sail. Mainsails usually have reef points constructed into them.

Regatta - A series of sailboat races.

Rigging - The system of masts and lines on ships and sailing vessels.

Rode - The anchor line, rope or cable connecting the anchor chain to the vessel. Also Anchor Rode.

Roll - A vessel's motion in a seaway in which it rolls from side to side about the fore-aft/longitudinal axis. An aircraft in a bank about its longitudinal axis.

Rollout - An aircraft's ground roll along the runway after landing. A return to level flight after banking.

Rudder - A steering device attached at or near the aft end of a vessel controlled by a tiller or wheel. On an aircraft the rudder is attached to the trailing edge of the vertical tailfin and controlled by foot pedals in the cockpit.

Run Up – An engine test at full power prior to takeoff.

Running Before The Wind or Running – Sailing with the wind behind the vessel. (See Points of sail).

Running rigging – The lines and tackles used to manipulate sails, spars, etc. in order to control the movement of as sailing vessel.

Runway - The paved surface of an airport designed for aircraft take-offs and landings. Runways are designated by the compass direction in which they are aligned.

Runway Edge Lighting - White lights, usually on stalks, on both sides of the runway.

Sail – A dacron or nylon fabric (formally canvas) designed and arranged so it causes the wind to drive a sailing vessel along. Sails are attached and manipulated by a combination of masts, spars (booms), and ropes (running rigging).

Sampson Post- A strong vertical post near the bow of a vessel used to support a vessel's anchor windlass and the heel (back end) of a vessel's bowsprit.

Scattered (SCT) - A meteorological terms indicating clouds distributed irregularly in the sky.

Schooner - A type of sailing vessel characterized by two or more masts with the mainmast being the tallest.

Scuppers - Openings in a vessel's bulwarks to allow seawater to drain from the deck.

Seacock - A valve fitted through the vessel's hull.

Sea Shanty – Song about sailors or the sea.

Shackle - A metal U-shaped device secured with a clevis pin or bolt across the opening used to connect rigging to an object or one piece of rigging to another.

Sheer - The curve of a vessel's sides.

Sheet - A rope attached to a boom or clew of a sail used to control the sail's trim.

Shoal - Shallow water.

Shrouds - Ropes or cables which hold and support a mast from the sides. Part of a sailing vessel's standing rigging.

Sloop – A sailing vessel with a single mast for a mainsail and headsail.

Solo – The first flight of a student pilot unaccompanied by an instructor, usually confined to the traffic pattern.

Speed Over Ground (SOG)- Speed of a vessel over the ground irrespective of its speed through the water. The speed of an aircraft over the ground irrespective of its airspeed. A vessel's speed over the ground is affected by tidal currents, while an aircraft's speed over the ground is affected by headwinds, crosswinds and tailwinds.

Speed Through The Water (STW) - Speed of a vessel through the water as measured by a speedometer log attached to the hull below the waterline. While STW indicates a vessel's performance, SOG is the relevant measure used for navigation.

Spar (Boom) – A wood or aluminum pole used to support rigging and sails.

Spinnaker – A large light fabric sail hoisted in front of the vessel when sailing downwind.

Spreader - A short spar positioned on both sides of a mast to deflect (spread) the shrouds allowing greater support of the mast.

Stall – A sailing vessel in irons. The position of an aircraft's wings relative to the surrounding air (angle of attack) at which lift is no longer generated.

Stanchion - Vertical posts spaced along a deck's edge to support a bulwark, rail or lifelines.

Standing Rigging – The combination of stays, shrouds, attachments and tensioners used to support masts and spars.

Starboard - The right side of a vessel or aircraft when facing forward.

Starboard tack - When sailing with the wind coming from the starboard side of the vessel. Has right of way over boats on port tack.

Stay – A line or cable running forward (forestay) and aft (backstay) from a mast to the hull to support the mast.

Staysail – A small triangular sail behind the jib or headsail attached to an inner forestay (between the head forestay and mast). On large vessels the foot of the staysail is usually attached to a staysail boom.

Steerage - The helm's effect on the vessel's steering.

Steerageway - The minimum speed at which a vessel will answer the helm, below which the vessel cannot be steered.

Stem (Stempost)– The upward extension of a vessel's keel at the forward end of the vessel, to which the bow is attached.

Stern (Sternpost) – The upward extension of a vessel's keel at the rear end of the vessel, to which the transom is attached.

Stick Shaker - An aircraft's stall warning system which when triggered by angle of attack sensors causes the stick or control column to vibrate. In small aircraft like Mike Daniels' Piper Seneca a stall warning horn sounds.

STOL – Short takeoff and landing.

Stow - To store or to put away personal effects, tackle, gear or cargo.

Straight-in - Approaching an airport's runway without executing any legs of the airport's traffic pattern. Also referred to as a long final.

Squawk - An identifier code which identifies transponder equipped aircraft on ATC radar screens.

Squawk Sheet - A list of maintenance items to be performed on an aircraft indicated in the aircraft's logbook.

Standard Pressure Setting - The 29.92 inch Hg altimeter setting universally used above the 29,000 feet transition level.

Superstructure - The parts of the vessel which project above the main deck not including masts.

Tacking – Turning the vessel's bow through the wind to bring the wind onto the opposite side of the vessel. Such a zig-zagging course is necessary to sail a vessel toward a mark in the direction from which the wind is blowing.

Tackle – The combination of rope passed through a pulley (block) or set of pulleys to provide mechanical leverage for hoisting, lowering or applying tension. (See also Ground Tackle).

Tailwind - Wind blowing in the same direction as the aircraft's direction of travel. The opposite of headwind.

Take-off Roll - The process of accelerating down the runway in order to take off.

Tarmac – Commonly used to refer to an airport's paved surfaces including runways, taxiways, terminal and other parking ramps. Short for tarmacadam, the name of the surfacing material.

Taxiway - Paved roadways for aircraft to move about an airport. Indicated by blue lights along the sides and named for letters of the alphabet pronounced phonetically.

Tell-tale (Tell-tail) - A light piece of string, yarn, or plastic attached to a stay or a shroud to indicate the apparent wind direction. Also sometimes attached to the body and/or leech of a sail to indicate air flow over the sail's surface.

Terminal Aerodrome Forecasts (TAFs) – Weather information similar to METARs but providing forecast information for an airport. Used by pilots during flight planning.

Terminal Control Area (TCA) – Controlled airspace around an airport used for departures and arrivals.

Threshold - The beginning of a runway usually marked by broad white stripes.

Thrust - The propulsive force generated by an aircraft engine; the other three forces which act on an aircraft are lift, weight and drag. The force generated by wind on a vessel's sails.

Thwart - A bench seat across the width of an open boat, like a dinghy.

Topping Lift – A line attached from the masthead to the aft end of a boom to control the boom angle and therefore the shape of the sail.

Topsides - The part of the hull between the waterline and the deck.

Touch and Go - A pilot training exercise in which pilots practice approaches and touch downs on a runway without rolling to a stop, instead taking off again for another circuit in the traffic pattern. This 'touch and go' or 'circuit and bump' is repeated several time in a single practice session.

Touchdown Speed - The airspeed at which the aircraft makes contact with the ground on landing.

Touchdown Target – A point on the runway a pilot aims for during the landing approach.

To Weather - The side of a vessel exposed to the wind. Turning toward the wind.

Track – The actual directional path (course) of a vessel or aircraft due to the effects of leeway, tidal currents or crosswinds.

Transom – The aft (rear) section at the stern of a vessel. May be vertical, or raked (sloped). Traffic Advisory – An air traffic control message advising a pilot of the presence of traffic in their vicinity. An advisory does not require pilot action but allows the pilot to visually locate and observe the traffic.

Traffic Pattern - A predefined flight circuit of the runway intended for landing consisting of downwind, base and final legs.

Trailing Edge - The rear edge of a wing, stabilizer or propeller blade on an aircraft. A sail's leech.

Transponder - A radio which transmits a coded response to identify aircraft on ATC radar. A mode C transponder also provides the aircraft's altitude.

Trim - Adjustments made to sails in relation to wind direction to maximize their efficiency. Adjustment of an aircraft's control surfaces to minimize control pressure on the yolk.

Turbo-Prop – an aircraft with propellers driven by turbine (jet) engines.

Underway - A vessel moving under control that is neither anchored, moored, tied up, aground nor adrift.

Vertical Speed Indicator (VSI) – A cockpit instrument which displays an aircraft's vertical speed, (rate of climb or descent) in feet per minute.

VHF- A marine and aviation radio using the very high frequency band.

Visual Approach Slope Indicator (VASI) – A system of 3 lights at the side of a runway which provide a visual descent/glide sloop when landing.

Visual Flight Rules (VFR) – Flight by visual references outside the aircraft in visual meteorological conditions (VMC). As opposed to Instrument Flight Rules (IFR) when flying by instruments in instrument meteorological conditions (IMC).

VOR – A ground based omnidirectional radio transmitter used for aircraft navigation. The intersection of two VOR radials provides the aircraft's position.

Wake – The trail behind a vessel caused by its passage through the water. The turbulent downdraft caused by the passage of a large aircraft through the air. Also referred to as wake turbulence or wake vortex.

Walkaround – An external inspection and check of an aircraft prior to flight.

Weatherly - A vessel which is easily sailed and maneuvered and makes little leeway when sailing to windward.

Weather helm – The tendency of a sailing vessel's bow to swing to windward.

Weigh Anchor – To pull up an anchor prior to sailing.

Weight and Balance – A document recording an aircraft manufacturer's approved weight distribution and center of gravity (CG) for that type aircraft. Required to be kept aboard the aircraft at all times. A pilot calculates weight and centre of gravity when loading the aircraft to ensure it meets the aircraft's weight and balance parameters. An overweight and out of CG aircraft may not get off the ground, and even if it does, it may be impossible to handle in the air.

Whaleboat (Bequia) – A narrow open boat pointed at both ends (double-ended) enabling it to move forwards or backwards equally well.

Whaler (Bequia) – A fisherman specializing in catching whales.

Wick Static Discharger - Located on the trailing edges of an aircraft's wings to discharge static electrical built up in the airframe during flight.

Winds Aloft – Forecasts of winds at altitudes above 3,000 feet. Upper level wind forecasts provide information on winds up to 39,000 feet for the polar jet streams and at higher altitudes for the subtropical jet streams.

Windward - In the direction the wind is blowing from.

Wing on Wing- A method of sailing downwind with the mainsail extended on one side and the Genoa extended on the opposite side.

Yaw – The tendency of a vessel's bow to swing off course in a seaway. The turn of an aircraft's nose left or right due to rudder input. The adverse tendency of an aircraft's nose to swing left or right, controlled by rudder input or a yaw damper.

Yoke – The control wheel and column in an aircraft cockpit.

Zulu – Used in marine and aviation radiotelephony for Universal Coordinated Time (UTC), also Greenwich Mean Time (GMT).

www.ingramcontent.com/pod-product-compliance
Lightning Source LLC
Chambersburg PA
CBHW060339260626
47160CB00006B/2134

9 780099 140083 6